D1826334

MILELE SAFARI

AN ETERNAL JOURNEY

JAN HAWKE

To Linda
Enjoy your journey
Jan Hawke

Copyright © 2013 by Jan Hawke. All rights reserved.

This book or any portion thereof may not be reproduced or used in any manner whatsoever without the express written permission of the publisher except for the use of brief quotations in a book review.

ISBN 978-0-9927472-0-6

Published by DreamWorlds Publishing
Printed by Lightning Source

www. dreamworldspub.org.uk
milelesafari.blogspot.co.uk

This is a work of fiction. Names, characters, businesses, places, events and incidents are either the products of the author's imagination or, where based on actual events, used in a fictitious manner. Any resemblance to actual persons, living or dead, is purely coincidental.

Dedication

To my parents, Ronald and Patricia Gove.

More than I can convey, thank you for teaching me how to look, listen and ask questions: and for always encouraging my interest in books, writing and drawing, and in this beautiful, but very messy world.

CONTENTS

Foreword

This was always going to be a tale about journeys and inevitably, in common with most first novels I suspect, there are elements of my own life's journey mingled in there somewhere with the principal voice of Sophie Taylor. My true love in literature has always lain with fantasy, sometimes to the point of obsession, so my choice of subject for this novel might at first have seemed a little strange to the people who know me best. However, for someone who has perhaps led an outwardly quiet and sheltered life, I have seen a lot of dark times, places and people from all walks of life, some of them very strange indeed and what better place than the 'Dark Continent' to let experience roam about looking for devilment, passion or redemption?

Like at least three of the main characters I have also had dark shadows in my head and certainly it is that experience that gradually gathered influence on what I was writing. It started out in theory as a kind of Canterbury Tales for modern Africa, to cover various themes that I could link into a safari progression, to places I've been to for real, or in dreams. Anyone who falls for the tourist-trail beauty of sub-Saharan Africa must also eventually reconcile themselves to the appalling problems it suffers from on every possible scale in terms of human existence - and that of course is what adds spice and depth to the whole kaleidoscope of life in what was likely the cradle of humankind.

One could not write a series of stories on the 'pilgrim path' without touching on deeply negative, if not altogether evil subjects and so these are mostly contained in Sophie's journey over thirteen years, leaving the lighter travellers' tales sprouting on the safari bases covered. So Harry's robust adventures in conservation and trophy hunting contain echoes of civil war, and Luey's background encompasses sexual plague and enforced exile, as well as Sophie's own mix of experiences as an aid worker and doctor.

War and famine also must find their place within the weave and of the many conflicts in Africa I could have chosen, Biafra and Rwanda were the ones that 'called' me most. Biafra because that was my first realisation of the enormity of the gulf between Africa and most of the industrialised world that I had growing up; long before LiveAid and Bob Geldof, with starving children 'dying in my living room' on a still black and white TV, as footage of the devastating famine in eastern Nigeria began to shame the world. It is not for nothing that Teresa Olatunde could have been born in the same year as I was.

Rwanda happened at a time when I had been a frequent visitor to Africa and only finished a month or so before I went on a road trip to Namibia with my husband, his brother and his wife. The flights for that trip had been on the verge of cancellation because of the terrible events there, even though it was nowhere near the areas we were to visit. The central incident at Umbeke was partly referenced by a report I'd read in 1994 about non-Rwandan aid workers at a church being killed by fires set by the mob and I vividly remember reading this and thinking how can 'they' let this go on any longer. Sadly it had been going on too long even before it started in some senses, and so the tragedy of Rwanda's Holocaust, that would have far exceeded the one in Nazi Germany if it had not been stopped, was always going to be something

I couldn't skirt around once I had decided to write about Africa and 'all human life'.

Zyanda. It is not truly Rwanda, but it is based on what happened there in 1994 and on elements of incidents that really took place and the people who might have been involved. Two accounts in the BBC online archives by neighbours, one Tutsi, one Hutu, in particular became a kind of keystone for me on how to convey the duality of the various tragedies that unfolded during the ensuing three months of genocide, where ordinary people literally made war on their next door neighbours. People they saw every day and whose children played together. In terms of human cost, in loss of lives alone, it was of course an almost unparalleled catastrophe. One that really defies dramatisation, because the truth far surpasses perception of what went on during that short, but wholly brutal period.

To be honest when I set out to write these stories it was not my intention to plumb the depths of all possible depravities and so the 'moral gymnastics' of a nation that had sunk itself in atrocity on a monumental scale and then somehow scrambled back into a semblance of a sane society, instead became the focus of David Mukuga's and Verity Beleshona's storyline. Having said that, I had no wish to write a totally realistic war narrative, so I decided that whilst this obviously had to be based on what happened in Rwanda, I needed to retain the fictional aspect, even though I wanted to be fairly authentic and so the idea of Zyanda began.

There are naturally many parallels between fact and fiction, but the main changes I made were in swapping the tribal origins of the two main factions, so the fifteenth century Horn of Africa migrant pastoralists became the majority

9

underdogs of colonial times as the wholly invented Matu, and the equally fictitious Lutse became the Bantu farmers who were the elite minority favoured under European rule, which was left fairly loose, save as to being Francophone, instead of specifically Belgian.

The other reason for making fictional rather than bare factual adjustments was that the genocide as started in 1994 has not gone away, but merely relocated into other parts of central Africa, especially to the Eastern Congo, where the murder and rape has gone on and evolved like some terrible epidemic to infect other countries and create further refugee crises that are barely containable.

Because of this, the places closest to Sophie Taylor's personal story are all fictitious, although they are again based on real locations, which I won't name, but can be found on a map if you care to look. Google Earth was invaluable in this respect, especially for the journey from real-life Mwanza, Tanzania into fictional Umbeke on the mythical Zyandan border formed on the Mgakera River - which does not exist, but if it did would eventually flow into Lake Victoria close to Tanzania's border with Uganda. There is a river roughly thereabouts, but mine is a more peaceful flow and the Mgakera Enclave is a kind of Camelot model for semi-permanent refugee camps and co-operative communities.

There are denationalised proto-communities with similar aims and purposes to the Mgakera River Enclave and I have no doubt that real-life David Mukugas, Christian Kamates and Verity Beleshonas work there. My enclave is entirely imaginary and probably far too well-run and supported. That's why this book ultimately isn't based in the real world, just one close enough to strike the right notes and focus on what's ultimately good in the human soul and in the aspirant fellowship of nations.

Which brings us back to the nature of inspiration. While the working title of The Safari Tales stood me in good stead using several viewpoints and perspectives, in the end it was not a terribly original name in the scheme of things. Finding another one was something of a headache since the safari theme was so strong, but of course the solution lay in the language that belongs to the place where the story of human survival on the continent was first discovered, starting with Homo Habilis. In the late 1980s I visited Olduvai Gorge Museum in Tanzania and saw the casts of those few small cranial relics found by Louis and Mary Leakey in 1931. Up close, they really do evoke a feeling of just how fragile and remarkable our species ascent into sentience, and the onward journey to civilisation in every corner of the world and beyond, has been. Whilst our progress has been astronomic, in essence every generation experiences the same tenuous trail of endeavour to maturity and thence to make sense of our brief existence on the planet. So in the end 'milele', literally meaning forever, presented itself as the summation of all journeys, whether fictitious or actual. Swahili is a sensible and musical language - milele, is pronounced me-lay-lay, and just seemed to suit that endlessly circling path through life's beginnings and endings, however it is woven.

In real life there are rarely happy endings and good intentions seem not so much to go a long way, as take a less than scenic route through psychological no-go zones and ethical minefields. So in the end this is pure fiction, in which the human spirit, whilst perhaps not triumphing, does try to make a good attempt at tying off ends and endeavouring not to make the same mistakes over and over. Although the book is not an 'easy read' in places and at times was difficult to write (or achieve the right tone anyway - I have an annoying habit of charging blithely through moments of high drama or tragedy), I hope that people find enjoyment along the way and much to interest in this journey through one of the most frustratingly beguiling and stupendous jumble of cultures and breathtaking collections of eco-systems on this jaded old world.

Acknowledgements

The internet is featured in these stories as a means of communication, but it has also been a bounteous source of information, if not one hundred per cent reliable at times, for some of my research, with an extra special mention for the always fascinating and rarely voiceless Wikipedia and its various portals. Where would we be without our online libraries and encyclopædias these days? Whatever I needed to look up from scratch I found at least a few lines on there about such diverse subjects as EMDR therapy (eye movement de-sensitisation and re-processing), Operation Noah, the circumcision customs of the Maasai and even a hugely interesting article about using gopo berries to counteract the dangers of the bilharzia parasite. So a plug there for a non-profit organisation and others like it, that survive on donations, which I happily subscribe to and would never begrudge a more formal acknowledgement for contributing so exhaustively, to my various avenues of investigation.

Some subjects of course needed a lot more than research and the world wide web, whilst being a very useful tool, isn't always too helpful on the detail needed to bring these stories to life, so of course I have people to thank and I must start with those who specifically gave me much needed background information and opinion in the areas where my own experience and memory were of no pertinent use.

The medical side of things was particularly vexed in some respects, even though I didn't always get too graphic, particularly in relation to the central fictional incident at

Umbeke and the section dealing with the war and ensuing famine in Biafra.

For the nursing side of things I am indebted to comments and suggestions from my friend and excellent staff nurse, Linda Mavin, especially in relation to pressure sores, dehydration and the cleansing of infected wounds.

My GP, Dr. Chris Anthony, was also kind enough to put me straight on the consequences of gunshot injuries and medication and dosing for prevention and/or treatment of malaria that was available, or effective at specific points in time, as this varies widely from region to region in Africa. Also on the efficacy of various drugs after certain periods. For the scenarios I cobbled together for Teresa Olatunde, age ten in Nigeria and then at the age of thirty six, for her and Tom Harrison in Umbeke and for Sophie Taylor in Zambia, Dr. Chris' insights were truly useful in determining just how nasty I could get with the two women in particular.

Of relief work and workers and PTSD (post-traumatic stress disorder) and how one survives personal disintegration... Some of this is drawn on personal experiences in Africa and in England, during my travels or at work. A lot of it is again based on case scenarios in news media archives, but also from my time working in the courts of the Family Division at the High Court in London. These days regrettably children even younger than Teresa Olatunde are subjected to physical and sexual abuse as serious and callous as those I subjected her to in fiction. Not just during a war, or in a so-called uncivilised Third World country.

For the more pragmatic exigencies of wartime atrocity and mindsets I am indebted to comments and reviews from my dear father, Ronald Gove and to my online friends 'Laifana', who served in Bosnia and, more recently, Afghanistan and 'Calon' who was stationed in Angola in the late 90's, on 'battleground' scenarios and behaviour for David Mukuga and his militia comrades.

My forum friend 'Penfold' was also a great sounding board for game guiding anecdotes, especially from the dual perspective of eco-tourist and game spotter, as he once worked with the guides on a South African game reserve for free, to go out with the paying customers. Sadly he doesn't drive so couldn't comment much on the vagaries of truck driving, but we'd been well versed in these by an ophiophobic guide in Kenya (ever see a black guy's skin go grey? - this chap's did when we came across a puff adder wending its way over the trail!) and numerous breakdowns of the tyre variety on a memorable self-drive holiday in Namibia. Africa isn't kind to any sort of motor vehicle, no matter how robust...

To John Leach, Operations Manager at Shelterbox in Helston, Cornwall, I have to say a big thank you for his time and patience in answering my questions and giving me a wealth of information and anecdotes on the logistics of getting aid to where it's needed as quickly and efficiently as possible; the type of people they need to do that; the other organisations that help them get aid where it's wanted and not sitting around in some container port; and some of the obstacles they have to deal with to get their so necessary boxes of tent and home-making supplies to those who don't have any. These insights were especially helpful as background for the *Hard Rains* and *Angels of the Abyss* chapters and even though I'd already 'invented' CAMEO by then, it was very reassuring to know that there are real life equivalents out there (such as ACTED - Agence d'Aide à la Coopération Technique Et au

Développement) doing such necessary and dedicated work. Also thanks to John for recommending *Emergency Sex (and Other Desperate Measures)* by former UN workers Ken Cain, Heidi Postlethwait and Andrew Thomson, which helped with some of the background for the genocide aspects and insights into the mindset of the perpetrators of racial massacres and, perhaps more importantly, those brave souls who have to go in and literally pick up the grisly pieces.

Finally for my expert contributor, Linda Winn, an amazing drama therapist and EMDR practitioner, was my much-needed core piece of the jigsaw for the therapy research in relation to the ravages of PTSD. The connection between this devastating mental and emotional disorder and military excursions is by now well-established, but I already knew about EMDR from a friend in relation to less martial areas. Victims of violent physical and sexual crime have also benefitted from this increasingly applied type of therapy. The whole issue of how to care for and reintegrate people who have been dehumanised and violated mentally and emotionally, as well as physically, is a subject that demands justice and authenticity in its portrayal.

I needed a lot of help in other words and Linda was able to give me a lot of pertinent and very useful feedback on the character backgrounds connected to the Umbeke incident, and practical steering on the actual mechanics of EMDR as undergone by David Mukuga. Some of the specifics have been glossed for the sake of pace, but are still there implicitly in David's and Sophie's journals and in terms of the 'safe place' sufferers are encouraged to construct, which can of course sometimes rest in other people, or a state of mind, as well as a visually realised 'somewhere'.

On general reading services I have several people to thank for reviews and feedback, not least my truly excellent editor Sue Bridgwater and other friends and writing partners on DreamWorlds and other online forums for their insights and encouragement.

These include, Galen, Nurbor, Dagrun, Deldaisy, Doughnut Jimmy, Juggler, michelanCello and raisindot. Off forum there was also my long-suffering husband Peter, Janine Hawke, Mike Billingham and my mother who stood over miscellaneous friends and neighbours and threatened to sulk royally at them if they didn't have a read of some or all of the writing as it progressed.

Having such a wide and varied cadre of reviewers was more than helpful in keeping me writing on the sometimes difficult content, as responses were in general positive, despite it being very different to some of the reviewers' general personal preferences in reading matter. Guys - your time, insights and feedback have all been appreciated so much!

Finally my heartfelt thanks and appreciation to my sister, Tina Rendle for agreeing to do the final proof read and critique for me. Having decided to take the independent road to publication, this task was of course absolutely vital and one which I could really only ask of someone related to me by blood and roughly equivalent literary affinities, since we are both SF&F nuts (although we differ in our tolerance of Dickens). I guess I must also thank Mum here again, for always insisting that Tina and I apologise to each other whenever we fought as kids. Who knew we could grow up and still be friends, just by liking the same books?

Inevitably I will have forgotten somebody, therefore an apology for doing so naturally and a general, but very sincere thank you to everyone for your assistance, kindness, honesty and thoroughness throughout the process of my writing the book. I've already said to individuals and generally online how this whole endeavour has given me the most marvellous experience. I literally could not have had such a wild and exhilarating ride without the help and support of all the people mentioned here.

Smoke and Thunder

Sophie's Diary: Thursday 26th April ~ near Livingstone, Zambia

Amazing! We walked across the actual lip of the Falls from the Zambian side almost as far as Livingstone Island. This place is different every time I come here. I remember seeing the Falls just after the rains last time all those years back, when I'd never really regarded water as an element that defined Africa, except in a negative way. Tom was with me and it had such a profound effect on us both (not just the emotional-sexual side although that made it so memorable of course) that I could never again forget the power and beauty of water and how much it sums up every part of Africa and its people and their economies. Perhaps that was because my earliest travels took me mainly to land-locked farming communities where water was far more precious than gold during droughts and the children listened to my stories of rain that fell gently and steadily for days on end with longing in their eyes, and of snow with open-mouthed disbelief. In those areas a lack of water was at least well understood but a surfeit – flash floods and suchlike were almost more dreaded than drought and much less predictable of course. Too much water or nothing like enough – an eternal dilemma for African farmers. I had never thought deeply on how much abundance of water could be such a boon if it could be controlled even a little until I visited Victoria Falls, but at the time all I could think of was how truly beautiful and spectacular the Zambezi was.

How would I describe the Falls? I suppose it would depend on what time of year you went to them. In dry seasons they are still impressive and, to some people, more beautiful as the constricted river flows in ethereal, lacy ribbons down the various gorges. People from North America scoff that 'Niagra beats the pants off this', conveniently forgetting that their connubial resort's attraction is firmly under control and almost completely tamed by dams and hydraulic engineering. But if they try to say that just after the rains you won't be able to see or hear them for the heavy mists and the rumbling, tumbling roar of the Zambezi as over half a million cubic metres of water career hundreds of feet downwards, across a span over a mile across and seemingly through a thousand channels and chasms. Dr. Livingstone was right you inevitably conclude if you experience the Falls at this time when the Zambezi is swollen to its limit – Angels would indeed pause in their flight. Mosi-oa-tunya.

The Smoke that Thunders…

… 'My first time here?' Sophie gave a small twisted smile as they all sat about the 'campfire' in the lodge later that evening. 'With my parents when I was fourteen I suppose. But it was the dry season then and I don't really count that as my first time - the Zambezi is a little pussycat then. No. My first sight of it in almost full spate was about four years later and I was with…' She gazed into the fire for a few moments before speaking again. 'Sorry. I was with a good friend. The river was really high and fast and some of the extreme sports firms wouldn't run their rafts in certain parts of the rapids because it was too dangerous – more than a 'five' anyway – too much of an insurance risk.' She grinned at the two cameramen. 'We were staying on the Zimbabwe side – before it started going badly over there and their petrol prices were really cheap so the Zambians were swarming across the bridge to trade for things they just couldn't get hold of at home. We had a couple of days break from work so we decided to stay in town and do the whole tourist thing. We went to the Vic Falls National Park, which is a really nice little reserve – you can get right out over some of the chasms if you're careful. But when the river is full like it was today – and the time we were there - you almost become a part of the Falls. The air is thick with misty droplets, so fine and light that sometimes you're breathing them in…. and the sound is stupendous. The ground shakes and you can feel the impact of the cascades in your throat and the percussion rising up through your legs. It's visceral… primeval even. It was so beautiful and wonderful that we both cried…' Sophie fell silent again and others began to talk about their own experience of the great waterfall. The general consensus was that it was awesome in the true sense of the word.

They had all gone to bed now except for her and the driver, Adam, who had come back to talk to Reception about some forward booking that had gone awry. Sophie had turned at the sound of his quiet low voice and smilingly waved him over to join her when he was done. They began to talk about small things, how Livingstone had changed since the last time she had been there. Anything so she didn't have to go back to her room just yet. She didn't want to be alone and certainly didn't want to go to sleep yet, or rather go to bed and lie there restless in the dusky blue light of the full moon, rippling through thin curtains, thinking about Tom. How blissful they had felt not two miles away across the great gorge in one of the basic but very spick and span lodges. That truly wonderful, magic night they had made their future plans and been so, so happy and so much in love…

… She sat bolt upright in her bed, shaking violently, still half in the nightmare, her face wet with soft tears. Sophie leant her hot forehead against her knees and tried to breathe slowly and deeply as the memory of the bad dream faded into her past again. After a few minutes, feeling calmer, she got up and went onto the patio and sat down on one of the smartly cushioned garden chairs, smiling at the banality of the little area with the neatly trimmed shrubs – she could be back in Surrey, or the Med perhaps. Until you looked up at the night sky. The moon had set and the heavens were strung with unrivalled starlight against deep blue-black velvet such as you never saw in Britain. Here in the tropics the Milky Way blazed opalescent as morning mist on the moors and the sky was huge with the light of suns, billions of light years away. They were tiny sky-diamonds that glittered like celestial frost, mocking the sultry warmth of the rainforest at night. It always moved her. She and Tom had loved to stay up late and gaze and gaze at them, wrapped up in each other's arms. She squeezed her eyes tight shut and willed the tears back. She had known visiting the Falls would be a trial, but she hadn't had the dream for so long now she had thought she would be spared on that count at least.

It always began so beautifully, with her and Tom making love that night – well it was barely the evening actually - when they had run all the way back from the Falls to their little lodge about a mile upriver out of Vic Falls. They had both felt so humbled, yet excited by the mighty roaring and reverberation that filled every sense just as she had described earlier that evening to the others. And they had both cried a little - well Tom had shed a few manly tears pretending there was grit in his eye - she had wept buckets and he had held her tightly, comfortingly in his arms. Then, with the closer contact they found they could feel the Falls in each other and began to get so aroused by the sensations. The vibration

23

from the rock underfoot and the warm damp mists from the cascade falling like a caress on bare shoulders, arms and legs, that it completely set their libidos alight as they stood at the edge of the southern cataract wall of the gorge, with a dozen or so others. Before they really knew it she and Tom were kissing and touching passionately. Someone had coughed meaningfully and then someone else had started giggling and they had abruptly recalled where they were and run off, cackling like hyenas. They had kept on jogging, hand in hand, until they tumbled back into their little room at the Lodge and then fell onto the bed, barely bothering to pull off what clothing they had on and the sex hadn't stopped for hours and hours – they had missed dinner at any rate and could only get cold room service when they had finally stopped to get their breath back.

But it was after that hurried meal that the dream replayed, when they were so soft and gentle and loving. They had lain together whispering quietly to each other, tenderly kissing, stroking warm skin and tasting each other everywhere, hardly able to bear a second when they weren't touching each other somewhere. It was when they both knew they would never want to be apart again ever. It was the night he had asked her to marry him. And it was the night that she had conceived, although of course she hadn't known that at the time. They had gone on whispering and stroking and kissing until they had fallen asleep in each other's arms, spent and blissfully tired, still listening to the dim thudding of the Falls in the distance, with the starlight falling on their beautiful nakedness.

It was not the time that she had been bitten and caught the disease. That had been several weeks before and it was still incubating then. She had started being sick occasionally,

24

feeling vaguely ill, but hadn't realised what was happening to her. It was enough to stop her contraception working anyway. But by the time she had found out she was pregnant and had contracted malaria it was far too late because by then Tom was dead and her life was over or so she thought. The life of their baby was over before it had even started – she had miscarried after only six weeks, devastated by grief, feverish and exhausted by the insidious disease, so like a bad bout of gastric 'flu, but poisoning her blood and invading her womb, befouling the placenta. It had killed the darling baby that was all she had to hold onto after the news had come through that Tom and Sister Teresa had been murdered by terrified 'soldiers' in a tiny refugee camp on the Tanzanian border with Zyanda. She couldn't remember much about that time because she had fallen into a minor coma the day after the dreadful news came through, and, when she came around a few days later, she had lost the child as well. Her co-workers had already sent for Claire and begun to make the arrangements to send her home to England where she could recover properly and then heal her grief. And of course she did recover eventually, but she doubted she would ever heal fully.

But the dream mercifully left out that bit, although in a way she would have preferred to linger over those awful days to what it did move onto. Always the same. That perfect end to the night and then she dreamt she woke up and everything was white. She was always alone at first. Tom wasn't there and she was just sitting on the ground and gradually the white light turned golden and someone touched her lightly on the shoulder. It was Terry. She hugged Sophie and kissed her lightly on the cheek. Which was very strange because they had never really been friends at all. But it felt right in

25

the dream up until the kiss, because that was when Sophie realised that Terry wasn't wearing her nun's habit, but a tribal dress and that she had great wounds in her chest and on the left side of her face. Terry smiled as much as she still could and whispered 'I'm so sorry Sophie. It was my fault, but I could not stand there and do nothing.' and then she was gone, and that was always where she began to cry because someone else was coming.

It was Tom of course, but she couldn't see him properly at first as the golden light was so intense. It worried her that he didn't seem to have any lower arms, until she realised he was holding something... someone. Someone very small. He held them tenderly and seemed to be humming softly at them. Then she could see him properly and his head and torso was covered in blood and so was the baby. Their dead unborn baby, but it seemed to be alive and smiling at her. He came and knelt down in front of her and leaned over to kiss her softly on the mouth. She could always taste the blood, his blood from the wound on his forehead that had trickled all down his face. She never looked at the baby – she couldn't, but she knew it was there because it brushed her breast with its little hand. Tom spoke to her too. Just a few words 'It's OK Soph – I'm looking after her. Don't worry babe.' And then he was gone too, with the baby, and then she would really wake up, sweating and crying frantically, her lip or her tongue bitten and bleeding.

'Don't worry babe.' Those were his last words to her when he left, with Terry looking so sanctimonious and noble up in the lorry cab, driving drugs and medical supplies to the agency's distribution depot in Tanzania. She rubbed her lower lip thoughtfully. At least she hadn't bitten it too hard this time. She let the tears come finally – they were a release now and maybe she would be able to get a few hours sleep at least. How glad she was that they had to come to the Livingstone side. It would have been too awful to stay in Vic Falls. Well she wouldn't have come on this trip at all of course if they were staying on the Zimbabwe side. She had never been back there since those wondrous few days that had meant so much to them both.

So far as her poor heart was concerned she did not wish her memory of that time to be disturbed and tarnished. Some wounds never healed. But she didn't have a monopoly on grief – that had been her mantra for a while back in England - she wasn't the only person who had lost the dearest, truest thing in their life. The one person she wanted still after all these years. And it was good to see the Falls again and remember something so beautiful and honest and fine. But not from the same place, because she couldn't go back there. It was lost to her and she had already let it go a long time ago. Some things are worth remembering though, even if it gives pain. Some pains are supposed to hurt and should never be forgotten.

Sophie woke with a start and grabbed the telephone which was buzzing annoyingly. Adam's voice crackled down the line. Was she joining them for breakfast and then a short excursion over the bridge and lunch at the Victoria Falls Hotel? She told him no for both breakfast and trip and said she'd meet them all in the lobby later in the afternoon, when they departed for Lusaka and the next leg of the safari. Before flopping back down on the pillows she reached over and turned the fans up a little and watched the wicker struts making flickering shadows on the ceiling. She smiled at another memory. The yanks would love the Vic Falls Hotel that still pulled in rich punters and their much-needed currency even now in the bad times – it was so beautiful and so incongruous. Maybe they still had a steel band playing in the lovely, lush tropical gardens every lunch-time? You could sit out there and eat very thinly cut cucumber sandwiched between immaculate slices of fresh-baked white bread on fine china, sipping hot Indian single estate tea that arrived in steaming silver teapots. Then carry on relaxing out on the verandah, or under the enormous thatched umbrellas and listen to 'Yellow Bird' or imagine you were sitting on the 'Dock of the Bay' with cape doves and the 'wireless' birds providing a weird backing track to the ridiculously kitsch metallic warbling of the steel drums; trying to decide whether to have a dessert now or wait until it was time for afternoon tea and scones with thick cream and fruity jam, or even lemon curd, or ginger preserve! Her mouth watered slightly at the thought of the English-inspired delicacies that seemed so right still in such a different climate and culture. In a different century now as well. Anyway, she would hear all about it when they got back later on. She didn't need to go there herself, her memories were enough.

No. She would stay here and sleep on a little and then read her paperback, or write in her diary, out on the little patio. She had inspected the room service menu very thoroughly the day before and she could order Assam tea with cucumber sandwiches and plain scones with ginger preserves and cream for her self-indulgent solitary luncheon. It would be good to be quiet and keep her own company in peace for a few hours out there, where, if she cared to look, she could just see the rise of the great smoky white towers of water-mist over the top of the rainforest and listen to the thunderous voice of the Zambezi rolling on forever. And remember how truly good it had been for them both.

Watching

Sophie's Diary: Saturday 28th April ~ Kafue, Zambia

Hot and humid during the day out here by the confluence of the Kafue and Lufupa rivers, but so beautiful. It reminds me of Vutare a little, down by the garage - the view across the river anyway. There are mostly Twa[1] living around here and some working in the camp as well, though most of the guides and drivers are from the south and look to be from more mainstream farming communities - the fishing here is pretty good, some yummy perch last night for dinner. Thankfully we're in rondavels[2] on the hill so we get the breeze off the river at night and they do night drives as well. We spotted some aardvarks last night which was interesting as I'd never seen them before. Porcupines too and a darling little civet cat. They have leopards here as well and we've been told we're almost bound to see at least one while we're here. Can't wait for that - they're my favourite big cat...

The salt blood from the kill had given her a raging thirst. Although the impala ram was barely adolescent, it had put up more of a struggle than she had bargained for and the early afternoon heat was not a good time for a full-blown wrestling match. She had to slake her dusty throat before she started the tiring business of dragging her prize to safety. The river

---

[1] **Twa** ~ one of the more ancient tribes of central Africa who range west and south into Zambia. They tend to live in wetlands and trade with the more numerous Bantu farming tribes. These are not to be confused with the Twa of more central parts of the Congo who are pygmies.

---

[2] **rondavel** ~ a circular hut, usually built of mud or wattle and a conical, reed-thatched roof.

was close by, so the chances that her food could be stolen away were low, as the pride and the hated pack would still be farther back in the bush, dozing in the shade whilst the sun was high.

She lithely climbed the bank once more, her aching jowls now cool and dripping, froze, and then flattened herself slowly into the long dry grass. Several tall-apes, chattering and making uncouth hyena coughs around one of their enormous smelly zebra-striped beasts had appeared on the edge of the glade where her hard won meal lay. It was not unusual to see the tall animals inside the belly of their strange huge roaring beasts that always seemed to be close by these curious almost hairless creatures. However, the sight of them walking around their monstrous mount in her river range was disturbing, even though she knew she had little to fear from them. She could see that they had not spotted her kill and knew no other predator would approach whilst they were making such a racket. Crouching low on the crest of the bank, secure in the knowledge that they could not see her through the long grass, she settled down to watch and wait patiently until they left.

The strange apes were much taller than their crooked-tailed baboon cousins who lived in the rocky country to the east of her territory. They always moved around on their hind legs; a lurching, ungainly gait when compared to her own graceful athlete's stride. Their garish coats, all differently coloured or marked, were even more outlandish and offered poor camouflage, which was surely dangerous for such a seemingly defenceless animal. However, she knew better than most of her kind that the tall-apes were not weaponless and, using their stinking striped monsters, could easily outrun a zebra or even a cheetah over distance. She would not confront these raucous, arrogant creatures, especially a whole troop of them, unless her own life or those of her cubs were in gravest jeopardy.

At last, with a rumbling fart and a cloud of dark smoke, the tall-apes' malodorous beast began to make its usual monotonous roaring sound. The apes all gave loud barks and coughs of triumph and climbed back into the belly of the monster. She knew they would soon leave, so she glided slowly away from them, keeping downwind and below the edge of the bank, intending to circle back to her impala as soon as they moved off.

As she left one of the older males got out again to retrieve a tool he had dropped whilst working on the engine. As he climbed back into the minibus cab he glanced back at the river and caught a flick of her pale tail fur and its distinctive dark tip as she slunk behind a stand of dusty acacia. From his higher vantage point, his sharp tracker's eyes also took in the flattened area and the lifeless twist of impala horns not far from the bank where she had struggled to bring down the ram. He knew she would be back for her fallen prey as soon as they left. They would return to this area later, as his safari clients would be impressed to see leopard on a kill.

Once she was satisfied that the tall-apes had left the glade, she took a firm grasp of the ram's neck with her powerful jaws and began the arduous task of getting the carcass into deep cover. Luckily she was dragging the kill into wind and was able to hide it in a tangled mass of fallen thorn browse not far from the clearing and close to where she had left her two cubs earlier that morning. Hungry from her exertions she tore hair from the rump with her rough tongue and took a few ravenous mouthfuls of prime meat before she went to fetch her sons.

They greeted her with delight, licking the drying blood and flecks of meat from her mouth and neck and squirmed with pleasure as she in turn rubbed her face over their chubby little bodies. Then, with an upward flick and sway of her long black tipped tail, she turned back on her tracks and began to lead them to the still new and delicious experience of a meal of fresh meat.

When they arrived at the hidden stash, still free from the recent spoor of rival carnivores, she efficiently proceeded to eviscerate the ram and pull out the juicy nourishing vitals that her young would find easy to digest. They tumbled energetically nearby, inflicting inexperienced but nonetheless sharp nips and ripping blows, learning how defend themselves whilst looking for the chance to make a decisive strike. One day their exuberant games would allow them to hunt and kill as proficiently as their mother. A soft growl from her quickly drew them back to the serious business of mealtime and the portion of delectable soft warm liver that she had saved for them. Only half-weaned, the cubs could not eat much meat, so she was able enjoy her own meal without having to keep order over who got what tasty morsel.

Eventually, sated by the rich food, the cubs began to nuzzle into her soft belly seeking milk, warmth and sleep, leaving her free to lie deep in the shade, stripping hair from a haunch she had detached, savouring the tender flesh. She was starting to feel drowsy herself when once more the low rumbling roar of the tall-apes' beast was heard in the distance. Realising it was getting closer she shook her cubs away and started to pull the ram further into the protective depths of the fallen brush. Calling urgently to her young she retrieved the leg and they all crawled under the shelter of the dense thorn of the branches as far in as they could go. She hoped it would be deep enough to shield them from the tall-apes notice.

The minibus driver-guide had found their feasting place with relative ease by returning to the killing ground and following the drag marks and bloody traces to the leopard's stash site. After his first glimpse of the leopard, he'd taken his clients a little further into the bush to view eland and giraffe and follow a family of elephants before starting back to where he'd seen the leopard and her kill and radioing his firm's co-drivers to direct them to the area. This gave him a little more time to track her and get to the stash first and bag the best vantage point for his guests – this would almost certainly be the highlight of their safari and earn him a nice big tip. He settled back in his seat with the engine off, happily enveloped in the lucrative sounds of whirring motor drives and the fat clicking of expensive cameras, waiting for the inevitable questions about the leopard. This was an excellent end to his day as he happened to know a great deal about this particular animal and knew his guests would be enthralled by her history.

The leopard's opinion of this turn of events was very different. However, she realised they had no alternative but to stay put – at least they had food close by and the sun was now low in the sky so the tall-apes would leave before it had sunk below the trees to get back to their lair in the twilight. She hardly bothered to look at the monster as she knew it could not get closer and turned her attention to cleaning her sons' grubby faces with her rasping tongue and then tearing more skin from the haunch.

The barrage of noise from the tall-apes and the strange black and silver pebbles that they held to their heads as she performed these seemingly mundane domestic tasks did not really bother her until her elder son started to get interested in the intrusive racket. She quickly gave him a warning cough but he'd already fled back to the protective curve of her downy belly as his few hesitant steps towards the striped beast had provoked even more noise and mad flapping of arms. She snarled her displeasure at the impertinent apes then pulled herself up and around the cubs and the food, putting her body in front of them so only her back faced the unwelcome gaze of the apes. Giving a last low growl of irritation she lay down again, glaring over her shoulder occasionally, but remaining otherwise unmoved by the arrival of a second and then a third and fourth monster.

After twenty minutes or so the guide decided that they ought to make room for other minibuses, as word had obviously been passed around the lodge's clientele and he could hear several more vehicles coming over. He hoped that his colleagues would soon follow him back to their evening base but knew that the leopard family would attract even more attention before the afternoon was done. The little clearing now looked like a small parking lot with around eight minibuses greedily clustered as near to the leopard's refuge as they could get and at least ten more circling the area waiting for their turn to get close. He felt a small twist of guilt for the cubs, wondering whether this unwelcome intrusion would stress them, but that was the safari business these days – the clients craved the Big Five and if they saw a kill and cubs then everyone was happy. Consoling himself with the knowledge that his guests were ecstatic at being the first to get their unhurried photographic trophies of this heaven sent opportunity, he blessed the dirty sparkplug that had caused their breakdown by the river, not five minutes out from the lodge. He'd be the envy of the other drivers tonight and, best of all, have the fattest wallet at the end of the week.

Dusk: first of nearly thirty entries in the Kifaru River Lodge game log

Spotted upriver from the Lodge - Female leopard (Lyssa) and 2 cubs. Lyssa, (the orphaned leopard raised by the famous wildlife author and pioneer conservationist Joanne Eveman) has not been seen at the night bait tree for several weeks so her absence has now been explained. Both cubs appear to be male, around eight weeks old and were nursing and taking solids.

The Land of Nod

... Cain rose up against Abel his brother, and slew him... And Cain went out from the presence of the Lord, and dwelt in the land of Nod, on the east of Eden.

Gen 4:8 and Gen 4:16 **(King James version)**

Extract from Sister Teresa Olatunde's Journal:
14th May 1994 Dragoman[3] distribution depot Mwanza, N.W. Tanzania

... so tomorrow the work begins in earnest. My heart is at once heavy and hopeful about the challenges ahead, but dear Tom will be with me a little longer at least and that is a great comfort to me. He wanted to get back to Sophie as she had been taken very ill again when we left Vutare, but we've just heard on the radio 'phone that she is much improved and is pregnant. Strange really, because I was beginning to think she had malaria, despite her almost manic obsession with taking her pills and repellents, but I guess it was just the usual drinking bad water and consequent gastric problems. It would certainly account for her getting pregnant I suppose as she had been vomiting so much. God has ways to overcome the strongest oral contraception! Tom is very pleased really and went into Mwanza yesterday afternoon to buy a beautiful tanzanite and diamond engagement ring for her. He said

---

[3] **Dragoman** ~ very large robust trucks of the types used by Aid Agencies and haulage companies in places like Africa, to carry supplies of food, fuel, medicines and other supplies, including people, where they cannot be flown in due to the roads being rough or non-existent, or because of other environmental and/or political prerogatives. Travel companies also now use similar vehicles for back-packing style holidays all over the globe.

the tanzanite was the same colour as her eyes on a sunny day – hopeless romantic that he is! Sometimes I wish Sophie liked me more – I see the hurt in Tom's eyes when she looks daggers at me, but I suppose she does not understand how it is with us and thinks I am some kind of rival? She does not understand that he is like my poor lost little brother to me and maybe the only true male friend I will ever have.

I felt horrible asking him to take me on to Umbeke, but Jacob has come down with a really bad dose of dysentery and there were no other drivers here that I trust, so he said it was no problem. I feel a little guilty about delaying his return but I must admit I am very glad he will be at my side for the first few days or so. I thank the Lord for sending this work to me – helping those poor women and young girls and their children. It will be so hard at first but He will send me strength and I shall not falter nor abandon my sisters to their undeserved degradation and awful despair. Sweet Jesus grant me the will to help them unreservedly, as I was helped, to bring them back to the light and maybe to find happiness again....

This was just terrible. Terry was shaking like a leaf beside him, the scarring on her face paler than ever, but she refused to let him comfort her and had shaken his arm away when he tried to put it around her shoulders. The German couple, grey-haired and in their late fifties so far as he could tell, appeared to be calm enough and he was glad that they seemed to be able to talk haltingly to the militia men in their own dialect and a little more in French. His hazy schoolboy French couldn't keep up with the furiously fast flow of orders that the soldiers' leader kept barking out. On the drive over Terry had told him that the couple were her godparents and had 'saved her immortal soul' when she was a young girl. They were career aid workers and were rebuilding the old mission to use as an emergency refugee camp under the sponsorship of a branch of the UN. So he would have been impressed with them anyway, but now he was truly relieved they were here and seemed to be keeping Terry from unravelling altogether.

The armed men were gesturing for them to go back into the school house now, at least the two with automatic weapons were. The militia men, Matus he assumed, were either very old or very young and most seemed almost as terrified as the huddled group of women, teenage girls and children that they had corralled under the rusty iron-roofed canteen. Not all of them wore uniforms, in fact one looked as though he was a clergyman of some kind. He seemed to be in charge of these ragged 'soldiers' and had a dog collar on under a flea-bitten camouflage jacket. They were all armed but mostly with pangas.[4] There were only about a dozen of them and of those only three had elderly hunting rifles apart from the two men with the AKs or whatever they were. Tom wondered if their weapons were even loaded, the whole group looked so down at heel and disorganised. But they were very jittery and he knew the best thing was to try to keep the situation as cool as they could and not antagonise them too much.

The Germans had turned and were walking back to the school building, but Terry was still almost rooted to the spot, shivering like a beaten dog. Gently but firmly he took hold of her arm, ignoring her violent flinch and almost dragged her back with him to join the couple and their male helper. He'd forgotten all their names already.

'Come on Terry – you're stronger than this, huh?' He kept

---

[4] **Panga** ~ a large heavy-bladed knife like a machete. Generally used in Africa for cutting through thick vegetation, or butchering carcasses of bush-meat.

his voice low as he pulled her into the school room 'Where's the lady who saved me from the sleepy snake during the engine-check this morning?'

Tom smiled as naturally he could at her as they went inside but the nun broke away, fled into the German woman's maternal arms and broke down completely. He rubbed his own watering eyes as his whole world seemed to turn upside down and stared at his friend in disbelief. She was always so cool and professional. He had never, ever seen her remotely upset by anything, no matter how bad or heart-rending, but as soon as she had set eyes on those women under the kitchen roof and the soldiers guarding them she had gone to pieces on him. Thank God Sophie hadn't come with them, even though she had been mad as hell with him for refusing to let her. He held onto the little trinket box with the engagement ring inside his jacket pocket like a talisman, turning it over and over with his fingers.

The older man turned to him and spoke in passable English. 'Snakes are one thing to be brave about my friend, but even heroes can be laid low by bad memories.' His pale blue eyes were worried too, but Tom appreciated the effort and smiled ruefully at him.

'I know. I'm Tom – Terry did tell me your names but... er... I'm afraid I'm not used to being held at gunpoint and I've forgotten them.'

The German smiled at the sad attempt at humour. 'I am Henryk and this is my wife Helga. And this fine young man, Christian, is our interpreter. His father was Zyandan. Matu. I am so sorry we could not warn you in time to turn you back – you saw what they did to our poor Aaron.'

Tom nodded, trying not to think of the other young Tanzanian who had run out to 'greet' them, or so they had thought, as they drove into the centre of the little group of old mission huts. Aaron had tried to warn them, but they were already out of the cab, unable to understand him and smiling in bewilderment, until he had been dragged away by three of the militia men and knifed repeatedly, whilst they both looked on in horror and confusion as more soldiers appeared and levelled rifles at them.

'God rest his soul.' Helga spoke English more hesitantly than her husband. 'Shush little Teresa. The Lord's will be done however hard that may seem. Remember you are his instrument and he will preserve you if that is his will. You must find courage and faith – for others as well as for yourself.'

Amazingly this seemed to calm Terry. These were obviously aid workers of the old school and he felt a little uncomfortable hearing the unpretentious and unfashionably pious words. Tom watched as the nun visibly relaxed and gathered herself in again. His own breath eased and he smiled sheepishly as she looked at him apologetically.

'Sorry Tom – like Henryk said. Bad memories are overwhelming sometimes.' She was his bold, forthright friend once more, her soft low voice steady again, her eyes clear and unafraid, though tears still trailed down her face. She came over to him and squeezed his hand gently. 'I am well now. I will be strong for those women and their babies.'

He looked into her dark, dark eyes and thought he understood. He nodded at her and ran his fingers through his sun-bleached brown hair and laughed softly. 'Terry – no wonder that snake skedaddled when he saw you coming this morning!' Her grip on his hand tightened and she smiled at him like an angel.

'What are they doing out there now Christian?' It was two

hours later and Henryk was looking tired and old, sitting down at the trestle table, sagging visibly in the heat and humidity of the school house. Christian was looking out of the one tiny glazed and mud-stained window and shook his head, turning towards them sadly.

'They are still talking to one of the older women. I cannot make out what they are saying but she is weeping now. She is on her knees before the one with the white collar. He is very angry to her.'

Terry sighed with impatience. 'We must be able to do something surely?' It was the fiftieth time she had said something like this since she'd pulled herself together Tom thought. Henryk appeared to concur as Terry joined Christian at the window. The old German spoke with authority still despite his dejected looks. 'So long as they are just talking we should wait. If we interfere it may make things worse. You know this as well as I Teresa...'

Barely a second after he said it both Christian and Terry jumped and drew breath sharply. 'He is hitting her!'

Christian's appalled exclamation was drowned out by Terry's outraged shout 'Stop that you filthy animal!'
Nobody was quick enough to stop her as she hurtled past an open-mouthed Tom and out of the door, deftly evading the one militia man left guarding them. Briefly he trained his weapon after her, but the others were all on their feet and Tom was halfway towards the door himself. The young Matu was wide-eyed and frightened and swung the gun around nervously as Tom came to an abrupt halt with the three others cannoning into his back. They could all hear Terry yelling like a banshee and the clergyman screaming back at her in rapid French. Their guard was getting a grip and gestured fiercely for them to get back. They all hurried back to the

little window, all four of them craning around to try and see what was happening outside.

'They are not wicked! They are frightened you devil-spawn!' Terry's eyes blazed with fury. 'What did they ever do to you?' Her French was suddenly fluent again after all these years. She was still scared as hell, but her anger was aflame now and it carried her on, passionately determined to stop this craven traitor who dared to declare himself a Man of God, no matter what it took.

'Keep out of this you snivelling worm!' He snarled. 'These women are less then pigs and they must come back to Zyanda with us!' He snapped at one of the men with a rifle. 'Get this stupid foreigner back inside or kill her!' He turned his mad eyes back on Terry. 'Go back to your no-good ghosts before I really lose my temper!'

'Sister – come. You cannot help them.' Terry spun and looked angrily at the mildly-spoken old man who nonetheless raised his rifle expertly. He had used guns before. But he was hesitant and her rage was flowing like wildfire through her veins now. In her head she was a scrawny, starving ten year old again, but with all the knowledge and strength of a survivor of war, rape and callous torture. She was no longer a terrified victim. She was not even afraid anymore. Her Lord was in her heart now and this was what she had to do.

'Why do you follow him?' She spoke rather than shouted the words at the other Matu men, pointing at the false priest, but her voice carried as far as the school house. 'He is Cain – a murderer! The blood of the innocent is on his hands and he will lead you all to Hell if you do his bidding!' The rifle-man looked at the priest shiftily and back at this unhinged nun who looked like a fiery angel and had no apparent fear of his useless weapon. They had run out of bullets long before they came over the border. He frowned at the woman, keeping the redundant rifle steadily aimed at her heart. He admired her bravery but it would be safest for everyone, even the Lutse women, if she stayed with the Europeans.

'It would be best if you went back to your friends Sister. Best for everyone, huh?' he spoke very quietly in laboured French, his eyes hard, belying the turmoil inside. He was sick of the killing frenzy. All he wanted now was to go back to Zyanda and try to forget all about the disgusting carnage that had swept over them these past few months. This holy woman was right. They were all murderers and carried the mark of Cain. They had killed the Lutse men, women and infants even, over and over until he was sick of the sight of blood, the sound of crunching bone and metal cutting flesh. The pathetic screams of agony. And now they were hunting terrified women and babies – a few of them were not even Lutse, and it was one of these Matu 'traitors' that the mad priest was still beating.

His voice lowered and he held the little nun's glare regretfully 'Please Sister. I do not want to kill you. We have no quarrel with you or the other foreigners. Go back to the school house and all of you will be safe. You have my word.'

'What is she saying?!' Tom was frantic, feeling completely powerless. Helga was hanging onto his and Henryk's arms. He did not know who was trembling more, her or him. Henryk's and Christian's eyes were fixed on Terry as she stood before a lanky old man who looked more soldier-like than the rest of the other Matu.

'She called them all murderers. Now she is saying they are not men if they make war on defenceless women and children.' Henryk's face was pale now and he pulled nervously at his full grey beard. 'Christian – please tell our friend at the door that we could help. Bring her back inside at least.' As the beanpole Tanzanian did as he was asked, talking softly but urgently in the boy soldier's dialect, Henryk turned to look up at Tom.

'Are you a gambling man Tom? There is something in the way these men are holding themselves. The ones with the rifles. They are too... what is your word...? Nervous? No. Uncomfortable. I think their guns are not loaded.'

'I thought that earlier too.' Tom's voice was quiet, although he was sure the guard knew no English. 'What about this one with us? He's certainly nervous but he's just a scared little kid with a big automatic – what if he still has ammo?'

'Maybe. And they still have their pangas of course. Let us see if Christian can persuade him to let us go outside. Helga my dear you must stay in here please. Christian can stay with you – it only needs Tom and I to talk to Teresa. Please my dearest. For our grand-children.'

Helga was sobbing openly now but nodded obediently and sat down heavily by the trestle, and covered her face with her hands. She was praying quietly. Tom was once again relieved that Sophie had not come with them. He wished fervently that he had stayed with her, but maybe he and Henryk might yet be able to extricate Terry from this awful mess. He sent out a silent prayer of his own to any deity who might be listening, that all the guns, manual or automatic, were indeed empty.

The voices by the door were growing more animated even as those outside soared back and forth in anger and outrage. Tom's eyes were torn between the two young Africans and Terry who was still refusing to be cowed. The soldier-priest had come over again and was yelling at her and the old guy with the rifle.

'You know why Terry is behaving so recklessly Tom?' Henryk's heavily accented English was harsh with stress.'

'I think so – she's doesn't like to talk much about her childhood. In Biafra. It was too brutal. I asked her about her scars so she told me about that and some other bits.' About how she was repeatedly beaten and raped then finally shot and left for dead after the Nigerian soldiers has used her as an ashtray. And he had thought they were tribal scars! His face flamed with embarrassment at the memory of her matter of fact explanation of the puckered white marks they had made on her thin little face and all over her emaciated ten year old torso and arms. His breathing was ragged now as it hit him. How truly hard this must be on her – not just this current horror, but what she must have felt when she was assigned to this project. But she had been really incandescent with excitement about it, saying how she had wanted to do something like this for so long. No wonder she had lost it earlier. And was so charged up now…

Tom's gaze strayed to the window again to the women and girls cringing away from the Matu guards. They were looking at the nun as though she were mad. Never, never again did he want to see people that petrified with terror. He turned back to Henryk and saw his own concern echoed. 'She is my best friend and the kindest, strongest person I know. I love her like my sister and I'll do anything I can to help her.' Henryk smiled up at him. 'She deserves to have such good friends Tom.'

'He says you can both go out to get the lady.' Christian's voice broke in on them. He looked worried and tired too. 'He says his grandfather is the one holding the rifle – that he will not hurt her, but the other one – their leader – he is a very angry man who will listen to no one. He will kill her himself if she does not stop. You must hurry.'

Henryk sighed and looked at Tom then back at Christian. 'Thank you my friend. And tell the young soldier thank you also for us please. You will look after my wife for me until I get back?' Christian smiled shyly and nodded his head at the two Europeans.

'You take much care Pastor, and you my friend.'

Tom forced a big smile at the quietly spoken young man and at the guard as he and Henryk walked calmly out of the school house into the strong African noonday sun.

* * *

It was three days later. Christian and Henryk looked wearily at each other as the inspector paused and put his biro down on the closely written statements. The policeman emptied the carafe of water into his own glass and handed it to the silent constable to refill it for the two aid workers. It was hell in these interview rooms with the fans cutting out all the time. Henryk thanked the constable in perfect Kiswahili as the young man freshened his glass.

'So you went outside the school and were walking towards Dr. Olatunde and the old soldier with the empty rifle. Who was it who struck her – the soldier or the priest?'

Henryk looked at the inspector calmly. He was only doing his job and probably did not know or care that he and Christian, Helga too, had been going over and over the horror with various authorities ever since the police had roared into Umbeke, far too late after Christian had finally been able to radio out for help. It was hard to go over such terrible events once more but he owed it to Teresa and to Tom and Aaron to make sure the truth was made known.

'The priest. Only the priest. The old man with the rifle was the one who kept his head - and he is the reason why we are still here to talk to you.'

The German took a large swig of the cooled water and talked on for nearly an hour, with Christian supplying corroboration where needed. How their young guard had only fired over the heads of Henryk and Tom as they ran to stop the priest. That it was the Matu with the other AK who had gunned down Tom as he ran towards Teresa, and the priest who carried on striking wildly at her with his panga whilst she lay huddled and still on the ground at his feet. The nun was probably already dead by then, half her face hanging off where he had first struck at her relentless accusing mouth. There was no way Tom could have saved her, but Henryk was too slow and too appalled at the sight of such frenzied hatred directed against his god-daughter to think of trying to grab him or hold him back.

It was weird watching Tom running away from him towards Teresa. Everything seemed to go so slowly. He too had started to run shouting after the tall Englishman who was howling in disbelief, his friendly northern accent distorted with rage and fear for his friend. The lad who had been guarding them in the school house had fired several bursts wildly over the back of his own head and he had pulled up sharply, realising it was too late for Teresa. His ears still throbbed from the horrible staccato pulsing of the other automatic weapon trained on Tom, following his sprint, firing all the while and finally felling him about twenty-five metres from where Teresa lay bloody and lifeless in the dirt. There had been silence for a few moments and then more shouting as the priest had turned on the old soldier who was standing beside the other Matu with the AK.

'Christian must tell you how the priest died as I did not see it. I was with Tom who was trying to talk. He was crying out for someone. Sophie. Saying he was sorry. I don't know who she is, except he loved her. I could only hold his hand and promise him I would tell her. He smiled at me and tried to get something out of his pocket. A little jewellery box. I got it for him… and he held it as he died. Like it was the most precious thing in the world…'

Henryk paused for a few moments and wiped his eyes trying to let go of the memory of the young man's face covered in blood from the wound to his temple. 'There was a betrothal ring inside – I gave it to the officer in charge when the police arrived afterwards. It should go to the young lady he was talking about. Also Teresa's journal should be returned to her order back in Vutare – after your people have finished taking copies of what you need of course.'

Inspector Abdullah listened to the old German with respect. He had read a short profile on the man from the District Commissioner's office before he came into the interview and knew that this German and his wife were distinguished professional aid workers who had helped co-ordinate dozens of campaigns and travelled all over Europe and the USA, raising awareness of the fight against apartheid in South Africa. They were even personal friends of the old statesman. Normally he had little time for aid workers who did their three year stint or however long it was 'doing good' and then went back to their privileged western lives, but this man knew Africa and had spent his life trying to make a difference – and they were even going back to Umbeke next week after everything that had happened there. The very nasty murder of the medical assistant, Aaron Umbatu and this ordained lady doctor Teresa Olatunde – the German's god-daughter. A Nigerian nun of all things. The other victim, an Englishman, Tom Harrison had been her friend apparently and shown a lot of steady courage before the Matu had attacked the nun, according to the German. Even though his last actions had proved futile. What a hellish mess! This morning the press had been all over the aid workers wanting to know more about the thirty-seven pathetic and traumatised women and their children as news of this atrocity had come to light. Other Europeans and an American had been burned to death in a chapel by more rampaging Zyandans a week ago, but that had been within their own borders and barely registered alongside the other horrors that had been going on inside that benighted country. This incident had taken place on Tanzanian soil - just - but the furore would last a few more days as the truth began to come out about what actually happened. In a way it might even help. The awful scale of the carnage and genocide could not be ignored any longer if it was spiralling out of control in Zyanda and spreading to neighbouring countries. The Umbeke encampment was right on the border of course, but something would have to be done by the international community now.

'I will read this back to you Mr. Kamate and then you can sign it if you are satisfied.' Inspector Abdullah looked at the interpreter sympathetically. The young man was lucky to be alive – if his Zyandan parent had been Lutse he would probably have been killed on sight by these rogue soldiers. The policeman took his time and paused whenever Christian made some comment that had to be added or corrected. If these Matu were ever found alive and brought to trial Christian Kamate would be a key witness as he had given very detailed descriptions, in particular of the young schoolhouse guard and of his grandfather, who seemed to have brought the madness to an end. Too late for some unfortunately. If it were not for this old man's refusing to obey the mad cleric the Zyandan women might all have perished as well as the Tanzanian, the Nigerian and the Briton – and these two men and the European lady too. In fact it was amazing that only four people had lost their lives. The inspector started to read from the handwritten statement.

Abraham was standing between the clergyman and the other man with the big gun and he tried to pull Sister Teresa away from the priest, but he had gone mad and was slashing about too much with his panga. No one could have saved her then. Abraham's rifle was not loaded. Then the priest stopped striking Sister Teresa and yelled at the soldier with the AK to fire at Pastor Henryk. The Pastor was tending to Tom then. Abraham used the rifle like a club to knock the AK out of the other soldier's hands before he could fire at the Pastor. Abraham snatched up the automatic and then turned on the priest and with his other hand hit him very hard behind his head on the back of his neck, with the rifle he was still holding. I think the rifle broke his neck. It was only one blow but it killed the priest straight away. Then Abraham fired the big gun up in the air and yelled at the other soldiers to put their weapons down on the ground and get away from the women in the canteen...

Inspector Abdullah put the paper down a moment. This was a crucial point.

'What were the refugee women doing at that moment Mr. Kamate?' Christian's dark brown eyes were tired and heavily tinged with red as he tried to remember things he would far rather forget.

'They were not doing anything really. They just stood

50

there like they had done ever since the Matu had told them all to go over to the kitchen. Some of them were crying I think but they were all very quiet. It was too far away for me and Mrs. Helga to see their faces properly through the window. We were still in the school house.'

'But you could see how this Abraham disarmed the soldier with the AK and then attacked his leader?' Inspector Abdullah's voice was quiet and patient.

'Yes we were close enough to see that. Mrs. Helga was very frightened for the Pastor.'

'Thank you Mr. Kamate. This is an important matter as you may guess. Did this Abraham at any point threaten Dr. Olatunde, Mr. Harrison or the Pastor.'

'Only Sister Teresa – with the empty rifle. He just pointed the gun at her. The priest told him to bring her back to the school house, but she would not go. And then she would not stop protesting and shouting at the priest and so he ordered Abraham to kill her. But he had no ammunition. He lowered his gun and said no he would not shoot her or hurt her. The priest tried to hit him with his panga but Abraham was too quick and he dodged it. So the priest went at Sister Teresa instead. It was very horrible.'

'You are doing very well Mr. Kamate.' The policeman gave him a small smile of encouragement. 'Just a few more things to clear up – another half hour at most and then you can both get back to the hotel and rest.' He took up Christian's statement again and read on.

The soldier who guarded me and Mrs. Helga in the school was Abraham's grandson. His name is David. He put his automatic weapon down straight away when his grandfather fired in the air and told us to come with him to help the Pastor and Tom. We had seen that the Pastor was talking to Tom

still, so we thought he was just badly wounded at first. I went
outside with Mrs. Helga and David came with us. Abraham
told him to bring the gun with him – I think he was afraid
the other Matu would try to kill us or the women still and
needed somebody else to have a weapon to help him.... Mr.
Kamate?'

Christian was looking down at the floor. He spoke, his soft
voice cracked with emotion.

'Tom was covered in blood all over his body and on his
face. The Pastor's shirt and arms were red where he was
holding Tom. We were nearly there and heard the Pastor
praying for him and then Tom began to shake and then he
went limp. He died. All he wanted to do was help Sister
Teresa and they killed him for nothing. He had no weapon.'
Christian's hands covered his face. Gradually he got himself
under control again.

'We have all we need on how Mr. Harrison died from the
autopsy and from Mr. Zimmerman thank you. I need to go
over what happened next with you Mr. Kamate. What this
Abraham said to you and to Mr. and Mrs. Zimmerman. I am
sorry for your distress but this is vital evidence.'

Christian looked at Henryk, who nodded and patted him
on the shoulder and rubbed his back sympathetically. The
policeman was waiting patiently. His matter of fact manner
was kind in a way – he almost made it feel as though they
were talking about something that had happened in the distant
past, not just three days ago. Abdullah went on reading from
Christian's statement.

Abraham asked if Tom was still alive. His French was not
so good so I asked him what he wanted in the Matu dialect.
I told him that Tom was dead. He is a very old man and said

he had been a soldier all his life. He said he was very sorry that the nun and the European man were dead. That it was a pity the nun had not stayed in the school house with the rest of us. He said that he and all the other Matu had not wanted to come over the border but the priest had argued with them and then persuaded them that it was their duty to pursue the women, even though they only had ammunition left for the AKs. It was because there were Matu liberals who had fled with them and helped the women to escape from Zyanda. He pointed to the woman the priest had beaten and said she was Matu and so were five others who were in the canteen with the rest of the refugees. I said we already knew this. That it made no difference to us what tribe they belonged to. The other militia men began to gather behind Abraham and David. They all looked like they were shocked at what had happened and would not look at the bodies of Sister Teresa or Tom. Not even the man who had killed Tom. He was shaking and looked very ashamed. David was holding onto his gun very tightly but his grandfather told him to put it down and get the other weapons, the pangas too, and then leave them by the school.

The Pastor asked me to try and find out what they would do now. The militia men. I asked Abraham and he said they would go back to Zyanda. He said the Matu ladies could come back with them if they wanted or stay with the other refugee women if they were too scared to go back. He asked what was in the lorry that Tom had driven. I told him some food, petrol and medical supplies. He started to talk to the others and then they went to the lorry and began to unload most of the drugs and medical equipment and a few gallons of petrol – we have a Land Cruiser and a smaller truck. Abraham said they were not thieves but there was very little food and *fuel in their township. He said they would only take the lorry and the food and the petrol and leave the medicines as there would probably be more refugees coming into Tanzania. I translated for the Pastor and his wife and they said to tell Abraham that they were welcome to take whatever they needed so long as they would promise not to harm any of the Matu ladies who were prepared to go back with them.*

Abraham told me to go over and tell the women what their options were. None of the Matu ladies wanted to go with the soldiers. I told them this and Abraham said they were sensible women. That they would be safer here with us. David gathered all the weapons including the AKs and the rifle that he and Abraham had been carrying and put them all in the school. He got into the lorry cab behind the wheel and his grandfather got in with him. All the other men stayed on the back of the lorry. Abraham spoke to the Pastor, Mrs. Helga and I very slowly in French so we would all hear. He said they were not bad men. That they had been caught up in the madness but now they were ashamed and did not want to kill anymore. They wanted things to be normal again but knew they had sinned and done terrible deeds. He said that he was very sorry the Sister was dead. That she was very brave but foolish and that he would have stopped the priest attacking her if he could have. He said not to think too harshly of the man who had obeyed the priest's orders and killed the other man. Tom. The Pastor told him that Sister Teresa had a great heart and had suffered much in another war long ago and could not bear to see the women treated so viciously. He said he realised her actions had caused things to happen as they did but that the women were safe now because of her bravery in trying to stop the priest. Even though she had paid too high a price. He said that God knew how and why these events had come to be and that ultimately mercy would be shown to those who had themselves acted mercifully and in good faith. Abraham nodded and told David to drive away. They headed for the Zyanda road. We did not see them turn back.

The inspector put the statement down. He looked at the two men appraisingly. The young African and the old European, so different to look at but bound by faith and the work they had undertaken. 'Gentlemen – nothing I can say to you will change a thing of course. What happened in Umbeke is terrible but as you told the Zyandan soldiers in the end, none of the women were badly harmed and only four people died. It could have been so much worse. Dr. Olatunde did a stupid thing for the right reason and died because of her own sense of courage. It is a pity that Mr. Harrison was there in the first place and an even greater one that he was shot down. A great pity. We have found out from CAMEO [5] that another driver was to accompany the doctor but fell ill, so he ought to have been safe back in Zambia by now. Perhaps if the other driver had been able to come as planned, only your medical attendant, the doctor and the soldier-priest would have lost their lives.' He sighed and shook his head, stood up and came over to Henryk and Christian and shook their hands firmly.

'Thank you for your statements Mr. Zimmerman, Mr. Kamate. You're free to go back to your hotel and to Umbeke next week as you have planned already I believe. So long as you do not leave Tanzania until this investigation is over. My office will be in touch with you very soon on that score I hope. If these Zyandans are ever brought to justice we will be in contact with you again of course, so we'd be very grateful if you could let

[5] **The Co-ordinated Aid, Medicine and Education Organisation** ~ an entirely fictional logistical umbrella group for several humanitarian organisations working all over the world.

us know if you are posted elsewhere, or where we can contact you if you have to leave this area. I hope you will have no further troubles of this kind at least. Like this Abraham said to you – there will be many more people fleeing across that border so your work there is most valuable. May your God go with you – you have my full admiration for the work you will do with these poor people.'

Onwards and upwards…

Sophie's Diary: Sunday 29th April ~ Kafue, Zambia

We had a truly glorious day today, driving around the Kopjes and looking at some really splendid Baobabs down by a little creek. Tons of Marabous, herons and cranes in the water meadows as well, on the hunt for frogs and snakes. Poor Eva's face when she got a good look at the storks through the bins…

'Oh-my-God! I never knew they were so ugly! Ugh! Phil – you gotta dump all my boas as soon as we get back to Santa Monica!'

So funny! I didn't dare look at Adam who was nearly choking on his cola. He was brilliant today as well. Kept them all enthralled – well me too actually – with his patter and anecdotes.

When we were driving back through the bush, Adam slowed right down when he realised we were close to a Dik Dik midden – he'd been talking to the camp guides in the staff bouma last night and they'd told him where to find one. Anyway he found it and went off road a little and there the stinky little heap was. Of course everyone was not too impressed until one of the dear little antelopes dutifully showed up and obligingly performed for us. The cameramen were beside themselves and the motor drives were being caned like mad, as the titchy little thing scaled what for him was this two storey bathroom.

Adam had turned the engine off so we sat there spellbound for about a half hour, just watching this darling little creature, only about the size of a small spaniel but so, so slender and delicate. And then Adam began to talk very quietly, telling us the apocryphal tale of the Dik Dik and the Rhino…

In the beginning of times all animals were friends with each other but, of course, they all had to eat and so the plant eaters and the meat eaters soon drifted apart and took different paths. Now it is well-known that some plant eaters like gemsbok, zebra, gnu, kudu and giraffe will come together when they drink, or even graze or browse together, but then this is easily seen for they are all large creatures and favour the more open lands. But not all large browsers like to be in the open and the Black Rhino is one of those who prefer to browse more privately and in peace in the brush and woodlands. And so, still long ago, it came to be that the great powerful Rhino befriended one of the smallest browsers of all – the quiet and tiny Dik Dik.

Now you may think this is very strange my dears, that such a great clumsy creature like a Rhino would be good friends with such a shy little antelope, but there are very good reasons for this. Most important is that the poor old Rhino does not see too well, but the Dik Dik has very sharp little eyes as well as good hearing, so he could tell the Rhino whenever a big cat or hunting dogs were about and his friend would not be taken by surprise. And of course the Rhino, being so big and strong, need not fear any predator once they are grown, so together the two animals found that they were, as often as not, left to browse in peace by the meat eaters.

Rhino became very fond indeed of his little friend, for Dik Dik was neat and clean in his habits as well as being very gentle and quiet. So the small and the great browsers spent a lot of time together wandering the woodlands, eating and sleeping and drinking close by each other. After a while however, Rhino began to get somewhat curious about his little friend's habits for he never saw the Dik Dik drop his spoor save in the one spot, which, incidentally, was one of the

Rhino's favourite places too – except he of course, ranging a little farther afield than his friend, had many places where he liked to drop spoor. Now this peculiar habit of Dik Dik's began to dwell on his friend's mind and one day Rhino just had to know why the antelope was so precise and particular over something most others would not think twice about.

'Tell me little brother Dik Dik - how is it that you only have one midden? Forgive me for asking such an impertinent question of you, but I have been puzzled about this for some time…' Rhino, for all his clumsy appearance and ways was a sensitive animal, as you can tell, and so he was a little embarrassed to be delving into his friend's personal areas. 'Why is it that you will only ever drop your spoor in the one place? I think you must be the only one in the whole forest who does such a thing!'

Dik Dik looked a little surprised to be asked such a question, but he was a sweet-tempered sort and he could see why his friend should be curious, for it was indeed an unusual habit.

'Well my good friend,' Dik Dik looked up at Rhino a little shyly, 'we are not always together, but when I am with you, I am always safe from the meat eaters. Have you ever noticed how predators choose the places to ambush our kind very carefully?'

'Not really, but then they leave me alone pretty much of course.' Rhino chomped on his browse thoughtfully.

'Well they do! They choose very carefully!' Dik Dik shook his beautiful little head sadly. 'Anywhere they know you might have your mind on other things, or are doing something where you may not be able to run away so quickly… like when you are drinking… or when you drop spoor. And if they can smell your spoor then they can track you too.'

'But why just the one place then my friend? Surely that means they always know where to find you?'

Dik Dik smiled ruefully at the great creature. 'Well yes they do, but they also know that you are often with me in that place, for you use it too and they can smell your spoor as well! And so you see, they know that if you are there too, they would be foolish indeed to try and come after me, your best friend, for you would surely trample them with your great hooves, or gore them with your sharp nose horn if they tried to eat me!

Rhino thought about this for a few moments, he was not the quickest of animals, but he was a very wise one and so he began to laugh at his little brother's cleverness.

'O, Dik Dik! You are indeed a sly one!' Rhino huffed and puffed in merriment for a good while and then looked kindly at Dik Dik, 'Well I shall certainly continue to drop my spoor beside yours in that place, for I would be sad indeed to lose you my dear friend.' And he did. Every time they visited Dik Dik's one and only midden he always made sure to drop some spoor as well.

Now in this early time the Dik Dik did not try to build great towers of spoor as they do now, but just spread it around the area a little like most animals do, to let the dung beetles do their work easily. And for a little time after their conversation Dik Dik carried on in that way. However, Rhino had been thinking very hard about what Dik Dik had said and wanted to be of even more help to his charming friend, for he did not wish for him ever to be taken by a predator. So in the days that followed Rhino was as good as his word and made sure to drop his own spoor as close to Dik Dik's as possible.

The little antelope was very glad he had told his friend of his clever ruse, but as time went on he got a little concerned about Rhino's new habit of dropping spoor right beside his own. Now you may of course guess the reason for Dik Dik's worry, but if you cannot I must tell you that one day the inevitable happened. They came into the glade where Dik Dik kept his midden and this time Rhino got far too close to Dik Dik just as he was dropping his own dainty little spoor – and splattered his poor friend with his own large, hot, steaming droppings... To be fair to Rhino, he did not mean for this to happen, but then, to make matters worse, as Dik Dik tried to flee his friend's droppings by dashing away under Rhino's big belly, Rhino then began to urinate too and the unfortunate Dik Dik had another, more liquid, dowsing.

Once poor Rhino realised what had happened, he apologised profusely again and again, mortified that he had gotten his dear friend so dirty. Dik Dik was naturally not at all happy, but he knew Rhino was truly sorry and had not meant to humiliate him, so he forgave him.

'Well, well... accidents will happen I suppose. You had better come back with me to the waterhole so I can bathe and get clean again though! Just see that you are more careful the next time please!'

And this is what happened of course. Although it has to be said that Rhino, being half blind and a more than a little clumsy, had several more near misses, but Dik Dik, having been befouled the once was not about to let it happen again any time soon. So, every time the two friends went to their joint midden, Dik Dik kept a very careful watch on Rhino's behind and thus avoided any further embarrassing incidents, although there were a few more close calls. However, as time went on and the memory was fading a little, one day Dik Dik was not as watchful as he generally was and lo, the same thing happened again. And once more Rhino was very apologetic and Dik Dik was as understanding as he could be, although he was very cross and slightly annoyed with himself, as well as Rhino, for forgetting to be vigilant.

Now as you know, Dik Dik was a very clever chap and so he began to think hard about how they could prevent this happening for a third time and I can tell you that it did not take too long for him to come up with a solution. The very next day when they visited their midden, Dik Dik chose a good spot, not too sunny, fairly shady but not overgrown so much that Rhino could not use the place as well, and then did his business as usual. Then every time after that, when they were at the midden, Dik Dik always dropped his spoor in exactly the same spot as before and this went on for several days. Well of course Dik Dik soon had quite a pile of droppings growing there and Rhino began to notice this and wondered what his little friend was up to now. However he was still very ashamed of himself for twice making his friend dirty so he said nothing. After several weeks of this, as the pile of Dik Dik droppings grew and grew, higher and higher, Rhino's curiosity was more than he could stand and the next time they went to the glade to drop spoor he finally asked his friend what he was doing. Dik Dik smiled and then looked his big friend in the eye, for they were now at the same level as the little creature perched on top of his great pile of spoor, hardly able to stop for laughing.

'Well my dear friend. it is quite simple. This way you cannot ever make me dirty again can you, for on top of this tower I am too high am I not?!' Rhino laughed and laughed with his friend.

'Ah Dik Dik! You are a clever fellow and I would never have thought of that myself.'

'No indeed!' the little antelope chuckled, but nevertheless

gave his friend a penetrating glance. 'But just you be careful my friend, for accidents can happen. And maybe one day my midden will be high enough for me to make you dirty! So just watch you do not get too close to me when you drop your spoor in future please!'

And so, to this day the Dik Dik and the Rhino are still the best of friends, but they are also very careful not to make the other dirty when they make their droppings in the same spot.

Kwashiorkor...

... is a profoundly distressing dietary disease caused by protein deficiency. It is particularly disturbing in small children under the age of five. It becomes prevalent in areas ravaged by famine and/ or war and takes hold when the most poverty-stricken levels of society of the Third World, in Southern Asia, Central and South America and, most commonly to western eyes at least, in Africa, when the people have consumed the animal population and their by-products to such an extent that protein sources including milk are scarce or non-existent.

The condition first came to global notoriety in news coverage near the end of the war in Biafra, in the Ibo province of Nigeria. Disturbing film footage of toddlers under the age of five was seen on television screens all over the world. These unfortunates, with their huge balloon-like bellies, stick-thin limbs, bones clearly visible, hair and skin discoloured with a reddish tinge and enormous haunted eyes, traumatised, literally dying in front of the horrified reporters and cameramen, finally pricked the conscience of the international community, eventually contributing to ending the civil war in newly independent Nigeria.

But of course, during a war and resulting famine, protein is not the only thing that is hard to come by - and other innocents suffer as much as, or more than very young children...

Why were they pulling at her? Could they not see she was dead? She heard a thin tormented shriek, then realised the voice was hers. She gasped and was silent, dreading the consequences of the noise she made. Soft hands were holding her close, brushing at her face, chest and shoulders; hurting her because her parched skin was on fire and flinched at the merest touch. They were speaking to her in a strange language, or perhaps were talking about her. She groaned and her eyes fluttered open. A man with a tawny-gold, silver-streaked beard was looking at her with water in his eyes. They were blue eyes, light as the sky and his skin was pale as milk. He looked like a picture she had seen in a book at the mission, long, long ago before her world had changed forever.

'Am I in heaven Lord?' her voice was a hoarse whisper and caused more tears to flow from the kind eyes. His hand gently caressed the back of her head, yet still she cried out softly at his merest touch that tore at raw feverish nerve endings. He spoke to her and this time she understood him.

'You are alive child. It is a miracle but you are alive.'

She began to cry, though no tears could fall.

'No! I cannot be. I must be dead.'

'Hush little one. You are safe now. We will make you well again.' One of his tears fell on her hot, scarred little face, landing on swollen cracked lips. She felt the salt sting a little but that did not hurt as much as his hands. Her tongue, swollen and wooden, slowly lapped at the moisture.

'I am thirsty Lord.' She murmured then cried out as he held her close and stood up. The pain was too much and she spiralled back into the warm blessed darkness where nothing could reach her. Nothing could hurt her. Except her dreams.

* * *

Henryk laid the child down on a clean bed in the large airy tent they had set up for the triage team. There were only a handful of other wounded villagers in here. She was the youngest, looking to be around ten or eleven. The girl had fallen back into unconsciousness and for that he was grateful as he knew he had hurt her, try as he might to be gentle. His wife came over with warm water and sterilising fluid and motioned him away whilst she set up a saline drip, then deftly injected a little morphine infusion to keep the pain at bay, as they tended to the injuries great and small all over the child's body.

'I got most of the maggots away from her head wounds, but she has old blood all over her genitals and thighs... I think she may have miscarried but there was not much left of the foetus.'

He shuddered, recalling the shock when he had realised she was still alive by the heat of her skin as he had pried the dried corpse of a much younger child, maybe four years old at most, out of her arms, disturbing hordes of buzzing flies in the process. Helga looked at him, not knowing what to say. They had seen many truly awful things over the last few weeks, but this little waif's predicament was heartbreaking. The military liaison people had told them that the atrocities suffered by this village had ended about a week ago. And this child had lain with the dead ever since, wounded and broken, clutching a little boy who had had no injuries on his body save the ravages of kwashiorkor.

'It is the Lord's will she endured and lived. Poor child. There is only one bullet wound on the breastbone. They cannot even have cared whether they killed her or not.' Helga's warm eyes roved over her husband's tired face and she smiled weakly at him. 'Go and get some drinking water my love. Three cups. For all of us. She will wake again as I bathe her other wounds, but it must be done. You can help her to drink and then at least her thirst can be tended to. Youssef will want to remove the bullet as soon as we can get her ready.'

Carefully she sponged the caked blood, dust and fly-blow from the bullet wound on the girl's chest and from the cigarette burns on her face, her head, neck, shoulders, back and budding breasts. A few years ago she would have wept as she did this, but she was too used to this kind of thing now. The only difference this time was that this ruined body was still alive. So young though. No wonder Henryk had been so moved. She had reached the girl's loins now and the blood was black and full of eggs and maggots on her mons. The smell made Helga retch a little, but she carried on as gently as she could because the child was beginning to regain consciousness now.

Henryk was right about the aborted pregnancy and she thanked the Lord for his mercy that the child could have been no more than six or eight weeks along. The umbilical was still attached and she worked quickly as she felt the heat of fever and reeled from the stench of infection, using the sterilising fluid almost neat now to get the disgusting mess around the girl's labia and vagina as clear as she could so that Youssef could work as cleanly as possible. This poor creature was not safe yet and even if she survived this horror, she had lived through God alone knew how much torment for two months or more before the soldiers had moved on. What would her life be with all her friends and family most likely dead or taken, forced into an army of the damned. As if reading her thoughts the child shrieked out and, as used as she was to the suffering and plight of the victims of war and famine, Helga groaned in despair as she reached out to grasp the child's feeble, shaking hand, needing to give some comfort to her. As the child clutched at her fingers weakly Helga realised she was barely as old as their youngest daughter.

Her husband put his hand on her shoulder as she vomited outside the tent. She took the cool cup of water from him and drank gratefully. They went back inside. The child was lying awake and whimpering now, her skin on fire and her eyes too bright with fever.

'I need you to help me turn her so I can clean her back Henryk. I hurt her so much just washing her poor little loins and I cannot bear to make it any worse for her now.'

He nodded grimly. The top sheet was befouled with her blood and worse so Henryk waited as Helga unsealed a clean paper sheet, then he swiftly, but as gently as he could manage, slipped his arms under the girl's bony shoulders and skinny thighs and swept her off the makeshift bed. Quickly Helga laid the new sheet straight and he put the girl down on the nearest edge of the bed as his wife reached out to roll the child towards her, moving her as softly and slowly as she could so she was now lying stomach down on the bed.

Trying not to show his horror as they saw more burns on her shoulders and raw oozing pressure ulcers all down her thin frame, he took the girl's head and tenderly moved it slightly to the side so she could lie more comfortably. The huge brown eyes blinked at him and the parched lips tried to smile.

'Thank you, Lord.' Her voice was not even a breath and he saw rather than heard the words. He smiled back at her then took up the cup of water he had brought for her and a little sponge.

'I have something for you to drink child. While we make you clean again.' He dipped the sponge in the water and wiped it across her lips.

As she opened her mouth, he squeezed the water a little at a time onto her bloated purple tongue. She sighed softly then gasped as Helga began to work with another sponge taking the last of the crusted filth away. The pained eyes fluttered shut again, but she was still conscious and he kept on dipping and squeezing, in between her little cries, as Helga worked as gently and quickly as she could.

'I am sorry this pains you, but once you are clean you will feel better little one.' Henryk carried on talking to her, trying to distract her from the pain, keeping the water dripping into her ravenous mouth as she swallowed it slowly at first then with more vigour. 'You are very brave. I am called Henryk and this lady is my wife Helga. What is your name my dear?'

She shut her eyes and her mouth closed. His hand froze between the cup and her lips. A few drips fell on the pillow. Helga looked over at him, her face fierce, nodding at him to keep talking. He tried again. This at least was something he knew he could do. 'Tell me your name child?' Her eyes opened again and this time there was a trace of tears.

'I died Lord. I have no name now.' Her voice was a little whisper and he smiled softly at her. She was a fighter and his hope began to gather again.

'Before you died little one? You had a name then did you not?' He waited as the dark haunted eyes closed.

'Yes… but I am not me any more. I am dead.' Her mouth stayed open and quickly he squeezed the sponge onto her tongue. The swelling was beginning to go down a little.

'I never knew a dead person who needed to drink, my little angel.' He stroked a finger gently against her cheek, avoiding the half-healed burn from a cigarette butt. She winced but did not cry out.

'Maybe…' she croaked then tried to smile at him again. 'Maybe I should have a new name then? You choose Lord. I am too tired.'

He looked at Helga and she nodded for him to carry on. Henryk smiled at the girl and thought frantically of female names. She spoke French so he assumed she was Catholic as the mission here had been run by Carmelites. They had a new saint he remembered – The Little Flower. Teresa. She had been sickly and died young but was strong in her faith and had found the courage to overcome her bodily frailty. He smiled at her again.

'Your smile is like a tiny flower opening up for the rain little one and so I think you should be called Teresa. Do you like that name?'

The enormous brown eyes gave a flicker of pleasure before the pain returned as Helga sluiced sterilising lotion into a burn on her spine. The child moaned softly but then spoke, her lips trying to curve.

'I like flowers. I am Teresa then. Thank you Lord.'

* * *

The dream came and she was happy because she would see Adie again. When he was a proper baby brother and laughed when she cuddled him and played silly talking games with him. He was her youngest male sibling and although she knew she should love all her brothers and sisters the same, it was Adie who loved her the most, so she had to love him most too. Her three elder brothers were grown and all worked in the city in those days, rarely coming home but sending money regularly, so that was all right. In a few years it would be her turn - unless she was a mother and married by then. She squeezed Adie just to hear him laugh and thought that she would like to be a mother if all her children were like her little brother…

It was later now and everything had changed. All her elder

brothers and her father had been taken by the soldiers and her mother had said they would not be back. They had all been killed she said. But still Adie was with her and that was something, even though he cried constantly these days. Femi and Demi the girl-boy twins, two years younger than Adie had died last week and she had had to finish the digging of their grave, for her mother could barely stand some days. She was inside their little hut now, trying to feed the infant boy who grizzled fitfully at the empty breasts. Adie snuggled into her, still crying with hunger and she hugged him gently and kissed his hot little head.

'There will be maize porridge for us tonight Adie I promise – when I have seen the soldiers...' She was crying too.

She did not like to go to the soldiers, but her mother said she had to or else they would have nothing at all to eat. The soldiers had taken everything and hoarded it – eking it out amongst the villagers. They were hungry too, the soldiers. They always took more of the food but they shared some supplies that came to them on a big truck. If she went to them and lay down with some of them they would give her more food and her mother, who seemed to get thinner and thinner by the hour, said she was a good girl if she brought extra grain home for them. For a while she would feel happy for her mother would smile at her then, even if her face was very sad, and said she was so sorry that she had to go to the soldiers. Her mother, Adie and the baby depended on her now and, even though she was sick every day and the soldiers always hurt her so much, she was proud to be supporting what was left of their family. She had to go to them now. Adie knew she would be back as she took his hands from around her neck, stroked his little cheeks and patted his taut round belly. At least he seemed to be thriving a little now, although the rest of his body was still painfully thin, almost as thin as their mother's…

… later still and the men were all jeering and shouting at her. Everyone else had run away a few hours ago after the soldiers had all been drinking. Not the native beer that her father and elder brothers had to drink sometimes – they had no milk to make that anymore. The soldiers had drunk glinting brown liquor from glass bottles and it had made them all mad. They had frightened everyone and fired their guns. An old woman and two boys, younger than her had been killed. That was when the few villagers left had bolted and now it was just her and Adie. She would have run as well but she was not strong enough to carry her brother, even though he was so light now. So she had dragged him, half asleep and moaning into the old schoolhouse, where it was quiet at least and left him there, not daring to stay with him when the soldiers started to call for her, their voices slurred with sleepiness even though it was not time to sleep, and getting angry when she did not go to them straight away…

… they had all gone now and she was so glad. She was still lying where they had left her and she knew she was dead now. Nearly dead anyway. She was glad of that too. Except Adie was still calling for her. He sounded so sad and tired and finally she could not ignore him anymore, even though she ached all over and knew she could barely move for the great pain in her chest and the sharp, raw wrenching hurt inside of her stomach and in her intimate places. She could not walk but managed to drag herself out of the sun more or less onto the porch of the schoolhouse, trying to get back to Adie. He was still inside. Surely he could come to her if he tried?

'Brother… Adie… I am here my dear. Just outside. You

must come to me… so tired Adie…'

She must have slept a little for Adie was with her now. He had crawled into her arms whilst she was asleep and was hugging her. He was very still and quiet and she gathered him closer to her. He was not breathing and she knew he was dead, but then so was she. Or soon would be. That was all right. They were together now and God would look after them.

* * *

Youssef had just finished writing up his notes on the last patient of the day, a ten year old girl that Henryk had named Teresa. The young doctor leaned back in his chair, exhausted but still sipping at his coffee as he would be awake again this night anyway. At least the caffeine would allow him to do something useful with the insomnia that he had succumbed to these past few weeks. No wonder medicos burned out in this job so quickly he reflected, but he had volunteered he reminded himself. Had wanted to 'make a difference'. What an idealistic young idiot he had been, but he was making a difference, he knew he was – and learning a lot about pathology into the bargain he thought bitterly.

What a hell-hole of a country this was! And every time he thought he had seen the worst of the atrocities that one person could inflict on another, along came something… someone else to prove there were no limits to the degradation that human beings could sink to. He passed a trembling hand over his eyes and gave way to the weeping he had held back whilst he had fought to save the little girl's life. He had won that battle, but he wondered what sort of a life she would have now, poor child. Silent and shuddering he reached for the battered, well-thumbed Qur'an and began to read haphazardly, trying to wipe away despair and find a place where he could summon the strength to carry on for another day.

The German couple had cleaned the child up as best they could. Today he was grateful they were here but they surely tried his patience sometimes. At least they had a lot of knowledge of this wretched continent and were experienced aid workers. Helga, a trained trauma room nurse, was amazing in triage, although he could never quite convince her about the efficacy of maggots in cleansing wounds and preventing necrosis. Western Europeans in general annoyed him a lot, especially some of the more unctuous Christians, but he had to admit that Henryk also was a useful person to have around, even though his medical skills were strictly limited to first aid procedures. He did have a lot of rapport with the Africans and seemed to be able to communicate with them in a genuinely caring and sympathetic manner. Youssef found that very difficult to emulate in himself at times.

What was that Christian saying they were always laughing at in University? Physician - heal thyself! He shook his head and shut the holy book with a snap and opened the drawer of the little travelling desk. He looked at the unopened half bottle of whisky for about a minute and then slowly shut the drawer again. It was not his bottle. His predecessor, also a follower of Islam, had said he had left him a 'present' in the desk drawer and had smiled at him ruefully. Youssef did not know whether the older man had left him a new bottle, having drunk previous ones. Maybe he had kept it there, like he did, undrunk, as a reminder and a challenge to his willpower and his faith. Youssef no longer knew which of those kept him from opening the bottle. He had so little of either left now but he had not succumbed yet and after two years he hoped he never would, but some nights it was hard to resist. And getting harder all the time. It was this place. It was cursed by God.

Almost dawn and still he could not sleep. It was that little girl. Her plight had torn at his heart. Helga had immediately got her on a penicillin drip, but the hysterectomy had been essential. Inevitable. As it was they had only just been in time to save her life for the sepsis had begun to run rampant through her circulatory systems. At ten years of age! He shook his head and poured himself another glass of bottled water but this time he did not attempt to put her from his mind. Henryk had found her and helped Helga to prep her for surgery – it had been obvious to her that there was a severe internal infection of the vagina and, of course, the womb because of the partially aborted foetus. Henryk had said it was a miracle the child had lived and Youssef had exchanged a look with Helga. They had both known Teresa's survival was by no means assured, even though her outer wounds had been cleansed well enough. The flies and excreta had done their work too and were the cause of the infection in her outer genitals, but the causative trauma… Never! Never again did he want to see a body, an innocent child's body, so desecrated…

It had been easy enough to remove the fetid umbilical once the child was under anasthæsia – he was grateful that Helga had done her work as thoroughly as she had, for he could well imagine how much pain this child had suffered. Like Helga it was the foul stinking wounds to the inner labia, and partially, to the pitiful, semi-pubescent clitoris that had revolted him most. Those animals… pigs!

After he had seen to the removal of the tiny infected placenta and the uterus – there was nothing he could save – he had to return to the outer genitalia to finish the botched circumcision the drunken soldiers had tried to 'perform' on this god-forsaken child. 'Make good' their terrible mutilations, simply to ensure that the damaged, gangrenous tissue was taken away and what was left to the poor soul could heal cleanly. It had been that trauma that had likely triggered the spontaneous abortion, although even there he had seen evidence that they might have assaulted her with a knife or bayonet, for there were wounds to the vagina that were suspiciously clean-edged. They had been in time to save Teresa's life at least, but these obscene injuries could never be undone.

He had not known the details or history as he worked, and perhaps he should have been grateful for that. Henryk had been asking questions of their other patients about the child whilst he and Helga had been in surgery. It was the first and only time Youssef would see the German look at all angry. Apparently one of the women whose child was being nursed to recovery from the severe protein deficiency disease - kwashiorkor - had asked if the soldiers' whore had died. Meaning this child... And so Henryk, barely able to hold his temper, had learned what happened as the woman had delighted in telling him why the girl was better off dead. How Teresa's mother, repulsively haggard from long years of childbearing and with starvation, had to instead send her ten year old daughter to prostitute herself with the soldiers so she and her other four surviving children could have enough maize to live on. The family was all dead now except for Teresa. The small boy Henryk had found her with was her little brother. On the last night they were in the village, the soldiers had all got drunk and started shooting people. Everyone had run away into the bush, except for Teresa and her brother, who had been too weak to walk. Teresa had refused to leave her brother but was not strong enough to carry him to safety. As it was he had probably been only hours away from death...

He could guess the rest and his stomach had turned at the thought of what the child had been subjected to, then shot and left for dead after months of what amounted to rape and defilement, reviled for her actions by the rest of her community, simply to keep her family alive. And then to lie in a coma brought on by the mental as well as the physical trauma for almost a week. A whole week! With no one to help her or even bury her disease-ravaged little brother, though the villagers had started returning to their homes for brief periods a few days after the shootings, still afraid the soldiers might return. But they had just left the two children there. Untended. Assuming they were both dead. Incredible! An unbelievable hell-hole...

* * *

It was past ten in the morning when Henryk found Youssef, sprawled across his desk, a full tumbler of whisky near his hand and a recently opened bottle with the top off close by. Also a bottle of sleeping pills knocked over. Alarmed at first, fearing the young doctor had taken an overdose, Henryk frantically shook him awake. Youssef's breath held no trace of alcohol and he laughed when Henryk asked how many pills he had taken. Just two. With water of course. Relieved, the German laughed with him now and asked what was with the whisky for he knew Youssef was an abstainer.

'The whisky? Just a test of faith my friend. Or willpower. And I passed this time. I passed!'

After the Rains

Dearest Ma,

I put Sophie on the plane for London about an hour ago. Physically she's much better than she was earlier this week, but still pretty shaken up as you might imagine. The CAMEO area co-ordinator for Vutare couldn't have been kinder to us - by the time I got there he'd already checked the outgoing flights to both the UK and to Harare for us, as well as making all the calls for me to confirm bookings etc.

Oh Ma - Sophie's really in a state, so they've sedated her as far as they could for the flight. They had one of their medical staff, a Dr. Youssef Jettou, who was going to be travelling to London on leave last weekend, but postponed in view of what happened - he's a long-standing friend and colleague of the Zimmermans and Dr. Olatunde trained under him when she joined the organisation apparently. He met us in Lusaka last night and he was so good with Sophie. I feel much better now about not being able to come back with her, but as you know Grant's out in Virginia for at least another fortnight, so I have to get back to the kids. I'll ring you as soon as I get back to Harare, but they cancelled the bloomin' flight (again!) and I'm stuck here for another rotten night. So this is in case I get bumped onto an overland transfer, although I'm on standby for a Zambia Air flight early tomorrow. Hopefully we'll have talked by the time you get this.

You'll have seen Sophie by then anyway, but I wanted to pass on something that Alma (Sophie's boss) was at pains to point out to me the day that I arrived. When the news first came through to them in Vutare Sophie was still pretty groggy with the first bout of malaria, but also the morning sickness of course. Well you can see that anyway because she's so skinny at the moment. Ma - she collapsed in hysterics and they think that's partly why the coma came on so suddenly. She's blaming Dr. Olatunde for everything. Apparently Tom had been close friends with the Dr for at least a year before Sophie came out there. Nothing romantic at all - the woman was a nun after all and apparently did not get on with men too well. But her and Tom were the best of friends it seems and so when Sophie came on the scene there was a lot of friction as Sophie got very jealous of the Dr's influence on Tom.

There's no information coming out of Mwanza
just now, but when it first came out the police
were in touch with the Carmelites in Vutare
over the Dr's assignment and why Tom was there
with her as he was supposed to return to Vutare
via Arusha after getting her to Mwanza.

Sophie's got it into her head that the Dr guilt-
tripped Tom into going with her to Umbeke and so
it's all her fault! It wasn't Ma. Tom volunteered
to go to Umbeke because the driver scheduled to
take her had come down with a whopping dose
of dysentery and there was no one else available
- it was all the most terrible bad luck.

Alma's promised to get as much information as
she can on what really happened to me asap -
apparently CAMEO are good that way with letting
colleagues know what went on in situations
like this, because of the close relationships their
teams have. Closure or some such buzzword. But of
course they do such grisly work and people do need
to know what happens to friends and respected
colleagues, especially when it's something so awful.

Sophie's talked to me a little about Tom - how I
wish we could've met him beyond the photos of
them she sent from when they were in Vic Falls!
He soun seemed wonderful - just the sort of chap

who would've really looked after her. Certainly not the kind of lad who'd be chasing other women, let alone a nun nearly twice his age right under Sophie's nose. She said that the Dr made all the running so at least she's not got that jumbled, but she said some really awful things about the poor woman to me and Alma says it's simply not true or grossly exaggerated, as the Dr was a very professional person with strong principles - it couldn't have been true. There's no question that she made Tom do anything against his will. Alma's asked me to make sure that this is made clear to you as Sophie will need a lot of support back in the UK, for which the organisation are offering professional therapy/counselling as part of their care package for employees in situations like this.

Youssef also talked to me a bit last night after Sophie got her head down - she was exhausted after the journey. He told me that from his own friendship with the Zimmermans, who were Dr Olatunde's godparents apparently, that they were all very dedicated people and he was sure that everyone caught up in the standoff would have done all they could to minimise the danger they were in at Umbeke. He did say one strange thing though - that he was surprised that Dr

Olatunde had been given the assignment to head
up the reception clinic for the Zyandan refugees.
Something about her background in Nigeria?

Anyway - I've just seen the length of this letter!
I'd better go and get some shuteye myself - I have to
be back at the airport again at 4 am in case I can
get on this ruddy milk run flight! Much love and
kisses to Dad - tell him we're all fine and hope to
be over with you again come suicide month. Will
be wonderful to get away from the hellish heat
of Zim to the lovely damp English autumn!

Claire - xxx

10 years later ~ Royal College of Surgeons, London.

Why the bloody hell had she let Youssef talk her into coming
to this conference? She adored him, but he could be a real
pain in the bum at times. Especially about CAMEO, but then
it was his job. His life more or less. Although he was getting
better now he'd got this jammy gig as a consultant lecturer
on tropical diseases at King's as a sideline to the day job. She
got off the tube at Holborn and walked unhurriedly around the
corner into Lincoln's Inn Fields and headed for the familiar
late Georgian facade skirting the mostly immaculate green
swards of the fenced gardens, though the bushes sometimes
showed signs of a hasty beery supper or makeshift cardboard
blanket for some homeless soul. Raggedy people were all
over the world, just in some places you couldn't see them
so well but they were there all the same. And some of them

didn't look raggedy on the outside, she reminded herself sourly.

She was there and Youssef was waiting for her by the gate.

'I knew you'd be early!' He greeted her as always with a friendly hand on her shoulder and a light kiss on the forehead.

'Keen as always, boss!' They laughed and went up the steps into the building past a banner proclaiming the conference being hosted there - 'Modern Aid for a Modern Africa'.

'So how is general practice in a garrison town suiting you these days?' Youssef smiled at her as they sipped coffee in the reception room.

'Interesting. Now the MOD recognises PTSD[6] as a proper medical condition I get some psychiatric referrals too.'

'Also interesting?'

'What do you think? Nothing really changes does it?'

'No. All you can do is try to help if you can.'

'If you have the strength. That's why I'm still in civvy street and staying there thanks.'

'Ah, Sophie...' He ran long surgeon's fingers through mostly grey hair. 'You don't have to meet them you know. They'll understand, but they'd like to meet you. Especially Henryk.'

'I'm here, aren't I? Of course I'll meet them. As for the rest...' Cool blue eyes looked warily into deep wise brown ones. '... we'll see Youssef. I can't promise anything.'

People were beginning to filter into the exhibition area and this was where Youssef had arranged to meet Henryk and

---

[6] **Post-traumatic Stress Disorder** ~ a severe anxiety disorder that is sourced from any situation where a psychological trauma is caused. Often the causative event involves physical or emotional violence and occurs most commonly in personnel returning from active service in conflicts, or in cases of domestic violence especially if rape is a factor.

Helga Zimmerman, so she and Youssef made a move as well. The CAMEO stand was of course impressive and Youssef steered Sophie to the various sections he knew she'd be interested in. It was whilst they were talking to the PR lady in the emergency surgical teams section that the Zimmermans arrived. Youssef's face lit up with pleasure as he introduced Sophie to them.

'It is good to meet you finally, Sophie - you are looking very well!'. Henryk shook her by the hand, smiling broadly, then put his arm around his petite wife. 'Helga's a little deaf these days, so make sure she can see your face.' Sophie smiled and took the old lady's hand gently.

'I'm very pleased to meet both of you at last! I hope you had an uneventful flight over here?'

'It was OK, thank you. Left on time and landed safe, thank the Lord. I do not like flying so much - never did!' Helga's English was more halting that her husband's, but her expression was so kind Sophie immediately took to her.

'I know what you mean! I hate being cooped up on long hauls. But working out in Africa you have to put up with that of course, even if you're not leaving the continent!'

They looked so old, but upright and vigorous still, she thought. Considering their lives had been given over to various humanitarian causes and war zones and they had only been retired a couple of years, they looked pretty good for seventy odd. These days the German couple lived fairly quietly in South Africa and did the occasional bit of consultancy work on the seminar circuit, so this was a working holiday for them, that they were fitting into a longer vacation that took in visiting relations in Holland and Germany. They all moved on to look at the other stands, talking easily, until it was time for lunch. The Zimmermans had made plans to dine with another friend, but, before they left the two doctors for the while, Henryk asked Sophie to get them some seats together in the Lecture Hall as Youssef was one of the speakers.

'We are very much looking forward to hearing about the latest practices in the treatment of post-traumatic stress disorder - heaven knows it's needed badly and not just in Africa!'

'All over the world, Henryk.' Youssef gave a rueful smile to his old friends. 'I'm thankful to Sophie for some parts of my piece - she's quite the expert on EMDR[7] .'

'Give over, silly!' Sophie glared at Youssef, a little flustered that he'd brought up her input into his presentation in front of them. She'd been happy to help him out, but this had been the beginning of him nagging her, saying that she could really do some good with her expertise out in Zyanda right now. 'And I'm not an expert, just a well-informed practitioner. Take no notice of him Henryk!'

'Sophie is too modest, not only is she having a lot of success with it in her psychotherapy clinic down in Aldershot, but she's also undergone the therapy herself.'

Sophie had gone beetroot-red and threw another furious look at Youssef as Helga asked what EMDR was. To add insult to injury he nodded to her to reply.

'It means 'eye movement desensitisation and reprocessing' - a little like the movements your eyes make when you're dreaming? That's called REM - rapid eye movements in dream-phase sleep.'

'Like a trance or hypnosis then?' Henryk had been listening

---

[7] **EMDR** - eye movement desensitisation and re-processing. A type of psycho-therapy that is deemed to be effective in treating people suffering from persistent dysfunctionality as a result of PTSD.

carefully to her. She laughed and cringed inwardly because it sounded so brittle.

'Not really. The client's conscious throughout and simply follows the therapist's finger, or a pencil they hold up and move from side to side, whilst the person's focussing on a specific visualisation of their particular trauma. This helps them to confront the worst memories 'safely'.'

She saw the elderly couple look at each other doubtfully. 'It's really simple to do, but hard to explain - Youssef's presentation will probably make it clearer. Let's get lunch over shall we? I promise I'll get you some good seats near the front!'

As good as her word, Sophie was one of the first people to get into the lecture hall and made a bee line for the front row, managing to get the end of the line that was handy for the exit, as she wasn't sure she wanted to stay the full hour for all the presentations. She'd probably have to now though as Youssef was the last speaker but one according to the programme on her seat. Henryk and Helga joined her almost immediately in high spirits.

'This is such a lovely place - the catering is very good isn't it?' Henryk beamed at her and she laughed.

'In this country the medical professions tend to be gourmets I think - and wannabe sommeliers too!'

'We have some good wine down in South Africa now!' Helga was looking a little merry and her eyes were twinkling at Sophie.

'Oh, I know - I love the Chardonnays.'

'Ah, well if you are coming back to Africa you must come to see us some time and we will get some of our local wine in for you to try.'

Sophie almost gasped at Henryk's first words, then

managed to calm herself and answer him sensibly, if a little stiffly.

'Coming back? No, you've got that wrong I'm afraid.' Bloody Youssef! She'd get him for this later. 'I've no plans to go back, not even to see my sister in Kenya.' She must have sounded rather tart for Henryk was immediately contrite.

'I am sorry, I must have misunderstood what Youssef was saying the other day.'

'It's alright it's not your fault. He's been trying to get me interested in some project for Zyanda for a while, but... well, I don't want to go there.'

Henryk nodded, but there was a stubborn look in his eye. 'Understandable, my dear.' He was going to say something else, but a look from Helga silenced him for a moment. His next words took another turn entirely.

'I don't know if Youssef told you, but we have brought something for you - copies of the transcripts of the police statements myself and Christian Kamate gave right after the Umbeke incident. Our friend at lunch is staying here at the College and he has invited all of us to have drinks and dinner here with him later. Our hotel is just up the road so I could go and get the transcripts and bring them back here for you? They're yours to keep - I have my own copies.'

She was speechless almost. Luckily the hall had filled up and it looked like the talk was about to start. 'Well... let's decide about that once this is over, shall we?'

'Of course. I should have mentioned it earlier.'

The lights over the audience were dimming as the Chairman stood up to make brief introductions and the first slideshow started, so they all gave their attention to the lecture. Sophie was ill at ease still and fiddled with the white gold ring she wore on the middle finger of her right hand throughout. It had an elegant cluster with a raindrop tanzanite stone, surrounded by nine little diamonds.

* * *

Homicide of:-
Harrison, Thomas (UK Citizen);

Mbrame, Rev. Jean-Batiste (Zyandan Citizen);
Olatunde, Dr. Teresa (Nigerian/SA Citizen);
Tamale, Aaron (resident)

18th May 1994

Part 2:- Events pertaining to Dr. Olatunde & Tom Harrison

I knew Dr. Teresa Olatunde since she was around 10 years old in 1968. We met during the course of my work as a surgical team orderly and liaison officer in Biafra, now south-eastern Nigeria. She was in a semi-comatose state and had been shot in the chest, was covered in cigarette burns and heavy bruising and had suffered a spontaneous abortion as well as general ill-health due to long-term malnutrition and dehydration. She needed immediate surgery as there was advanced infection and a hysterectomy had to be performed as the internal infection was life-threatening. Subsequently my wife, Helga Zimmerman, and myself sponsored Teresa's transfer of residency to South Africa for convalescence in a Carmelite nursing order, which also operated an orphanage and school.

We continued to support Teresa financially throughout, including dual citizenship for her in South Africa and in Nigeria once order had been restored there. We also set up a grant for her college training at medical school in Kenya. On leaving college, she took holy orders with the Carmelites and worked in South Africa and then Zambia in various locations. I think she was stationed in Vutare for almost 12 years as chief medical officer, running a general clinic for childhood inoculations, sexual health and obstetrics and for medical education and drug distribution for malaria and other tropical maladies; later on she also introduced a contraception advisory service against the wishes of her order, but with full backing for the initiative from CAMEO, who had the final say on services offered at the school and surgical unit. She had applied to CAMEO for transfer to work with refugees and/or in war zones at the beginning of 1993 and was initially unsuccessful due to her background, as it was thought her mental fortitude was compromised and, being tiny physically, there were also doubts over her strength and energy levels to withstand the demands of working in extreme field conditions. However, with the situation over in Zyanda escalating in April this year the decision was...

Sophie sighed and closed the file. The train was only a few stops from Aldershot now and whilst some of this was new to her, she didn't need to read it. She had heard most of Terry's early history from Youssef years ago, after she had emerged from the worst period of spiralling depression when she'd returned to the UK. Although she'd long ago got over her own misplaced resentment towards and unnecessary rivalry with Terry, she still found it hard to do the doctor-nun justice. As she put the file back in her bag, Sophie reflected on how her attitude to Terry had changed since that horrible day back in Tanzania. The nun should never have been given the Umbeke job but, with the urgency to get some aid and shelter set up for the terrified people who were spilling out over the Zyandan borders, the Zimmermans actually asked for Terry to run the emergency clinic in Umbeke during the setup phase for them. The placement had more or less gone through on the nod, since the camp was in Tanzania and not Zyanda. It had been like sending a little kid to war with a wooden gun and a 'willing attitude'. Sophie knew that Henryk in particular felt responsible for Terry cracking up, although of course nobody could have foreseen that the Zyandans would have started to come through at the old Umbeke mission settlement so soon.

The rest was simply consequential of the bloody mess of old colonial favouritism and tribal antagonism - except it wasn't of course. Something cataclysmic had happened in Zyanda. The death toll alone was horrific. Getting on for one million people, just ordinary people, not even soldiers for the most part, had been slaughtered in only three months starting in April and finishing in June, whilst the rest of Africa and the world looked on in stunned denial. Until Umbeke.

Other places in the Congo, Burundi and Uganda had already begun to get blank-eyed, traumatised refugees seeking asylum from the madness. Where Matu neighbours were killing Lutse children who had played happily with their own sons and daughters only weeks before it all kicked off. But in Umbeke 'foreigners' had been killed on another nation's soil and of course that changed everything. Only four people had died, one of them the leader of the Zyanda militia group who had pursued thirty-six women and children, including a half dozen sympathetic Matu women, who helped their friends escape over the border. A Tanzanian medical assistant, Terry and her poor Tom, all murdered. For nothing more than trying to help people in the direst need at the wrong place and the wrong time.

T. I. A. This is Africa folks. A sodding hopeless, never-ending series of disasters waiting to happen. The train had arrived and she got off and headed for the taxi office. She'd read the rest of it tomorrow...

.... we should not have pressed for Teresa to come and help us set up the clinic. Everything is clearer with hindsight. Aaron had broken away from the men guarding us to warn Teresa and Tom Harrison and make them turn back and get help for us. The Zyandan men had burst in on us only 5 minutes before the supply truck arrived and we were all still in shock and fearful for the women and children naturally. Aaron was so brave and he nearly succeeded, but Teresa and Tom were puzzled by his frantic waving and shouting so they got out of the cab, all smiles, thinking he was greeting them and by then of course it was too late. Aaron was hacked to death with pangas. This is when I first came to suspect that their rifles at least were not loaded.

We could all see straight away that Teresa was in difficulties - she was very pale and trembling as the Zyandans marched her and Tom over to us. He was relatively calm considering, but I could see he was very concerned about Teresa. As soon as she saw the refugees she was frozen. Tom tried to console her but she pushed him away. When they marched us over to the old school house he had to drag her with us. Once we were inside Teresa was almost collapsing with fear and shock, but my wife held her and talked to her and then Tom and I talked to Teresa as well and she came around to her normal self.

We could see the canteen where the Zyandan ladies were all gathered from the school house window. It was hard to hear what was being said but the priest, Mbrame, did a lot of shouting which we could hear. He interrogated one of the Matu women, forcing her to kneel before him and asking why they had helped the others. She was the head-teacher of the town school, Mrs Beleshona. She had been the one who had gathered the mothers of some of the younger Lutse schoolchildren together and had persuaded them to get out of their settlement and come across the border. Mrs. Beleshona is a very strong person and argued with Mbrame. He got very angry and started to strike her and she fell to the ground. Christian, our translator, Tom, myself and Teresa all saw this through the window, but Teresa was the one who reacted quickly and managed to dodge past the boy who was guarding us and ran out shouting at Mbrame to stop hitting Mrs. Beleshona. Both Tom and I tried to stop her, but David, the young man with the AK, levelled it at us and we had to go back to the window.

I cannot say that Teresa entirely brought this on herself. What she did was foolish in the extreme, but it did bring matters to a head with Mbrame's squad who had been feeling increasingly mortified by the killings. Most of them were only there because Mbrame had bullied them into following the women to Umbeke. Some of them had not even realised that they had crossed the Tanzanian border. We found out this afterwards when it was over and we talked to Abraham, the man who killed Mbrame and took over command of the other militia men.

We went back to the window anyway. Teresa and Mbrame were shrieking at each other in French and it was hard for me to follow what was being said, but Christian was translating for us as it became clear that Teresa was in trouble and perhaps endangering everyone else. Then we saw Abraham brought in, pointing his rifle at Teresa. Both Tom and I were now convinced that the men were short of ammunition - why else would they use pangas to kill Aaron when they were all carrying rifles? There were the two AKs of course, but we were not so sure of those. Anyway Teresa was still yelling despite having a rifle almost in her face and so we had to do something to help her. I asked Christian to talk to David, the guard and ask if Tom and I could go out and try and bring Teresa back in. This is when we were told that Abraham would not kill her and what made us take a calculated risk, as we wrongly thought that none of the guns were loaded.

David listened and agreed to let Tom and I go out. I asked Christian to look after my wife and we went out. While we had been negotiating with David the argument had got worse and Teresa and Mbrame had squared up to each other again and were screaming nose to nose almost. Teresa and Abraham both had their backs to us but as we came out of the school house the other men turned to look at us. I remember watching some of the men's faces - they all looked ill at ease, even frightened. We carried on walking towards them but then Mbrame gave a great roar and slashed at Teresa's shoulders then back again with his panga, this time at her face and neck. I think he stabbed her several times as well but it is confusing because so much was happening at once. Teresa fell to her knees screaming with pain and Abraham tried to pull her away, but Mbrame was in a frenzy and he had to back off. Teresa had fallen to the floor completely and I think she may already have been dead. I am not sure though. I was just standing there for maybe a second and so was Tom, and then he had sprinted a few metres from me, howling and shouting to Teresa. As Mbrame yelled at another of his men, the one with the other AK, to shoot at Tom, I began to run as well shouting at Tom to come back. The AK man was to the side of us and about 10 maybe 15 metres away from Mbrame.

There was the noise of the gun but Tom was still running for several more metres, though I saw him stagger twice and then he fell and sprawled on the ground. As I ran to him he tried to get up and made it to his hands and knees as I got to him and bent down to help him. He turned to me and I saw the blood as one of the bullets hit him on the side of his head. On his temple. He put a hand out to me and I caught him under the arm and waist, then we both went down and I turned him onto his back so I could see where the other bullets had hit him. I think it was silent for a few moments before the priest was shouting again. All my attention was on Tom then. Christian said Mbrame was shouting for the AK man to shoot me as well, but I did not hear because Tom was trying to talk to me. He asked what was happening to Teresa. I said I thought she was dead and then we both were crying. Then he said something like 'Thank God I stopped Sophie coming.' ...

She turned the file over and wiped tears away. Standing up she went to the cabinet and poured herself a brandy, her hands shaking a little, and she went into the conservatory, more tears streaming down like the late spring rain on the windows. It wasn't as though she hadn't known this. She'd seen other reports after all, including the autopsy for both Tom and Terry. Friends in high places were useful and Youssef had kept to his promise when he had come back to see her again shortly after they had flown back from Zambia. He had had to give up field duty himself five years earlier when he had started work with the after-care services for CAMEO and had just been made head of department when she had met him with Claire at Lusaka.

Back in England, Youssef was practically the only one who had understood how she was feeling, since he had also had a very bad burnout working up in Eritrea that had put an end to his mobile surgical career when he knew he was becoming too unstable in and out of theatre. If it hadn't been for Youssef she didn't know how she would have made it, let alone get her own act together and find a way to work through her own grief and nightmares. Regain some purpose and control in deciding to train as a doctor, instead of a teacher, as she and Tom had planned when they'd gone back to Vutare after their wonderful time in Vic Falls.

Catharsis. It still eluded her no matter what she tried. The EMDR therapy had been the only thing that helped her come to terms with the sorrow and outrage. In a way her grief was made worse for her not being there. Not actually there where it all happened. It was more what had been taken away from her. Her love, her baby, her future. The therapy had helped her to rationalise her true loss. Had let her remember without too much distress. It didn't help with going on though. Not entirely.

That was where Youssef had come in. Her team boss in Vutare had told Claire that any questions she had about Umbeke could be answered when she was over the malaria attack and better able to cope with everything. Youssef had confirmed this almost as soon as he met them in Lusaka. She had been barely conscious, zonked with painkillers and sedatives, but she had felt reassured listening to his low, soothing voice. The following day on the flight he had held her hand and started to tell her about the Zimmermans and about Terry and how all three of them had saved the nun's life out in Biafra, twenty odd years before. Saying farewell to her at arrivals in Heathrow after making sure her parents were there and understood about the medicine that she had to take. Telling them about the appointment card for clinics at the Hospital for Tropical Diseases at University College in London, he'd taken her hand again and said he'd make sure they got any more information on the killings as it became available, through Claire, or from himself whenever he was back in the UK on business.

About eighteen months later Youssef had arrived on their doorstep in Guildford with the engagement ring that Tom had bought for her in Mwanza...

... he knew he was dying. I had taken my jacket off and tried to compress the worst wound on his groin, but it was hopeless and he was bleeding badly from the head wound; from his ear, nose and even his eyes. He told me to stop so I did but still tried to keep wiping the blood out of his eyes. His voice was very weak then and I had to lower my ear to his lips to make out what he was saying.

Ring

Pocket

Sophie

Hers

The ring

He had been putting his hand in his jacket pocket every so often whilst we were in the school house and finally I realised what he has talking about. I found the little box and held it in his fingers for him. He could not hold it himself as he was starting to shake badly. I could not see his face anymore because of the blood and my own tears. He was a blur to me but he was still trying to tell me something. I put my ear right to his mouth. Blood was bubbling out there now as well. I could barely make out the words.

Love her

Ring

I promised him I would give her the ring. I was still holding his hand and the box. He brushed the back of my hand with his finger. Then the spasms began in earnest so he could not speak at all. He died in my arms.

I had been oblivious to everything that had gone on around me. I had not even realised Mbrame had ordered the AK man to shoot me as well. Helga, my wife, she came and knelt with me and put her arms around me and Tom as well. Christian came and squatted down beside us. We were all crying. Helga said I was a mess and I looked and saw the front of my body was smeared with blood. It was all Tom's blood. I told Helga I was not hurt and she slapped me hard on the face. She said not to be so stupid, then kissed me and held my head to her chest.

There were two other men who came to us now. David the boy who guarded us in the school house and Abraham, his grandfather, who had tried to get Teresa away from Mbrame. They wanted us to take Teresa's body out of the heat. Abraham said it was not fitting for him or the other men to do this. Christian said he would go. Helga said I was to stay with Tom. She went after Christian. Abraham could speak a little French and he said he was very sorry that Teresa and Tom had been killed. He said he wished he could have got Teresa away from Mbrame but the man was insane and he feared him so much. He said he had been weak and so stood and did nothing. I told him I had seen him trying to help. That the Lord knew who was responsible for all of this and would be merciful to those who had tried to stop it.

Christian had come back to us and overheard this last part. He said that Abraham had saved my life and killed the evil man. Christian told me this as we carried Tom back to the school house and laid him on the big table beside Teresa. I could not look at Teresa again after that first glance. My wife was sitting beside the body. Helga was holding her head in her hands and I could see her shoulders shaking with her sobbing but she made no sound really. The next thing I knew I was outside on the veranda and Helga was crouched in front of me holding my head between my knees. She was still crying but her voice was soft and normal. She said I had been sick and had collapsed so Christian and David had carried me outside into the shade.

After a little while Christian came and gave us both some little plastic cups of water from the cooler in the office. Abraham was with him. Christian told us that he had called the area police over in Mwanza and they would be here around dusk. He said that Abraham and the other Zyandan men would now leave as soon as they could. Abraham wanted us to come and talk to the women. He wanted the six Matu women to return with them. I told Christian to tell him that was for the Matu ladies to decide for themselves. As Christian translated for us Abraham looked at me and I saw the sorrow and regret in his eyes. He is an honourable man at heart I think. He nodded and there was a stream of local Swahili that I could not follow. Christian said they were content for the women to stay here if they wanted to. He gave us a few more minutes and then we...

This is Africa. She knew the rest. It was sometimes hard for westerners to understand Africans. Henryk and Helga did. They saw past the poverty and the hunger and the seemingly ignorant refusal to stop living in the day and make provision for the future. They could see the good still in this old man who, despite his compassionate behaviour that day, had nevertheless slain who knows how many innocent, defenceless people over those last bloody weeks. They let them go free, leaving their guns and rifles behind, in the hope that they might do more good back in their own land, or at least would no longer do evil.

Abraham, David and the others disappeared. They were never brought to justice and were probably dead, especially if they refused to be part of the hateful carnage that had gone on for another month or more before international pressure and intervention finally came and brought the atrocities to an end. It was far too late for all those Lutse and the Matu who had tried to intercede for their friends and neighbours, whose only crime had been to be born into the wrong tribe.

It began after the rains and ended in the dry heat of June. The madness ended, but its legacy was still being paid for by the survivors. Women without their men. Mothers without their sons. Those who had been drawn along in the mayhem and hysteria and become something unspeakable as mob rule invaded their hearts and minds. They paid too. They had to live with the nightmare reality of their own creation. Had to live alongside people without limbs, bearing terrible scars that went far too deep, until they were all victims of a malevolent cancer that had torn their nation savagely apart and cast them all into perdition.

Genocide. The pain goes on and on. T. I. A.[8]

---

[8] **T. I. A** - This is Africa. The plaintive cry of many a frustrated ex-pat of whatever hue, or hailing from any other corner of the world, who comes up against the multitude of problems that beset the continent to make the absent heart pine for their own native soil.

Trophies

Terra Incognita for me, but back on the Zambezi. Whatever you think of the politics in this country they really have looked after their National Parks. The lake itself is stunning, especially at sunrise and sunset, and the camp Claire's booked for us in the Sanyati Gorge is gorgeous. Eva got a little puffed going up the hill from the landing stage but it's really hot here so I think she's OK, although she was feeling sick last night. Probably too much biltong[9] yesterday. I told her to have a good drink of water after eating it but as usual she knows best, or rather her personal 'stylist' Phil does. So of course now she's swearing off Kudu meat forever, despite stuffing it down like it was going out of fashion, saying how tasty it was. Then she wonders why she's got stomach cramps because she wouldn't take a pint of bottled water to swish it down like everyone else had.

Anyway she's back on form tonight now her new best friend Harry's arrived. Honestly these safari guides are just one big cliché sometimes - I swear he's modelled his bush outfit on Stewart Granger in King Solomon's Mines! Except for the shorts. These Zimbabwean bush camps are solid with tanned hairy male legs and I swear it's because they're allergic to long trousers! Actually he's a very nice guy is Harry - knows his stuff and he's been great company this evening, so I guess he's worth his astronomic fee. Gareth and Keith are off with him at dawn tomorrow to canoe up the gorge a way to a bee-eater colony and then go croc watching - hundreds of the damn things on this river but they want to get some stock river shots for the art director. Eva and I have passed and are

---

[9] **Biltong** - strips of dried meat, a little like beef jerky. In many people's opinion Kudu meat makes the best game biltong being rich-tasting and not too tough.

*going out on the pontoon for the late afternoon cruise - we've both
fallen in love with the malachite kingfishers. Beautiful little things -
like tiny flying jewels, but they're so quick and therefore quite hard
to photograph...*

He laughed warmly, eyes crinkling with merriment, even
though the 'Ark' gag was hardly novel. 'Well Eva, you saw
the lake from the air - it's man-made and it's only been full
of water since the late fifties and early sixties. We needed
a reservoir, simple as, and there was the mighty Zambezi
with lots of tributaries joining it from the south and in the
north from what was Northern Rhodesia and Nyasaland, or
Zambia as it's known today. So hey presto - let's make a
dam!' Harry grinned as he sucked on his pipe, sending up
little sparks of tobacco, glittering in the dark as the match
took a hold. ''Course it took almost five years for the valley
to gradually flood and they had to move the Ba Tonga people
and all the animals on as the water levels rose. Most of the
people went and resettled around the south-western end
of the lake in Binga District, or went to the Zambian side,
but the wildlife mostly ended up on the south eastern side
of the lake here and we got the Matusadona National Park
as a result. And the Tiger Fish thrived in the water - game
fishing fans love 'em! Not to mention all that lovely hydroelectricity as well. But there had to be an Ark - lots of 'em
as well, because the animals got stranded on the new islands
like Fothergill and Spurwing. It was a little bit like a wildlife
Dunkirk, with everyone who had a boat chipping in to help
Rupert Fothergill, who'd started Operation Noah...[10]

---

[10] **Operation Noah** - ran between 1960 and 1964 and was organised by
game reserve warden Rupert Fothergill. Over 8000 large animals and
snakes were moved to safety on the surrounding high ground to the north
and south as the Zambezi levels rose to form Lake Kariba.

'Harry! Watch yourself! You saw the crocs not ten minutes ago. They may have looked sleepy on the sandbars but they wake up pretty quick if they see something moving that looks tasty!'

He grinned cheekily at his Ma but pulled his hand out of the water all the same and joined her at the front of the boat. She was looking at the cormorants and darters, already drying out their wings from the first hunt of the day in the naked Leadwood trees.

'They seem to like the dead trees more than the live ones don't they?' Helena smiled at her nine year old son and he nodded without much interest. She sighed, shaking her head 'Go on then - take the bins...'

'Thanks Ma!'

'Just put them down every so often - the rubber will go all sticky around your eyes when it gets hotter!' Helena laughed, then carried on watching the birds on the skeletal remains of the drowned Leadwoods, thinking how eerily beautiful they looked in the early morning light.

He scanned the foreshore with his mother's light but powerful binoculars looking for buffalo, which he found without too much trouble, but hoping for elephants. It had been all over Kariba Town last weekend that Mr Fothergill, despairing of getting a herd of females moved from one of the rapidly shrinking islands, had got them to the southern edge and had been surprised to see them all wade out into the water and then start to swim for the southern shore towards the Matusadona Hills, despite having four very young calves. They'd apparently been in the water for about twenty minutes and out of their depth for about half that time. Harry had been enthralled with the account in the newspaper and had pestered his mother all week to be allowed to go out with her on Saturday to help with the rafts for the smaller animals, but of course hoping to see even one elephant swim...

'I never saw them swim that day, but about a month later I went out with mother again and saw three bull elephants take to the lake. Very impressive sight! Seen them swimming many, many times since. They're pretty good at it but better snorkelers - and yes, before you ask, they do keep their trunks out of the water, so they look a bit like sea serpents with their noses up and then you see a bit of their heads and then their backs.' He stopped for a puff of the pipe and watched the smoke curling up into the night. 'The calves take to it quickly - but they're all water babies are ellies. They love it!'

He stared into the flames for a few moments and then began to answer more questions about the making of Lake Kariba. The moon was rising high now but there'd be no night drive - the Sanyati Gorge was too rugged for vehicles to negotiate safely, even during daylight. Canoes and Shanks's pony were the classy mode of transport up here and he had an early start... 'I'd better get some kip in now I think. See you at six, chaps - someone'll bring you some tea around five-thirty!'

* * *

'Hiya Soph!' Gareth hailed her from the path. Sophie looked up lazily from her Jilly Cooper and smiled at the cameraman as he walked over to the pool.

'How'd it go? Did you do OK for croc shots?'
'Fine, ta! Listen - can you get a hold of your sister later on today?'
' 'Course - what about?'
'Keith wants us to come back to Kariba at the end of the tour. This guy Harry, he's a sodding goldmine of info and he

says he can take us out hunting with bows at this game ranch just over from Bumi Hills!'

'Should think that's doable, yes - but what's that got to do with the movie?'

'Nothing at all, luv, but Jack's next project is a fantasy thingie and they go hunting with bows an' stuff. Tons of CGI, so Keith wants to get some footage for that as well. Harry's cool for it, but says he wasn't contracted for that and so it's too late for him to book it whilst we're here.'

Sophie laughed 'OK - I'll give them a call after lunch.'

'Cool! If they can do it, Harry says he'll give her a call when we're finished here and make the arrangements this end!'

Claire was nearly collapsing with hiccups after laughing like a drain.

'Oh, Sophie! Harry's such a whore! Honestly - I'm going to build an introduction fee into this gig! Hang on a mo...' Sophie could hear a hasty exchange going on in the background, presumably with Grant, Claire's husband and then she was back on. 'Yes, we should be able to arrange the flights back to Kariba from Nairobi OK, but they'll have to go via Harare. Tell Harry I'll give him a call with the dates and who'll be going after I've had a chance to talk to Jack's PA, but it might not be until the weekend now. We've not dealt with these Bumi Hills people before but I think they have a very good rep - they must have if Harry's tight with them. Tell the old robber hello from Grant and me!'

'I will do - thanks Claire and give Grant a big kiss from me.'

* * *

'Whoa, whoa, whoa there, Eva!' Harry had just had a good telling off from the actress on the evils of hunting

105

rare animals, which he'd mostly borne with good grace, but enough was enough and there was only so much uninformed flak he was prepared to take from anyone, least of all someone who'd barely set foot outside of California. 'I'd agree with you every time on threatened and rare animals - it's a tragedy when they're hunted to extinction and believe me, most African governments these days would back me up and mean it...' He smiled good-humouredly at Eva, she just didn't know what she was talking about and he was about to put that right. Winking at Sophie, who'd worked in villages in or near game reserves over the border in Zambia, he carried on explaining the realities of wildlife management. '...not because they're bleeding heart tree-huggers, but because wildlife is literally a big revenue industry and they need the money that international tourism brings in. And that includes hunting for food for the locals, as well as issuing licences for trophy hunters. These days, with giving over ownership of the reserves to the farmers and herdsmen communities, they're actually encouraging them to look after their wildlife.'

'I just don't see why there has to be hunting any more, Harry? This safari and the movie will be bringing in a lot of revenue surely and the regular trips must bring in steady income?' Eva wasn't just a pretty face and she truly did love all animals.

'Yes, the photographic and green safari dollars are an important part of that, but some of these people are dirt poor and profits for the flights and the travel company side of tourism doesn't reach them necessarily. That's where the hunting market comes into its own - the fees from licensing mostly goes straight to the district councils, then into building schools, clinics and better accommodation, even churches. That way they're really incentivised to look after their game instead of poaching the reserve for the pot, or for ivory or rhino horn. There's still a market for that out in the far east, and we still have a goodish elephant population down here...'

He'd already had this conversation with Gareth and Keith on the river and yeah, he'd got them fired up with going bow-hunting over at Bumi, which was something he enjoyed himself. Much better than Hemingway style as he termed it, with state of the art hunting rifles, which, although he did guiding on that too, was cheating in his book.

'How's it cheating, Harry? The Big Five[11] are hardly defenceless are they?' Keith's northern drawl cut in.

'Because it's not 'real' hunting is it? You go out with the intention of bringing back a trophy don't you and half the time that 'trophy's' been bred to be just that. All you're really doing is using a rifle instead of a camera, safe in the vehicle, holding a state of the art gun that virtually can't miss for you! With the horned animals you might as well take the client to a local slaughter-house because mostly all they're interested in is the trophy they've effectively already bought. Some of them don't even want to track the animal they're taking to the point where they're almost stepping out of the shower, shooting the animal, then going straight back to get dressed for dinner. They deserve to get royally ripped off for licences and taxidermy and all the other little 'add-ons' that the game ranches rake in!'

'So why's bow-hunting any better then? They use spiffy modern compound bows don't they?'

'You can use traditional longbows as well. It's because

---

[11] The top 5 animals that people want to see on safari. Lion, leopard, rhino and elephant are nearly always included on the checklist, with hippo, buffalo or cheetah making up the numbers depending on what's 'hot' at the time or where you're based.

you have to get in much closer. You have to track, keep quiet and concentrate on what you're doing. It's just so much more authentic and the balance is 'right', because you're on a par with your prey and because anything could happen. You might get hurt too, even if it's just providing something for the fly population to chomp on whilst you're getting downwind without breaking cover. It's hunting for real, or as close as you'd get to it these days.'

He'd nailed their interest now with the 'authentic' pitch - and it wasn't even stretching the truth that much...

'What can we hunt at your place then, Harry? Any chance of an elephant?' Gareth had been talking guns and hunting with Harry last night.

'It's possible, yes, but I'd have to pass you on to another guide. I don't kill ellies anymore.' Harry did have his own code and elephant were never on his hunting trip list.

'Why not if they're bred for it?'

'Because they're not - you have to own a hell of lot of land to support even a couple of elephant. A whole herd and you'd need to own a National Park and they're protected there of course. Ellies go where they like effectively.'

'But last night you said you'd culled elephants when you worked in the Parks?'

'That's why I don't kill them anymore Gareth. They're sacrosanct for me now. Too intelligent and social, plus I had a bellyful of killing whole families when they still culled them up here.'

'Why whole families?'

Harry coloured, but not from anger. 'Because they're like us - they mourn their dead. If a calf loses its mother - even if it's weaned, you might as well kill it too, because they'll not be able to survive without her. So if we found a herd we'd take them all. It was a lot 'kinder'...'

Culling truly was sickening, even though there was reason back then, when the farmers were still trying to get their crops back in after the civil war. He shook his greying head sadly. 'Then there's the dwindling black rhino, although we have the largest wild population in the world down here in the Matusadona. Back in my game warden days I saw enough of how the poachers butchered them, and the irony is that you can farm rhino horn - it just keeps on growing if you cut it off carefully.'

'You could really farm it?'

Keith's eyebrows had disappeared into his hat!

'Uh-huh!' Harry grinned broadly at both of them. 'Rhino horn's like your hair or toenails - just keeps on growing. If you want to grow trophy-sized horn then you'd get around three decent lengths in a general life-span. And if you're farming for pharmaceutical purposes then you can take the growth down several times a year! You could make a bloody fortune out of it!'

'We're in the wrong game Keith!' They all laughed.

'But you hunt the other, less rare animals don't you?' Harry nodded patiently at Gareth. Hunting was where he made his big money and he made enough at it to pick and choose what he would and wouldn't hunt.

'Hunting other sustainable herd animals - no problem at all for me. They really are bred for it after all. Carnivores, even lion and hunting dogs on the same premise, as they can breed well in captivity too of course. So long as it's on a kosher ranch, or licensed game area, it's just a much more lucrative way to ensure the wildlife's looked on as an asset. For the horned beasts it's positively easy money and actually good for the animals, as only the best and most magnificent are wanted for trophies. The females and young thrive with no natural predation and the big males all make it to maturity for starters, safe from poachers and siring several generations to ensure those big horn genes stay in the breeding group! And that all happens just because some rich old guy from Tennessee or wherever, wants a nice set of kudu horn or something over his fireplace.'

It was money for old rope almost and the client paid through the nose for literally everything - the pro hunter's fee being almost the least of it. Silly prices, and paid at source, where it did most good and everyone, including the precious animals, benefitted in some way. Gun hunting was just not something he enjoyed doing anymore, however great it was for easy money. It was too crude and if the client was a bad shot it could get very distressing, especially if they didn't miss but botched the shot and hit a non-fatal area...

... He was swearing under his breath as he tried to balance himself to take yet another shot at this bloody buff. Bloody client more like! Big Mr. 'I am', and he was 'gonna git himself one of them big motherfuckin' Cape bufferloes'... Flaming idiot! He should have listened to his instincts and refused to go out with Marjulies today - the amount the man'd put away last night it was a wonder he made it to lunch, let alone breakfast, but there were only two full days left of their stay here and the old dugga[12] bull they'd found down by the river should've been feeling sluggish so late in the day...

---

[12] **dugga boy** - Southern African slang term for a single or small groups of male Cape Buffalo, usually elderly animals (or sometimes adolescent) who have left, or been driven out of the herd by the dominant male. Because they may only just be past their sexual prime these mature males are usually still powerful animals, of irritable temperament and are generally carrying trophy size horns. They are thus highly prized by game hunters.

... 'Shit!'

The blasted animal had literally charged and nutted the tree trunk so hard he'd nearly fallen out and his shot had missed by miles. Harry reloaded quickly, his face grim. He'd have to chance it and get back on the ground because he sure as hell wasn't going to get a good killing shot in sitting up in a tree bole with this useless clot of a client, who'd managed to drop his weapon even before they'd both had to take shelter from the maddened buff in this ruddy tree. He looked up at Marjulies, who was rustling the leaves on the next branch up he was so shit-scared.

'Stay put and try to be quiet - I'll have to get down if it backs off again.' Dear God, the man was actually crying now... 'I mean it! Stay there.'

The old bull was puffing and blowing again. This one wasn't going to let things lie and not because by rights it should be lying dead several yards off. All they'd done so far was get it so pumped up with adrenalin it was literally running on spite now. It had moved off a little at last, but was still glaring up at them in the tree. Harry raised his rifle and used the telescopic sight to assess the damage he'd inflicted so far. Despite himself he was impressed - there was blood everywhere down the forequarters, so he'd got it in the chest at least once and judging from the way it was spurting blood he'd hit a major vein, if not the heart. That was buffs for you - mean as hell and long on retribution. This old boy wasn't too far past his prime either. He'd hate to meet up with the new guy who kicked him out - must've been bloody monstrous.

Very, very slowly he put his weight on the right leg and slid his left down and behind the trunk until his foot rested on the stub of an old branch, still looking at the bull. Finally it turned away and trotted off for fifty yards or so, breathing hard now. He only needed those few moments to drop lightly to the ground with most of his body hidden by the tree trunk. The buff had stopped, its chest heaving with the effort of its final strength, but it looked back at them, angling around so he had a choice of a head shot or one more to the chest. He had four shots and those should do it he thought as he raised the Browning.

'Burton! Behind us!' Marjulies hissed at him loud enough for the buff to bellow out its anger and turn full on again. Harry slewed his head towards the slight movements from nearby mopane brush in time to see a battery bird fly away.

'Shut the fuck up!' he growled viciously as he swung back and revised the low shot he'd contemplated in favour of the head. The wounded buffalo snorted aggressively and its muscles bunched in obedience to its final crack at vengeance. Hold tight Harry... Keep your focus... but this had gone beyond rationality now. He let off two shots in quick succession and still it came, even though both times he saw skin and blood flying away and the white of bone between the buff's eyes. Another shot, another hit, into the eye itself this time and at last it stumbled as he began to lower the Browning. There was a scream above him from Marjulies that joined the echoing gunshots reverberating in his ears as, unbelievably, the animal heaved itself back into the charge. Harry inhaled and held it in a mixture of fury and fear as he took careful aim with his last shot, knowing he'd need to be bloody lucky to have time to reload if it didn't go down this time. Wait. Wait. Make it count. Let it get close. He fired.

He breathed out and stood his ground as the old buffalo finally crumpled forwards onto its knees and slowly fell onto its side

as the rear legs splayed and faltered and then were still. It was
about two yards away from him. He could smell its blood and
sweat, saw the ever-present flies rise up with a buzz, then fall
back onto its face, feasting on fresh blood and brains. His legs
were shaking now and he breathed in sharply, squatted down
on his haunches and bowed his head, trying not to throw up.

'Why'd ya shoot the bastid inna head! Ya could've spoilt
ma trophy!'

The punch he landed on Marjulies' ugly yellow mug smashed
his nose almost to a right angle. It was worth breaking two of
his own fingers and the mocking laughter back at the Lodge
when the trackers asked him which one of them had really
shot the buff's tail off...

'First rule in the Pro Hunter's manual - follow up the
client's shot PDQ and be prepared to say yours was the one
that missed, if you want your tip.'

'Did that awful man pay your fee after you broke his nose?'
Eva's voice was a little faint with emotion and the shocked
looks of admiration she was giving Harry were certainly
more and more obvious.

'In a way yes, but I had to earn it the hard way - he pressed
charges for assault and I got fined and banned from guiding in
South Africa for eighteen months!' he laughed ruefully. 'Still
paid my fee though - I told the little squirt I'd counterclaim if
he reneged and I wouldn't be telling the version he'd touted
around the Lodge that night... It was a very good trophy
though - one hundred and thirty-five inches from tip to tip,
the long way around.'

* * *

'Sophie! Can you spare me a minute please?' She smiled
at Jim, Eva's agent and third husband, who was also English

and seemed rather too calm and studious for his lush and demonstrative wife.

'Of course, as many as you like. What can I do for you?'

'Don't laugh... I've run out of anti-histamine cream and I got bitten to death on that blasted walk with Harry 'I'm so bloody macho' Burton!' He put out a red bumpy arm as evidence for Sophie to admire. She dutifully examined it but got the giggles at his comment.

'He is a bit full on isn't he, but I think most of these top guides are bound to put on the big white hunter act for the punters - it's almost obligatory. He does know his stuff as well - I loved his talk about the water hyacinths...'

Jim snorted and rolled his eyes. 'Yeah, right! And all the lovely minutiae about sodding Bilharzia as well. I'm bloody mozzie bait down there and he's banging on about ruddy worm fluke infested water-snails, snacking out in your bladder - I'm sure he did it on purpose! It's not that funny, Sophie!' He tried and failed to stifle a smile as Sophie's giggling became contagious. 'You've got a really unsympathetic bedside manner, Doctor Taylor!' He was laughing now as well as Sophie rummaged around in her bag for a spare tube of anti-histamine cream.

'Come on now - he did offer you a couple of squirts of his insect repellent!'

'When we got back, yeah! Fat load of good it's gonna do now! And bloody Eva's all over him, saying how 'caring' he is...'

'Oh, that's not fair Jim. I thought it was rather sweet of him, and anyway you still need repellent up here.'

'I have some up here!'

'And it wasn't his fault that you forgot to put any on before you went out, now was it?'

'No - that was Eva saying to hurry up and not keep him waiting!'

'Or that you both overslept slightly.' Sophie admonished him gently, though she was finding it very hard not to laugh out loud now.

'Well. He's got far too much to say for himself around her and I'm getting pretty fed with up it, I can tell you! He even looks at me in that 'aren't I great' way when she starts going googly-eyed at him!'

Sophie pursed her lips and then spluttered, unable to repress her laughter any longer. 'Oh, Jim - why'd you think he's looking at you and not her?'

'Because he's a bloody sadist, that's why!'

'Because he likes you more, that's why. It was quite funny how he kept falling back to walk up here with you.'

'Trying to justify bringing his bloody rifle out with him, more like! I mean, I ask you - like he needs to carry it around with him so near to camp. He only brought it with him to show off!'

She sighed and shook her head, though her lips were still curled up in amusement. 'Actually he did need it, quite apart from it being part of his job when taking clients out, especially on foot. This is Africa, not Hyde Park... besides, didn't you hear that leopard in the night? He even showed us the paw prints down by the landing stage. But I forgot - you were hanging back again so you probably didn't hear him.'

'I thought it was more crocodile crap he was pointing at.' Jim had the grace to blush and finally Sophie decided to put him out of his misery.

'You know, you don't have to worry about him flirting with Eva at all. It's just his job to be pleasant and to entertain you all.'

'Well I wish he'd stop staring at her the whole time.'

'He isn't! I told you already - he's looking at you more than her. Haven't you wondered why there's no Mrs. Harry Burton?'

'Because he's shagging his rich lady clients and probably half of the bored hausfraus in Kariba Town as well?!'

'No.' She felt she was going to burst controlling the giggles. 'Because he fancies *you*, Jim.' Why did you never have a camera handy for these classic moments?

'Oh!'

* * *

'So, Harry - I can see why you'd have to carry a rifle whilst you're out with your hunting clientele...' Jim had been a lot friendlier since the morning walk and Harry sucked on his pipe, smiling lazily at him across the campfire, '... but why did you need to take one when we were just wandering around here?'

'To be honest, I'd be astounded if I had to use it in anger around camp Jim. But it's a good habit to have when you know there's wild animals about, as you just don't know what's watching you. In places where they have hippo and crocs nearby it's not unusual for them to come into the perimeter - hippos more than crocs, especially at night when it's cooler, but it's too steep here for either of those away from the immediate shoreline of the Sanyati. Leopards would be a problem, except they're smart and they don't tend to get close to camps like this when there's a lot of people about, so on the busier paths you're perfectly safe so long as you don't stray too far out of the complex. If you do get into a confrontational situation then usually an overhead shot will do nicely to scare most beasts off. So long as you don't run - just stay still and don't panic, then slowly back away and keep going. Most animals won't go for you if you keep your head but some are very dangerous and firing a warning shot to give them something to think about is a quick fix. Even lions or elephants will generally leave you alone then, but leopard, buffalo and baboons are notoriously unpredictable - they can be real buggers to scare.'

'Baboons?!' Jim's eyebrows disappeared into his hairline and then he laughed 'But they're just monkeys who go around in biggish groups surely.'

Harry chuckled. 'Ever got a good look close up at a male baboon's teeth?' he looked around at the others and saw Sophie was grinning already. 'Their canines are enormous, bigger than a male lion's and every bit as sharp - lions won't hunt 'em either. The only predator they have trouble with is the leopard, and that's also the reason why leopards are so dangerous for humans too. They know the trick of how to kill an animal that goes about on two legs. They don't go for the throat first - they go for the body and eviscerate instead. To a leopard we're just bigger baboons and therefore a nice big meal as well...'

He let that sink in a little for they'd all heard a male leopard around camp during the night and seen the spoor down by the landing stage on their little stroll. 'But there aren't any baboons around here - most safari camps will try not to encourage them to settle too near or to tolerate them coming in 'cos they're menaces - get into the stores and even the guest accommodation - break stuff or take it if they think it's edible.'

'It's a bit like all those warnings not to stop or leave your car windows open back in the safari parks in the UK really - little devils'll snap aerials and windscreen wipers and try to get in the windows if they can.'

'That's the sort of thing, Sophie - they're like the worst

gang of vandals you can imagine and they're really strong and fast too. They have a pack mentality with opposable thumbs - not as smart as the great apes of course, but they're vicious brutes and ruthless with it.'

'Chimpanzees and gorillas are meat-eaters though, aren't they Harry?' Eva was a tireless supporter and fund-raiser for a simian rehabilitation institute in Uganda.

'Yeah, although not gorillas so much, but neither of those species are found down here in southern Africa outside of zoos. You're going up to the Congo for gorilla-spotting after this aren't you? Or was that Zyanda, Sophie?'

'To Uganda, Harry,' Sophie's voice was quiet and thoughtful somehow. 'We're not going to Zyanda.' Not on this trip. 'But going back to carrying firearms in Africa, out of the townships it's not just the guides who go armed is it?'

'Certainly not, most farmers carry rifles as a matter of course and have to use gameproof fencing to stop all kinds of wildlife getting into the crops, or taking domestic animals. Rifles are essential really and woe betide you if you forget to take them out with you - and ammo too of course...'

... Carl'd had a bitch of a day and, although the evening had made up for things a bit, he'd had to leave his mates back at the bar when his aunt had phoned the pub to say could he come back tonight instead of tomorrow morning. But right now he really was up shit creek, drunk as a skunk, no spare tyre for the slow puncture because he'd used that on the blow out he'd had on the way into town, and he'd gone and left his rifle back at the bar under his seat. At least that's where it probably was. He was a bit hazy on where he'd left it but it was no use cursing himself over it - it wasn't in the truck and the truck wasn't going anywhere because he'd also run out

*of sodding fuel. He'd fouled up big time and he'd never hear
the last of this for a year or more.*

*He was only about four miles from home... The moon was a
day or so shy of full so it was bright enough to see where he
was going and his big solid torch was new if it got too dark
in places. And heavy enough to use as a makeshift club if he
needed to swat anything away. So of course he'd decided to
walk the rest of the way rather than stay with the vehicle and
risk the ire of his uncle in failing to help him with the herd at
dawn tomorrow. If he'd not had so much to drink he'd have
at least paused to consider his options but he was tired, hazy
and just wanted to get home and sleep it off. So, like an idiot,
he'd slammed out of the cab and stomped off up the road...*

*He'd been walking for about a quarter of an hour when he
first heard them. They were ahead of him, but off in the bush,
not on the road. It was just hunting calls he told himself and
they were female, so they were probably after something else.
And game didn't like coming onto the road. Then he'd heard
the terrified yelping of a bushbuck that cut off abruptly. The
sound quashed the more mellow effects of his skinful of beer
and suddenly he was stone cold sober and listening as hard
as he could to what was happening up ahead, wanting to
know how close to the road it had been brought down. He
knew better than to go faster than a walk, so he kept going,
glancing nervously off to the side, hoping not to see anything
because it was too far off. Far enough off that they wouldn't
be looking for anything for dessert too soon.*

*There were growling and slathering noises. They were close.
Then came a much longer, more aggressive grunt and a
brief snarling scuffle as a male introduced itself to his worst*

nightmare. A cloud that had briefly obscured the moon floated off and, out of the corner of his eye, Carl glimpsed two dark tawny shapes loping out of the depths of the brush, then slowing down to a softer, almost silent pacing through the undergrowth, still heading towards him.

The last effects of his beer began to make its presence felt with twisted glee, but Carl did his best to ignore it and walked on at the same pace, resisting the urge to turn his torch on the two lionesses who were padding along parallel to him about twenty yards away from the road. All he could realistically do was to keep going and try to keep his head, which was now painfully clear. Also to ignore the urgent signals coming from his achingly full bladder.

He kept telling himself that he'd be OK and just to keep going, not turn around and hope they'd lose interest. However, the need to take a leak was almost overwhelming but still he attempted to stave it off, trying to think of other things to take his mind off the merciless pressure. He'd been through what Kipling he'd had crammed into him at school and was down to lists now. A-Z of male names; same for females; English counties and African countries then finally, in desperation, he started on the states of America. That became his undoing as he decided to try that in alphabetical order and promptly landed himself in trouble in the C's, wondering if DC was a county, or a state within a state like the Vatican... Before he could move onto the other D's after deciding that DC fell neatly into the equation as a D, even if that was for District because Columbia came after Colorado anyway, he heard the sound of running water in a storm drain beside the track and passed the point of no return.

With no option but to obey the imperative to start peeing,

*since it was now cripplingly impossible to resist any longer,
he fumbled with his zip as quietly as he could, whilst still
keeping up the pace. Too late. He'd started even before he
managed to free himself from his Y-fronts, so he was already
sopping wet and the bloody wind was blowing in his face too.
The simple relief of emptying his bladder was momentarily
worth it though, as the padding in the scrub beside the road
had stopped...
Jesus! Thank you for that!*

*Carl was about to stop and turn around when he heard the
soft athletic thud of two sets of feline paws on the sandy road.
The bloody animals were having a good sniff of his urine!
Miserably, cooling clammy shorts clinging unpleasantly to
his groin and thighs and tickling drips down his bare legs into
his boots, he trudged on, hoping they'd not like his scent and
give it up but, knowing his luck, he was completely buggered.
Sure enough, pad, pad, pad behind him again and he thought
they were gaining on him. Stay calm. Keep going. He was
really starting to sweat now but he knew he had to be within
a half mile from the big meshed gates onto the farm and there
was anyway no choice but to keep going now.*

*At first he thought he was hallucinating when he saw a flash
of light ahead, but about a half minute later he heard the
sound of a motor and got another glimpse of the spotlight
mounted on the Land Cruiser, that promptly disappeared as
the vehicle turned into a kink in the road which meant that
he was nearly at the gates! Thank God for Aunt Helena! She
must have realised he was overdue and come out to look
for him. The road curved around too so he didn't see the
spotlight, but he could hear the engine still and it was getting
louder. A low growl from behind almost had him pissing*

121

his pants again, and suddenly his timely rescue seemed to disappear like morning mist as the gates came into view and the spotlight flooded the road, then doused altogether. The headlights went out too. Carl didn't know whether to laugh or cry now but wisely remained silent and carried on walking. Helena's bushcraft was second to none and he sent up another heartfelt prayer. Please God let her have seen them. Please God let her have seen me!

He kept walking. The vehicle was bathed in moonlight and he saw the driver get out. Oh, you beauty! She had a rifle with her. But why was she waiting? His answer came soon enough as he saw her raise the gun holding it up at an angle, but still she did nothing. Carl's nerves were completely shot now and he was about to scream at her to fire when she spoke to him in a conversational tone as though she was asking whether he wanted a biscuit with his tea.

'Keep walking, Carl. I'll fire overhead but you'd better get to the side quickly if they stick around. Nod if you heard, lad.' He moved his head frantically and another, louder growl came from behind him.

Time slowed. He saw her aim high, the stock almost touching her chin and then smoke. He squeezed his eyes shut. Then there was the crack of the shot passing harmlessly high over his head. A half second of silence, then an echoing snarl as he veered to the right, finally looking back at his tormentors. Both of them were turning on themselves, deceptively soft, tawny muscles bunching with the power of adrenalin and panic. Then his own instincts kicked in as he began to run as fast as they were but in the opposite direction towards Helena and the Land Cruiser.

'Get off me - you stink to high heaven Carl!' He hugged his Aunt again anyway, but then pulled away and hung his

head in shame.

'I'm sorry Helena. Thank you so much for coming out - I was terrified!' She was laughing softly now and he joined her guiltily, feeling like an idiot.

'I gathered that. Silly boy *- why the hell didn't you stay with the vehicle? I got the shock of my life seeing you in the road like that!'*

'Of course Cousin Carl ought to have stayed with the truck, but he wasn't too smart when he was sober, let alone when he was three sheets to the wind!' He laughed at the memory of Carl's ashen face when his father had got in the next morning after spending an anxious night watching over the cattle in the lower meadows close to the lake. 'He got the bollocking of his life when Pa came back and he had his pay docked for the petrol in the end and two replacement tyres too, as Ma had to take the Cruiser back into Kariba Town the next morning. But I came out of it OK as I got to go in with her and then I was allowed to drive the Land Cruiser back when we'd fixed the truck. I was twelve and it was the first time I'd ever driven on my own. I fell in love with Cruisers that day and that's part of the reason why I wanted to be a Park Ranger, and then a Guide, because they're such a pleasure to drive, even though they're tougher than hell - and, for a 4 by 4, they're comfortable inside too.'

He grinned at the others and started to fill his pipe again. 'Talking of good drives are you all set for an early breakfast tomorrow? There's rhino and elephant over on the west shore from Spurwing Island so we can take the boat over. I have a vehicle there we can take out and have a safari drive along the foreshore for the rest of the morning. Then back in the boat to have a late lunch or afternoon tea over at Spurwing camp. We can come back to Sanyati for a mini cruise and have our sundowners, then home in time for a shower before dinner? You're frowning at me again, Jim - you don't think that's a good idea?'

Jim looked over at Eva a moment, then smiled slightly, 'Sounds marvellous Harry, but I don't know about being out on the trail in the midday sun. Won't it get a bit too hot?'

'Mad dogs and Englishmen, not to mention fair skins, huh?' Harry laughed. 'It'll be OK, I promise. We'll have some cool winds tomorrow off the lake and my vehicle has a canopy so you'll have enough shade. The boat's loaded up with lots of drinking water so we'll be alright and the game viewing will be well worth a little sweat, if the wind does drop. Just make sure you get your camera equipment charged to the hilt tonight though, Keith!' Harry turned to look across the fire at Sophie. 'And how about you young lady? I can find us some of your wee little malachite kingfishers on the way back but there's all different sorts of birds over on Spurwing - Goliath heron and Egyptian geese, pied kingfishers and I know you said you love the ellies...?'

'Oh, go on then Harry - you've twisted my arm... I want my malachites though!'

Harry laughed and stood up. 'I am a man of my word, Doctor! I'll see to it you'll get in close for some good photos as well - but only on condition that you lot are very quiet.'

'Better do that before the sundowners then!' Jim was laughing along with them as he and Eva stood as well 'Well we're off now in that case - take it we'll get a knock a bit before breakfast Harry?'

'About half five, yes. I'm ready for bed too so I'll walk you both back up to the rondavels. Sleep well, everyone!' Sophie's voice drifted over to them again as they began to walk up the steps 'Don't forget to bring some sunscreen with you Eva! And the repellent and anti-histamine Jim!'

* * *

The rasping scream echoed all around the camp.

'Jim! Don't touch it! *HELP!!*'

This at least meant most people weren't getting out of their beds as they knew Sophie and Harry were immediate neighbours to the movie star and her agent husband. Harry got there first as he was already dressed (or rather he hadn't undressed), and his arrival caused more havoc as Eva was in her undergarments, huddled in a quivering foetal position on the bed. Jim was on the floor, completely nude, flicking his belt at something under the bed.

At the sight of Harry, Eva screamed again and flipped the sheet over herself then started sobbing.

'Oh, friggin' hell woman! Stop bloody stressing and keep still...'

'Morning, Jim. What've you got there?'

Sophie arrived in her dressing gown and flip flops in time to hear a soft thud as Jim's head connected with the bed-frame. Harry started laughing. More expletives issued from the floor as Jim's arm flicked his belt again and something small and black shot across the stone tiles into the bathroom.

'Fuck!' This curse came very faintly from Harry.

'Bugger!' Jim recoiled and leapt to his feet. 'Where'd it go?'

Sophie just managed to avoid Harry stepping on her flip-flopped feet as he backed out of the doorway, his face white as a sheet. 'What is it, Harry?'

'Scorpion! Can't stand 'em!'

'Oh dear!'

She turned and screamed at Jim. 'Stay put - it's a scorpion!'

125

'I know that! Where'd the little bastard go?'

'I'll tell you, but not until you put something on your feet. It could be poisonous!' Jim turned to face her, his jaw dropping.

'Better yet, put some pants on - and do it carefully in case it had a friend...'

... She found Harry stripped to the waist and finishing his shave.

'Coast's clear now Harry. It wasn't a big one... I never had you down as an arachnophobe...' She tried hard not to chuckle. She failed, but only because Harry looked so relieved as he put his razor down.

'You're sure? 'Cos they're tricky little buggers and it could have hidden anywhere in that bathroom.' He blushed brightly but met her eyes and tried to smile at her.

'I chucked it out of the bathroom window myself.'

'Sorry. It hadn't stung Jim or Eva had it?'

'Nope! It was a thin-tailed one[13] anyway so it wouldn't have caused too much damage if it had. But maybe I'd better do the 'shake out your clothes and boots before you put 'em on' lecture again at breakfast? Or do you want to do it?' She began to giggle.

'Ha ha - very funny.' He was laughing anyway now, and wiped away the last of the shaving soap. 'I've lost credibility there somewhat so you can take the honours my dear Doctor. Anyway - I thought arachnophobia was fear of spiders? They don't bother me at all by the way.'

---

[13] Thin tailed scorpions in Southern Africa are non-venomous to humans, though the sting is still painful. Their pincers are generally more impressive than their tail stingers and venom sacs. In the thick tailed scorpions, the sting is toxic and in one variety found in Zimbabwe, the *Parabuthus transvaalicus,* can be fatal if not treated swiftly.

'Just as well - far more of them around and I'm not getting into an open top vehicle with you if you're phobic with them as well. All that tall brush and gossamer across the road... OK - I'll give them a rocket. As for arachnophobia - scorpions are arachnids too - eight legs, see.'

'I wouldn't know - I've never kept my eyes open long enough to count the legs...'

* * *

Eva and Jim arrived for breakfast in time to miss Sophie's rather more strident admonitions on the advisability of checking shoes and boots and shaking out clothes before putting them on, especially if you'd already been wearing them the day before...

Keith was saying that he wasn't bothered about snakes, scorpions or assorted creepy crawlies so long as he didn't have to be around Jack the morning after a real bender. Sophie laughed along with the others, except for Harry, who was drinking his coffee over by the fire and looked over at them irritably. 'It doesn't matter if you're not scared of the little buggers - they bite you and you're just as poisoned or even dead.'

'Listen to Harry guys - he's had second hand experience of a bad scorpion bite and it's not at all funny.' Sophie looked over at the guide sympathetically. 'For a start spider bites and scorpion stings really hurt, even if they're not venomous. So be sensible and try to remember to keep your used clothing off the floor - boots too if possible so they're not so attractive to scorpions or snakes. One thing I do religiously with my boots is to stuff my dirty rolled up socks into them - I'm not going to wear them again and they bung up the way into your lovely warm and fragrant desert boots...'

Harry went over to Jim and Eva as they sat down to eat their fruit and yogurt. As usual, despite looking subdued and pale still, he came straight to the point. 'Just here to apologise folks. Sorry I wasn't much help, but at least Sophie was about to sort you out properly.'

'It's OK, Harry.' Eva was also still very shaken and feeling empathetic, 'I was really stupefied with fear when the little varmint dropped out of my pants. Won't you join us for a few minutes if you don't have to get the boat ready just yet?' Jim was chuckling, but he also nodded his own invitation and smiled warmly as Harry pulled a chair out.

'We were wondering whether it was the sight of us both naked and screaming our heads off or the scorpion that gave you the willies, Harry.'

'Definitely the scorpion, Jim - I was enjoying the view until it decamped into the bathroom.'

'Just as well you weren't there first off when the bloody thing scuttered out of Eva's trousers - I think I've got a couple of perforated eardrums from the screaming. Not that Sophie's being too kind about that of course.'

'I'm sorry honey - but I was petrified.'

'Pity your vocal chords weren't!' Jim gave her a comforting squeeze on the hand anyway, 'But what's this about you having a too close encounter with one Harry?'

The guide made a face. 'Long, long time ago. I was fourteen...'

Shit! Shit! Shit! Helena examined her hand minutely, although there was no difficulty in locating the puncture wound as her skin looked red and angry already. Bloody sod's law that this would happen today with Wayne's mother flying in this afternoon. She'd already killed the scorpion that had leapt on her from underneath the bed in the spare room as she was trying to sweep the dirt into the dustpan. She brushed the nasty specimen into the dustpan and stood up.

'Harry! Come here a minute.'

'What is it? I'll miss the school bus, Ma!'

'This is more important...' She walked out into the hall as Harry came out of his bedroom doing up his shirt. '... I've been stung - can you look this thing up in your spotters book for me?'

Harry's eyes grew wide as he took in the dark mangled head and torso with the unimpressive pincers and the relatively undamaged, wide, shiny tail carapace 'Christ, Ma - I think that's a poisonous one!'

'She nearly died, despite doing all the right things. My Ma was a really tough lady and bush savvy so she stayed very calm - but she had an allergic reaction. By the time I'd ID-ed the animal - it was a black thick-tailed scorpion, she'd had a bath and called for me to come with her to the hospital. Her right arm had gone numb and she couldn't grip with her hand, so I had to drive her and she started having convulsions on the way. I was so scared I can't tell you...'

Jim was also looking pale now as it dawned on him what a vulnerable position he'd been in. 'Bloody hell, Harry! No need to apologise, man. I'd have buggered off with you if I'd known!'

'You were so brave, honey. You're my hero!' Eva kissed him on the cheek, then stood up. 'I need more coffee - can I freshen yours for you, Harry?'

The guide handed her his mug, looking a little bemused since she normally had Jim running around after her for such menial tasks. As she made her way over to the groaning breakfast buffet, Jim smiled. 'She's not that spoiled really -

her parents ran a diner in Sacramento and she used to wait tables evenings and weekends.'

'And here was I thinking she's got you well and truly hen-pecked.'

'That's tinsel town for you - all show and posing outside! She's a sweetie really. You should see some of my other clients - the rock stars are hell on wheels compared to Eva. And I guess she loves me!' Jim tried not to look too self-conscious.

'Well, you'll be able keep cashing in on this for a good while I'd say. Ignorance is bliss, especially when you're facing a potentially deadly creepy buck naked!'

'Shush!' Jim started to laugh 'I nearly fainted when Sophie told me it could be venomous and then asked if it had bitten Eva!'

'Heroism's overrated my friend - ignorance and adrenalin are far better allies when you're in that kind of situation!'

* * *

Harry clapped his hands to get everyone's attention. 'C'mon folks - the sun's up and we need to get off now. You all got your sunscreen, insect repellents and bite creams, because this is your last chance to go get them until this evening...'

'Oops!' Jim turned and ran back up to the rondavel to fetch the day bag they'd left behind. The others had started to go down the pier when he came back at a trot but Sophie was waiting for him.

'Sorry to keep you!'

'No problem, Jim' Sophie winked and patted him companionably on the shoulder. 'Nothing like getting back to normal to get over a shock so early in the day. Try not to frighten the living daylights out of Harry or I for the rest of it though...'

'So long as Harry concentrates on vertebrates, preferably mammals today, I'll be good. I promise, Doctor Taylor!'

Perfect Day

What a day! It started badly when our wake-up call really was a bona fide alarm, with Eva screaming the camp down after a scorpion dropped rather grumpily out of her trousers where it had been having a nice cosy snooze! So my day began with rather too much flesh on display (Jim's) and poor Harry unexpectedly wimping out on me because he's phobic about scorpions of all things! Anyway, I cornered the wretched arachnid (not poisonous thank goodness) when it fell into the sunken shower tray - luckily they have nice deep slippery ones here and I managed to grab the little brute by the tail from behind, then threw it out of the bathroom window. So glad they put the generator on here for early calls - I don't think I could have faced doing all that in the semi-darkness!

The rest of the day, which I had been dreading as always, was simply wonderful! Harry thoroughly redeemed himself and I don't think I've ever been out on a better safari drive. His pleasure in all the animals is so obvious - even Phil began to enjoy himself instead of fussing about Eva's hair the whole time. Kariba is just - words fail me actually. It's not dramatic like at Vic Falls, but it's just so beautiful - the colours of the water and the earth and vegetation with the red ochre Matusadona hills as a backdrop. Simply stunning. And we saw ellies swimming too! Whatever happens now on this trip and afterwards, I'm so glad I came out here. That'll please Claire and Youssef - the 'I told you so's' will be endless, but that doesn't matter anymore. I can't wait to get the photos downloaded - Keith did us a playback of his footage today before dinner and it's marvellous. So many smiles!

Harry laughed warmly as he turned the boat out of the gorge and into the pale pure sunrise, slipping effortlessly through the drowned, petrified skeletons of the leadwood trees.

'Welcome to my world, folks!'

The sun, blushing through the clouds like a showy tea rose, was just pulling clear of the hills with Spurwing Island looming towards them and he smiled gently back at Sophie as she turned slowly to him, her eyes shining with wonder at the dawn in her face.

'It's magic time! Thank you Harry.'

Her voice was husky, barely audible above the motor and his heart went out to the doctor as her head went down for moment and a hand dashed away tears. He wanted to say something but hesitated, knowing something of her story from her sister, and wondered what she was remembering, poor kid.

The moment passed as Jim turned and grinned at them 'Looks like another great day in paradise!'

'It's so beautiful...' Phil's prissy LA drawl was softened in genuine amazement for a fleeting moment. '... such glorious colours - pink and aquamarine on the waters and in the heavens. It's biblical almost!'

'Finally, he sees it!' Eva laughed teasingly at her stylist, delighted that something had impressed him at last.

'Yeah, yeah - don't get used to it honey. I'll find something new to bitch about soon enough, don't you fret!'

'I got y'down on disk, Phil - what's it worth not to show you enjoying yourself to the 'girls' when we get back?' Gareth, cackling away at Keith's dry comment, drew a snort of contempt from Phil. They were all used to the back and forth between him and the two cameramen by now and far more interested in where they were headed as Harry steered them smoothly through the dead tree sentinels, then out into deeper water heading for Spurwing Island, shining in the soft dawn.

As they drew alongside the jetty, a couple of Shona lads

appeared out of nowhere and lots of smiling and nodding went on as Harry launched into a rapid Q and A in the local dialect. The consultation was brief and ended in laughter and friendly waving as Harry retrieved the painter and backed out, taking the boat into the western channel and they were on their way again. 'Well, we're all set up for a late lunch on Spurwing. They do some fantastic fish dishes, and I've got some snacks and cola in the coolbox for elevenses, so that should keep us going on a good hard game drive, guys.'

'In this humidity I'm surprised at anything staying hard!' Phil's muttered comment got a laugh from Jim and he hugged Eva in the breeze as they picked up speed.

'Harry's promised us cool winds today Philip - keep your pecker up!'

'Hah!'

* * *

'Do you see the ellies, Sophie?' Harry nodded towards the shore and handed the bins over to her.

She could see them bare-eyed, dark against the red earth as they made their way down to the water, but put the binoculars up to her eyes and smiled 'They have babies!'

'Well that's a great start for us then! Should be several calves with this group I think - some of those old girls are highly sought after!'

'Top elephant totty?' Sophie giggled and looked back at him.

He grinned at her 'Did you get a load of the ivory? Some of those cows are the daughters and grand-daughters of the Chura Bull.'

Sophie smiled 'A famous stud was he?'

'I'll say! He's dead now but he was a big boy all over. Massive tusks - getting on for 11 feet long. Even starred in a movie with Clint Eastwood when he came out here on location in the late eighties - doing a movie about the filming of *The African Queen* and John Huston.'

Eva and Co all turned round at this remark, eyes wide with interest and the next several minutes were filled with questions, which Harry answered cheerfully until they were getting close into the shoreline.

'OK guys, let's turn the volume down a bit and get a load of this herd - I think they're going to have a little water fun so we'll stay out here in case any of them decide to swim...'

The chattering died away as they all focussed on the group of females and calves or, in Phil's case, on the water patterns and the reed beds as he made swift sketches and notes on the subtle colours and shadows in the little notebook he always had on him. Sophie was glued to Harry's binoculars for a while as the boat idled slowly towards the huge, yet strangely vulnerable and gentle creatures. Finally the bins were lowered as one of the cows with a very young calf softly caressed her baby's ears and shoulders with her trunk and then nudged him on the rump slightly with a front knee, trying to encourage him down one of the shallower banks into the sparkling water. Again Harry happened to glance at the doctor and caught more tears before she put her sunglasses back on. She was evidently taking pleasure in the scene so, once again he said nothing...

'Try to get back to sleep for a while, babe...' Tom kissed her hot cheek sweetly. His warm brown eyes looked at her with concern as she tottered back from the bathroom with a bottle of water. He sat down beside her on the bed and stroked her sweaty fair hair away from her face, tucking the strands behind her ears, then put his arm around her thin shoulders.

'We're not going until after breakfast and I'm only doing the engine checks and filling up. I'm worried about you, Soph...'

'I'm fine - really!' she made herself smile at him, then took a quick swig of the water so he wouldn't catch the scent of spew. 'Honestly - Terry said yesterday it's probably just another dose of the trots.'

'I heard you throwing up, Soph.' Tom's chiding was gentle and he pulled her closer, stroking her cheek and laying his head on hers. 'And Terry's worried too. She's told Alma to give you a good check-up today, OK? You've not been right for weeks now - ever since we came back from Vic Falls.'

Damn! Bloody St. Terry, the interfering cow... 'I'm keeping the sodding fluids up! It's not as though I haven't had a dose of this before...' she trailed off, biting her bottom lip, afraid she would lose it and start crying.

'Not with being sick all the time as well, you haven't! Oh, Soph... Look, I know you want to come with us but we'll be doing some hard driving and you're just not up to it, babe. I'll be back before the end of the month, so you rest up and get yourself well. Mwanza's got some great shops, so I'll get you a really lovely ring and we can start making plans for going back home when I get back, yeah?'

He got up and leant down looking into her tired eyes. 'If you promise to go back to bed after we're off, then I won't stop you coming with me for the checks, OK? Make a change for us to see the sun come up together, anyway!'

She got up as well and hugged him tight 'I promise! Won't be a jiff!'

Tom smiled happily as she got into her shorts and a fresh Tee shirt at lightning speed. He reached out for her hand as they made their way outside...

This day. That last day together, all those years ago and the sunrise had been as pure and golden as this... Sophie came reluctantly out of the memory, smiled and turned to hand the bins back to Harry. 'Thank you!'

'Keep them a while - some of them are almost certainly going in to swim.' Harry grinned at her but spoke in a near whisper. 'I'll have to manoeuvre a bit so we're downwind and not too close to them - keep an eye on that big cow with the out-turned tusk, looking right at us now. She's the boss, so I'm going to back off a little more behind these leadwoods, so she doesn't get too concerned about us. Pass the word down to the others - we all need to keep very quiet for a bit.'

The garage canopies and fuel stores were down by the river under the fever trees. The river ran quite wide here past the township, but on the eastern shore it was still undisturbed and wild and there were several converging game trails that came right down to the waterside. It was Tom's favourite place in Vutare and, even when he wasn't working, he was often down there fishing with the Zambian men and their children, or on his own, bird-spotting, before she met him. She was into birds as well and so one day, not long after she'd joined the teaching support team, she had asked to join him and that was how they had fallen in love, so naturally and quickly.

That morning, in the half-light, before the sun had fully risen, a dozen or so elephants, cows and calves like these, were just coming down to drink. Tom watched them with her for a few minutes and then sighed and lifted her up onto the back of the truck. 'Work time! Stay here and watch them some more love - I won't be long!'

What he meant was that he was doing an engine check to
make sure there were no snakes or other small animals
who'd decided to curl up under the bonnet or wheel arches
overnight. She was terrified of snakes so she made no protest
and was content to keep watching the family ablutions across
the water, as the sky gradually lightened and the clouds
became edged with jewelled shades of peach and gold, above
the eerie misting over the canopy of dark trees...

* * *

'Oh! How wonderful.' Eva's voice was so breathless with
excitement it was barely a murmur.

'It certainly is - be as quiet as you can still, people. The
wind's shifting and we may have to back off soon.'

Harry's hushed warning was as light as the breeze and almost
unnecessary, for they were all spellbound as the matriarch
strode past the other cows and their young into the deep
channel and disappeared altogether for a few moments, save
for the tip of her trunk peeking out of the water. She was only
about ten meters away and they could easily see her as she
emerged, side on to them, water streaming away from her
head and ears down her crinkly hide. Truly swimming now,
for her shoulders and then her ridged back undulated across
and just below the surface, almost like a gigantic dolphin,
then again dipped out of sight altogether momentarily.
Keeping the end of her trunk, snorkel-like, still visible out of
the lake, she did this five or six times in succession before her
feet evidently found firm ground and she rose, puffing water
out of her trunk and mouth like a hissing kettle until she was
standing steady again, with the water lapping almost up to
her shoulders and mouth and shook herself enthusiastically,
ears flapping wildly, diamond droplets spraying out in all

directions. She had turned back towards her sisters and children and gave a massive gurgling snort, then slammed her trunk into the water again, making a huge splash as it dipped down and another, curling back in again towards her body as she scooped water onto her ears and short neck.

Time seemed to freeze as Harry held the boat motionless, making minute adjustments on the rudder so they didn't make too much noisy impact on the leadwood trunks, as the others drank in the sight of the huge cow having an obviously enjoyable bath. Another female, then two more, and finally one of the adolescent males, all followed her across the deep water onto the former hillock that now formed the lake bed, and the serious bathing gradually gave way to playtime as they all splashed around each other. At last the spell was gently broken as the original cow swam back to the bank, then turned and looked over very pointedly at the boat, her trunk held high and swaying slightly, trying to fix the unnatural scents of the engine and the creatures floating too close now.

'Time to go folks - she doesn't like our scent and they won't hang around too much longer.'

Harry opened up the throttle gently and reversed regally around a tree trunk then headed back into the channel, slowly increasing their speed as Sophie and the others still looked back for some final glimpses and last photo opportunities.

'Good?'

'Bloody marvellous, Harry!' Sophie had turned right around to face him, her face split with a huge grin as she finally gave him back his bins. He smiled back, his eyes holding hers in concentration.

'You OK today, sweetheart? You were looking a little sad earlier.'

'I'm alright - just memories. Happy ones.' A little embarrassed, she looked past him for a few moments. 'They're all out of the water now.'

'Yep - the wind changed and they don't much like people about. I keep forgetting that this isn't your first time on safari, but that's a rare sight even here - elephants swimming.'

'I love them - always have. I'm glad we saw them!'

She was looking at him nervously now so Harry took a deep breath and decided to come clean with her.

'You know what an old gossip I am - Claire told me that you might not be on top form whilst you were with me, so I got nosey as to why. She said that your fiancé died in May, several years back - out in Zyanda?' He stopped abruptly as the doctor squirmed uncomfortably in her seat, though she did not turn away from him. Just as he was about to apologise for bringing it up she replied, her voice quiet and composed.

'It was on the Tanzanian border with Zyanda. The second of May... that was the last day we were together. He was killed up there on the fifteenth.'

The connection was a little crackly, but they could hear each other well enough.

'Nothing much to report on the journey really - we only lost one tyre and made good time once we crossed into Tanzania... Anyway - are you feeling any better, Soph? Over.'

This was so frustrating because she was longing to see his face but she just had to tell him. 'Not exactly better, but I'm feeling really happy. Tom... we're having a baby! Over.'

There was a crackle over the last bit and he frowned.

'Say again, Soph? Over.' He could hear her laughing like a loon and shook his head at Terry who was sitting opposite him, waiting to talk to Alma.

'I'm PREGNANT! Oh Tom - I'm so happy!' She chuckled as she heard him whooping at the other end... 'Over... Oh no! Wait a minute. Alma thinks I'm nearly two months gone! Hahaha! Over now!'

'Soph! That's fantastic! Hang on a moment... Just telling Terry - she says congratulations and that she's very relieved!'

There was another loud crackle and Sophie broke through again. 'What was that? Never mind - we got pregnant at Vic Falls, I think!!! Over.'

He laughed like a drain. 'Well that'll make a good story for wetting his or her head - or the wedding! Which do you want first? Haha! I wish I could hug you. I love you so much, babe! Listen though. Terry thought you were showing signs of malaria - she's delighted for us, but says Alma should do some more blood tests, just in case, OK? Over.'

Sophie rolled her eyes in annoyance. Alma tutted at her.

'OK - yes. We'll check it out before you get back. Over.'

'Erm - yeah you will. Look, I'm sorry, but I'll not be coming straight back to Vutare. The driver who was supposed to be taking Terry to Umbeke with the med supplies has come down with a whopping fever, so I'm taking her instead. Over.'

'What?!! What did you say?! Over.'

'I have to take Terry to Umbeke - the only other driver's got a fever. It's only two or three days out of my way really, so I won't be that delayed. Over.'

'Awww!' Sophie's eyes crossed and she poked her tongue out, resulting in more glares from Alma.' Well I suppose it can't be helped. Alma needs to get on to talk to Terry, so I'd better go. Come back soon, you hear! I love you! Over.'

'Ditto! I'm going into Mwanza later for that beautiful little ring! Can't wait for you to see it! Love you, babe - look after that little bairn! My bairn! Haha!'

Another crackle at the other end.
'Here's Terry now, Alma. 'Bye Soph! Over...'

* * *

'It was a long time ago now.' She shook her head and smiled a little. 'But I still miss him.'

Harry nodded at her. 'That was an awful time they had over there, though. It took a lot of getting over, I expect?'

'I'll never get over it - not really.'

'Hell! I'm so sorry, sweetheart - that was a fatuous thing to say.' Bloody idiot! he screamed inwardly at himself, his face flushing furiously. Sophie shoulders were shaking, but then she laughed out loud and shook her head at him.

'No, really - it's alright, Harry. How would you have known - it's hardly that common though is it? Even for Africa.' A white dragoman driver getting killed during a tribal genocide atrocity in a border refugee camp. Not common, just bloody terrible. 'I wasn't there, but... it destroyed me. I was a mess for years afterwards.'

He nodded, still angry at his stupid gaffe, but he'd seen times almost as bad during Zim's civil war and, as she seemed to not mind talking now, he motioned for her to come and sit next to him. The throttle was wide open now and he had no intention of continuing this conversation over the engine noise. The others were all nattering, or checking out the foreshore on the mainland so they had some privacy for as long as she wanted to off-load. He could at least listen respectfully.

'I lost someone - very dear to me, during the war here. I was in the police force then. There was a mine... But that Zyandan thing. Utter madness!'

'Good things came out of it. In a way. And I survived. Done things I wouldn't have if it hadn't happened. But I lost so much.'

'Talking helps a bit I suppose. But it doesn't bring them back.'

She nodded, twiddling with her hair. 'Did Claire tell you I'm going there to work - when this safari's over?'

'No...? To Zyanda?!' He was genuinely shocked.

Sophie laughed again. 'Yeah - I'm nuts! Officially!'

'That's a hell of a thing, Sophie! Whatever made you decide to do that?'

'I was nagged into it mainly. By a very old and good friend. And other kind friends who forced me to see that my life wasn't over. That I could really make a difference for other people who were still suffering and in true need...'

'Oh, thank god!' Claire's words came out in a sob that rang through her skull. 'Sophie - I was so scared!'

Her vision was blurry and when she tried to speak it came out as a garbled moaning. A coolness ran across her forehead and liquid trickled into her right eye, then down the side of her nose like icy tears. She squeezed her eyes tight shut and moved her hands floppily. When her eyes fluttered open again, Claire was leaning over her and arms were snaking under her shoulders and armpits from both sides of the bed. They moved her into a more upright position and Claire gently put a cup of water into her hand and helped her bring it up to her mouth.

'Take it slowly, darling.' Claire's voice had firmed into nursing tones as she steadied Sophie's hands. She smiled benignly at her younger sister as a tiny tentative sip was taken and swallowed. 'You've given us a real fright the last couple of days.'

'My head hurts...' her voice was raspy. Claire took the cup from her and looked past her at someone on the other side

of the bed.

'You went into a coma, Sophie dear. It was the malaria - and the shock too.' Alma's soft Irish drawl floated in and Sophie slowly moved her aching head towards her boss and friend.

One bleary look at Alma's strained, exhausted face and it all crashed in on her again. Someone was screaming. Hoarse and raw with grief and pain. Calling for someone who could not answer. Would never answer...

... 'Alma had to give you a sedative, Sophie. Please don't try to talk yet. It's important you stay calm else you could slip back into the coma again.' Claire's voice was muffled but she could feel her soft fingers stroking the back of her hand. Her hand hurt though and she must have winced.

'You're on a drip, darling. We just want you to be comfortable and quiet until you're a little stronger. You're going home, Soph. Back to Guildford - Mum and Dad are going to look after you, as soon as we know you're up to flying back.'

'Do they know...'

'Hush, darling. Rest. Don't upset yourself.'

''M'OK. Just tired.' She saw Claire open her mouth to protest again and flapped her hand dismissively and pressed on. 'Do they know about the baby?'

'Yes.' Somehow Claire stopped herself from crying because, whilst her answer was true, Sophie still did not know why. She forced a smile onto her face and squeezed Sophie's other hand. 'They can't wait to see you. They would have come out but Alma's been wonderful and got me here so they don't have to travel at all.'

'But my contract's not finished yet...'

144

'You've been really ill, Sophie. You won't be well enough to work for a long time.' Oh hell, hell, hell! This was unbearable and she didn't even know she'd lost the baby yet... Claire's hand came up and caressed her sister's sunken, burning cheek. 'Try to rest as much as you can. If I'm not here, Alma will be. OK?'

'Am I dying?' Her lovely blue eyes were anguished with fever and fear.

''Course not!' Claire's voice caught, but she pulled herself back and bashed on. 'You're going home, Sophie. You're going to get well again.'

'For our baby. Yes!'

Her lids came down and her breathing softened as she sank back into true sleep again. Claire waited until she was sure Sophie was asleep and then walked over to Alma's office in despair.

Alma was on the phone and motioned for Claire to take a seat while she finished. 'Thanks, Stefan. Sophie's sister's been frantic here because her husband's going to be in America for another fortnight or more, so she has to get back to Harare for the kids...'

Claire burst into tears at that point and Alma rose hurriedly and, still holding the phone to her ear and knocking some files off her desk in the process, came around to hug her tight as she finished the call. 'What's the doctor's name again? Youssef...? OK... Yeah, I've never met him, but I know of him. That's perfect almost. Thanks so much for setting that up. 'Bye now!'

She hugged Claire with both arms and smiled broadly. 'Don't worry anymore - Stefan's sorted it. One of our doctors was going back to London the day after it happened but he postponed because he's a close friend of the Zimmermans.'

Claire looked at her blankly. 'The couple who tried to help Teresa and Tom at the camp. He's been up to Tanzania to help them and the refugees, but he's flying back to Lusaka tomorrow and says he'll escort Sophie back to Heathrow himself when she's able to travel. He's called Youssef Jettou - he used to be a field surgeon but these days he heading up our Staff Welfare and Medical Assessment group. I don't know him personally but he's got a terrific reputation and I'm sure he'll look after Sophie like she's his own daughter.'

Claire nodded numbly and wiped the tears away. 'She was asking about the baby, Alma... I couldn't tell her.'

'That's OK. It's alright, Claire. That can wait until we've got her properly stabilised. She has enough to take on board for now. I can tell her if it's too hard...'

'No... No. It's alright Alma. I'll do it later on, when she's stronger.'

* * *

He was lost for words now. She wasn't crying but the silence was tense. Finally he had to break it. They were getting close to the southern shore of the lake. 'Nearly there. We may have to pass on the rhino, but the guys said there's a good-sized herd of buff not far from where the Land Cruiser is.'

'Your favourite!' She laughed, remembering his story about the trophy bull.

He chuckled with her. 'They are really - when I can keep my distance and don't have a git client to look after. For grazers they're bloody smart and mean as hell with it - just as well they aren't carnivores, else we'd be in real trouble!'

'Them and the elephants!'

'Doesn't bear thinking about, does it? A predator with more than half a brain! I'm happier facing down a lion, or hyenas, that's for sure!'

146

'Leopards too!'

'No...' He smiled wryly. 'Leopards are solitary hunters and strong as a hyped up heavyweight boxer. They're bloody ruthless and if they're coming at me ever, then I shoot to kill. Never take chances with buffs, ellies or leopards.' He was chuckling, but Sophie knew he meant it.

As they were chatting they'd again been slipping past the ubiquitous skeleton trees and the others were beginning to get their things together as Harry slowed the boat and neatly curled the painter around a mooring post on the narrow little jetty that poked out into the lake. The foreshore looked to be deserted aside from birdlife and Harry's open-top land cruiser parked about fifteen metres away from the jetty. They could hear the cape doves monotonous cooing in the rising heat as Harry secured their mooring and reached for his rifle.

'Wait!' The guide called out softly to Gareth who had stood up, hefting the bigger of the cameras over his shoulder, ready to get off. 'Me first, guys - you can't see everything from water level and this isn't a busy camp mooring, so the animals are more relaxed here and we could spook 'em.'

He put his hat on, pulling the strap toggle tight and stepped onto the jetty, scanning the bank and foreshore ahead to both sides and then to the borders of the brush and mopane trees. He looked back at his charges and gestured for them to disembark, but frowned at Phil. 'Lose the cap, Phil - I've got a spare khaki hat if you haven't got one.'

The stylist's head was aglow in bright cerise and he pouted mightily.

'Alright, already! For fuck's sake - that gorilla's got no style at all!' He muttered crossly to himself as he burrowed into his silver and black backpack. 'This do you, Tarzan?' he asked tying a camouflage patterned scarf around his shaven head.

'You look adorable, Jane - and gorillas hate pink that much they'd pull your head off!'

Sophie winked at him as Phil put his hand out to help her onto the jetty, 'It's alright - no gorillas in Zim, Phil... There's buffalo around apparently though - they don't like pink either!'

'*Why* is this friggin' place so butch!' Phil moaned theatrically, then winked back at her and sashayed off the jetty behind the rest of them.

They all piled onto the Land Cruiser willy-nilly as every seat had an excellent view, being tiered so the back row was tallest and the front the lowest. Harry started laughing as Phil chose to go on the back with Gareth and Keith, despite the amount of equipment they had. 'Hey, Jane! How are you with cobwebs? You're likely going to get a mouthful of them up there - I'll be the first vehicle through the brush this week, so the wigglies will still be floating across the mopane...' Harry broke off, unable to hold back on laughing at Phil's horrified face.

'Is Tarzan making sport, Doc?' Phil rolled his eyes like a pro. He might love his creature comforts but he wasn't particularly faint hearted except for dramatic effect.

Sophie chuckled. 'Don't think so, Phil. Here - we can make room for you in the middle anyway.'

'Little one coming through!' Phil trilled happily as he stepped over the seat back after Gareth kindly unhooked his foot from a holdall handle.

'Sophie - you come and sit up front with me if you want. Little Jane's been overdoing the eggs benedict this morning!' Harry winked as she climbed onto the front passenger bench while Phil squealed and tutted at the vicious, but justified slur, then turned back to hiss at Gareth.

'What the hell have you got in that bag anyway?! It's like a friggin' ball and chain!'

'Never you mind, boyo. You'll find out later on!'

Harry drove off slowly into the brush and onto a sandy well-worn trail that hugged the foreshore for a little before dividing north-west and east. He took the east fork still within sight of the lake occasionally and also heading back to the Sanyati river.

'Looks like the luck's in - been more ellies along here recently so not too much gossamer across the track!' Harry shouted back to Keith and Gareth. 'I'll give you a yell if it looks like you'll get a face full of spider, OK?'

'Ta, Harry!'

He grinned over at Sophie, who was leaning back in her seat looking relaxed and happy. Strands of her fair hair were escaping from under her battered straw pith helmet, which was held on with two grubby string ties and her collarless green khaki shirt was billowing in the cool breeze of their passage. 'I'm enjoying their company very much! Keith was using one of their mic' poles yesterday on the water to shift a monitor lizard! Never thought movieland bods were so inventive.'

'I think they go into all kinds of rough territory for Jack - Keith's probably seen worse wildlife back in Moss Side, mind you!' Jim chipped in as he leaned forward for something in his camera bag and grinned at Sophie briefly.

Harry lifted his eyebrow ironically. 'Moss Side?'

Sophie laughed. 'Deepest, darkest Manchester. Drug barons, that kind of thing.'

'Ah, right - I knew there was some reason why I prefer the bush... Your side, Keith!' Harry steered off to the side slightly so the hand-sized spider wouldn't get whacked too

149

much.

'Tom would have definitely agreed with you on that, although he came from Bolton not Manchester! He loved it out in Zambia...'

Sophie broke off as Harry slowed to a crawl, leaning over the driving wheel and looking off to the right into the brush. As they came to a halt, engine still running, Harry slid back and stood up on his seat as he brought his binoculars up to his face looking through gaps in the dusty foliage. Grinning now, he put a foot on the top of the door, jumped down onto the trail and took a few paces back towards a pile of dark grey-brown droppings about the size and shape of a yellow turnip. Squatting, he felt for heat and softness and his grin lengthened as he stood again and banged the side of the Cruiser, shouting up to Gareth and Keith to unstrap the canvas canopy and pull it over the roof-frame.

'Little help here, chaps!' Harry smiled broadly at Jim, Phil and Sophie as he opened the driver door this time, and again stood on his seat. 'That's it - just keep it straight over the cage and then get the sides strapped up around the supports.'

It only took a couple of minutes to get themselves a good sturdy canopy and then they were on their way, buoyed up by the news that they'd see rhinos today after all.

'Buffalo first though, huh?!' Harry was still grinning, in his element as they picked up speed again. 'This is a big herd and they'll be down in the creek this time of day, so it'll get a little bumpy, OK? Hang onto the straps, or the poles if you're getting too jolted.'

'Won't it be too marshy for the vehicle?' Sophie was also smiling, as though at an in-joke.

'Nope - water levels have fallen again last couple of days

down here and we don't have to cross any feeder streams. You'll have more trouble with the dust and the flies!'

'Oh, good!' This came from Jim, but he was laughing as well. 'I thought we'd see hippos and lots of mud flats this close to the lake, Harry?'

'We'll see them better from the boat on the way back - this is water meadow territory now... Get your cameras ready!'

Harry turned a corner and halted briefly after cresting a hillock that brought the lake back into full view almost. They could see the large herd of dark buffalo through the thinning trees as the vista opened up before them. 'OK guys - I'm going to try and keep the revs down where I can, but we need the 4-wheel drive in case the ground's too waterlogged, so we also need to keep the chit-chat down low when I douse the engine. You'll get some great photos as close in as I can get us. We're downwind but they have good eyes and hearing too and they can be very dangerous if we annoy them, so we need some hush!'

So saying he drove into the long grass. The wind off the lake blew the smell of warm earth and dung mingled with green watery smells towards them, but it also helped keep the noise of their approach to a minimum, so they were already taking some distance shots when they all, even Harry, sucked in their breath in wonderment. The buffalo had seemed oblivious to them but then, one by one, the closest cows looked over towards them and suddenly hundreds of snowy egrets that had been mingled in amongst the herd on the ground, or even standing on the mud-caked backs of the great bovines, almost simultaneously rose into the air and drifted slowly upwards like feathery balloons. The white birds weaved in outward spirals on the breeze, effortlessly floating over the curving horns of the buffalo like white thistledown; and then as gently descended back into the lush tall grass and promptly busied themselves with catching frogs and insects once more, or went back to work on the buffalo, with the oxpeckers, searching out juicy blood-rich parasites.

'Beautiful!' Eva's hushed whisper was echoed by Keith and Phil. Harry, who had stopped and turned the engine off as soon as the birds had taken off looked back and grinned at them all.

'Now you know why they call them snowy egrets - looked just like snowflakes didn't they? I'm glad you all saw that - it doesn't always happen, but it's breath-taking, huh?!'

'Yes. It always is. Like it's the first time.' Only Harry heard Sophie's comment and didn't press her because once more she was lost in another memory, in another land.

How many times had they watched the egrets down on the river rising out of the trees, swirling and circling out over the water and up, up again, to float lightly back onto their perches like huge dandelion 'clocks'? Tom had laughed when she'd first made the analogy and it had been an in-joke with them ever since. Now, here she was in the departure lounge in Lusaka and there were the egrets floating up out of the marsh into the sky after a Boeing had just roared past them, brakes screaming in reverse after landing. But this time there was no one to ask her how many 'o'clocks' she could see. The tears were hot on her face as the last of the birds descended back into the reeds.

'I know it's a big cliché, but don't try to hold back the grief, Sophie.' Youssef's clipped public school English was gentle as she used a soggy tissue.

'I'm not. I'm just fed up with crying all the sodding time.'

The words came out more petulantly than she'd intended and she felt herself flush spectacularly. Her already heated cheeks must have been blotchy as hell.

'I... I'm sorry. You're very kind, but I don't want to talk right now.'

And down they bloody came again. 'I'd better go buy some more tissues...' she mumbled ungraciously, but Youssef's hand was on her arm pressing her softly back into the plastic seat.

'I'll go get them for you and get us some more coffee. That was our plane landing I think but we'll have enough time before they call us to board.'

He'd come back and not said a word as they both slowly sipped at the hot aromatic local blend that came in those horrible foam cups with the silly plastic tops with slots for a stirrer. She was feeling chilled again and held both hands around the container, taking comfort in the last heat of the coffee, shivering just a little.

'Here, child.' Youssef put her jacket around her shoulders and looked over at the information board. 'They'll be calling us soon I think so you might want to put that on when you finish your drink. They usually have the air con going full tilt on the plane.'

She nodded mutely but made no effort to talk for now. This was not how she'd imagined going home. It was too soon for one thing, except that really it was far too late because Tom wouldn't be with her. She looked down at the coffee sloshing about the bottom of the cup, trying hard to hold it steady, when two firm hands enclosed hers and stayed her trembling, then took the cup from her altogether and put it on the little table in front of them.

'Up you come now.' His voice was soft as he reached out to help her stand and put her jacket on, then put his arm around her and lowered her back into the seat. He sat down as well, still holding her gently and let her put her head on his shoulder and cry some more as her head pounded with the fever. 'Not quite time for your medication but I'll get the steward to bring us some water as soon as we get on board, so you can settle down and sleep for a while.'

'Sorry. I don't want to make a fuss.'

'You're not. They know you're unwell and need to keep your fluid intake up. You just do as the doctor orders, hmm? Not everyone gets the personal Jettou in-flight service y'know.' He smiled down at her. 'I can never read books on planes and their movies are always tiresome, so I get very bored on long haul. Looking after you will give me something to do. If you're a very good patient I may not have to tell you my life story...'

What would she have done without Youssef that day, when she thought she had turned her back on Africa for good?

* * *

'Are you ready for the main event now?' The cameras hadn't clicked for a while and Harry was good at assessing boredom thresholds in mixed 'specialism' groups. He knew that Keith and Gareth were itching to use the little toy they had in their heavy holdall and that the buffalo herd just weren't cutting it on the cinematography front now they'd settled back into ignoring them thoroughly. Phil and Eva were getting fidgety too, though Jim was still peering about with the bins and Sophie was off with her own strange thoughts. High time to go really, if only to stop her brooding too much.

'Yeah! Rhino time, Harry!' Gareth remembered to keep his

voice down still and Harry grinned to himself again, pleased with the way the cameramen were really getting into the wildlife and environments. He turned the key, slipped into reverse and moved off as quietly as they'd come in and back onto the trail again, still following the spoor he'd found there earlier. They picked up speed for a mile or so and then turned off road and headed inland and uphill slightly, the terracotta Matusadona Hills wavering over the trees ahead of them in the midday heat haze. The brush was patchy and he knew that there was a small clearing up ahead which just might... Yes!

He cut the engine and coasted to a stop in the dappled shade of some taller acacia, thankful for the cover as the lake wind was lost to them in the interior. The tree shadows and the land cruiser canopy would also help to keep their visibility down from the two poorly-sighted cows, because again they'd struck gold.

'Very, very quiet this time, guys. You're really fortunate - these two are sisters and they...' he kept his head towards the dusty grey shapes nibbling quite delicately on the leafy browse, but his eyes were darting around the deeper, lower cover and he stopped talking for a moment, not wanting to scupper the luck.

Catching sight of a muddy snub nose with the tiniest horn through the leaves, about six feet away from the rump of the furthermost adult cow, Harry gave a low chuckle and finally turned to the others.

'You see the one on the left? Look back into the brush behind her. Can you see the little horn...? It's a bit stubby, right?' Gareth and Keith were on it already and Jim suddenly stiffened and was tapping Eva on the shoulder. 'Now don't point or wave your arms around please. They have poor eyesight but they can pick up on sudden or unusual movements and their hearing is excellent.'

Satisfied that the wind was again in their favour and nobody was going to get over-excited, he went on in a 'carrying' whisper. 'Like I said these two girls are sisters and they're quite unusual in that they stick together a fair bit, but the best thing is that they both had calves about two months ago and... yes, there she is. Isn't she sweet?'

As he was speaking the baby rhino tottered out into plain view and promptly attached herself to her mother's teat, burying her blunt little nose into her side. 'Try not to bash the motor drives too much and one at a time please, else they may take exception to our presence. And here comes number two calf - little boy this one.'

Again he paused as the others focussed on the newcomer, who also made a beeline for mum, proceeding to rub himself against her foreleg almost directly opposite Eva.

'Ohhh! Harry?' Sophie stirred softly in front of him, looking back into the thicker browse again.

Harry smiled to himself as the adolescent cow trotted out into the clearing. 'That was going to be my surprise! Here comes the little girl's big sister! She's nearly three years old. If she'd been male then she'd have probably been 'encouraged' to leave by now, but like I said these two ladies are quite sociable and so she's still tolerated by mum and her auntie. She's been shaping up as quite a nice little nanny to the two babies, so she might stick around for a good while yet.'

'When will she be old enough to fend for herself?' Jim's voice had a smile in it too.

'She could manage well enough right now but, unless she starts getting stroppy with the little ones, she could stay with the group for a year or more. She'll be ready for her first boyfriend in about two years time I should think and so she'll definitely leave them around then, when she comes into season. But after that she might come back for extended visits with her ma - I hope so because these rhino really are in trouble as a species and greater socialisation always helps in the survival stakes.'

A hush fell on the party as they watched the little family moving slowly around the acacia grove, the tiny calves both nursing whenever their mothers stopped to strip leaves off the shrubby mopane and thorny scrub. The teenaged calf seemed to be more interested in nuzzling her little sister but eventually started to browse as well.

Harry was watching the group intently when he looked back at Keith and Gareth who had started to fish around in their mysterious holdall. Gareth looked over a little guiltily.

'Will it be OK, Harry? It doesn't make much noise unless we run it fast.'

'I'd be happier if you left it for another five minutes chaps. Let them settle - they may even lie down in the shade over there now the sun's right up.'

'You're the boss, Harry. Promise we won't scare them and let it get too close.'

'What are they up to now?' Sophie whispered the question that the other three wanted to know the answer to and Harry laughed quietly.

'They've got a remote control camera mounted on a little carriage that they want to try out. Wait until you see what they've done to camouflage it! So funny!'

'Will they scare the rhino?' Phil rather surprisingly joined the conversation. 'Can't they get pretty aggressive if something upsets them, especially with babies around.'

'It should be OK, Jane - they tried it out yesterday

afternoon down on the beach where it's sandy and it's pretty quiet so long as they don't make it scoot around too fast or get too close. It's hot and they'll all be looking for a siesta about now... and, to be frank, rhinos aren't too blessed with imagination so I doubt they'll take much notice.'

They were all having trouble trying not to giggle as the mobile baby boulder trundled at barely a snail's pace towards the cow who had two calves. They had fortuitously settled nearest to the land cruiser and where the terrain was relatively flat and free of obstacles and were side on to the safari group, so it couldn't have been more perfect for the boulder-cam's first proving run.

'Wasn't there something like this on one of the UK wildlife docu-series a few years back, Keith?' Jim asked as he came around the back of the vehicle after setting the remote control camera on its way. Gareth had put the monitor where Keith had been sitting on the back seat so the others could watch the visual feedback whilst he operated the console, guiding the fake boulder towards the sleepy rhinos.

'Yeah - but this one's state of the art. It can switch to caterpillar track like a tank, or standard wheels depending on the terrain and its little motor can be set to 'silent-mode' when it's on battery. The downside is it doesn't take much of a charge, so this is ideal to test it out in field conditions.'

'Impressed with the silent running, guys - you ought to be able to get it within a few feet of them so long as they don't get too interested in a trundling rock!' Harry was keeping an eye on both the mothers who were looking relaxed, but not too inclined to go to sleep.

'It's got a good zoom so we won't push it right under their noses - don't want them to freak and squish it.'

Gareth was enjoying himself with the controls and decided to angle in towards the sleeping baby girl who had her chubby chin propped up on her mother's foreleg, so they could see the stub of her nose horn and the little bump where her posterior horn would grow a few inches behind it.

'Try switching to the zoom now, Gareth - the wide angle's not really needed with it right out in the open like this.'

'Right-o, Keith... whoops! Sorry that's the fish-eye... there!'

'Oh! She's adorable!' Eva was fascinated as the monitor screen filled with the baby rhino's face even though the trick boulder was still about twenty feet away. 'Is her skin really that rough, Harry?'

He laughed softly. 'Not quite. That's mostly mud where she's been rubbing it down at the salt lick, but they do have very tough hides, even when they're infants.'

'Still not very black - but then white rhinos aren't really white either, are they?

'Nope. It's *wijd* rhino in Afrikaans - meaning wide. The white rhino's got kind of a wide squared-off upper jaw, because they're grazers primarily. They're almost like a lawnmower sometimes! You can see this baby's got a pointy, beak-like lip really well now - when she's weaned it'll get progressively more flexible, almost prehensile, like a stunted elephant trunk, to help with grabbing leaves and seed cases. Next time we see them eating have a good look at their mouths with the bins.'

* * *

An hour later they were on the way back to the boat, having had quality rhino and boulder-cam time and a few colas to toast the slumbering giants. But just as they came back to the turn in the trail for the jetty Harry jumped on the brakes slightly and sharply diverted to the far side of the tree line that came down to the foreshore, looking over into the lower boughs and slowing as they drew near the canopy, where they could see long gourd-like shapes hanging down from the higher branches.

'Behold the sausage tree! Otherwise known as *Kigelia Africana*,[14] or better yet, 'the maiden's prayer' tree - for obvious reasons!' he paused for the mandatory tittering. 'The only species in its genus, and only found in Africa. I won't go under it, 'cos its sausages look about ready to drop and they bloody hurt if they hit you, but also...' He turned and grinned broadly at them 'what d'you think of that very long, thin, spotty sausage hanging down over there?'

He nodded towards one of the lowest branches that hung out almost at right angles to the trunk, shaded by the upper leafy boughs and more sausages. They all looked in the direction he'd indicated and, almost to a man, went for their cameras, except for Phil who simply whistled in admiration. 'Well hellooooo, leopard lady!' and then grabbed his pencil and started scratching away in his notebook like a demon.

'Guys - she's a pro and will pose quite happily for close-ups. Just don't get too animated, else she'll go higher up and sulk at us from a distance.'

'You know her then, Harry?' Sophie asked, smiling broadly.

'Oh, yeah! She's Moll - after Moll Flanders. Quite an adventuress she is, but she's getting on now and loves her afternoon naps down by the lake. This is her favourite tree. She's usually higher up but if you look, you'll see there's no sausages above her? They've already fallen, see.'

---

[14] **Kigelia Africana** ~ known as the Sausage Tree has long pendulous fruit shaped like short-link sausages, hanging from long rope-like vines or peduncles. The 'sausages' are similar to gourds, but are in fact woody berries.

'Damn, Harry! Why didn't you bring us here first?' Keith growled.

'Because you already have those great shots you showed me last night of that leopard and her two cubs up in Kafue. Moll's retired anyway and the black rhinos are almost 'last chance to see' these days. Always be plenty of leopard around - they're survivors. She's certainly photogenic, I'll grant you that, even though she's an old tart! She won't budge from here, so fill your boots for five minutes and then we'll get off. I'm ready for some lunch!'

* * *

'So... are we going to be allowed to have a look at your sketches then, Jane?' Harry and Phil had continued their acerbic role-play assignments all the way back to Spurwing, but the needle factor had waned somewhat in the sultry heat. Now they'd had a very good lunch and were lounging under the fans in the bar overlooking the lake, they were all chatting contentedly about the day so far.

''Course you can, Tarzan. No charge!'
Phil slid his notebook over to the guide and went back to his rum and cola with a mischievous glint in his eye as Harry started to leaf through, idly at first and then really intently, forgetting all about his pipe that he'd been puffing on since they'd finished eating.

'These are really excellent, Phil - and I've seen some great wildlife artists rough work in my time, but...' he trailed off and quickly looked over at Sophie who was deep in conversation with Eva and the others, leaning over the balcony rail admiring a pair of goliath herons down by the jetty. '... I'm not sure if Sophie'd thank you for this one though.' Harry moved his chair closer to Phil, lowering his voice and pointed to an exquisite little study of Sophie looking sad, chin cupped in

161

her hand when they'd been looking at the buffs.

'Well, no. But I'm letting you see it, not her. I couldn't resist and she was much more interesting than the buffalos. She's been through some tough times I'm guessing?'

Harry nodded but didn't say anything more.

'It's alright - I'm not fishing. But she's been up and down all day and I got intrigued from afar whilst you two were having your serial tête à têtes.'

'I can see. You've caught her mood very well.' Harry moved on more hurriedly now, feeling rather awkward, but then slowed again as Phil's focus switched back to the wildlife. 'These ones of the baby rhinos are wonderful.'

'Well, Gareth's monitor helped a lot there.'

'You have a very good eye for detail even so.'

'All in the job description Tarzan, darling. I'm not a top stylist by accident! I've won awards I'll have you know!' He winked theatrically and Harry chuckled.

'Have you now?! So you're not all permanent waves and highlights then?'

'Sauce! You've been about us enough to know I don't just do Eva's hair. I trained in set design and I have a fine arts degree and a masters in art history.'

'Well it certainly shows in these sketches. Seriously - I think they're first class. Do you paint as well?'

'Not any more, no. I can't be as good as I want to be and the fine art world's a real bitch if you're not on top of your game - I should know after all! My analyst would be a billionaire if I had to sell my art for a living. Strictly a hobby this kind of drawing but it comes in useful for work as well. My other half's an art director - now he really is the family genius! Regular Michelangelo.'

'Your eyes met over a crowded prop room?' Harry was back on his pipe again, grinning through a swathe of smoke.

Phil waved his hand fussily but laughed. 'Make that a rock benefit, but yeah - we met on set.'

'Somehow I didn't think Tarzans were your type, Jane.'

'Damn right! Jungles play merry hell with your skin, although I suppose the humidity's good for the pores... Oh, to hell with it.' Phil sighed and motioned to the barman 'Two more beers here when you're ready, Solomon!'

He turned back to Harry with a slightly embarrassed grin '*Ice Cold in Alex*'[15] had its moments and if Sylvia Syms can do it, so can I'.

'Man - you are priceless!' Harry roared with laughter. '... and only a beer will get Matusadona dust out of your throat. So you like old British war films too?'

'What's not to like? I lurve upper crust men doing what they gotta do and to hell with the gals! Plus I hate being stereotyped, though I will admit to liking *Whatever Happened to Baby Jane*? And listening to Judy Garland, naturally.'

'My ma looked like Joan Crawford. Could shoot like John Wayne did in his films though.'

'Adorable! She sounds like quite a lady. Is she still with us?'

'Nope. Hell - I'm only just the right side of sixty!'

'Too much in-for-mat-ion!' The beers arrived in bottles and they lapsed into silence as they poured them out.

'So are you enjoying this safari against your better judgment? No offence intended but, aside from these

---

[15] **Ice Cold in Alex** ~ A 1950s British WW2 movie set in the Sahara desert. An ice-cold beer in Alexandria, Egypt is the fantasy that keeps a stranded group of soldiers and nurses going as they try to pass enemy lines.

extraordinary drawings, you weren't giving off too many happy vibes up until today.'

'All a performance, Tarzan. We Hollywood types can't help ourselves half the time don't you know?'

'Bullshit!'

'Quite!' Phil took several long pulls of his beer. 'My, that's good! No bullshit. This isn't something I think Eva should be doing but she wanted me along, so I came because she's my best friend for real. That, and to make sure that Jack doesn't mess with her head too much.'

'But he's not even here? And surely Jim can look after her? Wait - Jack is her ex, isn't he?'

'With bells on, yeah. And believe me, he doesn't have to be on the same continent to screw Eva around. Jim's not bad at heading him off at the pass generally but he fancies himself as a Hemingway type, so he wasn't about to pass up on this little trip once Eva had expressed an interest in taking the part.'

'She's really excited about it I thought? Is it not certain she'll be in the film?'

'Oh, she'll do it in the end and be brilliant in it, but Jack'll make triple sure she is. That's the trouble. He pushes her around way too much and... let's just say I don't like blood sports of the gladiatorial persuasion and Jack always bleeds her white to get an 'authentic' performance out of her. Did you ever hear the stories about Katharine Hepburn when she filmed *African Queen* with Huston?' Harry shook his head. 'Well she got really sick while they were on location and had to have a bucket to vomit into between takes - hell the whole crew were throwing up out in Uganda except for Bogey, and that was only because he was drinking whisky non-stop instead of water!'

'But that was back in the fifties. Things are a lot better these days and even sleeping sickness isn't too bad if someone's otherwise fit and healthy. Besides, I thought there wasn't going to be that much location work?'

'Ever heard of method acting? Eva takes all that crap seriously and really she needs to focus on other stuff right now... It's up to her anyway, but Jack is always a bastard to her eventually and yet she still idolises him, even now.'

'They've made some fantastic movies together, haven't they?'

'Sure.' Phil shrugged. 'But you don't see the cost necessarily. Let's say if I was married, I'd want my husband to be a little more concerned for my emotional welfare, even if there was the possibility of an Oscar. That's why I came along, to make sure she remembers why she divorced the rat, and also that an Oscar won't kiss you goodnight - or hold you when your world falls apart. She hasn't signed yet, you know.'

'Ah - so this trip is a sweetener then?'

'Of a kind, yes. Sorry. It's been great with you and what you've shown us today is amazing, but this is a vacation with a sell your soul clause and she has other things she wants to do with her life. She doesn't need this role to do them, plus she has nothing to prove anymore for this kind of movie after the *Red Dust* remake.'

'I preferred the original - that Mary Astor was beautiful.'

'Gable was better! The machismo...'

'Well I'm just glad Gary didn't have his halitosis problem for the smooches...' Eva chuckled as she left Sophie and the others to their bird-spotting and joined them. 'Can I have a sneak look at your sketches too Phil?'

'Sneak away honey - you don't have to ask.'

The movie star, obviously familiar with Phil's work, flicked through a little more quickly than Harry had but then rewound and ended up on the same little sketch of Sophie that Harry had worried over.

'Did he break her heart do you think, Harry? You were talking about someone very intensely back on the boat.' The famous dark blue eyes were aglow with curiosity.

'I don't think he ever did that. Maybe it would have been better if he had. It's sort of a sad anniversary today apparently. We haven't really talked much about it - very private and sad, but her sister told me to try and keep her spirits up when I was with you all. That's all you're getting out of me though ladies - my lips are sealed from this point onwards. Mainly because I don't know the details and I'm not asking about them.'

'You're no fun Tarzan! Don't tell me you're not wildly interested?'

'Wind it in Philip - it's not fair on Harry.'

Eva smiled gently, but was not quite done with the subject and came at it from another direction. 'Her sister seemed so nice when she was on the phone going over meeting us off the plane in Nairobi. She's older than Sophie, I think?'

'Claire? She was a forty year old at birth!' Harry laughed warmly, then went on, the affection in his voice made plain. 'I've known her husband, Grant for years - he's American, but he was based out here in Harare when the tobacco trade was still going strong and used to come out to the company's hospitality accommodation in Kariba Town most weekends. They left in the nineties when things were getting too uncomfortable politically. Set up their executive safari business over in Kenya with their payoff - he was top brass.

Based there, but not just centred on East Africa as they both have a ton of contacts here in the south still. She dotes on Sophie like she's one of her kids though.'

'Age difference about ten years?' Eva was smiling thoughtfully, glancing over at Sophie who was in fits over something Gareth had just said.

'Are you a witch, Eva?' Harry was laughing. 'Thereabouts - Claire's nine years older I think.'

'We met her, remember? But I'm an older sister too - only Amy's thirteen years younger than me.'

'Trouble is, darling Amy's decided to stop at age thirteen too!' Phil's eyes rolled in disgust.

'That's enough mister... she can't help it - some of the time anyway. She had a rough time after I left home and some of that's left her a bit vulnerable with certain types of people.' She glared at Phil, who seemed about to interject again, but reconsidered when he saw the warning look in her eyes. 'But she's a good kid at heart and I love her.'

'Family, huh? Can't live with 'em, can't live without 'em. My pa and I had some fights after I finally came out. Ma was fine with it bless her, but pa was one of these 'Grand Old Men of Africa' types and he couldn't get to grips with it properly.'

'Oh my! How wildly exciting!' Phil perked up again at the thought. 'White hunters are too hetero for words in general, I suppose?'

'You'd be surprised then... well no - probably you wouldn't, Jane, but my trouble was more a generation thing of course. My dad was the original regular guy - very Trevor Howard, stiff upper lip, etcetera.'

'Nothing queer about ole Trev! Oh! How adorable! I can just see you as poor little Lord Greystoke brought up by a big gorilla daddy!' Phil was almost crying at the imagery and the others of course had to know why. The gossipy threesome thus increased to seven again and so the conversation turned in less intimate directions until it was time to leave for Sanyati.

* * *

They set off with two hours to spare before sunset, to allow plenty of time to slowly skirt the south shore of the lake and then the eastern side of the Sanyati gorge for the last of the day's heat as the sun disappeared below the western cliffs. As promised they saw pods of hippo, crocodiles and waterbuck as well as more buffalo and elephant again, off in the distance away from the foreshore. Jim was hankering for a good close-up of a hippo with its mouth wide open displaying its tusks.

'Well, Jim - we can try, but best not to get too close as they're getting a little restive about now. Nearly their dinnertime, so they're looking to get out of the water and there's a fair number of calves so the cows will get pretty ratty if we're too near.'

'Also they stink to high heaven, James!' Phil already had a hand over his nose and mouth. 'And I bet their breath is as bad!'

'You'd better believe it!' Harry laughed. 'Actually, if you can get a hippo yawning then that's a better picture really - if one's baring its tusks in anger then it's getting ready to bite, so you have to be damned quick to get a decent shot.'

'Pug ugly, vicious brutes the lot of 'em.' Phil was dousing a neckerchief with cologne now as the less than fragrant smell of hippo fart became more pronounced.

'I won't get us any closer than this, Jane, so stop your dripping!'

After their bonding session at Spurwing the banter had mellowed considerably and the group was, anyway, winding down now as the time for their sundowners was fast approaching. Giving up on the hippos, Harry headed for deeper water for a while and increased the speed before turning back in towards the gorge, but then slowed as they approached a small 'forest' of skeleton trees in which were perched a veritable flock of soon-to-be-roosting cormorants and a few darters. He angled the boat around so they could get the falling light levels reflecting in the water behind the gnarled, bony branches and let the engine idle so their wake gradually subsided.

'There!' Harry pulled the catches free off the replenished coolbag. 'Beer time again folks - you'll get some fantastic pictures in a minute or two.'

'No thanks, Phil.' Eva shook her head as he was about to hand her a beer. 'I'm on sodas for the rest of the trip.'

'My God! Are you sickening for something?' Even though Phil was joshing, Sophie turned to look at Eva quizzically, suddenly realising that she hadn't had any alcohol at all since they'd come to Sanyati and that the movie star had been feeling rather queasy that day.

Eva just laughed and helped herself to a lemonade. 'I decided to go on a health kick is all. Lots of water and juice for me from now on - it's more refreshing anyway.'

'Let me know if you start chucking up again Eva - it can bugger up your malaria protection,' Sophie smiled, but her voice was earnest, 'it's so easy to lose immunity if you've got a tummy bug, no matter how careful you are.'

'Have you seen the amount of insect repellent this woman puts on, doc?' Jim guffawed 'No wonder I'm getting bitten raw, I can't get near our gels and the sprays make me sneeze like buggery.'

'The gels are best and I've got plenty to spare if any of you need them.' Sophie spoke a little more tartly. 'Seriously, all of you, you have to be careful about your routine on a long trip like this, especially near the water. I've had a bad dose of malaria in the past and nearly died - it's really not worth taking risks.' She sighed a little as Phil made another of his faces, but laughed good-naturedly at herself. 'OK - lecture over but I'm not kidding either. You all should take care with your malaria meds...'

'Get your head down, Sophie - your body needs the rest.' Finally they were airborne and on the way home. Good as his word, Youssef had got one of the stewardesses to bring them some water so she could take more painkillers and her next dose of mefloquine[16] before take-off. Sophie was mortified at the unusual attention but, as they'd been given priority boarding with the rest of the 'walking wounded' as Youssef joked, the Zambian stewardess was quick to put her at ease and had ensured they had pillows and blankets within easy reach if they needed them before the rest of the passengers started to pile on board. They were also in a side aisle with a spare seat between them so they wouldn't be disturbed and Youssef had insisted Sophie take the window seat to minimise any jostling as people moved about during the flight.

'I'm not really sleepy, Youssef - and I keep having horrible dreams when I do, so I'd rather try and stay awake and watch the movie maybe?' To tell the truth it was the icy blast of the air con that had woken her up, even though Youssef had tucked her up nice and snug after she'd taken her drugs.

---

[16] **Mefloquine** ~ a synthetic type of quinine, widely used in tablet form to prevent and treat malaria.

He shook his head but grinned at her. 'OK - but humour me and try to take a nap after they serve lunch, huh?'

'Promise.'

She looked out of the window and fell quiet for a while, watching dusty Lusaka recede as they turned and climbed up into the clouds and onto the flight path for home. She always liked to watch the clouds below them on planes, where the sky was deep blue with the earth far below and remote as they drifted past fluffy fields and misty towers of cloud. A world of cotton wool - just what she needed to wrap herself up and soften all sensation, all pain. But the fever was still there and she needed to distract herself, so she soon turned back to Youssef.

'Why did they switch me to mefloquine?'

'Because the chloroquine [17] you were taking had failed to keep your immunity up. You know that the treatment for full-blown malaria uses the same types of drugs that help prevent it?'

'Sort of... Was it the chloroquine that made me miscarry?' The question had been circling around and around her head, ever since Claire and Alma had quietly and calmly explained about the 'spontaneous abortion' she had suffered back in Vutare.

'No. That was the malaria, pure and simple. The reason the chloroquine stopped working was in part due to your getting dysentery so much - that also stopped your contraceptive pill working too, of course. I'm afraid, Sophie, if you're looking for something to blame for losing your baby, then it's down to dirty water and/or your own shoddy hygiene habits at fault.'

Sophie flushed more deeply with temper and tears threatened.

---

[17] **Chloroquine** ~ another synthetic preventative and treatment type of quinine in tablet form

'I was always very careful with washing and putting on insect repellent - and I always used a net whenever I could. I only got bitten once or twice on the legs the whole time I was there!'

'Then that was enough, my dear. I'm sorry Sophie - you were just very, very unlucky.' The trolley was coming around with more drinks and he broke off to get some more water for them and then, to Sophie's surprise, ordered a double gin and four tonics, but no ice. 'Don't look at me like that, missy! They're both for you anyway.'

'I don't want them!'

'Yes. You do. It's medicinal.' He'd got three cups and let the middle tray down to plonk everything down. Quickly he poured water into two of the cups and opened up the gin and two of the cans of tonic for the other. He pushed the drink towards her and then caught her very firmly by the wrist as she tried to push it back.

'Take it easy, Sophie! Like I said last night, the gin will help you relax and the quinine in the tonic will do you good.' His voice was calm and soothing, no trace of irritation showing, even if he felt it. 'And yes, I will have a whisky myself, just like I did last night, but with my lunch, thank you. I'm not an abstainer, as I'm no longer a believer, so don't think you can throw hypocrisy at me - this is for you, OK?' He let her go and sighed as she petulantly folded her arms. 'And I'm immune to tears too. You have to keep taking your fluids, so you can have the rest of my water instead if you want to sulk... but no ice with anything. '

They started the first film not long afterwards so they ignored each other steadfastly whilst she tried to watch and he looked through some papers from his briefcase and the latest issue of 'The Lancet'. After about half an hour's low-key fidgeting,

Youssef tried not to smirk as he saw her reach out for the gin out of the corner of his eye. The film was obviously not holding her attention so he put the magazine down.

'No good?'

'Not in the mood for it. Mel Gibson gets on my nerves a bit.' He laughed and stood up. 'I'll keep you company then and go and get that whisky now - do you want some more peanuts?' She nodded stiffly, still not quite ready to get matey again. He was soon back and cracked open the little bottle.

'I see you get ice then?'

'I don't have malaria, do I! You're shivering enough as it is without putting the cold inside you too. Truce, now? Please?' he winked at her and was relieved to see she was smiling at him again. 'So, what shall we talk about next then?'

'You choose - you're the doctor, aren't you?'

'Prescribing conversations is not one of my specialities, I'm afraid. Do you really want my life story? You may miss dinner through falling asleep from boredom you know? That's better!' She was laughing now and he raised his drink in salute.

'I'm not going to argue with you again...' Sophie was suddenly shy and her eyes dropped. '... but what you were saying about Teresa last night...? I wasn't really listening to you, to be honest.' She stopped and bit her lip, then looked at him anxiously, her eyes begging him not dismiss her question. He didn't say anything but nodded slightly, wondering what she was going to say next. 'I didn't like her... maybe a bit at first, but... once I was with Tom, I thought she was a real pain... and he idolised her the whole time.'

'She was his friend. Before you met him, I think?'

She nodded miserably. 'He used to yell at me for being so bitchy about her... I was jealous, I suppose. I felt left out -

they practically finished each other's sentences sometimes. But she always called him 'little brother' and he said I wasn't to make fun of her because that was how it was - that it wasn't her being all religious...' She paused and the next words were whispered. 'The last few days I've been having this awful dream and she's in it... Tom is too, but she's there first.' Two fat tears skittered down each side of her nose as she took a big mouthful of gin. 'She hugged me and then said sorry to me - in the dream. Said it was all her fault. Was it her fault?'

'Do you think it was?' Youssef spoke softly, taking her hand in his because he could see that this time Sophie was genuinely wanting an honest answer, trying to make some sense of it all. She shook her head and shrugged.

'You were listening to me a little, weren't you? Last night?' There had been a bit of a 'scene' back at the hotel when he'd met her and her sister Claire, and had started to tell them what he knew about events up in Tanzania, as he'd just got back from there earlier in the day. There was the smallest of nods from Sophie and he didn't wait for her to reply any more than that. 'OK. I can only tell you a little about what happened because I only talked to Mr. and Mrs. Zimmerman you remember, and they had already been questioned enough by the police, so I don't have the full story.'

'But you're their friend... and you knew her too.'

'Yes, but in respect of Teresa, I didn't know her very well, not really. She was my patient a long time ago, when she was still a child.'

'You said you trained her, last night?'

He nodded slowly. 'Yes, I did. But that was a long time ago as well and she was only one of many students.' Was this a good idea he wondered? Another long look at Sophie convinced him she was trying hard to be rational and clearly was desperate to try and understand what had happened to the man she loved and the woman she had been so jealous of, however little grounds there had been for that.

'I think, yes. It was her fault that things happened as they did. She set things in motion is what I mean. But it was not her fault that she was killed, or got your Tom killed too. The man who killed Teresa and who ordered one of the other soldiers to shoot Tom down... and to fire at Henryk - Mr. Zimmerman too, he was the one who was responsible for their deaths. One of his own men killed him finally and then they pulled out. Stole the truck and ran for the border, leaving the Zyandan women there unharmed. Henryk told me that he thought the rest of the men had sickened of all the killings and just wanted to stop, so they could go home. Teresa had screamed at them that they were like Cain - murdering their innocent brothers and sisters...'

Had it really been that simple? They had just needed someone to point out the 'error of their ways'? The ringleader, a Catholic priest, had been the one who urged the men into following the women to Umbeke. The other men had let him browbeat them perhaps, but they were still as culpable as he was - following orders wasn't a defence for genocide after all. However you cut it, it was a slaughter of the innocents, even if there had been cause for the Matu to rise up against the Lutse 'elite'. That the two tribal groups were largely indistinguishable from each other these days made not a scrap of difference once the mob fury had been roused. How many times had he seen it happen in front of him virtually. People who had lived together as neighbours amicably enough, worked together, even inter-married, had gone mad. And it only took a 'wrong' look at a crucial *moment, or a word in the 'right' place and off people went with whatever lethal weapon they could lay their hands on. Everybody suffered for it, even the aggressors. It made no sense, but then it never had, even back when he had started working out in Nigeria. When Teresa had been found and they all were sickened at how that could happen. How it could happen over and over still, after all these years. And people like him were still trying to find the words to explain this to someone like Sophie, knowing that it solved nothing. The innocent dead had no noble cause, no saviours.*

'What is happening up there defies logic. Not even in terms of warfare and political imperatives. It is simply madness. Utter and unreasoned insanity. Evil, perhaps. It was her fault that it happened the way it did, but I also think that Teresa could not help herself. She had to act in the way she did, because of who she was, and what she was... and most of all, why she was that way.'

Sophie was quiet, seemingly speechless, but just as he was about to go on she spoke, her voice bleeding confusion. 'What way? Why was she like that? What happened to her?'

He told her about the ten year old child who had been brought to him almost dead. How she had been starving for months and abused in the worst and most degrading of ways, then left for dead, ignored by her neighbours, people who had known her and her family since she was born. How she could still have faith in the same god he himself had forsaken, in part because of her, because she thought her life had been redeemed, instead of destroyed. He told her why he thought the little girl, who had lost almost everything she had to live for, instead chose to serve and save others as she had been 'saved'.

'She tried to give others what she had been given. Mercy

176

and the chance to live a 'good' life. And when she saw those wretched women and their children in that camp, she was so distressed she could not speak at first. And then she got very angry, so that was her own fault. She should have stayed with the others. Not tried to challenge the men who were terrorising those refugees. She was 'brave' because she lost her reason in her fury. She wouldn't help herself because she wanted to fight for them - as someone should have for her, all those years ago in Biafra...'

'She couldn't stand there and do nothing...?' Sophie's face was white and drawn as the words, dreamt in fever, passed her lips.

'That's all it was, really. She felt she had to do something, so she did. And it got her killed.'

She wanted to scream the agony out. Tom shouldn't have been with her! He shouldn't have gone with her at all! But all she could do was sob and sob, and all Youssef could do was hold her tight, until she had no more tears.

* * *

'Now do you see it?' Sophie was laughing at Phil again.

'OK! OK! I admit it - they're super cute and sooooo pretty it makes ya wanna puke!'

Harry was creased up, jaws aching and the object of all the praise had long since flown off in terror at the vehemence of the conversion of its latest admirer. 'Oh, Jane! Don't even attempt to mock the size of the Malachite Kingfisher with this woman - she's unhinged over them.'

'Why shouldn't I be? They're the most beautiful little birds in the world!'

'Oh, I beg to differ - what about Pygmy Kingfishers? They're even tinier and have lovely little purple heads...'

'Oh, my god! They don't?!' Phil was out of control now and on a roll, so the bird watching was well and truly over for the day. 'They do!!! Where are they? I demand you find me one this IN-stant, Tarzan!'

'Shush - settle down, Jane! You'll have to wait until tomorrow now, 'cos you've just frightened the entire avian population in this part of the gorge off!'

Harry couldn't keep up the gruff game guide act up and started chuckling again. 'Seriously, man. They're really tiny and nothing to write home about - and they're more of a sort of indigo than purple.'

'Awwwww!'

'And they only eat insects so they live back in the bush more. I'll see if I can find some for you tomorrow afternoon - it's a trip to the Dam in the morning, isn't it?'

'I think so - unless we can skip it?' Jim's voice was hopeful.

'It's worth seeing, y'know - one of the wonders of modern African engineering and there's a whole mythology behind it too - quite a spooky one.' Harry grinned at them all broadly, back in the raconteur mode he so enjoyed.

He took them effortlessly up to the camp jetty whilst they all started asking questions and shook his head at them after he'd tied up. 'No, you'll have to wait until tomorrow now because you need to be there and see the mighty Zambezi tamed to appreciate the tale. If you're lucky I might find an old medicine woman to tell it to you properly...'

'All I can think of are feathery purple heads now - you've totally lost me, Tarzan!' And so it went on, all the way up the path and around the camp fire over drinks, before they went off for their pre-dinner showers.

Sophie was about to set off down the path again when Jim called her over as she passed their rondavel. 'Sophie - can

178

we grab you a minute, please? We need to check something with you.'

'Of course.' Sophie smiled at him as he stood back to let her into their room for the second time that day. 'So long as it's not another scorpion.'

'No, nothing like that. But you've put the wind up us a little bit with what you were saying about our malaria meds? And with Eva's little 'stomach upset'...'

The emphasis on those last words had Sophie leaping to all sorts of conclusions and so she wasn't entirely surprised at what Eva had to say next.

'Well, we're not too worried because our doctor back in Palos Verdes was pretty thorough but, as you're quite the expert in a very hands on way, I just wanted to be sure, and really...' she smiled happily at Sophie 'to reassure you as well. Because you see, I don't have a stomach upset as such at all. I'm pregnant, I think...'

'And we just wanted to double check that the meds we're taking won't hurt anything?'

Sophie nodded, partially relieved, but needing to be professional for a few moments before observing the customary congratulations. 'You're taking proguanil and chloroquine in combination aren't you? Daily?' They both nodded. 'Then you should be fine - it won't harm the pregnancy. In fact it'll help your immune system and the baby's and still do its job in protecting you from the malaria strains. You really don't want to catch that while you're pregnant, as it infests the placenta...' She stopped, aware she was being too clinical and might cause some unnecessary anxiety. 'Sorry! I'll take my quack hat off and just say congrats to you both.' She smiled as she gave Eva a little hug. 'Your family doctor knew you were trying for a baby when you went for your other shots, I assume.'

'Yeah - we had some trouble getting pregnant, so we didn't want to take any chances when we said we'd go on this vacation. But this was a bit of a surprise to us really, and it wasn't until the other day when Eva started to throw up before she went and made a pig of herself with the biltong...' Jim was prevented from going on by a flying pillow from his dear wife, who was giggling happily.

'And I've thrown up first thing every morning since, whether or not I've been a pig - except today... Well, not until after the scorpion was evicted...'

'You've done a test? Because we could probably pick one up in Kariba Town tomorrow if you haven't.'

'Honey - I've had so many things to monitor this last year I'm in total harmony with my bod, whether I like it or not! I did an ovulation kit test before we left the US and we did the pregnancy one yesterday.'

'One of those ones that gives you a digital message and whistles and turns blue, then goes out and buys the kid a teddy!' Jim was holding Eva tight now and kissed her on the top of her head. 'We're beyond happy, as you might guess!'

'Well triple congratulations to the three of you then! And to Tester Teddy!' Sophie smiled at them both. 'And you're not to worry about the meds, just keep taking them regularly as you have been and in conjunction with your repellent sprays and creams. Let me know if you do start to get too ill during the day - take the tabs with breakfast still, but if you start chucking up after that then I can give you something to help with the nausea.'

'I'm very good at following doctors orders - you'll be the second person to know if there's anything the slightest bit wrong, Sophie. I've waited so long for this I'm not going to risk a thing from now on.'

'Hence the health kick thing? I should have twigged then, shouldn't I!'

'Puh! You know us tinsel towners! We don't need an excuse to be prissy.'

'But that's partly why we asked for a doctor to be on hand for this entire trip. Just in case.' Jim was still smiling but his voice was serious. 'Sometimes it's handy that the legal boys are heavy on the insurance risks. Jack isn't going to be so pleased though, I suspect.'

'Oh to hell with him! I'll have had it anyway by the time he needs me - this'll be in pre-production for soooooooo long he won't be doing the location work until this time next year. They can shoot around me if they get to filming beforehand.'

'We'll see - I don't know that I want you off on location at all.'

'OK, Mr. Ten per cent! I'll be a good little client...'

'You're a perfect client - and this is the end to a perfect day!'

Any further banter was saved by the dinner gong.

The Gathering of Water

Atika maanzi aatakwe buyoleke ~ once water spills you cannot gather it again.

Ba Tonga proverb

And of every living thing of all flesh, two of every sort shalt thou bring into the ark, to keep them alive with thee; they shall be male and female.

Genesis 6:18 - 6:19 (King James version)

Sophie's Diary: Thursday 3rd May ~ Lake Kariba, Zimbabwe

Gracious, what a kerfuffle during dinner last night! Well, afterwards to be exact, but 'the call' came for Sonya, our camp host, while we were eating and she came back to get Harry not long afterwards. Then he comes back just as we finished dessert and - well, to say the excrement hit the fan is putting it mildly... Turns out that Harry's little proposition about the bow-hunting over at Bumi Hills has caught Keith and Gareth's boss, Jack Hawkins, the big-shot Hollywood director's imagination and he's joining us tomorrow afternoon! Claire had an urgent call back from his office late yesterday and his secretary says Jack's currently in Cape Town on business and will fly into Kariba tomorrow p.m. to join us here in Sanyati and will stay on with Harry when we move on to Uganda at the weekend.

Luckily Eva and Jim seem amused by the news. Apparently it's 'situation normal' as Jack has these sudden impulses all the time. But Phil went into a massive hissy fit for some reason and Gareth's steaming because he was really looking forward to Uganda and now he and Keith have to stay here with Jack. Or rather not here, because apparently Sanyati Camp's not swish enough with their comms facilities, so they'll be staying at the big resort complex over at Bumi when we leave. Harry's pleased at the whopping fee Claire's got for him because of the short notice, but he seems to have spent most of last night trying to get Phil down out of orbit over it all.

We're off to Kariba Town now to go to the dam's observation point and visitor centre. Just me, Eva, Jim and Phil today - Keith and Gareth want to do some editing on yesterday's footage and work on the boulder-cam so Jack can have a look at that. Harry says he knows some of the old Operation Noah veterans up at the dam, so we'll get some local colour - hopefully that'll smooth down some of the ruffled feathers, at least until we go and collect 'Hotshot' Hawkins at the airport afterwards. I must say I'm quite intrigued by the interpersonal dynamics, given that Jack is Eva's ex-hubby squared - they married and divorced twice like Burton and Taylor!

You must understand that Nyaminyami is not a god, or rather he is not a god in the way of Allah, or the Christ. He is a force of nature, a Mudzimu, or Spirit who lives in memories and dreams perhaps and defies definition and proofs. He does not require faith or followers, because he is the Zambezi, and of the Zambezi, and so he does not need the prayers or belief of men. He is the guardian of the Great River in its aspect of the Giver of Life and Death, and so Nyaminyami is also the Lord of the Spiritlands. In times past he was just and bountiful in his wanderings across the great plateau and down into the vleis[18] and veldts to the eastern ocean, if the people held him in respect and did not begrudge him his share of food in

---

[18] **vlei** ~ a Dutch/Afrikaans word meaning a marsh, or shallow pool of standing water. Generally seasonal but sometimes permanent and, in drier parts of the continent, forming clay or salt pans that are mostly dry for years at a time and only occasionally fill during floods. Vleis may hold fresh, brackish or saltwater depending on the topography.

times of plenty. During the season of drought it is said that he would take the form of a great water snake with the head of a fish and, if the crops failed, he would allow the Ba Tonga people to take his own meat to fill their bellies in return for their observances in dance and sacrificial ceremonies, until it was time for the rains to swell the Great River once more.

For ages the Tonga lived in peace and harmony with Nyaminyami, the Great River Spirit and their herds and crops prospered in the long valleys of the Zambezi. Though Nyaminyami could be found anywhere along the river, he spent much of his time near a dwelling he made for his wife, Meenda-Musimbi[19], in a huge rock in the depths of the river gorge that was known to fishermen as the Kariwa[20], or 'the trap'. This was said to be one of the portals into the Spiritlands because the cliffs of the gorge rose high on either side of Kariwa, making the river run white and wild and, in places, deep and perilous. The fishermen stayed away from there because Nyaminyami, wishing to be left in peace with his beautiful wife, would cause great whirlpools and cascades to form and so their canoes would be broken on the rocks, or worse, dragged down into the black waters by the Kariwa never to be seen again.

Meenda-Musimbi was a gentle creature who cared much for the Ba Tonga and she would sometimes ask Nyaminyami to help them and make the river rise and flood the land enough to make it green and fruitful, so that the crops would grow

---

[19] **Meenda-Musimbi** ~ in Chitonga this literally means 'water girl'. Regrettably research has not revealed the name of Nyaminyami's wife and so some licence had to come into play.

---

[20] **Kariwa** ~ comes from the Shona language (alternative spelling is Kariva) and is also the root word for Kariba.

strong and tall and feed the Tonga people and their animals. Together the two Mudzimu of the Waters blessed the land and people of the Zambezi, and life was good.

Times change, sometimes slowly, sometimes fast. For the most part life changed little around the gorge of Kariwa and the Tonga were happy in their great valley, under the auspices of Nyaminyami and Meenda-Musimbi. A bad time was long in coming to the valley, but the cities of the Shona and Ndebele peoples grew larger and the British and Americans came to grow cotton and tobacco in the south, and to mine for coal and precious minerals to the west and north; and so their eyes were drawn more and more to the mighty Zambezi and its riches. They did not wish to know much of Nyaminyami and his wife, how they cared for the Ba Tonga and allowed the waters of the Zambezi to flow for the benefit of the people: but they did want to make use of the Great River so the cities in Zimbabwe and in Zambia would become even greater with the new power of electricity. They sent men to Kariwa who would build a great dam to hold back the waters of the Zambezi.

The Ba Tonga did not at first see this as a threat to their ancestral ways, until the District Commissioner told them that they would have to leave their homes because the great valley would be flooded and the river would rise and fill it for evermore. This seemed to be something ridiculous to the Ba Tonga, but when they protested that Nyaminyami had always made the river rise in its season, then recede so crops could grow, they were not listened to and were told they would lose their homes and their harvests if they stayed in the valley and that they must go and live on higher ground in Binga, or move away altogether.

Now, ever since the white men had come to the northern valleys of the Zambezi, Nyaminyami had not appeared in the river so often and indeed the Ba Tonga had rarely seen him in their grandparents' lifetime, and so they began to wonder if the District Commissioner was right and that they should move off their ancient lands. Chief Sampakumura tried to tell the people that Nyaminyami and his wife were still living in the Zambezi and told of two times while he was a young man when he had seen the Mudzimu's long snake-like body, as wide as an elephant is long with a huge head like a great Tiger fish, swimming far out in the deep river where the waters were stained red with his passing. More men, Shona and Europeans, came north to work on the building of the dam wall. This was where the Kariwa itself was located and finally the Ba Tonga were afraid because they knew that Nyaminyami, if he still was there, would be greatly angered by such a thing.

The clans once more held their ceremonies and danced for Nyaminyami, but to no avail. The rains came too early and with it a flood such as no one in living memory, not even in ten thousand years, had seen. The Ba Tonga, as was usual, had prepared to move further into the hills above the usual levels of the floodplain, but such was the speed and violence of the flooding that many people and their animals, as well as the men who had come to build the dam, were drowned, and the walls of the coffer dam and a great bridge that they had begun to raise were all washed away. As the waters receded it was discovered that many white men, who had been working near to the Kariwa, had completely disappeared. The Tonga who lived nearby were asked to help with the search for them, but they knew that Nyaminyami must have pulled them into the Spiritlands below the great rock of Kariwa, which of course was still there as it always had been. The tribe danced, many prayers were made and a white calf was sacrificed and set in the river before the great rock at sunset. When they came back there the next day the calf was gone and there, near the Kariwa, the bodies of all the white men were found, floating in the river where the calf had been left.

Nyaminyami had made his displeasure clear but the Shona and the white men returned to work soon after. Thinking that they had won this time, Nyaminyami and his wife decided to take their blessings to the other Ba Tonga lands and so the Great Mudzimu swam upriver to the west and Meenda-Musimbi went downriver to the east. The Zambezi in Kariwa receded and, once again, the men came back and started to re-build the dam wall, higher and stronger than ever. When Nyaminyami returned to the valley after the rains he discovered that the high wall had been completed and stood thick and strong, just beyond the Kariwa, holding back the Zambezi's waters so it was starting to rise higher than it ever did during the flood season. The lower reaches of the valley between the Batoka Gorge and Kariwa were already under water that would never subside. Worse was to come however. Meenda-Musimbi had not returned in time and was trapped on the eastern side of Kariwa below the dam wall and could not return to their home.

Now a Mudzimu is not infallible and Nyaminyami soon realised he had badly misjudged the determination of the Shona and the Europeans, for their desire to harness the power of the Zambezi had been very great. Grieving over the absence of his wife, Nyaminyami withdrew into the depths of the Spiritlands below the Kariwa. The plight of the Ba Tonga and the wild animals of the great valley became desperate, for the waters of the river continued to rise, driving them away from the old floodplain onto the high ground and stranding many of the smaller and slower ground-dwelling animals on little islands. The Ba Tonga at least had a place prepared for them at Chibwatatata, where the hot springs lay in the Binga Hills; but the animals, even the great buffalo and elephant, were in danger of getting stranded as the high ground of the central valley became swallowed up by the waters of the Zambezi.

If Nyaminyami was aware of the peril of the Ba Tonga and all the creatures of the valley, there was no sign that he would do anything this time. The tribes danced in vain, for he would not emerge from his dark home beneath the swelling waters and they began to think that the Great Spirit of the Zambezi had fallen into a dreamless sleep in the Kariwa and the despairing souls of the Spiritlands could not intercede with him on behalf of their wretched living children. But Meenda-Musimbi had not been forgotten by Nyaminyami. He could still hear her call out to him as he slept and, whenever she drew near to the wall of the dam, Nyaminyami could hear her weeping for him and this caused him to turn and moan deep down under the Kariwa. When he did this the earth itself rumbled and writhed beneath the waters of Lake Kariba, especially in the great cliffs around the gorge where the Kariwa still lies, far underneath the water.

Time for a Great Spirit runs differently than for the peoples of the Zambezi. Though fifty years have passed, Meenda-Musimbi still tries to come back to Kariwa, though she cannot pass through the dam wall and always she calls out her sorrow to her husband as he slumbers deep below the water. The Chibwatatata hot springs at times grow restive and boil and spit and the ground around the lake trembles and groans as Nyaminyami stirs and twists in his sleep, listening to his wife's crying. One day it is said, when the walls of the dam grow old and weak, Nyaminyami will wake and come out of Kariwa again and his wrath will be such that the Zambezi will finally break down the walls of its prison and the Great Spirit will at last be reunited with faithful Meenda-Musimbi and the Ba Tonga will finally be able to return to their ancestral homelands.

* * *

Luey Ogilvy grinned roguishly at the group, his dark brown eyes darting back to Sophie several times - he was always a sucker for natural blondes. 'So you had a good time with old Syamenga, I expect? Told you all the old legends about the River God... sorry, the Great Spirit of the Zambezi?'

'Folklore is always so interesting. I think it says a lot about people who have respect for their heritage.'

He smiled nicely at the famous movie star and nodded wryly. 'Oh, I think so too, believe me! You can't live in Kariba all your life and not have a good chunk of respect for Nyaminyami - have you seen him yet, by the way? No? Well, come along with me and you'll get a good look at the old boy.'

He led them further down a shady path to a low plinth overlooking the dam. 'Here he is! Of course this is only a scale model and if this was really him - well I wouldn't be standing so close naturally.' Luey patted the splendidly coiled sculpture on the head familiarly and flashed another bright white smile around the tour party. 'Now, if you thought I was making light of the legend that old Syamenga span for you, then you couldn't be farther from the truth. In fact I'd go so far as to say that, leaving out the wilder mythology and concentrating on the truth of the natural world, there's a hell of a lot of substance to Syamenga's story. Starting with this representation of Nyaminyami. See his head here - nasty long, sharp teeth, hah? Well, if any of you like sport fishing and go out on the lake with your fancy rods, then you might find yourself with one of Nyaminyami's great-great-grandchildren on the end of your line, because this bears more than a passing resemblance in the teeth department to our famous Tiger fish here in Lake Kariba...'

They were in the shade and a pleasant breeze was coming off the lake again as Luey carried on with his little palaeontology and geology lesson '... now the snake-like body of the Great Spirit, ten feet wide and way, way long - nobody knows for sure. Two theories here. Unlikely, but fascinating nonetheless is the 'Nessie'[21] solution.'

The blonde and the other Britishers in the group started giggling and he winked conspiratorially at them. 'Now that's not so far-fetched if you go back, say forty-odd million years ago, when there were early whale-like creatures called Basilosaurus who, from fossil records, we know were more eel-like in shape than modern cetaceans and whose heads resembled...?'

'The Tiger fish?'

Wow, that lady had the most amazing blue eyes! Pity they weren't staying in town. 'Tiger-ish anyway.'

They all laughed. 'But I kid you not. This animal did exist and from the specimens found over in the U.S. around Louisiana, here in Africa up on the Nile and in Pakistan, the articulation of their spines meant that they did swim more like snakes, or eels, than like dolphins and whales do today.'

'But even the Tonga wouldn't try to tell you that the river, remember, because there was no lake back then,

---

[21] **Nessie** - an affectionate diminutive for the apocryphal Loch Ness Monster

could support a gigantic whale-like creature without being a lot more obvious. Which brings us to a more likely, but nonetheless mysterious solution - what I like to call the Dagga Dream Alternative.' And pause for the usual titters, once he'd explained to them that dagga was the local name for the common recreational drug known as *cannabis sativa* that the Ba Tonga avidly smoked in calabash[22] pipes.

'Uncle Harry says you saw elephants swimming out on the lake yesterday? Well - imagine you've been hitting the dagga pretty hard all night and your old lady kicks you out of your pit to go fishing and... well you kind of drift in your canoe and then all of a sudden you see this big old shiny wet back, undulating away like some bloody huge freshwater porpoise! See! You get it too, huh? Hippos'd be good too I think, but they don't do the snorkelling thing really. The actual Kariba legend itself is another matter altogether, because that has a much firmer grounding in geology and climate theory...'

Luey was good at his job and took them through the making of the dam on a more modern and scientific basis, but he slowed down again when one of the group asked about the white calf and the return of the mysteriously missing bodies. 'Well - that's all true and so ceremonial dances and the sacrifice worked, didn't they? However, because of course there is a more pragmatic reasoning behind it all, the calf obviously went down some croc's neck, or more likely several as the ones that had survived the floods - they can drown as well of course - would all have been gagging for fresh meat by then because the floodwaters took a while to go down.'

---

[22] **calabash** - the bottle gourd, commonly used throughout Africa for bowls or drinking vessels, pipes, bottles and musical instruments.

'But that still doesn't explain the reappearance of the bodies - unchewed, but very battered and decomposing of course. Well, forensic medicine wasn't such an advanced art back then and 'T.I.A' so the burials weren't held up much for an inquest - the white men on the building detail who tried to get the plant out of the basin before the waters rose too high were mostly Italian and therefore Catholic. Anyway, no doubt Syamenga told you that this all happened down near the Kariwa right? OK, so old Nyaminyami's trap was notorious for sucking people down, so you have a pretty vicious current there to start with and this flood was a real bitch on wheels and there was a hell of a lot of water running past that would have pushed the bodies and trucks etcetera right down into the underwater gullies. Lots of pressure of course and that would have been sustained for a good while, so the corpses would have stayed down there until the water began to level off and then subside. At that point the debris would've started to loosen somewhat and things like body cavities will start to inflate with gas and so up they popped - right after the nice fresh calf had been scoffed. Being underwater so long those bodies would not have been too savoury at that stage for the surviving crocs, who are reptiles remember, and would have been stuffing themselves stupid on all the other animals that had been caught up in the flooding, so not hungry enough for finding well on their way to rotting corpses a tempting prospect. Makes some sense anyway, and is more likely than some conspiracy theories that say that it was the Ba Tonga, and not Nyaminyami, who finally let the dead Italians go...'

Luey took them up to the Chapel of Saint Barbara, patron saint of the Italian Navy and of military engineers amongst other things. This was where those killed throughout the period of the dam construction were buried or had memorials.

The latter were mainly for some of those unfortunates who fell to their deaths into the fabric of the dam wall itself and could not be retrieved from the wet concrete.

'In all eighty-six men, African and European, were killed during the construction of the dam, so some would say that the project was cursed from the outset because the cost in human terms was high, especially when you consider the problems faced by the fifty-seven thousand Ba Tonga people, north and south of the valley, who had to be moved away.

'Syamenga may not have told you about the one hundred spear-toting warriors who charged the police line back in 1958, when the first of the villages was surrounded prior to being moved out to one of the new permanent communities. There'd been murmurings against the relocations so, when the angry tribesmen got within fifty metres of the police, tear gas was used and spears were thrown in retaliation, but they kept coming. Eight of the Tonga were shot dead and thirty-four more were wounded before they disbanded and fled into the bush. Only one policeman was hurt from a stray bullet. The villagers were moved out anyway, on trucks towing the branches of baobab and mopane taken from the village trees. This was done so the Ba Tonga ancestors who supposedly haunted the trees could ride on the branches and wouldn't be left behind. The dead are very important to the Tonga because the living inherit their souls; so leaving their ancestors behind to the floods was really unthinkable for them and behind a lot of the resentment against the dam construction.'

'Were they compensated for leaving their lands?' Luey shook his head sadly at the little guy's question.

'Depends on how you look at it. The new settlements had schools and dispensing hospitals and the land was mostly an improvement on what they had before, except in the south they couldn't, or wouldn't, change their farming methods, despite government schemes with things like irrigation to help them. The Tonga on the Zambian side did better as they were still on colonial status in the late 1950's when the relocations were being made, so they were able to call some shots for a better deal. Different times back then of course. It was the plight of the animals that got more attention internationally of course, and no doubt Uncle Harry's told you a fair bit about Operation Noah?'

He smile good humouredly at the nods and carried on walking around the outside of the circular white walls of the chapel.

'It wasn't quite the conservation success story they wanted - or not at first anyway. Big, big learning curve, even for wildlife experts like Rupert Fothergill who was a game warden, because there'd never been a rescue attempt like it before, except of course in biblical times, hence the name for the programme.'

'Lots of interesting things came to light, such as impalas don't swim, monkeys are great divers and that lions and leopards will swim if they have to, especially when they know there's a bunch of trapped prey just waiting around to be devoured on the islands that were being made as the waters rose. The Operation Noah helpers tried several methods to round the animals up, including banging dustbin lids and trying to herd them into the water. They even experimented using nets - that wasn't such a good idea as it stressed some animals so much that they died, or got so frightened they injured the people who were trying to help them. Warthogs were the worst for that apparently - they're tough little buggers and those tusks are really dangerous and lots of people got slashed pretty badly. Buffs and ellies weren't too bad, unless they had really tiny calves as both species swim pretty well: but there were instances where they couldn't move the smallest elephant calves as their mothers would attack the rescuers and, if they couldn't get the babies off the islands, their mothers eventually killed them rather than abandon them to the water and starvation.'

'Pretty tragic all around as the islands started to get smaller and smaller. Of course the browse and grazing went and the animals had further than ever to swim to the mainland. In the end, especially with the larger, more aggressive animals like the rhino, who weren't keen on swimming, they eventually took to darting them and, from a medical perspective, they learned a hell of a lot about dosing with tranks and recovery times etcetera. In all, north and south side of the lake, they rescued around eight thousand mammals, birds and reptiles, especially snakes, over the course of six years between '58 and '64, as the lake filled up.'

He'd led them back down to the statue again, where Harry would be coming back to collect them. 'Well that about winds things up, unless you have any questions?'

'What about Nyaminyami's missing wife and all these bad-tempered rumblings?' The movie star's husband looked like he might have some sympathies there and Luey nodded sagely, brown eyes twinkling merrily.

'Mostly seismic activity - there's been a good number of earthquakes since the Zambezi filled up Kariba - about twenty that were a magnitude over five on the Richter scale, but you put two hundred billion tons of water where it wasn't before and you're bound to get a few geological repercussions! We're at the tail end of the Great Rift Valley here and have hot springs over in Binga, so there's always been some seismic activity going on up here, well before we had the dam. If the wall gave out then of course it would be a huge disaster, but it's still here fifty odd years later and outputting a good lot of hydroelectricity for Zambia and Zim, so it's obviously in our interests to keep it in good order...'

'... and here comes your ride folks!' he turned to look at Harry's snazzy top of the range 'about town' white pearl land cruiser that he kept for meeting his more exclusive clientele from the airport and for overland transfers. Luey's face split into a huge grin as the game guide got out and walked over.

'Best bib and tucker, Uncle? Your guys have been telling me you have a big shot Hollywood director coming out later?' Harry had been home to change and was looking even more like the big white hunter with a very spiffy-looking leopard skin trim on his mud-coloured canvas drover's hat. He laughed uproariously and caught Luey in a rather lazy armlock, then gave the slightly shorter man a noisy kiss on the cheek.

'Ciao, bello! Come va?'

Luey grimaced melodramatically at the tactile greeting, but was laughing as they parted with friendly shoving. 'Owww! Not so good now, thanks to you, Uncle!'

Harry grinned around at the group. 'Has this cheeky little Eye-tie been looking after you all OK? No luring you off for some dagga?'

'Nah - just telling us about the calabash pipes.' Sophie smiled at the two men as they all made their way over to the smart vehicle. 'My, this is swish!'

'Sweet, huh?' Harry was obviously in a good mood. 'What can I say - gotta love Cruisers!'

'Gotta lurve clients with pots of money then, Uncle!'

'Oh, you know I do!' Harry chuckled indulgently and winked at Phil 'So what d'you all think of this boy then - would he make a good Tarzan, 'cos he surely ain't gonna make it as a movie star if he has to act!'

'Like he'd have to with that bone structure!' drawled the stylist who'd been rather busier looking than listening to Luey's talk. 'So you really are a Luigi then, bello?'

'Sure he is, but he's only half Italian - this is my cousin Carl's youngest!'

'Up yours, Unkie Harold!' Luey scowled prettily, but then his lips curled affectionately again. 'Thank the gods there's no blood relationship - well not too close. And for the record I have never had any desire to be an actor!'

'Cousin Carl with the lions?' Jim stopped eyeing up the land cruiser and looked speculatively at Harry and then Luey's name badge and grinned at the young man's vehement retort. 'Very good instincts Luey - fickle bunch these movie types. I was wondering about the Ogilvy surname and thinking you were too ridiculously glamorous to be a Scot! So it was your mother who was Italian?'

'Yeah - grandpa was an engineer with Impresit who contracted for the dam and he fell in love with Africa. Brought the family out here to settle when mum was only a toddler, although he ended up working all over southern Africa. Uncle Harry was my momma's eldest brother's best mate.'

He'd been glancing surreptitiously at Sophie again and was a little surprised to see her throw Harry a questioning glance at his last remark. The old rogue didn't often give out on his personal life.

'So many interesting stories out here! I expect Jack'll be in his element with you, Harry.'

'That's what young Sophie's sister is hoping for, Jim!'

'Wait - you're Claire Lucas's sister?' Luey looked at Sophie in astonishment, blushing slightly under the suntan and gave a nervous chuckle. 'I used to have such a crush on her whenever she came up here with Grant on weekends - I was trying to think who you reminded me of earlier. Oh! Sorry...' he spluttered to a halt, appalled at what he'd just said.

'Yeah, we noticed you struggling!' Phil observed, rolling his eyes bitterly. Eva shushed him loudly and it was Sophie's turn to flush with embarrassment, though she was laughing like a drain.

'Well, Claire's always been the good-looking one of course - but then I'm much younger than her, so we never really competed for men.'

The wind was getting up and she was pushing her hair out of her eyes when Luey finally took in the tell-tale sparkle of an engagement ring and was about to get annoyed with himself for not noticing earlier when he realised it was on the 'wrong' hand. Or was she one of those annoying females who opted for the continental option of middle finger right hand? The thought barely settled into his head before it went straight out of his fool mouth and the poor woman was flushing like a beetroot belisha beacon.[23] He was almost incoherently apologetic and Harry was practically asphyxiating himself with ill-timed hilarity, which rapidly infected the rest of the group.

'Oh boy, Sophie! You realise you just pulled the most eligible bachelor in Kariba Town, don't you?' Harry, almost crying with laughter, finally managed to spare enough breath to wheeze out the odious notoriety, which wasn't entirely accurate and certainly not deserved as he rarely dated

---

[23] **Belisha beacon** ~ a flashing, usually orange globe light on top of a black and white pole found on pedestrian crossings in the UK and other Commonwealth countries

anymore. Luey had had enough and prepared to withdraw as gracefully as he could manage without actually throttling Harry on the spot.

'Please don't listen to the worst gossip-monger in town!' the agonised brown eyes pleaded with Sophie. 'It was just some wishful thinking on my part - I hope he realises what a very lucky man he is?'

'Huh-who?' Sophie was feeling quite dizzy, not knowing whether to laugh it off or burst into tears and had no idea what to do or say now.

'Your fiancé of course? Your lovely ring?' Her hand went up into her hair again, in alarm more than anything, and her wild raw gaze pierced him to the core as tears threatened in those beautiful blue eyes.

Harry stopped laughing and, finally looking appalled at the outcome of his mocking behaviour, stepped over to Sophie and put his arm around her, shooting a warning look at Luey to hold his tongue. More than ever now Luey wanted to punch his lights out and spoke out again anyway.

'Have I offen...?' But she was coming right back him, shaking her head and trying to pull away from Harry.

'It - it's OK. I over-reacted... You haven't offended me. Truly.' She looked up with some annoyance at Harry. 'And you can stop looking so nastily at him - how was he to know about the silly thing! I'm not engaged to anyone, but it was really nice of you to say... what you said.'

Harry let her go finally and mumbled a subdued apology to them both. The other three had also quietened and, as if by some magical polarity, somehow a gap opened up and Luey and Sophie were left to recover themselves. Luey, though still thoroughly mortified, was the first to regain his composure.

'I want to apologise though. I didn't mean to upset you - I wanted... Well, you're going tomorrow aren't you, so I thought I'd take a chance and then I saw your ring and - jumped to the wrong conclusion, obviously.'

'Not really - back home it doesn't ever get commented on. With it being the wrong hand of course.'

Her laugh was so brittle and sad that his heart went out to her. 'It really is a lovely ring.' He spoke gently, tempted to draw closer to her, but not wanting to make any more wrong moves. He settled for gazing deep into her eyes and just waited for her to take it on, if she wanted to. When she did he was sent spinning off-balance yet again.

'We'll still be here tomorrow. Flying out on Saturday.' Why, why, why did she sound like some stupid wheedling kid! She closed her eyes, hoping it would help. It did, though she still sounded a little unhinged.

'I was engaged, but he died before... Long time ago now. J-just so you know.'

Somehow, despite the awkwardness, she found a shy smile for him because he looked so concerned. Luey was almost speechless and could only look at her in bemusement for the next few moments. Usually he was good at talking to women but then that was before he'd been in love with Sarah. She'd done such a good job on demolishing his dreams of easy domesticity that he'd almost forgotten what is was like to look at a woman with more than passing desire. This girl really did look like her sister Claire though. He'd only been seventeen when he first saw her with Grant Lucas and was he ever jealous of that guy for more years than he cared to admit. He hadn't seen Claire, or Grant come to that, for years now but he'd never forgotten the feeling of looking at someone you knew you could never have and not caring, because it felt so good anyway. The implications of what Sophie had just said finally hit home and he flashed his brightest smile back at her.

'Can I take you out tomorrow then? I have a boat - well, Harry will let me borrow his. He owes us big time!'

She laughed properly at last, her eyes showing her pleasure.

'Yes he does. Let's get him while he's still feeling the shame!'

* * *

Sophie's Diary: Thursday 3rd May (evening) ~ Lake Kariba, Zimbabwe

OMG. Am sitting here stunned so I need to calm down before I make a bigger show of myself than ever at dinner. Luey Ogilvy and Jack Hawkins all in one day is a rather tall order I suppose, but Harry's been brilliant with me ever since he overdid the teasing back at Kariba Heights. Eva, Jim and Jack - it's like the Borgias! They're all absolutely super-polite to each other on the surface, but the underlying hostility! And Phil's been bitching like there's no tomorrow at every opportunity he can grab, which is all the time, naturally. And then there's Harry doing shuttle diplomacy that Kissinger would have been proud of between the lot of them and still taking time out to be nice to me and Luey. Luey's come back to Sanyati with us and is sharing with Harry tonight because he'll need the boat tomorrow to go off with Jack, Keith and Gareth up the gorge again. Luey will be doing another game walk with the rest of us here and then out on the Sanyati pontoon with the rest of us late afternoon and staying over to take us back for the flight on Saturday.

Luey. He's a little quiet and very, very kind underneath all the southern African machismo, but I'm not sure I can cope with the way he's looking at me all the time. Now I've had a chance to recover from this morning I can vaguely remember Claire saying how she had a handsome toyboy Italian admirer up here after they'd got married - it's a small world I suppose. Why couldn't this have happened earlier in the week? He's really so nice, but there's no time to get to know each other. No time - I'd better get showered and make a bit of an effort I suppose...

The Season of the Year

Till I took up to poaching, as you shall quickly hear,
Oh, 'tis my delight on a shiny night in the season of the year.

Traditional English Folksong

Sophie's Diary: Sunday 6th May ~ Murchison Falls, Uganda

I've hardly had a chance to draw breath - what with the late afternoon transfer to overnight in Harare yesterday and then the gruelling light aircraft flight up here from Entebbe. Poor Jim was airsick most of the way out from there, but Phil kept Eva's spirits up and if Eva's happy Jim's not too down, so all in all the journey could have been worse. Of course she's not showing yet, but she does seem to be 'glowing' already! Or maybe it's this glorious place - it really is stunning with the narrow strip rainforest up by the cascades and riverine woodland bordering savannah. Claire's done us proud with this one as it's certainly a unique environment - and as for this Tree Lodge! We're all wishing Harry had come with us for this leg because this really is Tarzan territory with bells on! Well - maybe that's an exaggeration as there's no gorilla watching up here, but these tree-house suites - they're utterly brilliant and almost totally eco-friendly. They've done an incredible job in balancing luxury with green tourism holy grails - natural everything down to the fully bio-degradable loo tissue and hand-made local papyrus and marula[24] butter soap - wonderful scent!

---

[24] **marula** ~ a tree that bears a succulently tart fruit of the same name and is rich in vitamin C (8 times more than oranges). Found all over Africa wherever the Bantu peoples have migrated, as it forms part of their traditional diet. The seeds are also edible.

No Luey though. I wish so much that he was with us still too. It's almost like a dream except I can still feel his touch, his voice - I've not felt anything this strong so quickly. It's frightening in a way - but very exciting as well. We called in at the house he shares with Harry on the way out and he gave me his new mobile phone - still in its box. He's put his old number on it for me and his email contact details - we're going to instant message each other, whatever that is. Never done it before! Phil was convinced Luey was going to 'pin' me! Is that some frat house thingie?. I'm missing him like hell because this has to be one of the most romantic places I've ever stayed at...

'You realise this is the worst timing ever?' Luey reluctantly stopping kissing Sophie, but drew her even closer into his arms.

She sighed contentedly and moved her lips close to his ear, trickling her fingers through his wavy dark hair and speaking in a breathless murmur. 'Hmmm! I'm an albatross I'm afraid.'

'A what?!' His laugh was so sexy! Like a teddy bear's growl.

'Thought you were supposed to be the wildlife expert...' she teased.

He silenced her with another long lingering kiss and then cuddled her into him and gazed out across the starlit lake, resting his chin on top of her head. 'I know what an albatross is, you minx. Just never met one with such a nice beak before! Nice everything...' He trailed his tongue lazily down her neck and she sighed with pleasure and then answered him properly.

'Bird of ill-omen. A bad luck booby!'

'Nothing wrong with your boobies either - and boobys aren't the same species as albatrosses. What are you on about woman? I thought it was only unlucky to kill an albatross - they're lovely birds.'

'Just that my romances always turn out jinxed.'

'Huh! I'm an albatross as well then! We'll just have to hope we cancel out each other's bad luck, won't we? Two wrongs make a right, kinda style?'

'Perhaps we should just go for it then? I have a nice big bed...'

Oh no! She'd blown it she thought, as he gently reached up and unlinked her arms from around his neck and took a step backwards from her. He was still hanging onto her hands though and he smiled lazily at her, stopping her groan of despair with another soft kiss on the lips. The full moon was coming up and he drew her around beside him to look out over the water.

'The rabbit in the moon.'[25] He spoke softly and let go of one hand, only to put his arm around her waist and pull her close to him again. She relaxed into him and laughed without having to ask him to explain. 'Nothing would give me more pleasure Sophie, believe me. It's just... I don't want to rush this? You're so lovely and I'm already there, y'know? Ordinarily I'd have hauled you off to bed as soon as we'd got through dinner - before that even, but...'

His turn to sigh as he looked down into those mesmerising sea-blue eyes. A finger stroked a tendril of silky fair hair away from her face and he kissed her softly on the forehead. Another shiver of arousal went through her body and she nestled into his shoulder and breathed into his ear.

'Well then...?'

He moaned with frustration and put his hands gently, but

---

[25] **the rabbit in the moon** ~ the 'Man in the Moon' looks like a rabbit down in the southern tropics

firmly, on both shoulders and pushed her back slowly so he could look her in the face. 'Will you please let me play the gent here a moment, Sophie? See, Uncle Harry read me the riot act before dinner - about how you'd had such a rough time before, and starting a new job after this and all?' His dark eyes searched hers anxiously, screaming out his desire, but trying to get across how much he wanted this to mean something more than a turbo-charged encounter for both of them. 'So there's that, and after this morning and seeing how you looked when I asked about... you know. This is probably coming out all wrong, but... I haven't had this strong an attraction to anyone for ages - years even. I've got some baggage too, babe and I don't want to rush in and take things that should be cherished and...'

He stopped abruptly as he caught the glint of tears when Sophie squeezed her eyes tight shut and buried her face in his chest. His heart lurched as he felt the wetness and her warm breath above his bush-shirt lapels and his voice sounded thick and fused with a sorrowful passion.

'Oh nooooo... Please, Sophie... sweetheart! I just want this to be special, so, can we go slow, for now? I want you so much, but...'

Her shoulders were quivering and he heard a muffled sob. Again his head dipped to kiss her hair then, all of a sudden, the world shifted and, before he knew what was happening, her wet lips fastened on his and the heat enveloped them. All the words flew away for what must have been hours, surely, until they heard a leopard's cough away in the distance and the world crashed back as they both tensed and pulled away from each other.

'We'd better go back, Soph. Sorry. You're right - we're both albatrosses! But then that means we're made for each other, doesn't it?' He forced a smile onto his face when she nodded compliantly and squeezed his hand gently. Keeping a hold of it, he led her back down to the firepit by the bar. The fire was still burning and there was the sound of laughter and late night talk from the dining boma.[26] Luey slowed and turned to look at Sophie in the firelight, not wanting to be with the others but fearing that she wouldn't want to be alone with him any longer. She gave him a slow, warm smile and his heart leapt as her soft hand came up and caressed his cheek, fingers outspread and trailing gently into his hairline. He leaned into her touch and sighed when she spoke.

'You're right. We shouldn't rush into this, but I want it to be just us together for a little while longer. Please?'

'Whatever you want, Sophie.' It was almost a gasp of relief and he looked up into the night sky, sending up heartfelt thanks to the moon. 'How about some star-gazing? That should keep us out of mischief, huh?'

'Better to pow-wow - safer that way!' She laughed, but it sounded rather wistful and her eyes were serious as she sank to the ground, cross-legged beside the guttering fire.

Looking over at the boma she saw Harry's lean figure come up to the low wall and smiled wryly at Luey as he joined her, knee to knee.

'I see... you want to play cowboys and indians do you?'

---

[26] **Boma** ~ also known as a kraal in South Africa, is a circular woven hurdle-type fence for corralling livestock but also for enclosing buildings or gardens. They are often roofed with thatch where there is a need for shelter from weather, etc.

The dark chocolate eyes were narrowed and glinting with amusement. 'I may have to lasso you later...'

'Not me kemosabe[27] - I'm no native American!'

'Not with that cut-glass Home Counties accent, no. Pity really. I had a thing for Pocahontas types - when I was like eight!'

'Silly! But no - we have a chaperone, I think.' She nodded over at the shadowed outline by the dining hall blaze and the puff of blue-tinged pipe smoke.

They grinned at each other like Cheshire cats and both laughed at themselves.

'Are we allowed to hold hands, Soph? I can't not touch you I'm afraid - self denial's never been my strong suit.' He reached out for her and she took his hands in hers again, stroking along his fingers. He shivered despite the warmth of the hearth and smiled ruefully as she laughed at him.

'De-Nile is a river in Africa - anything else and it's not good for you. I'm a doctor - trust me!'

'Come to that, so am I. Doctor Doolittle - I'm a veterinarian by trade. There you are. A proper introduction at last! See what happens when we take our time.'

'Really?'

The lovely fair eyebrows arched up and he smiled happily at her questioning look. 'Yup - not a game guide like Uncle Harry. The Ogilvy family had to work hard for their living and dad was a stock farmer - having a vet in the family made good economic sense at one time. Family rates - inoculating

---

[27] **kemosabe** ~ from the classic TV show The Lone Ranger. Usually applied by Tonto, the native American scout, to his friend the eponymous hero. It allegedly means 'faithful friend' or 'trusty scout' amongst the Potawatomi clan in the Algonquian language.

against rinderpest[28] cost a small fortune, but... times change. They packed it in and went 'home' to Italy at the tail end of the '90's.'

She nodded, but didn't say anything, glad that he wasn't asking her questions, though she wondered what Harry had been saying to him about her. He seemed to read her thoughts with his next remarks.

'Bad decade in Africa all round. They were chucked out more or less, but luckily mama has family over in Italy still, up near Verona and they farm as well. It would have killed them both to have to repatriate to the UK - they're both a bit rheumatic these days.' He paused and looked tentatively at her before going on. 'Harry told me about your fiancé - with the troubles up in Zyanda. I asked him, after what you said at the dam, and what with Grant and Claire having arranged this gig for him. He didn't say much more than that. Not quite the same thing here but my folks couldn't stay without a whole heap of strife. Some things aren't worth fighting for.'

'But you stayed?'

'I was born right here in Kariba and vets are always in demand, in or out of the game parks. Regardless of skin colour. I... had more ties then as well.' He stopped and looked down for a few moments, frowning, then seemed to come to a decision and pressed on.

'I came back expecting to propose but it all fell apart. So it was all over by 2000. With mama and dad leaving as well it was a hell of a way to see in the new millennium. Since then I've been fancy-free as they say. Just me and the cattle.

---

[28] **rinderpest** ~ also known as 'cattle plague' or 'steppe murrain', rinderpest was successfully eradicated world-wide in 2011. Previously it was endemic in Southern Africa into the late 20th Century prior to saturation vaccination.

The odd tourist every now and then, maybe.' He smiled ironically at her. 'Uncle Harry made it his job to keep me amused outside of work - I work part-time up here with the National Parks and they prefer Europeans for that still, so it kind of tied in with his business.'

'You're a wildlife vet as well?'

'Yeah - I trained some of the time out in San Diego and did an internship in the zoological parks there for three years. Grant helped me get in there actually.'

'Wow! It really is a small world!'

He felt his stomach flip at the smile she gave him. Oh man, this woman was the original irresistible force. He struggled to control the urge to pounce and kiss her breathless, but gave in to a wolfish grin. 'You been out there as well?'

'For holidays a few times - when they've taken the kids over to see the grandparents.'

'Hell! We must have missed each other by weeks at some stage! I was out there until '96'.

'I skipped that year...'

'Damn! We really have got our timing buggered!'

'I'll say!'

'Seconded!' Harry strolled into the circle of firelight, soft-footed as a lion and about as welcome from Luey's glare. Sophie gave Harry a sweet little grin anyway. She was feeling the need to keep herself in check and someone else to talk to was a good distraction, as she was having some difficulty trying to filter out old triggers when Luey had called her 'babe' or wanting to star gaze. Like Tom had done and with a similar expression in his eyes. Déjà vu came along unexpectedly by definition, but the conflicting pain and pleasure that went with the territory was hard to handle after a long and emotive day.

'Is it bedtime already, Harry?' asked Sophie, smirking a little.

'Nope! Phil just went into orbit, so Eva and Jim have shuffled him off to calm down and now 'Hotshot's' talking business with Gareth and Keith, so I needed something to sooth my romantic old soul. How are you both getting on then?' His eyes crinkled with affection, for he loved Luey like the child he'd never had, and it had been a long time since he'd seen him this enthralled over anyone. Ever, actually. He looked closely at the younger man and how he could hardly tear his eyes away from Sophie. This could turn out to be very interesting indeed!

'Mind your own business, Uncle!'

'Like *une maison en feu!*'

Their replies were a counterpoint chorus. Luey grudgingly joined in with the delighted giggles from the other two, as Harry settled himself on the other side of the fire and signalled to the barman, who'd followed him over from the boma, for more beer. The uncertain lovers shuffled around slightly to face the newcomer but, as Sophie moved closer in the process, Luey put his arm around her shoulders and threw a sheepish grin at his Uncle, who was looking at them with open admiration.

'You make a handsome pair - the timing however is truly lousy!' Harry shook his shaggy silver head. 'But you have a whole day on your own together tomorrow. If you want. Eva says she needs some down-time, so Phil's clamouring for a 'spa day,' whatever the hell that is. Anyway, Jim's going to come out with me and the others now - give you two some space to do whatever takes your fancy... Sonya says you can take their motorboat out if you like Luey, so long as you're back in time for sundowners on the pontoon. Ah - cheers Luther. Just the job!' He took the chilly be-dewed bottle from the barman and held it up in salute as Sophie and Luey took theirs.

'Here's looking at you, kiddies! Make sure to ask me about some of the best secluded coves on the Matusadona shore before we bed down, Luey - I'm getting a 4 a.m. call so I'll be out before you're up.'

'Who says he won't still be up before you're out, Harry? I might not let him get to bed at all...'

'Heavens - you young gels today! In my time a lady let the gentleman make all that kind of running!' Harry did a passable impression of Miss Jean Brodie, only just past her prime...

Luey started to laugh and ended up spluttering beer out of his nose as Sophie had to thump his back. When he finally managed to get his breath back, he caught her up around the waist and rested his chin in the crook of her neck, holding her back against him tightly with both arms and one leg crooked around her hips.

'Who needs a lady around here? Gimme a Moll Flanders any day!' He planted a noisy kiss on her collarbone and she wriggled appreciatively in his arms as Harry rolled his eyes.

'I can do without the incest thanks, but if you mean Moll the leopard, then I'll take that as a compliment, I s'pose.'

'You're too young and tender to be Moll the leopard. She's a decrepit old hussy!' Luey whispered hot in her ear.

'I'd better leave now then, shall I?' Harry chuckled indulgently, but made no real effort to move.

'No... No, Uncle you stay put. We already decided we're going to take this sedately - for tonight anyway. And I'll take you up on the secluded coves advice - been a while since I've been out this way. Usually I'm around Bumi Hills rather than Sanyati.' This last was for Sophie's benefit.

'More lucrative work that end of the Lake.' added Harry with a wink. 'Another time you should come out with us for a little cruise on a houseboat - that's great fun! My mate Barry's got a lovely old-fashioned one with a swimming cage - you can swim croc-free that way, off one end and do some fishing on the other. Then off to sleep on the top deck under the stars. Heaven! I stay at home for all my vacations.'

'No wonder!' Sophie nestled back into Luey's warmth, feeling distinctly mellow now and more than a little hazy with happiness. 'It's lovely here - I'm going to be sorry to leave you on Saturday, but I'm contracted for the whole trip. Anyway, it's good fun now Phil's getting into it, although it's just as well 'Hotshot's' not coming with us, I think. I don't really envy you that next part Harry, he seems a bit of a handful.'

'Nah! I've had worse believe me - he's gagging for the bow-hunting anyway, so he'll behave I think.'

'Getting back to his roots - isn't he supposed to be three-quarters Cherokee or something?' Luey was stroking Sophie's hair and trying not to pay too much mind to Harry's being there.

Harry gave a guffaw. 'I'm half Zulu in that case! Isn't some extraordinary percentage of the old world US population descended from Native American stock these days, Sophie?'

'Wouldn't know - racial genetics isn't my bag. Anyway, it's like saying I'm a Viking because I have blonde hair and my family's mostly from Northumberland. Most Brits are pure mongrel - no such thing as a pure-bred Englishman or woman. Never was, really. Same for white Anglo-Saxon

Protestants I'd guess - plenty of Pole and Italian mingling around in there, without the indigenous folks having a look in, necessarily...'

'Different for us Scots, och aye!' Luey chuckled and nibbled on her ear. 'Or should I say, ciao bella? I have impeccable genes on both sides, natch!'

'Watch out for him when he's wearing a kilt, Sophie! He gets very traditional about dipping into his sporran as well.' Harry fussed over his pipe, trying not to smirk too much. 'I prefer the Italian side myself, but then I would. This boy turns after his mama's side of the family actually. His Uncle Giovanni was better looking though...' He puffed heavily, sending a shower of sparks up and waiting for the inevitable riposte.

'Bloody cheek! Mama was the looker of the family!'

'Did I say she wasn't? Gi'anni was more to my taste that's all and your ma was always way too grown up for me anyway, even if she was five years younger!'

'See! See what I have to put with, Sophie!' She was shaking with laughter and he gave her a pleased little kiss on the neck, but then groaned. 'I wish we'd met on your first day here!'

'Well we still have the best part of two days, hon... we don't fly out until about 8 pm on Saturday.'

'Even so. No time at all.' He moaned.

'We must make the most of it then - we don't have to go off anywhere tomorrow.'

'I think we do - if we stay here, I won't be able to keep my hands to myself.'

'I told you that's not a problem...'

Harry coughed with mock discretion. 'Ah, young love! Look Luey - forget what I was saying to you earlier - if it's that strong between you, go for it. You're only here once, remember? The lady's a medic as well - she's fully equipped in the protection department, so no worries there. She kitted Gareth and Keith out back in Livingstone when they did the casino...'

'Oh, Harry! You bloody old gossip!' Sophie didn't know whether to lose it completely or laugh it off, so settled for a blustery fume in the interim. Luey was a little taken aback, but started to chuckle against his better judgement as his Uncle puffed away unconcernedly.

'Hey-hey! Calm down, Sophie - they told me. I didn't ask them!' Harry was grinning widely. 'Besides which you can't take chances on that sort of thing in Africa, 'specially if you're a hetero male. This is the only continent where gay men aren't in too much danger of getting HIV or AIDs, after all!'

Sophie tutted with annoyance and crossed her arms, but said nothing.

Luey decided that he ought to stick up for his Uncle a little. 'Well, that was one of the reasons, Soph. This was all a little hasty and I didn't have time to get some condoms...'

'Oh, shut up - the pair of you!' She tried and failed to frown at them, but ended up giggling as Luey whispered sorry to her, while Harry howled with laughter on the other side of the fire.

'Turn it down over there, boyo!' Gareth's amused voice lilted over the night air from the boma. 'Some of us are turnin' in - somebody said we had an early call or summat?'

Other voices were raised in hilarity and they saw Keith and Jack's silhouettes against the firelight, making ready to head for bed.

'I'm going up in a bit myself, no fear Gareth! Just finishing

215

up playing cupid here and I'm done...' Harry managed to reply, which elicited yet more witticisms from Keith.

'So much for the Italians! Some Casanova you are, Luey! Get a move on, man!'

'Don't answer that!' Sophie hissed at Luey, feeling her face flush a little. 'We'll never hear the last of it!'

Luey was laughing too much to say anything, but that didn't stop Sophie elbowing him in the side. 'Oww! What was that for?!'

'Yo, Luey. I thought you knew a bit about women?' Harry was still laughing, but not that loudly. Again he sucked long on the pipe and blew out a swirl of blue smoke that rose lazily on the night air. 'Sorry guys - *mea culpa*. They're right anyway, even if you two don't have to get up too early. Why don't we get some more beers and walk Sophie up to her rondavel and I'll bugger off, and you can come over to me when you're done, Luey - if you want. I won't wait up for you in other words.'

'Sounds like a plan? Sophie?'

'OK. You'll probably be sleeping on the floor wherever you end up though...' Luey chose that moment delicately teased the lobe of her ear. 'Maybe...' she murmured, as his warm fingers stroked her neck. 'Hmmm... We'll see!' So saying, she got up and looked over to the bar. 'Can we have three more beers please, Luther?'

'Sure, Miss - you want to take them from here, or shall I bring them up?'

'Well, I've finished mine.' She chugged the rest of hers quickly. 'We'll take them - save you a journey!' She handed him her empty bottle with a smile and scooped up the three full ones after he took the tops off.

'Coming then, chaps?' She didn't bother looking to see if

they were following and walked off up the torch-lit path, her ponytail swinging jauntily from side to side as she took the steps two at a time.

'Does that mean the jury's still out? Very mixed signals there!' Harry finally got up, trying not to look too amused as Luey was looking rather pensive all of a sudden.

'Dunno, Uncle Harry. I think I may be kipping on your floor after all. And you were on the right track too - about not rushing things. She's worth waiting for, whether I have to or not.'

* * *

Sophie's Diary: Tuesday 8th May ~ Murchison Falls Tree Lodge, Uganda

Blissful night's sleep! It's not too quiet up here what with being so close to the Falls, but then I haven't had much shuteye the last couple of nights. We're going out late morning for a picnic lunch in the game reserve away from the river. They've promised us tons of lions and kob and oribi - the two antelopes being the local niche species for impala and dik dik, although they're both heavier-built animals. Luey rootled them out for us in the wildlife encyclopædia back at Sanyati. Uganda's new for all of us, so we're feeling pretty excited about going out today.

I do miss having Gareth and Keith with us but not having Jack around is a big plus - I think Jim had 'words' with him when the guys went off with Harry last Friday, but he's not talking about it, or not in front of me. Or to Phil, although he says he'll winkle it out of Eva soon enough. The game guide here's another Brit, Frank Travers - Harry knows him slightly from the hunting circuit and said he's good, so we should have fun. He's married to Parvati, the marvellous chef here - the Afro-Asian fusion cuisine is just scrumptious and she cooks English-style puddings for Frank as well. Mango and marula crumble with delectable egg custard last night! Jim and I were in heaven and I'm going to have to watch my waistline here now Luey and I are an official item! We instant messaged each other last night - a first for me!

There was a light tap on the door lintel. 'You indecent still, Taylor? If so I'm coming in!' Luey's question was rather superfluous as he could hear the shower going, so he grinned to himself and took a seat on the porch instead, enjoying the early morning light on the lake to the north east. Soon enough the sounds of ablutions ceased and he tried again. 'Have you got your clothes on yet, woman - and can I come in anyway?'

'I'm a world champion changer!' Sophie poked her head around the door curtain and stepped soggily outside, wearing a light green khaki T-shirt that came down to mid thigh with white deck shoes. She sat down primly on the cushion edge of the other wicker chair, legs firmly clasped together, causing Luey to laugh out loud in delight.

'Liar! Or do you go commando every day!' He shook his head and raked a hand through his wet hair in frustration. 'Obviously my timing still sucks. Good morning, beautiful! Did you sleep well?'

'Did you?' She countered, smiling happily.

'Me? I always sleep like a hog. So Harry says anyhow. I'm surprised you didn't hear the snoring.'

'Just as well you didn't stay then - I'm a light sleeper. Phil woke me up. He and Eva are camping out in her rondavel until pontoon time - having an aromatherapy day apparently and she's doing his roots as well, so the most they'll be up to is having a swim before breakfast. That means I'm officially off duty and all yours, Doctor Doolittle!'

'Well then. How about you finish getting dressed and we can decide what to do for the rest of the day over some breakfast? I have to get some coffee inside me soonish...'

In the end they decided to take the boat out. Harry had suggested a nice little spot a few creeks to the west and told Luey about Sophie's penchant for water birds, so they took a rod with them from the camp store and went fishing. The idea being to catch their own lunch and stay out until late afternoon. Sonya insisted on packing them some rolls and strong Zimbabwean Cheddar cheese too, 'just in case the perch aren't biting!'

'So no tiger fish up here, Luey?'

'Nope - too shallow. They prefer the deeper parts of the lake. Not much eating on them either. Young perch are better for a meal for two - adult fish are bloody huge, but this creek's ideal for juveniles.' He was concentrating on baiting the line and Sophie smiled idly to herself as she watched him at the fiddly work, his strong tanned fingers securing the bait firmly.

'I warn you, I'm rubbish at fishing - and I don't do the gutting and cleaning either.'

'Wussy English girl!' He glanced up briefly, flashing her a big grin. 'Don't worry bella, you're in the hands of an expert! Uncle Gi'anni and Harry had me out with them when I was knee-high to a locust and mama always made us clean the catch before it went on the braai.'[29] Finishing off deftly, he popped the line into the water and handed her the bins. 'Now - you shush and do some wee birdie-spotting. Leave the fisherman stuff to me!'

'Yes, bwana!'[30] She said in a whisper and then trained the glasses on the rocky bank to start with. 'Will there be crocs up here?'

'Hmmm? Oh - here maybe, but we'll have lunch a bit

---

[29] **braai** ~ Southern African word for an outdoor grill or barbecue.

---

[30] **bwana** ~ Swahili word meaning master or boss.

further upstream, where it's too steep for them. They're probably off in the lake getting a late brekkie now, but we'll see some later I expect. You like crocs?'

'Out of the water - scary in it, especially if I'm in an inflatable.'

'Well no probs with this little bit o' kit. Just don't dibble your fingers about in the water without checking what's under us - they've been known to nip you even as the boat's moving.'

'No worries - I'm very attached to all my appendages thanks.'

Luey pursed his lips and resisted the temptation to come out with the predictable comeback, so they sank into a comfortable silence for a good while.

'Whoa-hah!' Luey gave a great whoop as the line jerked strongly. 'Bugger! I think I gotta catfish!' He looked over at Sophie in a slight panic as the boat wasn't too big and they had electric catfish locally. 'Can you see if they have a keep net in the box - I might need it.'

Sophie yanked the cover off and grabbed the net just as Luey gave another shout and then howled in relief.

'Woooo! Oh, man! S'OK it's a Butter!' He gave a grunt as he reeled back hard and pulled the fish's whiskery head clear of the water for a moment. 'Urgh! I think I can land it without the net thanks. Just try to... keep - out - of the - way. Hoooowrr! He's heavy!'

Sophie quickly nipped around so she was standing behind him. 'How's this? Shall I help you to pull back?'

'Ooof!' He gasped, but shook his head. 'Best not... Just - stay behind me if-yuh-can...'

He was bracing hard now, his arms bent, tight into his body and kept jerking his upper torso and the rod high and reeling back quickly as he leant over in a wide crouch, keeping his centre of gravity low. Sophie had to force herself to concentrate on where he was moving, rather than on his tensed biceps and the outline of his buttocks and straining thigh muscles under his beige shorts. She squealed with excitement when he again yanked the catfish's head out of the stream, just a few yards off the boat.

''Kay - he's comin' in!' Luey grunted and hauled hard on the rod, flipping the big-mouthed fish into the boat. His arm snaked out and his fist thrust down into the gullet to get the hook and then he held the catfish out at arm's length, dangling hopelessly and hardly moving after the struggle. ''Geez! That must be nearly two hundred pounds worth there!' Luey panted and put it down on the deck fairly gently, then groped around in the box for a hand-axe and a two foot square hardwood board. 'How are you with blood sports, Soph?' His dark eyes searched hers rather anxiously. She turned around abruptly to face the opposite direction.

''oooo! Just get it over with quickly!'

There was a scraping sound as Luey put the board beneath the catfish and a few moments of fumbling sounds as he got a good grip and then a rather grisly thwack of the blade. There were a few fleshy sounds and more splashing as he dumped the innards over the side and then a nauseating, grinding snap as he broke the top of the severed spine completely to make sure it was dead, or at least pain free.

'Is it safe to look yet?' She asked querulously.

'And here I was thinking I'd got myself a girl with a strong stomach!'

He came up behind her and his lips brushed her gently on the cheek. 'All done!'

She turned and kissed him hard on the mouth. His arms enfolded her waist briefly but then he released her with a sigh.

221

'Gotta tidy up - the flies'll be a bloody nuisance else. Luckily...' He gave the box a good yank by the handles on the side and it parted company with the wall of the boat and flipped outwards on its hinges to reveal a long plastic trough, that was just about big enough to take the catfish. '... Sanyati Fishermans Lodge are a top class operator! Neat, huh?' He laughed as he slung his catch into it and folded the box back up again. 'Well I reckon that'll pay for my board and lodgings up until tomorrow, and we'll have pan-fried, black-peppered Butter Catfish for dinner tonight! Sonya'll be pleased with me! But...' He sprawled out on the back bench and patted the seat for her to come and join him. '... it's cheese sarnies for lunch for us after all. Will that be all right for you, sweetheart?' Sophie laughed and sat down beside him, running a slim hand up his arm and pulling him in for another, deeper kiss.

'That'll be just right. Don't know that I'm that kind of hungry yet though...'

'Oh, really?' Luey's eyes were glinting challengingly and she made to move closer, but he twisted out of her grip and turned to start the motor.

'Time for a little dip first then - put an edge on that jaded appetite of yours...' He winked at her salaciously, but slapped her hands away as she tried to steal another kiss. '... plenty of time for that if madam's patient for five more minutes.'

'You're a hard man, Luey Ogilvy!' Sophie's pout was short-lived as he put his arm around her shoulders again, taking the tiller firmly and steering out into the middle of the creek and heading upstream.

'That's your good luck then, babe. Wait until you see what Uncle Harry's come up with for our dining venue!'

'Oh my! It's perfect!'

Luey smiled fulsomely at her as they ascended the natural staircase beside the series of waterfalls that washed down the cliff. 'Well it is, just about - it had a little bit of help and it's not finished yet though. Apparently Sonya wants to use it as a honeymoon suite, so they're working on the accommodation still.'

'How the hell will they have accom.... Oh!'

'Bloody hell! That is fantastic! Shall we?' Luey grinned and grabbed her hand.

They slipped past the constantly moving curtain of water and entered into the little pool and cave-like indentation hidden behind it, in a kind of recessed shelf in the limestone cliff. It was open to the sky above via a narrow wind-sculpted chimney that had huge gnarly roots and lianas and the shrubby branches of a fig tree growing up through. They both walked into the rocky chamber, mouths agape at the concept. Some decking had been put over the stony floor already and there was a kind of boulder staircase arrangement into the dark green pool, with the scrolling water patterns glinting off the cave walls. The falling curtain was quite ethereal in front, so they could look out onto the other side of the gorge with a glimpse of the lake further off to the side.

'Wonderful!' Both their voices echoed off the walls of the water cavern and they smiled happily at each other.

Luey swiftly unbuttoned his shirt and looked at Sophie encouragingly. 'Harry says it's guaranteed bilharzia[31] free -

---

[31] **Bilharzia** - is a parasitic disease also known as schistosomiasis or snail fever, as it is spread by flukes-infested freshwater snails in less developed countries on every continent except Europe and Australia.

look! They're growing gopo berries[32] in here too! Ah! This is brilliant!'

'I didn't bring my cossie - but neither did you, I suppose?' Sophie was giggling as she squirmed out of her T-shirt and bra and wrestled with her trousers. Luey was already naked and in the water and splashed at her playfully.

'Who needs them here! The water's lovely - hurry up! Look... you can stand up just abou...'
His dark head disappeared abruptly in a flurry of bubbles as he backed away to let Sophie down, then bobbed up again with a distinctly predatory grin closer to the foamy sill of the waterfall. Sophie took a few steps towards him laughing and, as she was out of her depth sooner, she stroked lazily over to him. His arms snaked around her waist and he circled around and pulled them both to a place where he could stand again, leaning against the rocks, holding her steady.

'Now isn't this nice, Miss Sophie...?' He nibbled tenderly at her ear as her arms folded behind his shoulders and her hands tangled themselves in his wet curls.

'Gorgeous - like you, my Fisher King.' She leant her forehead against his chin and sighed, her breath tickling his throat and the top of his chest that was just exposed to the cool air.

'But I forgot to bring the lurve insurance...'
He ducked his head around and kissed her deeply, then pulled her closer to him, his hands caressing down her back to the top of her thighs and lifting so she wrapped her legs around him, pressing his hardness against her belly. 'There

---

[32] **gopo berry** - the climbing African soapberry plant is lethal to the water snails that are carriers of the bilharzia fluke. It is also used in shampoo to kill head lice and in containing mosquito populations. In addition it has mildly contraceptive properties being a natural spermicide, and can be used for general hygiene.

are other ways, aren't there?' He murmured, his voice soft and thick with desire right in her ear, making her shiver. 'Half the fun of the mating season's in the display. We can postpone the actual moment a little longer, can't we?'

Her lips ghosted over his neck and her skin tingled as his hands glided upwards to her shoulders. He gently peeled her away slightly so he could drop his mouth to close around a convenient nipple, suckling delicately, his tongue flickering softly. 'Whatever you want, bwana!' She breathed raggedly as she melted away for him.

* * *

'Isn't that a fire over there?'
Jim's voice cut into Sophie's reverie sharply. She followed the line of his bins to the small open copse of acacia off on the distant hillock. There was the merest whiff of thin white smoke and a tell-tale orange flicker through the tall grass. Hussain, the spotter took the binoculars from beside Frank, who had been vaguely headed in that direction for a couple of minutes having spotted vultures and marabou storks by the trees. A flurry of rapid Swahili passed between the white and black guides and Frank went off the little trail and headed towards a stand of papyrus by a feeder stream that partially screened the acacias from view. He cut the engine and skewed around to face them as Hussain jumped down and headed into the reeds, still carrying the bins.

'We may have a bit of a dodgy situation here guys, so Hussain's checking it out.'

'It was a fire wasn't it!' Jim kept his voice as low as Frank's, who nodded grimly.

'If it's what we think it is, I'm going to have to radio the wardens and we'll need to wait around for them to get here - maybe an hour or so. Main thing at the moment is to stay in sight of the trees, but not look too interested, which is why I pulled in over here as there's some hippo about and birds, so we can look at those and have lunch maybe - depends on what Hussain finds out.' Frank gave them a not very relaxed smile and Phil hissed out what everyone else was thinking.

'Are we in some sort of danger here?'

'Probably not, but we're not about to take any chances.' He patted the rifle on the seat beside him and then grinned more apologetically. 'It's a two-legged mammal we're worried about, not a four-legged one. Hussain's trying to see how well-armed they are...'

Phil opened his mouth to say something, but Jim cut in sharply. 'Shut it Phil - let them do their job.' As he spoke, Hussain appeared again and jogged over to Frank's side of the vehicle. Again there was a swift exchange in Swahili and then Hussain climbed into the central tier of the land rover, standing immediately in front of Jim and politely asked him to go and sit in the front passenger seat . As Jim complied, Frank handed the rifle back to Hussain, donned the earphones and flicked the radio on, then spoke rapidly into the mic' in Swahili again.

Sophie only had a smattering of the language, but she caught one word she recognised 'mwizi'. 'Oh my! I think it's a poacher. Hussain?' She got up, grabbing Jim's bins, but Hussain motioned sharply for her to sit back down again.

'Please, miss. Pretend you are looking at the hippos in case he looks over here.' He was looking in the direction of the river himself now and holding the rifle rather casually and plainly visible over his shoulder, with the barrel pointing upwards. 'Frank needs to tell the wardens our position and then we're going to go over and arrest him - he's only armed with a panga and he's getting ready to leave, so we may have to move fast in a moment.'

As Hussain was explaining, Frank ripped the earphones off and started the engine again. He reached down beside his seat and the door and pulled up a shotgun, cracked it open then handed it to a rather startled Jim. 'Just hold it in plain sight - there's no shot, but he won't know that! Don't worry - just close it up and point it if I tell you to, OK?' As Jim took it from him, Frank was reversing back the way they'd come in and glanced back at the others. 'It'll be OK folks. The Wardens are already on the way over - this chap's mates are all in custody and Hussain's certain he's not got a gun.'

He put the land rover back into off-road mode and began to drive at a regal speed towards the trees again.

'No problem, folks.' Hussain was holding the rifle across his body now and leaning unconcernedly on the roll bar and scanning the horizon as though he was doing his usual job, but he looked over his shoulder and smiled toothily at Eva and Phil in the back. 'Just hold tight if Frank has to put his foot down.'

'Shall we put our seat belts on?' Phil's voice was laudably calm, like he was contemplating a trip down Rodeo Drive. Sophie resisted the urge to giggle as she was feeling more than a little hyped.

'If it makes you feel better, of course.' Hussain shrugged and went back to staring out across the grasslands.

As they drew closer, still keeping to a modest 'game-viewing' speed, it looked like the fire had been put out. But then they all got a look at a brief grubby blue blur of movement beside one of the acacias and then gasped as Frank picked up speed slightly, when a lanky figure broke cover into a slow jog with a strange twist of his arms.

'He's dropped the panga! Give him a warning shot Hussain! Cover your ears, folks.' Frank spoke urgently as he changed course slightly to overtake the man, who seemed to be in some difficulty and wasn't making much progress. The powerful hunting rifle cracked out as they put their hands to their ears and then Phil grasped Eva's hand comfortingly as Frank accelerated and swung around the now stationary and visibly quavering figure of the poacher, who had gone into a low submissive crouch with his skinny arms covering his sweaty balding head.

Hussain jumped down holding the rifle low and pointed towards the man and spoke harshly in clear English.

'Get up! Keep your hands stretched out in front of you where I can see them!'

Sophie heard Eva gasp as the man slowly rose, clearly in some pain. He must have been well over six foot tall, but he was as thin as a whippet and shaking uncontrollably. The grubby blue vest he wore was stained with sweat and full of moth holes and ill-repaired tears. Sophie's trained medical eyes travelled down his lower body, over equally filthy and threadbare grey canvas shorts that concealed his most of his long thighs. But even she was shocked at the state of his knees and shins, which would probably have matched the rest of his slender body if they had not been so swollen.

As his poor condition became apparent, Hussain lowered the gun and switched to Swahili. The man replied in the same language in a desiccated, frightened voice. As Hussain questioned the man, Frank switched the engine off and turned to Jim with a smile.

'You can stand down, sport. Well done! ' He held out his hand for the shotgun, which Jim handed over with some relief. 'Go back to your seat again now. This guy'll have to come in the front with me and Hussain.' He turned round to look at the others and gave them a cheesy grin. 'Exciting, huh? Poor chap won't give us too much trouble - I'll give the wardens another call to let them know we've got him.'

'I don't know about that, Frank - he's on the verge of collapse, poor bastard.' Sophie unbuckled her seat belt and pulled her bag over to get some water for the man.

'He's tougher than you think, doc. Just relax - let Hussain look after him.' Frank put his hand firmly around Sophie's wrist as she went for the zip and held her gaze knowingly when she looked like she would pull away. Satisfied that she wasn't going to make any more fuss, Frank went for the 'mic again, this time leaving the earphones off.

'*Asante. Kuwa huko hivi karibuni.*[33] Over!' The crackly exchange ended, so Frank started the engine as Hussain assisted the man into the middle seat and jumped in after him, sitting with the gun on safety across his lap. The rank peppery smell of unwashed fear flowed over them and Sophie heard a muffled gag and then Phil's cologne spray going.

'Shut up! He can't help it!' She hissed softly, then leaned forward to try and get a better look at the man's swollen legs, wondering how he'd got them into such a state. Frank was heading for the acacias where they'd first spotted him. As they drew up under the shade, the large mob of vultures and marabou storks that had stayed put when the man ran off backed off a little, but gradually crept back again and carried on picking at the long grass. Sophie was beginning to guess why they were congregated there, but tapped Frank's shoulder when he switched the engine off again.

'Look - I know you have to handle this, but he must quite old and he seems to be in a lot of pain...'

Frank held his hand up semi-apologetically, but cut her off

---

[33] Thank you. Be there soon

sharply. 'Sorry, doc. He'll be all right - it's just from walking down here. He probably came out of South Sudan.'

'That's over a hundred miles north of here! At least let me give him some clean water...'

'And some soap...' Phil muttered darkly. Eva shushed him and Sophie gave him a filthy look, but Frank was coming back at her.

'He's not lacking water here - or food come to that. Please, Sophie - leave it to us and the wardens. They'll be here soon. If we hadn't got here first, they'd have picked him up in a half hour or so.' Frank wasn't taking any more argument and motioned to Hussain. 'Best get him down to show us where the cache is.'

Hussain nodded and got out, again helping the old man down. They both walked slowly over to the small marshy stream that ran behind the acacias, as Frank pulled out the cool box from under the seat and plonked it between Sophie and Jim.

'This won't take long so why don't you folks grab some beers and start lunch. Watch the vultures - there's some Lammergeyers over there, if you've never seen 'em before.' He nodded towards a pair of huge vultures with buff coloured heads and breasts that were stalking around, slightly apart from the other smaller vultures.

'T.I.A. time with bloody knobs on!' Sophie fumed under her breath, grabbed the bottle-opener and started to open the beers, passing them to Jim to hand around.

'T.I.A?' Eva asked, whilst pointing frantically to a coke.

'Sorry...' Sophie put the fourth beer back unopened, pulled the top off the cola and gave it to Eva. She took a quick swig of her own beer and explained. 'This is Africa... T.I.A. It means shut up and don't ask too many questions, because this is the way it goes and there's nothing you can do.' She

230

sighed and angled around so she could look at the birds, but she wasn't in much of a mood for spotting and took another big mouthful of beer.

'Well there's no need to snap, honey - if the guy's come here to poach the wildlife he deserves what's coming to him, doesn't he?' Phil reached over and grabbed a delicate little samosa out of its pristine waxed paper and looked appealingly at her.

'Look. He'll not see sixty again I think and he's got a whopping case of œdema from having to trek over a hundred miles, across hot rough terrain, to work like a dog drying bushmeat out here in the middle of nowhere with nothing but a panga to play butcher with... What d'you think the vultures are hanging around for? The price of ivory to go up!'

'Bushmeat?! Ewww!'

'Nothing endangered. Just food to sell in the local markets.' She sighed again. 'Sorry - yes, he shouldn't be doing it here on a reserve, so they have to police it, but... Oh what's the use. At least he'll probably get a ride some of the way back home. It's just bugs the hell out of me that they treat them like dirty little children.'

'Can't solve all the world's problems, Sophie.' Jim offered her a samosa. 'But then you've worked out here before, so I suppose you've seen some nasty stuff in your time?'

'The thin edge of a massive wedge, yes. It's all so much sticking plaster half the time.' She took the pastry, then looked over at a fight that had broken out between the marabous. A flash of white skull and dark, ridged horns flipped up into the air. She laughed bitterly.

'What is it, Sophie?' Eva turned to look at the commotion.

'They were taking hartebeest. It's open season and they've been doing it for thousands of years. Nothing changes.'

Much, much later. Bit depressed now. Frank's talking to me again more or less. I apologised anyway - didn't ask what would happen to the man, but hopefully they won't send him to prison. Frank said that the others weren't in a much better state, just younger. They weren't a super-organised gang anyway and the wardens didn't find any serious automatic weapons on any of them. Apparently they said they didn't know they were on a reserve - big lie probably, but as they were only after meat for the pot, not even the market and they all came from one village up near the border with Sudan, they most likely weren't serious thieves. Frank thinks they'll drive them out to the north gate of the park and let them walk home with just slapped wrists. I wish I could believe that, but I bet they were given a sound beating before they put them on the truck. And of course the biltong our chap was making will be sold anyway. I suppose some of the proceeds will find its way into the local economy - they have an arrangement here so the villages can take a small percentage of game. It'll get channelled back in some way anyhow.

Managed to chat with Luey again before dinner. He's got his interview date for the job - Tuesday next week. Same day the hospital opens officially. They've given him a few more details about the various projects they have going and it looks like there's a couple that might be in northwest Tanzania...

* * *

The sound of quiet sobbing intruded on his dreaming and he pushed himself into consciousness, reaching out for a table light that wasn't there. Instead his hand swept onto a dishevelled, still warm pillow. Luey sat up with a start, remembering where he was and rolled over towards the door.

'Sophie, love - are you OK?' He got up hastily, seeing a

shadow move through the moonlit window and padded out onto the veranda. She was curled up in a ball on the wicker chair, but turned to look up at him. Her face was streaked with wet silver trails and he had a sick feeling deep inside that he'd somehow upset her without knowing it.

'Hey there...' He strode over to her and sat on the edge of the chair, pulling her gently into his arms and letting her nestle into him, feeling the wetness on his neck as she hugged him to her. He kissed the top of her head carefully and waited a few moments until he couldn't remain silent any longer.

'Are you alright?' He asked again, the worry making his voice shake a little as he rubbed her bare back, slipping his warm hand under the thin cotton jersey. 'Can you tell me?'
She nodded slowly, but made no other move. He waited patiently, though he was sure his heart must have been pounding, as he wondered where all this was coming from. It had been so perfect earlier and even better as they'd both sunk down into a pleasantly exhausted sleep, holding each other close.

'Just a bad dream...' Finally she could trust herself not to sob snottily all down him. She gave a pinched little laugh and looked at him, her eyes still a bit teary. 'I get them sometimes. But I thought...' She tailed off miserably and looked at him contritely.

His thick dark brows drew together, his face full of concern and he reached up and put a finger gently on her bloody bottom lip. 'Please don't tell me I did that?'

'Oh!' She squeaked and drew back from him slowly. 'No - that was me. That happens as well.' She hung her head and went back to burrowing into him.

He held her closer and waited again. After a few minutes had passed though, he gave a slight shiver and murmured softly. 'Wind's getting up. We can stay out here if you want, but I'll have to put some clothes on.'

'Let's go in then. Back to bed.' She started to uncurl, but he slipped an arm under her knees and lifted her up easily.

'Relax, Soph. Let me look after you?' She'd tensed up, but his soft gruff voice soothed her and she did as she was told, winding her arms around his shoulders and neck. He laid her gently down on the bed and pulled the sheet up over her.

'Won't be a tick - getting some water for your poor little chewed up lip.' He whispered and kissed her on the forehead.

He turned the oil lamp back up a little and was back with a glass and a soft towel almost immediately. Sitting down beside her on the bed, he patted expertly on the torn skin, his face a soft golden colour in the dim light.

'I didn't bite it too badly. Bit of salty water on it at breakfast and it'll be fine.'

'Shut up, woman - I'm doing the doctor stuff for now.' His teasing words were belied by his soft voice and his eyes were brimful with loving care.

She smiled, then winced so he took his hand away for a moment. 'Now what did you want to do a silly thing like that for?' He grinned soppily at her and went back to dabbing away the last of the blood, looking at the cut intently and stroking the hair off her face with his other hand as he leaned over her.

'I feel like a little girl now.' Her eyes were still watery as he kissed his fingertip and feathered it onto the side of the wound.

'Is that good or bad?' Luey looked at her seriously, going back to stroking her hair.

'Good mostly. Although it may make you a dirty old man if you get back into bed with me...'

Her eyes began to glint saucily, so he went with the joke and buried his head in the pillow beside her, coiling his fingers into his hair. 'La belle dame sans merci - what have I done to deserve this!' He wailed hoarsely, then turned to face her with a wink. 'Budge up Taylor - it's emotionally exhausting being with you and I need my beauty sleep, even if you don't!'

He slid his arm under her shoulder and she snuggled into his chest, stroking her fingers through the dark coarse hair. It tickled slightly but he lay still, enjoying the sensation and relishing the shared warmth.

'You have a very strong heartbeat, Mr. Ogilvy. You're not a Leo are you?'

'What?' His brow furrowed and he looked at her quizzically.

'Lionhearted... magnificent mane... keen on sex... good with cubs too, I expect...' she chuckled softly and lightly scraped her fingernail across his nipple.

'Mmmm... is this an audition to get yourself an alpha male, or are you just asking me what my star sign is?'

She smiled more carefully this time. 'Both I suppose. So when is your birthday?'

He rolled his dark eyes dramatically, then fixed her gaze intensely. 'October 31st - I'm a warlock. And a Scorpio. So what does that make you I wonder, Doctor Taylor?'

'I'm a midsummer baby - well midyear's day. June 21st. So we're both water signs more or less...'

He laughed. 'Just as well, since we're albatrosses too.' He pulled her closer and kissed her tenderly on the corner of her lips. The shining warmth in his eyes was like melting chocolate. 'I guess we're stuck with each other then. Would I scare you off if I said I love you?'

'Do you?' She breathed the question onto his cheek, but

gave him no time to reply. 'Because I'm pretty much there with loving you, Luigi Ogilvy. So no, I'm not scared at all.'

'Then I do love you, Sophie Taylor - but we're going to need a hell of a lot more insurance cover...'

His warm hand roamed over her waist and headed south, fingers caressing her rounded flesh. 'But first I think we need to do some more talking, don't you?'

'Talking's for fainthearts, not passionate Scorpios...'

'No, Soph. I'm serious. Why're you crying over a bad dream?'

'Not now...' She tried to kiss him but he drew back slightly, his jaw tightening with determination.

'We can do this in the morning if you'd rather, but if we're going anywhere with this then we need to be straight with each other, OK?' He smiled at her softly and pulled her closer. 'I want everything in plain view, babe. You've had a rough time and I've got scar tissue too, so I can go first if you like?'

She put her hand up to his face and traced over his cheekbone and down his jawline. 'Timing's still off, Ogilvy - but you're right. In the morning.' She tentatively brushed her lips against his and cuddled into him more. 'I need some more kissing better first, please.'

This time he was awake before her, but he made no move to get up. They were spooned together and he moved his head closer to hers, so he could breathe her warmth. The sunrise wasn't far off but the birds weren't making too much row yet, so he was content to lie still, listening to the wind in the trees and mulling over whether to tell her about Sarah yet, or concentrate on his future plans, which in some respects matched Sophie's. His gut told him that her nightmare was linked into her past. So, seeing as how she hadn't pushed him away at all and it was obvious that it wasn't going to interfere with what was growing so sweetly between them, he decided to leave the future to tend to itself for now and be upfront with her about his own previously disastrous love life. This time things couldn't be more different and that pleased him. He wasn't one for dwelling on the past, or a believer in history repeating itself come to that, but from what Harry had said about Sophie, he wondered how much she'd been able to move on from the tragedy that still seemed to haunt her.

He must have dozed off again as it was just light and she was stirring in his arms. Her breast brushed against him and his hand rose in reflex, pulling her close.

'Morning...'

He nibbled her neck and licked gently. 'Hello there, bella.'

'Thank you for a lovely night...'

'Ditto. No more bad dreams?'

'No - just the one full Technicolor™ feature. You wore me out for a repeat.'

There was a light tap on the door lintel. 'Coffee, Miss!'

'Oh! Thanks - can I have an extra cup please. I have a guest.' Sophie called out, still sounding sleepy.

'No problem, Miss.'

They heard the tray being put down on the table outside and waited a few moments before collapsing into giggles.

'Brazen hussy! What about my rep?' Luey teased, pulling her around and kissing her firmly.

'Oww! Watch the lip!'

'Oh - I'm sorry, babe.' He planted a softer kiss on her chin. 'But shush - I bet you he's only gone to get my cup from Harry's room!'

Sure enough they heard another creak on the veranda and both began to laugh silently, hugging each other in delight.

Sighing, Luey disentangled himself. 'Shower time and

then I'll have to go and borrow one of Harry's shirts.'

'What about coffee?'

'Shirt first, but I'll be back, no worries. You could come in the shower with me though...'

'So I could - is that an order?' He was getting out of bed, but turned to slap her bottom lightly. 'If you like! Plenty of room in there for two...'

By the time she'd dressed, put her hair up and settled herself out on the veranda, he was on his way back from Harry's with a fresh shirt slung over his shoulder.

'Ciao, bello! You're a sight for sore eyes, aren't you?' She smiled at him affectionately as he took the other chair and grinned at her.

'Need coffee - no talk yet!'

'You're not on a Tarzan kick as well, are you? Phil might get jealous of me!'

He took a big gulp of coffee and sighed hugely. 'Is your name Jane? I know I'm his type...' He stuck his tongue into his cheek and watched her blush.

'Pig!'

'Minx!' He laughed and swigged the rest of his coffee greedily. 'Harry's going to ask Sonya to send breakfast up here for us and he's not taking the others out until ten. If you want, we can stay here all day and I can help you pack?'

'Goodness - you're determined to pow-wow aren't you?' She sounded a little cross but she relented when he frowned right back at her. 'OK. Don't worry. We do need to talk lots now but it's not something I'm looking forward to. Anyway, I need to check with Eva and Jim as well, to see if they're OK with me goofing off again, but I can catch them as they come down - or after breakfast.'

'Well, there's Jim now...' He got up but before he could

call up to him, Sophie frantically motioned him back down. 'I'm not going to impugn your honour, Soph!' He sat back down with a grin, as she looked quite flustered.'

'Not that - it's a professional thing that shouldn't be shouted all over the camp.' She in turn got up and walked over to the couple's rondavel.

When she got back, Luey was fully dressed and looking rather sheepish. He greeted her with a bear-hug .

'I'm sorry I'm such a git. I just want to get this right before you go tonight?' He whispered softly to her as he released her.

She smiled up at him. 'You're not a git. I love it when you get all bossy with me, but work has to come first for now.' She flopped back into her chair. 'The good news is that I'm off the hook yet again, so I'm all yours until we have to go to the airport. Will you be able to wave us goodbye?'

He nodded soberly. 'I don't have to get the boat over to Bumi for Harry until tomorrow luckily. Sonya's going to do their transfer from here after lunch.'

'Well we have until then to go over my gory past in that case. In fact, we could probably get that done before breakfast, as you already know some of it from motor mouth...'

He laughed. 'Harry? Yeah, well don't forget he's related to the Ogilvys on his mother's side - and I've inherited the nosey gene as well. I intend to give you a thorough grilling, but I'll let you do the same in return. We have a deal then?'

'Like you said last night - we need everything in plain view. You want to do the dream analysis first?'

He nodded. 'Let me get us some water - thirsty work dream divination, I expect.'

'Yes, in a manner of speaking...'

The dream had been the same as always, except at the end

of it and that had been what had made her get up in such distress. She took a glass straight away and let Luey pour from the carafe for her, then roughly outlined what had happened with Tom and Terry and then the dream itself. Luey listened without interrupting her, realising she needed to get it out in one go. More and more she realised that they really did have a lot of natural rapport, but it was just so damned quick. It was harder trying to explain how the dream had been different last night, as she was still really trying to work through it herself. She tried again to get across what had changed last night and what it might mean in the cold light of day.

'I've been having it for so long really and of course, this being my stock in trade, I can usually ride it out OK. Up until I came out here to Africa again I actually haven't had it for a good few years. It was really what Tom said to me at the end that had changed...' She paused, searching for the right words, so Luey's sudden question threw her for a moment.

'You always have the same conversation?' He flushed slightly, but he wasn't sorry he'd asked because he was getting really spooked by what she was telling him. His thoughts about her being haunted seemed to be a little too close to the truth.

'More or less.' She didn't want to have a detailed discussion about post traumatic stress disorder with him just now, so she cut to the chase. 'It's part of the therapy - you organise your memories of how the trauma presents, so it's not uncommon to get this kind of echoing sub-consciously.'

'OK. Sorry. Go on, please.'

'Well - usually Tom says something like 'It's OK Soph – I'm looking after her.' Meaning the baby and then he says 'Don't worry babe.' ... and you've been calling me babe...'

'Oh, hell! Soph... Sophie...' He squirmed, as she looked almost stunned at what she'd just said. 'You should have said something to me...' He leaned over and reached out for her hand and heaved a sigh of relief as she let him take it.

She was shaking her head at him now. 'No - no, that's OK. It was touching - attractive even, though it made me cry at first when you... Oh please... No! Luey...'

It was her turn to squirm, as there were actually tears in his eyes. He'd pulled his hand away from her, so she hastily got up and knelt in front of him as he put his face in his hands. She gathered him into her arms and kissed his ear. 'It's OK. Truly it is. Luey... Look at me? Please? It's OK. You've been healing me, I think?' The words were soft, whispered into the thick dark hair. Gradually the tenseness went out of him and she drew back slowly as he put his hands down. She groaned as she saw how wretched he looked, then kissed each of his eyes as the tears escaped.

'Sorry...'

'Don't be...' She spoke softly and cupped his cheek in her hand. 'Let me tell you what he said this time, before you go wimping out on me anymore.' Her eyes scanned his with concern, willing him to see that he hadn't hurt her. He nodded and tried to smile.

She took his hand in hers and sat back again. 'He said 'Don't worry - we'll be OK, Soph. He'll look after you now, babe.' I think he - I mean the dream, meant that you will look after me. And you have, Luey. You have been, ever since we met up at the dam.'

'I have?'

''Course you have! Getting cross with Harry... Protecting me from phantom electric catfish... Taking me to romantic waterfalls... Making me doorstep cheddar sandwiches for lunch. Last night. Everything...' She felt like crying too now, except her tears were happy ones.

'You're sure? Not just saying this to make me feel better?'

'Nope. Cross my heart. Us albatrosses have to stick together you know.'

He was beginning to smile and it turned into laughter when she told him to pull himself together, because Luther was carrying the breakfast tray up to them.

He gulped down the last of the mango juice and just sat there studying the amazing lady who'd crashed through all his defences so unexpectedly and so very thoroughly. That it had been lust at first sight there was no doubt, what with his besotted teenage memories of her sister, but he had also realised that it was because she was almost the exact opposite of Sarah Ndaemin, both physically and emotionally, and that was how she'd wound herself around his heart so quickly if he was truthful. After what Sophie had just told him about herself, he was anxious to clear the decks and dispel the last remnants of the woman who'd betrayed him so callously seven years ago. All he wanted now was to get on with ensuring that Sophie could be his entirely and hang everything else. In fact he was seriously about to rethink everything that he'd got going for him. In a way the timing was actually very good indeed, as he'd not committed to anything in concrete with this new job and, if there was one thing he was sure of now, it was that he'd do anything for Sophie if she asked it of him.

So, he told himself sternly, even more reason to slow it down and keep a lid on unruly emotions, because he now knew how committed she was to this new job she was going to. They still had a long road before them perhaps? She had said as much as they talked over breakfast, when she told him more about this position she'd taken as a clinician and general practitioner at some new UN project on the Zyandan-Tanzanian border.

'It must be your turn now, Luey!' She smiled as she spread marmalade over the last piece of toast. 'I must have been gabbing about myself for an hour or more now. C'mon! Dish!'

'Are you giving me fair warning that I'm not the only one with nosey genes?'

'Damn right - I don't spill my guts for just anyone I'll have you know, Doctor Doolittle... why don't you tell me some more about this new job you're waiting to hear about. Or are you saving that for later and want to lay the ghosts of your numerous tawdry conquests of all those poor tourists first.'

'Tell me why I love you again, Doctor Taylor?' He laughed and blew her a kiss. 'And I did not have any conquests... Well not as such.' He blushed a little, but fronted it out admirably. 'Mostly one night deals if you want the truth and none of them were serious. I was hardly Don Juan either - can't have been more than...' He spoiled the effect by running out of fingers, but at least he made her laugh. Still grinning, he shrugged and poured himself another coffee from the pot, then settled back. 'Let's do my big tragic romance and get it out the way then.'

'Yes, bwana.' She smiled sweetly at him and crunched into the toast.

'And you can bloody well stop that too, if I'm to cut out the babes!'

'But it suits you! And I like you calling me babe, so don't stop.'

'Ah - yes. That's why I love you. All your old loves are amenable ghosts.'

'Well, some of them are still around and probably have

PhDs! I told you I screwed my brains out at uni, trying to blot it all out - sauce for the goose etcetera.' She poked her orange tongue at him.

'Hussy!' Luey shook his head in mock resignation. 'So that means we're quits on casual liaisons, does it?' He sobered then.

'OK - it's not a nice little story, so I'll make it short... Crushed by unrequited love for Mrs. Claire Lucas, the youthful Luigi fell like a ton of bricks for yet another older woman - by two weeks...' He winked at her. 'We take age differences very seriously here in Zimbabwe. Anyway... her name is Sarah Ndaemin and she's a South African Ndebele.[34] Her father moves in top government circles there. She married somebody else after stringing me along for over eight years. Most of the time I knew her I was at university - wasn't away in the US all that time. I did my BVSc[35] in Pretoria where she lived and she never cheated on me then - that I know of. But when I went to Davis - that's near San Diego, of course I couldn't afford to come back too often and she basically went off with several other guys, but kept me sweet with very passionate letters and her absolute and undivided attention whenever we did meet up. I wasn't exactly an angel in the US, but I did love her and I thought she loved me back, though she used to drive me around the bend. She could be a real bitch, but the sex was... cosmic.'

He made a sour face, then laughed at himself. 'When I came home for good in 2000, she was married and six months

---

[34] **Ndebele** ~ a tribe absorbed within the Zulu nation in the 1800s who migrated northwards into Transvaal, Southern Rhodesia and modern day Zimbabwe.

---

[35] **BVSc** ~ Bachelor of Veterinary Medicine

pregnant - I hadn't slept with her for almost a year, but she'd written to me every week more or less. Not a hint of any of it! She said she was sorry. That her father disapproved of her being with a white man and had 'made' her get off with Gabriel. Poor sap. That girl never did a thing she didn't want to do in her whole life... They'd got a house and everything. So that was that.'

'She didn't even tell you when she got married?'

'Would have been polite, wouldn't it? If only for her husband's sake... Nope. Don't know why - the letters were always... enthusiastic...' He rolled his eyes. '... and when I did manage to see her, she was always all over me like a rash, so I had no idea. Maybe she just liked having a tame white boy with his tongue hanging out for her.'

'I'm sorry.'

'I'm not. I had a lucky escape - her husband died of AIDs and tuberculosis last year and their kids were all born with HIV. She was the carrier, not him. So there was someone else before him too. I don't know who and I don't want to know. She finally got around to telling me about that side of it three years ago. Nice little reminder of everything, just as I thought I was over her.'

'Oh, Luey...'

He flushed a little and hastened to reassure her. 'I'm OK - don't worry. That was the first thing I did after I found out. I'm clear of it all. I always used something with her 'cos she was Catholic and paranoid about getting pregnant. Ironically as it turns out. T.I.A. Black guys don't like wearing condoms and their women won't make them.'

There was a slightly awkward pause in the conversation that Luey filled with pouring them both more coffee. Sophie tried again.

'I didn't mean that you had such a scare... The whole thing, her lying to you and then coming back to find her married and pregnant by someone else - it's just an awful thing to happen to anyone.' Sophie tried to get him to meet her eye, but he was studying his coffee ferociously.

'Yeah, well. It's not like it's gonna happen to me again. Sorry, babe. She broke my balls at the time - and you are, really and truly, the first woman I've looked at more than twice ever since.' Finally he met her gaze with a twisted grin. 'Probably doesn't sound too flattering put that way, but I dealt with it all long ago, so I don't like talking about it.'

'Sounds like it's festered inside you beautifully.' Her eyes were sympathetic even though her tone was rather dry. 'Sorry - you have your own way of dealing with things.'

He nodded self-consciously. 'And there's my pseudo-Italian male ego to contend with, of course. It's hard taking after mama's side of the family sometimes!' He ruffled his hair awkwardly and smiled thinly. 'Don't worry I know I'm shallow, but like I said, I did love her. It caused a lot of rows with my folks too - by that time they weren't too fond of the Shona and Ndebele around here. The star-crossed lovers aspect was probably wildly aphrodisiac too, if I'm honest. And with her family's politics I suppose there was an element of 'having' to toe Daddy's line, but honestly, she could wrap him around her little finger very easily - and he quite liked me in some respects. Vets being such a catch...'
He sipped at his coffee and grimaced as it was going cold. 'Compared with what happened to you and Tom it's nothing - it didn't exactly ruin my life or anything.'

'My life wasn't ruined, Luey. Not really. I took a long time to get over it, that's all, because it was all snatched from me so finally.'

'And you had some good people looking out for you, by the sounds of it? Youssef for one. Seems like he was a good mate to you?' Relieved to have got his own sordid baggage out of the way, he smiled over at her warmly.

Sophie however was concerned about his apparently still raw wounds and wasn't quite so keen to move on with the conversation but, as he seemed to want to steer back to her, she went with him. There was still time enough to talk it through later.

'He's certainly older and wiser than I'll ever be. Saint Teresa idolised him - but then she had good reason to.' Even now, knowing the whole background, she still felt bitter about the little nun. 'But yes, Youssef's amazing. He really understands what it's like to 'serve' in these disaster zones, even though he can't do it anymore himself. He was a burnout as well - field hospitals are no place for recovering alcoholics of course.'

'Is he still with CAMEO then?'

'Part time - well, on a consultancy retainer. He's based in London full time now and lectures at the Hospital for Tropical Diseases, and with University College London.'

'Did you train under him then?'

'No - he came to UCL after I was there. I'd started post-grad at Brunel for psychology about a year before he packed it in and came to England. That was when he remarried too. I did my EMDR training off-campus while I was at Brunel as well. Sorry. I'm waffling on here again - what about this job you're going for?'

'I don't know that I am now, babe. Meeting you and all...' He reached across the table and stroked her hand. '... I might just jack it all in. Follow you instead? These past few days - it all feels so right and after last night, Sophie... everything's kind of come together? Just as I'm about to cut loose here. I've never felt about anyone the way I do about you and, even though it's happened so quickly for us, I feel so good with you and it gets better and better by the second, babe.'

She nodded at everything he was saying to her, feeling like her face was about to split with smiling so much. 'I know the real thing when it hits and you're still blowing my mind in all the right ways, Luey. But we do need to be practical as well... What about your job here?'

'They know I'm leaving whatever. I have two weeks left and my contract expires.' He smiled lovingly at her. 'Let the half-Italian make the grand gesture in the spirit of La Forza del Destino! And I haven't accepted this new job offer yet, so nothing's settled there.'

'Run me through it again - it doesn't sound a million miles from what I'll be doing, only with you it's animals and conservation.'

He'd been really excited about the offer as it came to him through the National Parks rather than his commercial contacts. The wildlife veterinary side of things had always been his first love and had only blossomed when he'd studied over in California in a world class university. Parks had forwarded a letter from a conservation project office at the UN saying that his name had been given to them by Davis as a former high-flying alumnus working in Africa, outlining a new initiative needing the services of commercial farming and exotic species specialists in certain parts of Africa, to promote good practice stock breeding and also game management projects in tribal areas. The timing couldn't have been more perfect and exciting, as he was getting really sick of how things were all round and had seriously been considering leaving altogether and going to Europe and starting over, possibly in the UK and maybe trying to get into zoological or conservation area projects there.

Sophie watched how his face lit up as he was talking about the type of work that he might be involved in and wondered how he could say he'd give all this up for her. But maybe he wouldn't have to.

'From what you're telling me, these projects would probably come within the scope of what CAMEO does, Luey.'

He nodded. 'Yes - when you were talking about the place you're going to, I thought that as well. Do they get involved with the social and economic side of things?'

'Well it's not the division I've worked with, but it'd certainly come within the agricultural and community aspects they cover. Where do they have these projects?'

'I haven't got the full information yet - I only sent the expression of interest request back to them last month, but I should be hearing next week for an interview and get more info on the actual sites. But they have places in East Africa and the lesser known game reserves in Tanzania and Kenya.'

'I'm not sure if there's a game reserve where I'll be going, but there's bound to be farming there.'

'Whereabouts is it exactly?'

'It's on the border with Zyanda, so west of Lake Victoria. It's just under two hundred miles by road from a northern city called Mwanza. That's one of CAMEO's distribution depots. I think it's quite close to the Serengeti. Well, nearish.'

'Yes it is, but I think Tanzania has a corridor on the west end of the lake, up to the Ugandan border and there's one of the smaller reserves that way...'

'I don't know about a reserve, but Umbeke's on the main

route into Zyanda and one of the trunk roads from there goes up to Uganda!'

'We can grab Harry after lunch - he'll have a decent road map directory with him for sure.' He paused a moment, drawing in his breath sharply and then a great grin split his face as something else dawned on him and he started gabbling excitedly. 'There's Gombe National Park - right out on the western borders - that can't be too far to the south!' He sprang up and almost knocked the table over as he reached out for her and hugged her tight to him, kissing her manically all over her surprised face. 'Oh, Sophie! Love! This could actually work out!'

She started laughing and kissed him back enthusiastically, forgetting all about her sore lip. He swept her up in his arms yet again, making her shriek with excitement.

'Well now! Looks like Harry's lost his Tarzan crown!' Phil was walking down the path for the boat trip and paused in admiration at their antics. 'Can one ask what the commotion's all about?'

'Too early - we'll jinx it!' Luey yelled, but he was swathed in smiles and Phil clapped his hands in delight.

'Bags I be flower girl? Pretty please, Sophie?'

'Don't be ridiculous, Philip! Let me down, you brute!' She kissed Luey on the cheek and squirmed out of his arms, but held him close still. 'We just worked out that it might be possible for Luey to work within a couple hundred miles of where I'll be based. But we have to wait and see if he can get a placement.'

'That's worth all this furore is it?' Phil pursed his lips, but did look suitably pleased for them.

'Two hundred miles away is peanuts by African standards, mate.' Luey was almost hysterical with laughter still.

'Yes - but it could cost a fortune with a commute. Don't lets count our chickens yet...' Sophie warned.

He drew her closer still and whispered in her ear. 'There's something you don't know about me, sweetheart. I have a pilot's licence.' He turned around and looked sternly at Phil.

'Off to the boat with you, Jane! Tarzan's got pressing bedroom business with his new lady.'

'Well, really!' Phil screamed practically. 'Sensitive homosexual here! Eva! Jim! Save me! The heteros are freaking me out...' So saying he gave them a merry wave and headed for Eva's rondavel.

'I think this is a suitable point to retire indoors for a bit, Tarzan.' Sophie's lips murmured longingly against Luey's.

* * *

Quackers status: Available

Quackers
Luey - am I doing this right?

Doc Doolittle
lol - Quackers? What are you on woman?!
Yeah this is fine - v.g. for a newbie :-)

Quackers
Well you have a silly call sign or whatever they call it :-)

Doc Doolittle
Username? lol - if the cap fits I always say. ;-)
But what's Quackers supposed to be?

Quackers
Haha! Well I'm crackers and a Doctor? Quack? - Doctor?
Crackers - Quackers? :-P

Doc Doolittle
Hell - you are quite mad aren't you?! lol
Don't ever change my love ((hugs)) x
So... how was your day today? No more poachers I hope?

Quackers
No - just a great day for game viewing with nothing much to spoil it. We saw Shoebills!

Haha. Brilliant. And your favourites?

Quackers

Mallys? Not so far - the river's too fast for slow moving boats, but we'll go over to lake Albert tomorrow and should be able to go out there.

Doc Doolittle

Oh? So how did you see Shoebills?

Quackers

lol! They were just there by Phil's tree! He can see to the other side of the river and there's these big papyrus beds and there were about 5 of them. They're massive aren't they! :-)

Doc Doolittle

Yeah they're big even for storks. We get them down here too but they tend not to be around Kariba so much.

I'm really missing you sweetheart...(((hugs x 1000)))

..... let's try that again :-P

I'm really missing you QUACKERS!!!! rofl

Quackers

Oh thanks - rofl? Silly man! xx

Doc Doolittle

rolling on the floor laughing ;-) - roflmao = rolling on the floor laughing my arse off :-P

Quackers

Pity that - you have a nice arse :-D I love you xxx

Sent at 6:24 pm

Doc Doolittle

xxx

Oh - I went surfing today and found a whole load of info on NW Tanzania around Mwanza

Quackers

I wish you were here! want you so much... had to blow my nose :-(

Sent at 6:26 pm

Soph... This is torture in some ways. :-(
But it's better than nothing at all. Hell - I'm tearing up here as
well :-(

The letter with the interview date mentioned a couple of
reserves right by Umbeke - I mean literally all over that
border country and also an island reserve on Lake Victoria in
that little corner although that's a way over from Umbeke.
There ARE some projects in the area and it mentioned
CAMEO as one of the partnerships they've got going there
and other jargon that was to do with local governance.

Oh? That sounds v. encouraging... I have an information
pack back in my suite that Christian Kamate sent me and it
gives a list of contacts for the whole Community admin
setup - hospital schools and tribal thingies - would it help if
I gave you some names to drop do you think?

Sent at 6:35 pm

Can't hurt can it? I don't know if I can pick and choose like
that, but I don't have to take what I'm offered, although
it'd be a pity as the project work sounds really interesting
depending on the area it's covering - potentially anyway...

Yeah love - would you do that - and then I'll just be straight
with them and ask if it's possible?

OK - have to be tomorrow now though. Jim's here - he
needs to get through to LA with something so I have to go
in a mo :-(

chin up Quackers (((hugs x 1 billion))) all you tomorrow?

Please!!! xxxxxxxxxxxxxxxxxxxxx Love you babe

Be good. I love you too babe. Talk soon xxxxx

The Acts of the Apostles

And in the latter days new tidings of the gospel shall issue forth out of Jerusalem, and the hearts of the people shall rejoice, and behold fountains shall be opened, and there shall be no more plague.

The Acts of the Apostles 29:11
('The lost chapter' a.k.a. The Sonnini Manuscript)

*'You are **all** murderers! You are here to kill your sisters and their children! **You are all Cain!**'*

As usual David woke from the dream with a groan, sweating profusely. Long ago, in the beginning, the dream would have swept onwards and he would watch Mbrame slowly, slowly swing the panga back. Then it would be in real time again and flash like lightning in the noonday heat as the nun's blood spilled, spurting brightly around the metal into the air when the blade sliced an artery, gaping wide, the white of her shirt soaked and spattered with red. The panga would have kept hacking in at her head, her accusing mouth, over and over, just like it had in those last weeks, except this time he was watching from the outside. That was when it had all changed.

* * *

I swung my legs from under the cool sheets onto the floor and went over to switch on the kettle. Rubbing bleary eyes, I began the ritual of pre-dawn tea-making and then took the mug outside onto the veranda to watch the sun come up.

Another day alive. Another day to atone for not being dead and innocent. Feeling ancient and tired. This happened so often I'd brought the stick-backed chair from my quarters onto the decking as a permanent fixture. I sat down, still feeling weary, putting the mug on the floor. It was too hot to drink still.

Long ago I'd trained myself to wake up before I started to dream about the day Sister Teresa was killed. Long before I came back to Tanzania. The dream had been coming to me almost every night back then, starting the night we left Umbeke. Well, every time I'd been able to get to sleep. Night doesn't necessarily go with sleeping when you have chronic insomnia. It happens when it happens. Now the dream didn't come so often, but in a way that was worse, because I'd taught myself to accept the tortured memories as a just punishment for what I'd done back then. What we had all done. But you see, I was the only one left now. The last of the Apostles.

'You are mine. My own Apostles. Together we will rid this land of the Lutse scum. They shall pay - life by life! We are instruments of God and we do His Will!'

Even at the time it hadn't made any sense to me, but all the others there, my father and grandfather amongst them, seemed to be hanging on the chaplain's every word, shouting responses to the litany of hatred that poured out at us, like we were at church. Hell - we were at church! And so I joined in with them, the chanting echoing in my skull as the dagga smoke took hold, feeling sick even then, before all the real anathema had started.

I'd known about why we should hate the Lutse, but if I was honest and these days I have to be, I always knew there was not that much of a difference between 'us' and the Lutse people. Not where I was from. Most of my friends at school, at home too, could call ourselves Lutse or Matu depending on how we were feeling. When we were little kids anyway. The Headmistress at the school, Verity Beleshona, was Matu like us, but married to a wealthy Lutse man who ran a chain of bakeries. I was best friends with Misha, their only son. And Fleur, his younger sister. If all this had not happened I might have ended up married to her perhaps. She was a beautiful girl. The biggest smile and it got even bigger whenever she looked at me...

Misha had been there with me that night. At the church. He had chanted too. But that was the last time I ever saw him. Alive. That was another part of the dream. Before the bit with Sister Teresa. Misha and Fleur. Lying dead on the floor of another church, weeks later. Misha had tried to shield Fleur from whoever it was killed her. You could tell by the way they'd fallen. The machete had gone through his shoulder and cut into Fleur's skull - in across her nose and eye. Misha's head had been hacked off to a bloody stump. Probably it had been kicked away, but I knew it was him. There was that silly Mickey Mouse watch he loved wearing on the wrist of the hand that was cradling what was left of Fleur's head. She would have been thirteen years old in a few days. Misha had been talking about the party their mother was planning. I threw up when it sank in that it really was my friend I was looking at. My father rushed me away before Mbrame could see my reaction, muttering angrily at me not to draw attention to myself. That I could get killed too for showing such a weakness. But we were both weeping. My father had always liked Misha...

I picked up the dagga tea, as usual ignoring the tremor in my hands when I held the cup to my lips, drinking thankfully.

That was normal for me these days and the dagga saw off the shakes soon enough. I was always careful not to take too much, especially if I was driving that day. I never smoked it anymore. If I started that again I'd lose my job for sure and that was the only thing standing between me and insanity these days. Christian said it was only a temporary fix for the insomnia. That sooner or later I had to face down my demons and decide to start living again. Or stop dreaming about the past.

Easy said, hard to do. Easy for Christian anyway. He'd had no part of it, or rather he had, but it was the good part if there could be said to be such a thing. His father was a Zyandan Matu, but he lived with his wife's family here in Tanzania, so Christian didn't get mixed up in all the madness until we'd taken it to Umbeke. That was where we first met. The day Sister Teresa held a mirror up to Mbrame and it had shattered and everything had fallen apart. When none of us could avoid the truth anymore, though we had known it all along. We were all Cain. What was it Christian told me the second time we met, seven years ago?

'We are all marked like Cain. As long as there is fear and hatred in our hearts we will commit his sin in thought, if not in deed.'

More dagga tea. Drink it down, let it soak up the nerves, the memories and chase the darkness off for a little while. Christian was always kind to me, even back then. Sometimes we talked about how things might have been if we had been born into the other's family. Whether we would have done the same things.

Christian said that really I had had little or no choice. That I was a survivor and had people to protect as well. I hadn't killed any little children at least. But I'd killed the adults who

257

*were weaponless. Raped women in front of their menfolk,
before and then again after we'd killed them all. Beaten and
spat on them as I did it. We kept some of the younger women
'to breed on' Mbrame had said. The older ones that already
had kids, or were pregnant...*

Stop thinking!

Stop... remembering!

*But that was the trouble of course. I couldn't stop. The ghosts
wouldn't let me. I didn't even attempt to control the flow of
memories anymore, because of the deal I'd made with my
grandfather. Never lie to yourself again. And now the truth
was slowly killing me, little by little. I deserved it all.*

*I'd known it was wrong, but I did it anyway, because I
was terrified if I didn't it would be me getting bludgeoned
to death, then spat and pissed on. My mother and sisters
who would get raped and mutilated. Made limbless and
infected with disgusting diseases. And all the time there was
Mbrame screaming at us that we were doing the Lord's work.
That it was divine retribution. The Lutse had brought it on
themselves. They did not have the right to be called people.
God wanted them all dead.*

'Stop here, David.'

*We had crossed the river border into Zyanda a few miles
back. I pulled over, glad that my grandfather was wanting
to talk to the others about what to do next. We were all still
stunned by what had happened. About the nun more than the
Tanzanian and the European men we'd just killed. What she
had been screaming at us all wasn't too different from what
Mbrame had been doing - pulling the strings that the church
put on us all when we were barely out of the womb. As soon
as we were capable of understanding what was being said.*

Do as the Lord says and you will be good. Disobey and you are damned to eternal suffering. Except she was saying it all for the women. The Lutse. Showing us no mercy, just like we had done to the ones we had been butchering. Though it was only words she fired off at us, they hit most of the Apostles like the bullets and blades we had used on the Lutse and their sympathisers. People like Misha and Fleur. People like their mother, Verity Beleshona. She had survived the slaughter that took her husband and children from her, because that night, the night Misha and Fleur were killed, she had been out on the outskirts of town, meeting with some of the other Matu liberals in the area. A few weeks later, after weeks of hiding and moving them, she had led the dozen or so Lutse women and their smaller children, the ones who weren't even going to school yet, over the border to Umbeke.

They ought to have been safe, but Mbrame had had it in for the Beleshonas. Misha's father had been mayor the previous year and had threatened to stop some of the public funding because of Mbrame's increasingly hostile attitude towards charitable efforts in the Lutse community. Even though the President was Matu and advocating a more liberal approach across the board. Mr. Beleshona was one of the first to die, the day after Mbrame had 'christened' us all again and given us communion as his 'disciples'. Misha had been christened too. It had been just another day and we had been playing football together after school, when my father had called me over and said to go with him to a meeting at Saint Antoine's.

'You're old enough now, so it is right that you come with us.' *Grandfather Abraham, my mother's father had been there too. I asked if Misha could come with us and there had been a look between them, then grandfather had shrugged and said that Misha had Matu blood as well, so why the hell not. We all went together. And Misha chanted with us. We had both turned fifteen that January and it had seemed like an adventure. We sat there with the older men, trying not to gag on the dagga smoke, feeling like real men who were about to fight for the honour of our blood.*

I never saw Misha after that, but I guessed what must have happened. His parents, especially his mother, would have been mad at what he'd done. Mrs. Beleshona was not a Christian or a Muslim, but she was very well educated. She had taught History and Political Studies at the school and had encouraged Misha's friendship with me because I was a good student. She was my favourite teacher. Misha would have been told that the Matu uprising was wrong, ignorant and immoral. All of it lies. Evil lies that killed Misha's father and his two sisters. The lies had killed him too.

On the other side of the river, we all piled out of the lorry we had taken from Umbeke and there had been a big argument over where to go. Most of them had wanted to stay in Tanzania and head north for the Ugandan border where we'd probably have been safe enough. Grandfather put a stop to that right away.

'We killed three people - four counting Mbrame! The three were not Lutses - not Matus! They were foreigners. One white man. We stay in Tanzania, we will be treated as criminals! Murderers!' He paused, letting it sink in. 'Just like the nun said. We could make a run for Uganda, but they would come after us - even if we stay here in Zyanda, they may still come. We have the time now, while the police come to Umbeke. They will not follow us over the border. Not yet.'

'That Beleshona bitch recognised some of us! They will

come after us for sure. We shouldn't have given up the guns...'
My grandfather had knocked Paul, the one who killed the Englishman, to the ground.

'She stayed there. She's had enough! We've all had enough! Haven't we? **Haven't we!!!**'

I'd had enough long before. Almost before it started. And still I said nothing to support my grandfather as the fight went on, back and forth. In the end we agreed we couldn't go back to Tanzania, but then we couldn't stay in Zyanda either, unless we carried on with the 'cleansing', so we headed north into the Mgakera Highlands to hide out for a while.

Mgakera was sparsely populated but had plenty of game back then. Some of the others had been in the army like grandfather, so we lived off the land easily enough. One of the men had served in the district during the troubles the previous year and knew of a place where they'd cached some weapons from their 'friends'. By then we were having to range out further and further to set traps for bushmeat, so we looked for the dump and by some miracle there were still some rifles and ammo there. There had been another row that night as well. Three of the men had disappeared within hours taking some of the guns with them. They probably headed west, trying to join up with other Matu right wingers as the Zyandan National Party (ZNP) were advancing south from Uganda. We never heard of them again, so they were most likely killed, or else got out of the country somehow. The eastern parts had been crawling with UN patrols by then.

That had been the end of the Apostles more or less. A few months on and the rains were due, which would have washed most of the roads out, but we knew we couldn't hide for much longer. There were only eight of us left. Of the twelve who'd left Umbeke, Paul went first. Well he killed himself more or less. Jumped into the gorge. He'd been flipping out for weeks before Umbeke, ever since we got pinned down by ZNP snipers and my father and four others had got killed. Paul'd been losing it badly - probably he hadn't even meant to kill the Englishman. He just panicked when Mbrame gave the order and kept on firing because he was terrified of the priest. We all were. Grandfather thought Paul might have just walked off the cliffs in his sleep, except he'd not been sleeping much. Maybe that was right. Nobody saw what happened, or at least they said they hadn't. We were posting guards at night because we were travelling then, looking for a base, but none of us saw Paul slip away. I asked grandfather if someone would have pushed him off the cliff. He just shook his head and said that he hadn't done that, though someone else might have. He said if he'd wanted to kill Paul he'd have said so in front of everyone. We didn't lie anymore. Not to each other, but then we didn't ask too many questions either.

Grandfather and I went down into the gorge and buried Paul not far from where we found him. He looked better than he'd looked in a long time, except he was pale and cold of course. Maybe he had been sleepwalking. His face was peaceful-looking enough under the bruises and scratches from the rocks and branches. That was when my own nightmares had started to kick in really badly. I wasn't the only one suffering that way either. So by the year end with the rains threatening, we came down out of the highlands and gave ourselves up to the ZNP troops, who'd mostly secured the hill country by then. I'd been in prison for six weeks by the time my sixteenth birthday came around and by then it was only my youth that had saved me. The other Apostles, including my grandfather, had been summarily executed after a hasty war crimes trial.

None of them had said a word about being at Umbeke and now none of them ever would. Only Christian and Verity Beleshona knew my secret and, later, they said they would not tell because I hadn't killed or mistreated anyone. Not that time. Except I had done something. I had done nothing, like all the other times. I had done nothing to stop it. Nobody could forgive me. Ever. Not even God.

The birds were awake. I smiled at the Quelea swarming up across the dawn from the acacias. They're real pests sometimes, but I liked to see them flying in those huge flocks, out across the game park and then back across the river, again and again. No borders for them. The Cape Turtle Doves were off as well. Zy-anda! Zy-anda! Zy-anda! Or 'work-harder!'... That's the East African version of their soft cooing call.

I had always worked hard. My parents had been proud that I did so well at school. I was the middle child of eight and none of my older siblings had been interested in academic studies, much to our mother's annoyance. She wanted me to go to university and become a doctor. Mrs. Beleshona had said that I could do it, if I kept at my studies.

Afterwards, when we were in the Highlands, the night before we gave ourselves up, my grandfather had asked me about the future, if there was one for us.

'Tell me what to do, David. I don't know anymore, I really don't. All my life I have done what I was told to do. By my elders, the army. My wife even. I thought I was a good man. I tried to be, but now I know I wasn't. I just followed orders the whole time.'

'I'm the same as you grandfather. I always do what I'm told.'

The others had been asleep, but we hadn't been able to, so we got up and went over to the fire. We watched the stars. When I said that, grandfather wept and I didn't know what to do. All I could do was watch him. That was when we made the deal.

'Don't say that David, please. Not you. You can't be like me.'

'I've done the same things with you and father. I'm the same. I don't know what to do either, grandfather.'

'You didn't! Not really, David. I saw you - remember. Saw your face, even in the beginning. This was never you. Not really.'

'But I did it all the same!' *I had been crying then too.* 'I killed them as well. Blood is on my hands too.'

'You weren't there! I could see it in your face. That was not you. Not you David. Please Lord, say it wasn't, because if it was then there is no hope for us.'

'What do you want me to say grandfather? I was afraid. A coward. I knew it was wrong, but I still did it... She was right about me as well. I am Cain too.'

'Cain lived, David. You must live too. You are still young, hardly a man yet. There may be a future for you. You can maybe make us proud again.'

'How can I? What we have done is unforgiveable, isn't it? All I can do is tell the truth and ask for mercy. I don't expect I'll get it though.'

'You are the youngest. We will tell them that you had no choice in the matter. You didn't. Not really.'

'I didn't have to do any of it. I could have run away.'

'Where would you have run to? Don't lie to yourself anymore, David. You were with us because you had to be. There was no choice for you. Your father and I made it for you that night, at the church.'

There was nothing to be said. I was right and wrong whatever happened. But I could and did do that one thing for my grandfather's sake. I never lied to myself anymore.

* * *

'What do you want me to say? That I forgive you? I thought you had more intelligence than that, David.'
Verity Beleshona hadn't ever wanted to have this conversation, but David had been her Michel's best friend, so maybe she 'owed' him five minutes, especially if that meant they never had anything to do with each other ever again. Yes, that was the way of it. Finish the business and let it go forever.

'Well? Say whatever it is and then leave me alone.'

'My mother said I should come to you. She wants me to go to college.'

'Didn't you learn anything in prison? You - go to college! Why should you have what my children can never have? What all the other women here should have had for their children and can't. Killer!'

'I - I... have to support my family now. I want to. They suffered as well. You know they did, Mrs. Beleshona.'

'How dare you try to make me feel sorry for you! Why should I help you?'

'I said there was no point in coming. But my mother said that she wanted the son she lost, back. The son who would have been a Doctor.'

'Hah! Doctor Death more like! No. I will not help you recover your education, but if it is your mother who is asking, then I will give you some advice instead. Go away. Far away. Don't come back.'

'We need money - the younger children need food and medicine.'

'Money! Why should I make you rich? What are you even doing here? You should still be in prison. Or dead.'

'Sometimes I wish I was. You could have made sure of that at one time but you didn't speak out against me.'

'Because your mother begged me not to!'

Why the *hell* had Veronique sent him here? She knew how she felt about Mbrame's Apostles! They were almost six years down the line and just the sight of this young man made her want to vomit, even though he looked like hell, hollow-eyed and emaciated. What was he doing now? Grovelling there on the ground like he was praying to the Prophet.

'Get up! That won't work with me! You know I don't believe any of it. That ignorance and weakness. The perverted, power-tripping lies... Look at me! Look! At! Me!'

David knelt back on his heels but would not get up. He looked at her, his face exhausted of any emotion and utterly blank. She had been going to yell at him again but suddenly her anger seemed to drain away and instead she deliberately, slowly, studied the face of the man who had been a little boy in her class, hanging on her every word and really soaking it all in. He had been such a good student. One who could have gone all the way in whatever field he had chosen for himself. His family hadn't been wealthy, but she had told his parents that there were scholarships she could help him win so he could go to university in the capital, maybe even Paris, depending on what he wanted to study. Now here he was again at her knees, dagga-reddened eyes with pupils like lifeless black holes, and she shuddered at the thought that this man and her Michel had once been almost inseparable, in and out of school.

She remembered everything of course, including how she and Robert had yelled at Michel the night he told them that he and David were Jean-Batiste Mbrame's 'Apostles' now. Robert had wanted to beat it out of Michel, but she had pulled him off their son, screaming at him that he was only a child, that he didn't know what was happening. Robert had calmed down then and together they had sat Michel down and explained to their son how things really were. That night had been the end of her life because Robert had got himself killed the very next day, doing what he said he should have done in the first place. Showing Mbrame up for the idiotic fantasist he was. She had been so proud of him that morning and had kissed him goodbye. Wished him luck even. Now she knew better. She should have stopped him going at all. They should have got out of Zyanda that night. Just taken the children and left.

But that was when she had faith in politics and a modern day approach. Democracy even. What a gullible fool she had been as well. Even now, there was no justice. Lip service paid to the overwhelming dead, 'regretting' the genocide, but underneath it all the evil ones were still there, just over the borders in the Congo and Burundi, Uganda and Tanzania. Still killing and torturing. And now they were letting out the ones who had been caught and thrown in jail. Pathetic wrecks of humanity, broken with guilt and horror just like their victims, saying they would atone. Like this boy looking out of hell at her. He may have had a man's body, pitifully thin maybe, but he was etched into that vile past. Just like the people, the children he'd terrorised and persecuted.

He was still that little boy who had been so clever and dutiful in her class, eyes wide and hungry for everything she could teach. She had taken such hope from children like him. That one day they would help build a better country than her generation. And reactionary thugs and ignoramuses like

Mbrame had stolen him away from her - and, briefly, her Michel too - and made them rapists and murderers, over and over. Ravening animals.

She blinked away tears. They were one indulgence she would not allow herself, but nevertheless she was caught in David's pleading gaze, remembering the little boy Veronique thought she had the power to restore to her. Well Veronique had another think coming her way. Stupid, jealous women like her didn't deserve sons like David had been before all the evil had started. And then it was as though David had read her thoughts.

'I know my mother is fooling herself, Mrs. Beleshona. And I will leave - I was always going to anyway. But I will send money back to my family wherever I go, even if I never see them again. So I am here to ask for her sake. That's all. Her and my little brothers and sisters.'

Verity wanted to hit him. Scream at him. But what could she do to him that he was not already doing to himself. She could see it in his face, his body, the way he moved. So instead she asked him the question he had been dreading.

'Were you there when Misha and Fleur were killed?' She knew he had been. All of the Apostles had been there, with Mbrame sermonising the whole time, the holy book in one hand and a machete in the other.

'Yes.' he said in a broken whisper, 'I saw him and Fleur afterwards. I was sick.'

'Good! Did you kill either of them?' He said nothing but shook his head. She felt sick now, but she wasn't going to stop. 'Get up and look me in the eye!'

David did as she commanded. He was quivering like a whipped dog, his head bowed contritely, but he did look at her. She took a deep breath, willing the nausea back.

'Were you there when they took my Angelique? Cut her and raped her so many times she bled to death?' Angelique had been eighteen months older than Michel and David. She wasn't sure that David knew how she had died, but she didn't want him to go without knowing what had been done to her eldest child.

'No.' He didn't even flinch. He hadn't seen Angelique at all at the church though he had assumed she had been killed there, like Misha and Fleur. 'I kn-know there were some girls taken... but I didn't know... and I c-couldn't...'

'Why not?' Her voice lashed out at him like a scourge. 'You raped women as well as killed them, didn't you? Didn't you!' She held his stricken gaze now, glorying in his anguished expression, wanting to watch him squirm. He nodded at her, his eyes showing the agony of guilt he carried. 'I want you to tell me, David. I want to hear your voice. How many women did you rape?'

'I don't know. Not anymore.'

'Take a wild guess. Indulge me, David!' He shook his head raggedly now, looking at her like she was a cobra. Verity forced a savage smile onto her face and took a step towards him, enjoying the way he seemed to shrink back from her, although he didn't move an inch. 'How - many - women?'

He held her terrible gaze. He couldn't not. 'D-d-dozens! F-fifty... I don't know. I l-lost count. But I never saw Angelique. I n-never touched her - I swear it!'

'You wouldn't have. She died after Umbeke. Before I came back.' In spite of her anger she breathed a sigh of relief that he would not try to deny things she knew that he had done. He wasn't the only one carrying the guilt. There was no escape for her either. She had failed to protect her own children. His eyes escaped her finally but stayed on her face, falling to look in horror at her mouth, her chin. She realised she had bitten her lip and hastily licked at the blood, then smeared it away with the back of her hand.

'She wasn't there when Michel and Fleur were killed. I'd sent her south with some people trying to cross into Burundi, but they were intercepted by another militia. They had her for three weeks before she died.'

'I'm sorry...'

'Are you? Really?'

He really was. They both knew it but there was no point to it all. Nothing would bring their dead back because they never went away now. The ghosts walked alongside the living, whether they had been doing the killing or not, because they were all guilty in one way or another. She was no better than Veronique in her own way. What good had her high-flown principles done?

'You saved those women at Umbeke. You got them there.'

Had she asked the question or was he reading her mind again? 'No, I didn't save them. It was the little nun who did that. She bought our lives with her own. I was there, remember? Mbrame would have killed me and then the rest of us, if she had not come out.'

He nodded slowly. 'But you got them all to Tanzania. You did that.'

And left Angelique behind in Zyanda to shift for herself. To be used worse than the lowest whore and tortured to death. All she had to do was close her eyes and she would see the photographs at the grave site. Her eldest, her dearest firstborn, lying like a pale broken rag doll, amongst the other poor wretches, all piled in on top of each other. Massive cuts all over their bloated corpses. They had cut both her arms off above the elbow. The UN people said they did it to stop the girls trying to fight them off. Her baby mutilated and torn apart by filthy hyenas on two legs. But this man had not done that to Angelique. He had not killed Michel and Fleur. She believed him. He was not innocent, but at least he realised that. One more question. She had to ask it.

'Did you see my husband die?' She held her breath, wanting him to hesitate. To try and lie to her. She wanted him to and he knew it. Not for a single moment did he try to slide his eyes away from her. She watched his lips form the word. When the sound came it was clear. Almost pure.

'Yes.'

* * *

Robert Beleshona had been a big man in every sense. David's mother had worked in one of his bakeries before she got married. She didn't know him that well and he probably never even spoke to her. He was older than her so they never went to school together. In fact he hadn't gone to school in Zyanda at all because his father had been in the army and then the diplomatic corps. Robert had been educated in England. He had gone to one of the big universities there, got some spectacular degree in Economics and Political Sciences and then had come back and taught at the university in the capital.

That was where he had met his wife. The bakeries were left to him by his maternal grandfather and he decided to leave academia and make the family fortune work for the good of the country, mostly in the field of education. That had been Verity's influence of course. He had belonged to the same political clique as the President and was hoping for a ministerial appointment after the next election. He had stepped down as mayor specifically for that purpose. That day, when he was killed, David had gone out with his father and grandfather again. Mbrame had told them all to go to the hall where Robert Beleshona was campaigning. It was at another church hall, across town from St. Antoine's, in a more well to do neighbourhood.

Some of the other men who had been at their faux christening were with them and they had gone to another place first. They were given weapons. Because grandfather had been in the army he was given a rifle. His father had picked up a long-handled panga, so he had taken one as well. He had used one before of course. Cutting back shrubs and the grass at the church and the school. He liked helping out in the gardens, being outside smelling the jacaranda and bougainvillea, listening to the birds and the bees buzzing high up in the flowering trees. Misha hadn't come with them of course. He'd left before they'd arranged to meet, saying he was late and would get in trouble. David wasn't absolutely sure but he thought Mbrame had waited until Misha had left before telling them about going to the political hustings where Mr. Beleshona would be speaking.

As the Apostles walked to the hall they were joined by many other groups of Matu workers - it was a big town and he saw a few of the other priests there, wearing their collars but with military jackets on as well, just like Mbrame. There must have been about two hundred men there in all. It was like being in the army he said and his grandfather had laughed grimly and said he would soon see active service. It wasn't a big hall. They must have outnumbered them two to one, if not more. No women or children that time. He had thought it was odd, but Mbrame made a speech and the voices of the other men had been like the growling of mad dogs as he told them to do God's work.

Robert Beleshona had appeared at the door of the hall then. He had yelled at Mbrame who had yelled back of course. He couldn't remember what they were shouting because everyone else had started roaring, their faces screwed up with hate and anger. He was screaming too, but it was weird. Like he was watching himself, but in the thick of it as well. He and his father had been near the back and it was on slightly higher ground, so he had seen Mbrame strike out at Robert Beleshona with his panga. The same way he killed Sister Teresa. Smashing the blade into his neck and shoulder then back and in, again and again, always aiming at the face.

He hadn't killed anyone that day. There were too many of them and by the time they reached the hall they were tripping over bodies, severed limbs and headless torsos. All he remembered was hacking at people who were already dead, shouting with the other men, feeling angry and powerful, until he realised his hands and arms were slick with warm blood from his blade. Suddenly it had all gone quiet as they stopped and looked around at each other. His father's and grandfather's faces had been wet with splattered blood, their clothes the same. They had looked at each other and it was like they were strangers. Worse. It was like they were mindless animals, resting after ripping their prey apart. And then Mbrame spoke, quietly reverent. The parish priest once more, his voice soft, but carrying out to his bloodied flock.

'Lord Jesus Christ, you said to your apostles: I leave you peace, my peace I give you. Look not on our sins, but on the faith of your Church, and grant us the peace and unity of your kingdom where you live forever and ever.'

'AMEN!'

He had said it with the rest of them, accepting the blessing for the obscenities they had just committed and then there had been no going back, because they were all Mbrame's Apostles and his was The Way, The Light and the Glory...

'I was there that day, Mrs. Beleshona. I saw Mbrame kill your husband. I watched him and said nothing. I followed the other men and I desecrated the dead.'

* * *

She gave me a small nod and asked me to come inside with her. I couldn't believe she had asked me in, but she had turned to walk away and looked back when I did not follow.

'Come. I want you to meet someone.'

I went in. It was the same house, but the furniture was new and not expensive looking, like it had been in the old days. There were still smoke stains on the ceiling and some of the walls in the hall from when we had tried to burn the house down, but she took me into the kitchen, which had been repainted. Misha had loved it in there. He was always hungry and used to try and steal food from their fridge, finding ways to sneak past his mother and Angelique. There was no fridge anymore, no fancy oven either. She had a microwave cooker though. Strange the things you notice. She opened the window and called out to someone to come in. There was a laugh and a low happy voice responded, then Christian Kamate came in carrying a big kettle of hot water. I didn't recognise him, but then that wasn't surprising. I never looked at the men too much. The people we were going to kill. Not properly. But he recognised me and put out his hand for me to shake. He smiled widely at me. We were about the same height and build, but he seemed to loom over me because he was like an

274

athlete, standing tall and relaxed, his head only a few inches below the slowly turning fan in the high ceiling. I looked at Mrs. Beleshona and she laughed. Not with her eyes though.

'You remember Christian? From Umbeke? This is David Mukuga, Christian. The man who didn't kill anyone. That time.'

He smiled even more and took my hand in his.

'I always wondered if we would meet again, David. In happier times now, I hope?'

'That depends where you've been in the meantime. Doesn't it, David?'

They were both speaking in English. I understood them well enough, but all I could do was nod stupidly. She laughed again and told Christian to make some coffee and tell me why he was here in Zyanda. Then she went outside into the vegetable garden and I didn't see her again that day.

Now I knew who he was I did recognise him, but Christian acted as though I was an old friend. I felt like I was in some surreal dream for a good while as he walked around the room I'd known since I started school. Like he was Misha almost. I couldn't understand why he was treating me in such a friendly way until I realised that he only knew what I hadn't done that day. He thought I was a good man.

He talked to me as he made the coffee - he was fluent in French and used that, thinking I would understand more easily. We had spoken in that language in Umbeke when I was standing guard over him and the European people. He brought the coffee over to the table and motioned for me to sit down with him. I felt giddy by then and did as he said, still not saying a thing, just nodding and trying to smile back at him.

'Votre grand-père a été libéré de prison aussi bien, David?'
Had my grandfather been released from prison as well? The question was like a hammer blow to me and the mug slipped from my hand. Luckily it didn't spill - it was only an inch above the table. I was weeping I suppose. Everything had gone hazy and my face was wet. The next thing I knew Christian was crouching down beside me, rubbing my shoulders, comforting me and asking what he could do to help. He made to stand up and I knew he was going to call for Mrs. Beleshona, so I had to stop him.

'I can speak English. Please don't get her. She won't want to see me.'
It must have come out wrong because he stared at me in confusion. I took deep breaths, trying to calm myself down.

'Sorry... Please don't call Mrs. Beleshona back - it's not necessary.'
He laughed a little nervously.

'I thought... have I upset you?'

'No... a... a little. This has been such a strange day!'
He had drawn away from me and sat down again, looking at me warily now.

'So... are we speaking in English or French now?'

'English - I need the practice, I guess.'
He smiled at this and I tried to return it.

'My grandfather was shot. The others are all gone as well.'

It wasn't a lie - they were all gone, one way or another.

'He expected it, but they put me in prison. I was too young to be executed they said.'

'How old are you now, David?'

'Twenty two in January. At the Epiphany. The 6th I mean.'
That was something I had in common with Mrs. Beleshona

still. I had no faith left in anything, least of all in any god.

'Mr. Zimmerman was right then - you were only about fifteen?'

His eyes were full of sympathy and concern for me. Again I had this sweeping feeling of unreality and his voice sounded as though it was coming from a thousand miles away.

'The old man with the beard. He told the police that you weren't that long out of school. We both told them that your grandfather had stopped any more killings. And we knew that you hadn't killed anyone because you were with us all the time. You only shot over our heads and then you helped your grandfather.'

Did he think that had made any difference?

'No. We surrendered to the ZNP and were tried for the murders we did here in Zyanda. We never spoke about what happened in Tanzania. That was just the end of it all.'

'Your grandfather saved our lives! He was a hero.'

'He wasn't before that. We had to pay for what we did. What we did here.'

I couldn't look at his kind face any more. I pulled the mug back towards me and drank the coffee slowly. It had been such a long time since I had had decent coffee. Why was it all such an effort now? He was looking at me curiously and I knew if he said one more thing about Umbeke, or the war, I would lose my temper.

'I don't want to talk about that time. Mrs Beleshona said you should tell me why you are here. Please - we cannot change what happened.'

Finally he understood and nodded sadly. Then he told me he was here for his final year of medical studies in a teaching hospital in the capital...

He didn't tell me it all that afternoon in the kitchen. He was only staying with Mrs Beleshona for a few days, but he came to see me at my mother's house the next two days and that was how I came to work for CAMEO. They had sponsored his training in Dar es Salaam and then he had landed the internship in Zyanda. For him, Umbeke had been both terrible and fantastic. His Mr Zimmerman and Mrs Beleshona had both made a huge impression on him, but most of all it had been Sister Teresa and what she had done there in that village that had inspired him. On his last day in town he came to say goodbye and to give me his address at the halls of residence, saying he wanted to stay in touch and hear how I was getting along. Just before he left he gave me a message from Verity Beleshona. She wanted to see me the next day. He said he thought it was about a job I might be able to do - she was CAMEO's area co-ordinator for Eastern Zyanda, as I now knew.

I wasn't as sure as Christian was about the job, but he seemed to be enthusiastic for me and said that Verity was always looking for help with various posts as they still couldn't get many non-Zyandans to come and work in the country. That at least made sense to me, but I very much doubted I was going to get as good a position as Christian had. My mother had been completely dazzled by the Tanzanian and was convinced that Mrs Beleshona was going to help me to an equally dynamic future. We were both right but, regrettably, my mother had the bigger disappointment, because of course Verity had found me a career that would keep me out of Zyanda most of the time.

* * *

'I am not doing this for your benefit, or your mother's come to that, so don't thank me yet, David. And you're not going to university unless someone else sponsors you, but I think you've already decided that's not going be your future, hmm?'

He nodded miserably and she felt a stab of painful joy that he was still a clever lad who knew when he had had all the breaks he was going to get from her. Christian had been at pains to be David's advocate, saying he was sure the man had turned a corner and was genuinely remorseful and wanting to be of use to others. She had smiled and said she was sure of that too and that she would find something for David to do that made the most of his talents. Work that would eventually give him some peace of mind and a new purpose in life.

But first he had to do some more detention of her own devising, which involved him redeeming the lives he had helped destroy, even if he hadn't squeezed the trigger, or swung the blade.

Christian was not the only one who had been impressed with Dr. Teresa Olatunde and with Tom Harrison and Aaron Umbatu, the other two aid workers who had died at Umbeke. Verity had been literally floored when the nun had stormed out of the school house where the Apostles had bundled the camp operatives. As soon as they had seen Mbrame walk into the village square with his men she knew she was so much dead meat. In a way she had welcomed it almost and there was a solace of sorts in the looks of pure hatred he threw at her as he bullied and blustered at everyone with his usual sanctimonious rhetoric. She almost felt sorry for David Mukuga and Paul Induna, as they were detailed to guard the camp people and the Zyandan women. They looked almost as terrified as she felt when Mbrame finally stopped grandstanding and walked towards the cantina like some self-righteous, overfed predator.

Induna had actually been shaking more than she was when he had motioned with the automatic for her to come forward. Mbrame had wanted her to beg for her life. She had too, but only if that was with the rest of the women she'd hidden and comforted and finally made a desperate run with, over the border to the refugee camp that had been rumoured to be setting up across the river.

They had made it and these four wonderful foreigners had welcomed them with open arms and hearts. The German lady, Helga Zimmerman and Aaron Umbatu had set up an impromptu clinic within ten minutes of their arrival, getting water into their dehydrated youngsters and treating minor cuts and bruises from the horrendous trek they had made on foot for the last fifteen miles, when they had abandoned their stolen vehicle. They had been about a half a day ahead of Mbrame and his men, who had ironically run out of fuel in their pursuit and so lost the advantage of trying to outrun them to the border. She had been so certain they would not follow them over but, unfortunately for them all, Mbrame knew she was with the women and he was vindictive enough to risk the Tanzanian patrols. They must have sneaked upriver and then over to Umbeke. They had been in the village for about three hours and were just settling down to an early lunch of fish stew, having been told that supplies were expected any time, when the Apostles had burst in on them. Of course there were no weapons in the camp and then Aaron Umbatu had heard the supply truck and had tried to turn them away, to get help for them and... got himself killed before he could warn them off.

As she was shoved over to grovel before Mbrame the last person she had expected to come to her aid was this little scrap of a woman, who had looked so petrified as the Apostles frog-marched her and the young white man over to where Christian and the German couple were being questioned. When they were taken off to another building by David Mukuga the nun was obviously frozen with terror and she had dismissed her from her thoughts, fully convinced that she herself would be dead within the hour. And then, just as she thought the moment was upon her, as Mbrame had punched her in the belly and then kicked her in the jaw as she sprawled on the ground at his feet, this little nun had literally flown at him, screaming like a lunatic in perfect French but with a Nigerian accent. Quoting Genesis like a fury and giving Mbrame better than he could bluster back at her. By then she had been so petrified and half blinded with blood where he had split her eyebrow open with his bare knuckles, she had curled up in a tight ball and kept quite still, eyes squeezed shut as the shouting and insults flew thick and fast. Abraham... someone, David's grandfather, had come over and had started talking to the nun, but she had ignored him as well and kept winding Mbrame back with more taunts and barbed accusations and biblical rhetoric.

Later she was told what had happened because, mercifully, she had not been conscious when the nun had been killed. One of the other women saw Paul Induna knock her back down with the butt of his gun. She still had the scar running under the hair at the back of her head. When she began to come around she had heard the automatics firing and had almost fainted again as she braced herself for bullets that were never aimed at her. Then everything went quiet for several moments, except for the sound of people running and then the German lady calling out to her husband. Abraham had begun rattling out orders, saying for the men to put their guns and pangas down and then calling one of the women, Celeste, over to help her up. She had almost spewed up the fish as she caught sight of the nun's mangled little face laying a dozen feet from where she had fallen down. Then there was screaming and it was her, and she thought she would never be able to stop for the pain and the fear.

But she had. Celeste and the others told her what happened. Mr. Zimmerman had been out there still, holding the young Englishman in his arms, covered in his blood and all they could do was stare and stare at Mbrame, lying on the ground a little way away from where he had killed Doctor Olatunde. The bastard actually looked like he was still alive, with this kind of surprised look on his face, except his head was at a strange angle. Abraham had broken his neck. Mrs Zimmerman and Christian were carrying off the pathetic body of the nun to the school house and Abraham was yelling at two of the men to bring the body of Aaron over as well. It was hot but she had been shivering. Celeste had hugged her tight and thanked her again and again for bringing them here. Saying it would be alright now. But how could it be alright? People had died. Good people.

   'Hush' Celeste said. 'The Germans are talking to the Matus.'
Her jaw had been dislocated but she had mumbled painfully, saying that there were no Matus, only killers and the dead.

David had come over with Christian. Christian had done all the talking. Telling them that the Apostles were leaving and, if any of the Matu women wanted, they could go back with them. They would not be harmed he said. There had been no question they would go with them. She had started to laugh at the suggestion. Somehow she had slurred out an answer.

   'Are you mad, child? Why would we go back with them?'

And then David had turned to her and the look on his face tore what was left of her heart to shreds. Because she had seen it before, when he and Michel had got into some scrape and they both knew they would be in big trouble. She felt sick to her stomach as she thought of her own dead son and her voice soared away from her as the tears came back again 'They are already in hell - why should we join them?'

'Do you remember what I said to you and Christian? Back at Umbeke?

'That the Apostles were already in hell.'

'Are you still there, David?'

He nodded, though he had the grace to look ashamed.

'So am I. I don't need to explain that to you.' Finally she gave him a smile that held a little warmth. 'You were always a good boy, David. I was pleased you were friends with Michel - I think you were a good influence on him. He was always a little wild in his ways, like I was at his age. You reminded me a little of my husband, you know? Always thinking. Looking for reasons.'

She sighed and motioned for him to sit and join her at the kitchen table. What was she going to do with him? There were a number of options and most of them meant that he could leave the area. Whilst that would not please his mother, his wages could still be paid to her and the younger Mukuga children direct and he would be able to live all-found in accommodation on site, wherever he got posted. But part of her felt appalled at the waste of potential. Really she should be trying harder to place him on a more professional career path, whatever the justice of the situation, because that way he could contribute a lot more. She needed to be fair with him even now, for Michel's sake, if not hers and her daughters. This could so easily have been Michel sitting there looking like a bankrupted soul. Knowing the evil he had done, had been a part of, however reluctantly and knowing nothing he did now could ever scour him clean. But this boy had not had a Lutse father like her Michel and his mother had always been the sort who was resentful about how easy life would be if only they had more money or status, or both. If she and Robert had not taken the actions they had Michel might still be alive and sitting like this in front of someone else, wishing he had never been born. David knew he couldn't go back to what he might have been if he hadn't been taken to that meeting at St. Antoine's that night. Like the real Apostles, he had abandoned the path that had lain before him then and took another which had led away from a career in medicine, or politics, or educating others and landed him in this unholy mess. He was tainted in every possible way and he was incapable of retrieving any part of what could have been his. Even if she had been about to hand him a college degree on a plate he wouldn't have taken it because he knew he could never honour it properly. He simply couldn't do it justice any more.

'You like Christian, don't you?'

'Yes?' Why was she asking this? She kept looking at him so he went on, now knowing what she was after. 'I don't know why he would want to be my friend though.'

'He is a very kind young man. But then he knows no real ill of you. The day you both met, you behaved well, whatever your reasons.' She gazed down at the table, needing to stop looking at him because she knew she couldn't do this impartially otherwise. 'Do you ever think back to what happened that day? Not with me, or the women - with the people the Apostles killed. The Tanzanian? The nun and the white man?'

He looked confused for a moment, unsure what she was asking, but then he saw the meaning of what she was saying and nodded. 'I will never forget the nun. What she said. I still dream about her words - almost every night.'

'And the two men?'

'I... don't...' he stopped himself a moment. What was she asking him here? 'I don't think about the Tanzanian - he was there and then he wasn't. I didn't kill him...'

'Obviously - what about the Englishman?' She spoke in staccato, sounding annoyed.

He shook his head, feeling bewildered now. 'You know I didn't kill him either. What do you want to know?'

She slammed a fist down hard on the table, startling him with her angry glare. With an effort she tore her eyes away from him again and spoke rapidly, her voice harsh with emotion.

'What I want to know, David, is how you feel about these people that you'd never met, who had never done you the slightest harm. What I want to know is how you feel about why they had to die that day. For doing nothing wrong.'

Finally she could look back, needing to see if he understood why she was asking this.

He realised he was holding his breath and expelled the air in his lungs in a heaving gasp. Squeezing his eyes tight, he fought to hold back tears that he knew would only make her angrier. His thoughts were disordered, but he tried to hold them down and find the answers she wanted. She was waiting patiently now, giving him time. But he just didn't know what to say. He opened his eyes and looked at her. All he had, all he ever had was the truth. He told her, knowing it would not answer her. It was all he had left to give.

'The whole thing was like a dream? Happening to someone else? I - we all let Mbrame do our thinking for us... I was told to guard them. That's all. I did as I was told. I - I didn't recognise Christian the other day because...'

How could he explain? Would she even want to understand? He went on. '... because I wasn't there. Not me. I didn't even take any notice of the nun, until she ran past me - it took me by surprise. Then I had to do something and I stopped the rest of them following her outside.'

He stopped again, trying to remember what he was thinking when Christian had spoken urgently to him, begging him to let the two white men bring the nun back inside. It had been the Englishman he had looked at as Christian was talking to him. The way he looked so upset and frightened, and how it had dawned on him then, that the man was frightened for the nun, not for himself. He looked at Verity carefully and spoke softly.

'Christian said that the white men were the nun's friends. I watched them go after her - and I heard her words... I wanted them to stop her. I wanted them to get her away from Mbrame... I didn't want her to die as well and I hoped they would get her to come back.'

The silence between them was calm now and she took her time to come back on what he had said. It was going to be all right she told herself. He could find a way back, somehow.

'Did Christian tell you why he decided to become a doctor David?'

* * *

After that first afternoon Christian had told me a little about what had happened after we'd driven away from the village. Calling the police, all the questioning and then the newspaper and television people coming to Mwanza. That we had been in a foreign country just hadn't sunk in with me, but it had with my grandfather and some of the other men who served in the army. Even in prison I hadn't really thought about how the rest of the world would see what had gone on in Zyanda, let alone what we had done in Umbeke. Christian had started me thinking about things less personally, and in some ways it did me good, although it also made me feel even more terrible about what I had done. I felt small and horrible, especially when he told me that he and the Zimmermans had gone back to Umbeke the following week to carry on with the work they had started, and that they had taken in several thousand more refugees that year and processed more to go to other camps in Tanzania.

He had been hired as an interpreter and liaison assistant for Mr Zimmerman but in fact that meant he was kind of like an odd-job man around the camp.And he soon began to help out with the clinic that Mrs Zimmerman ran with the replacement doctor, a Kenyan, that CAMEO sent out when they re-opened. He had taken Christian under his wing and encouraged him to apply for a medical training degree course when the camp was wound down. But it was actually the 'pastor', as Christian called Mr Zimmerman, who had convinced him to become a doctor. He said it had really all started when they talked amongst themselves about Sister Teresa, Mr Umbatu and Mr Harrison, as they waited for the police to arrive. And it carried on when they came back from Mwanza, accompanied by Mrs Beleshona, who had talked to the representatives that CAMEO had sent out to support the Umbeke staff. She had got herself a job there as well, helping Mrs Zimmerman and the other medics with the clinic and teaching the children while they stayed there during processing.

Over those two days he had told me about why Sister Teresa had been so foolishly brave. How she had nearly died during a war they had in Nigeria in the 1960s. She was the only one left of her family. They had been killed in the fighting, or starved to death in the famine that went on at the same time. Mrs Zimmerman had explained to him that the nun had been through a similar experience to the Zyandan women. That she had been raped and badly beaten and shot by the soldiers who had come to her village when she was only ten years old.

My dreams came back worse than ever, though I never told him that then. I was too ashamed when I thought about the little woman who had screamed at Mbrame for betraying his faith. Who called us all murderers. She had been very quiet at first in that little building we put them in. She was crying and looked really scared, but the Germans and the Englishman had all comforted her, so she had recovered and looked out at what was happening with the women at the window with Christian. They had been talking in English and I hadn't really listened to them much until she got loose and they all tried to follow her. Now I knew what had happened to her when she was a child it made a lot more sense to me.

Christian said he had felt such admiration for her he had wanted to follow her example and help people like she had. Like the Zimmermans too. He said they were amazing people who had worked all over Africa and helped others all their lives, but that even they had been in awe of what Teresa Olatunde had achieved in her life, in spite of such a terrible start. I had been thinking about her and the three other people in the school house that day ever since meeting Christian again, but I was still in a kind of torpor over that whole time, so it took me a while to work out what exactly Mrs. Beleshona wanted from me.

'For this to work, David, I need you to be aware of how you can repay some of what those three innocent people at Umbeke sacrificed. For myself, I hold a different guilt to you. Because of that I felt the need to carry on with what they had given to me and to those women and children I brought to that village. It was the same for Christian, though he focussed more on Doctor Olatunde, naturally. For me it was Aaron Umbatu, the man who got killed in the beginning, because he had taken the greater risk in trying to turn the Doctor and Tom Harrison back. To get help for all of us. That's why I came back to Umbeke with the Zimmermans and Christian. They needed people like those three and I wanted to work - literally to help do the work they would have done there if the Apostles had never followed us. I blame myself too, you see. Just like you are starting to do.'

She had found other ways of 'repaying the amnesty' the three aid workers had bought with their lives for the Zyandans that day. She told me I was included in that amnesty and after she had explained what that really meant I was more confused than ever, but for the first time in all those years I began to see a future for myself. When the UN helped the ZNP back into power in Zyanda she had returned, before the camp at Umbeke closed, because as she said, she had other qualities to offer to help rebuild our country. To make certain that the genocide could not happen again. But it was hard - we both knew that the ones who had escaped justice were still doing terrible things in the Congo and other countries in central Africa. The killing of Lutse and Matu refugees who were too scared to return to Zyanda still went on, just in fewer numbers and the governments and even the UN seemingly turned a blind eye so long as it did not get too obvious.

'I have some hopes still of doing something more meaningful than just throwing aid - food and medicines at the people who are lost and frightened. Even for people like you David, because you do know that what happened was wrong and you need a way to atone for your own part in it. I did not kill anyone, or ask anyone to kill people for whatever reason. But I was part of it all the same, because I had a chance to change things - in the way you children were educated, but I wasn't careful enough and I thought enough was being done by the politicians that might have saved us from all of this madness.'

'You couldn't help that - the President was killed...'

'No - I don't mean that. This is hard - I told you. It's not simple how wars start, but one of the ways to stop them is to prevent ignorance and, as a teacher, that was within my power to remedy. So our children could know what was right and what was wrong. Be able to see the truth and recognise the lies. Do you remember when you moved to Junior School? I taught you History then. Do you remember the lessons about the old Zyandan tribes and the colonial attitudes to racial bloodlines?'

'That was the past. It is over.'

'No. It's not. It's things like that which got us into this mess and that is something that educators should explain - why history misleads and divides and lies. I taught you the science but not the heart and so I failed you, because you, and other children not as smart as you, did not learn the lesson properly.'

A lot of what she said went over my head then, but we wrote to each other sometimes after I left Zyanda and gradually I understood what she was trying to do. Christian would become a doctor, like the nun who died. She had done some of

290

the work that Aaron Umbatu would have done in the refugee camp, working in the clinic and helping Christian and Mr Zimmerman and then coming back to Zyanda and working to change how people thought and how they acted towards each other. Which left the European, Tom Harrison. She wanted his sacrifice honoured as well.

At first I couldn't see what I could do about the life of an Englishman, here in Africa. Mrs Beleshona pointed out that he had not thought the same. That nobody had forced him come to Africa to help the people here. He had been a truck driver, carrying various supplies, food, fuel, medicine and personnel in Zambia, Kenya and briefly in Somalia and Ethiopia, for about four years. Mostly he had worked in agricultural communities, but he had taken loads through war zones on occasions and was a valued mechanic and driver at a big agency base in Zambia when he'd been detailed to come to Tanzania with various medical supplies that needed distribution and couldn't be flown in for some reason. He had come on to Umbeke with the nun as a favour because someone had been sick.

'He shouldn't have been in Umbeke at all apparently, but he came because Doctor Olatunde was a long-standing friend and she asked him to take her. We found out after the police investigation that he was due to return to England eight weeks later. He was going home to be married to another English lady who worked with him in Zambia, but they were both intending to come back to Africa at some stage, to work in the schools and on engineering projects. These are the kind of people our war has destroyed. People who care how others live and want to help them. Not just our people. Our Lutses. Our Matus. Our Twa. None of them should have died like that. Because of attitudes that are based on lies.'

I did remember the lessons. She had taught us from old school books, but also about our 'new' history in modern times. She had us read about how the Germans and Belgians made political and economic alliances with the Lutses because they were more 'co-operative' and better farmers, whilst the warrior-caste Matu were seen as troublemakers and cattle-thieves. The missionaries had also reinforced those perceptions and defined the Matu as 'bad lots' because they had migrated from the Horn of Africa and had taken territory by conquest. Even though they were thought in those days to be descended from Ham, one of the sons of Noah, they were also influenced by the Arab slavers and Islam, and so they were made to appear of less worth than the Lutse, who had come south a thousand years ago, from the Sahara and places like Chad and Sudan. It was all a nonsense she said. Modern genetics had proved that racially there was very little difference between Lutses and Matus, due to the amount of intermarriage that had happened since the Matu migrated to central Africa five hundred years before.

Religion also had been of little account in Zyanda's past, until the arrival of the missionaries and Roman Catholicism was the most influential creed in the country amongst both warring tribes. The famous 'long' Caucasian noses supposedly found in peoples from the Horn of Africa appeared in both Lutse and Matu communities and the cattle raiding aspect had been redundant for a hundred years or more. The truth was that although our points of origin were different, we were mostly descended from the peoples of Ancient Nubia.

The Twa, the smallest tribal group in Zyanda were the only ones who were racially different, being pygmies and of course they also had suffered badly during the war. To say the killings had been about blood ties was a nonsense, because for centuries there had been little difference between Lutse and Matu, though it was true the warrior traditions of the Matu had meant an uneasy relationship during the last century with the colonialists.

I still could not see how I could take the place of a European. Mrs Beleshona became quite angry with me, thinking I was being deliberately stupid, but the simple truth was that I was so far gone in hopelessness the smallest effort to think for myself was beyond me after years in prison. Give me a routine - get up, work, eat, more work, eat then sleep - and I went through it without question, on automatic. I was smoking dagga all the time then. We had it in prison as well, because it kept us quiet and numb and as she realised this she was gentler with me, but even more determined to get me out of this dark and narrow world I was living in and have me doing something meaningful with the rest of my life. My mother was right after all - Mrs Beleshona was the one who could and would help me get back on my feet. Just not for the same reasons because, in those days at least, she still hated me and could barely stand to talk to me. But she kept on with it. She was always a very determined woman and the war had only made her more so because she had lost her entire family and the work for CAMEO had become her mission in life. One thing we did share though, was our sorrow and feeling of loss for Misha and I knew by then that she would help me, if only for his sake.

'You have more in common with Tom Harrison than you know, David. Think about it. What did you do at Umbeke that he did as well? It's not a trick question!'

'All I did was hold the AK and guard them. He was the one who tried to stop the nun getting killed.'

'How did he arrive there? How did you leave? Come on

David it's not that difficult and you're not stupid!'

'Driving?'

'Finally! Yes. We always need drivers.'

It really had been that simple. The terms of my release from prison was that I submit to the judgment and needs of the community I was returned to. The place that had suffered most from the crimes I committed. CAMEO had been appointed by the UN to place representatives in some parts of Zyanda who were doing much the same as Verity Beleshona, although maybe not quite so personally as in my case. She had a vision of what should be done to rebuild, with a view to union and re-educating and this involved our government, as well as the international element in the funding of the projects she was working on. Her particular interest was in trying to rehabilitate the thousands of women who had survived the genocide, but had been severely injured or damaged sexually as a result of the rape and mutilations that the militias carried out. Many had been infected with the HIV virus and had developed AIDs by then. Mrs Beleshona was determined that the implications of the atrocities would not go away just because the women affected were dying six years later.

There was nothing I could say or do to justify what I did. My grandfather was wrong. I did have a choice, even if it was one that was likely to get me killed. I could have chosen not to do anything at all. Not join the Apostles. Not try to stop the killings. It was cowardice and would probably have left me with as much, if not more of a guilty conscience. But at least I would not have had blood on my hands and in my head. The rest of it, the destruction, looting and the rapes were what had disturbed me most in the end, because I saw the victims all around me still, in the wrecked shops and businesses; in Verity's burnt rooms; with the women that I sometimes glimpsed trying to look after their children, or their homes. They had maybe lost their arms, or could not walk far anymore because of injuries to their spines or pelvises from wounds dealt by blades, or simply by the violence of the assaults on their bodies during months of sexual and physical abuse...

... It is still difficult for me to deal with, but I can't lie about what I did. The killing, with Mbrame exhorting us to do the Lord's work, was like being a soldier... it's a bad metaphor, but throughout history the Church has never had a problem with violence. I mean it was a part of being an Apostle and when we killed we were brothers. The rest of it - the wanton destruction and the hurting of women and girls, that was something we did together too, but for me, that was different. I was very young in all kinds of ways. Misha and I had been with girls at school before, but not that much - the girls were mostly very scared of getting pregnant and we both had sisters we loved, so we never pushed for sex. And there was Fleur of course. She was so beautiful, and even though I was two years older than her and really she only thought of me as another brother, I suppose. We liked each other a lot and if things had been different...

What's the use in thinking like that. What's done is done and I can't do anything about it for her. For me there is nothing to be done. I will never marry, or have children. I haven't been with a woman since I was in prison, seven years ago now. And before that even...

... I saw them both dead. Misha and Fleur. Like I said, he died trying to protect her. My father pulled me away - he was upset too, but he knew if Mbrame saw how we were we would

pay for our weakness. So he calmed me down and then we went back to where we were staying that night. We all used to smoke dagga and drink beer, or spirits if we were lucky in our looting - there were some rich people in our town. We got high, or drunk, or both. Some of us - Paul Induna was one at first anyway - got excited just from the violence and didn't want or need more stimulation after we'd done our work. There were always women there that we had taken 'for later'. Some of them would try to get away - those were the ones who ended up like Angelique Beleshona. We'd hit them with whatever we had there - our pangas, knives, guns - fire them or hit them with it, or our fists, sometimes bottles. Whatever was near until they were subdued. When we finished with one we went on to the next, passing them around like we were playing with a football. I did it. It was a part of being an Apostle.

The night I saw Misha and Fleur I couldn't drink or smoke, I felt too sick. Every time a girl was given to me all I could see was Fleur's face. Her dead face, covered in blood. My father was watching me, trying to make sure I wasn't breaking down again. So I tried. I turned them around so I wouldn't have to see their faces and I held myself to them, but I couldn't. It just looked like I did. Then I did throw up, but that wasn't unusual because I wasn't used to alcohol so much and everyone else was concentrating on their own 'fun'. Finally I had an excuse to stop and I lay down and pretended I had passed out. They were laughing at me. My father said I was still a little boy and needed my beauty sleep. Like it was a joke. They thought he was mocking me and laughed even more, so I rolled over and hid my face and I cried like the boy I might have been still.

The worst thing? I wasn't lying to Verity about the women. I honestly couldn't remember how many because it was like with not recognising Christian? I never saw them. Sometimes I was so off my head I couldn't remember a thing, but when I wasn't I'd always detached and just went along with whatever was happening. Almost like I was watching a movie, except I was in it of course. Not at first maybe, but very soon, because that was the only way I could go through with what we did. When I came out of prison some of the women I saw must have been ones I had violated, but I never recognised any of them and none of them ever confronted me, so maybe it was the same for them...

Hell... I'm kidding myself of course. They must have known who I was, surely? Or was it because I was still a kid then. Maybe they didn't know it was me for certain, but they knew who I was. What I was. No - the worst thing was that I came out of all of that almost unscathed physically. I picked up some cuts here and there, but nothing serious. The weeks that I was still taking the girls I got a minor infection. Not even the clap. It was enough to stop me being able to get an erection, but probably that was as much to do with that night than the rash. My body was perfect more or less, if under-nourished back then. I'm a true Matu in that at least. Tall and strong with lean-muscled limbs. Fast on my feet, with my hands and eyes. I'm good with a gun. Of course.

That came in useful when we were in Mgakera, when the game began to get scarce and would run as soon as they saw or heard us. At least killing to eat is honest. In some ways that was the best time of my life. I liked hunting, but the best thing was sometimes just sitting and watching the animals and birds. Even silly little pests like the Quelea. But also driving out in the truck. I loved driving. The rougher the terrain the better. Or fast. Flat out.

My father taught me to drive. He used to drive delivery trucks for Mr Beleshona. Long distance. He used to do the grain run up to Uganda before. The day after Misha was killed he woke me up early and took me out and showed me how to start up and we went out for a drive. He said he was sorry about what he'd said - my needing my beauty sleep. There was no need. I knew he was trying to cover up for me. He said that if I could drive then maybe I 'wouldn't have to do the other side of it so much'. Those were his actual words. That was how we talked about what we did. Like it was our job. So you see, I had on the job training from a professional. I'm a good driver and I know my way around an engine pretty well. You have to when you drive long distance in Africa.

Tom Harrison was a mechanic too. Christian's told me a lot about him over the years. The Zimmermans kept in touch with him when they moved on to their next assignment - or maybe they retired. I'm not sure. The more I learned about Mr Harrison the worse it got in some ways. Christian said that it was obvious that he was really good friends with Sister Teresa from those short hours they were with us in the school house, especially at first, when she was so frightened. He said he had held her close and helped her move when she was still in shock, even though she tried to push him away. And then, while I was standing watch, he said they seemed to be taking it in turns to keep the other one's spirits up and did the same for him and for the Zimmermans.

I couldn't remember any of it, up until when she'd run past me. The rest I can never forget. What she shouted at Mbrame. How she stopped him beating Verity and kept going at him, letting him know exactly what she thought of him. What she thought of all of us. A little Bantu lady shouting at the big strong warriors who were going to kill the defenceless and the weak. Telling us we were evil and would pay for what we were doing. She must have been frightened most of the time that day and yet she did what none of us could have done in a million years. She took Mbrame down. It got her killed, but she did it anyway.

My grandfather said she shamed us all with the truth. He said she gave us a reason to stop, so she saved us as well as Verity and the other women. Verity says it was the same for her. I don't truly see why she blames herself so much for what happened to her and her family, but then her burden isn't so obvious as mine. She says she may not have killed anyone, but she didn't do enough to prevent it happening. Not as much as she could have done. But then how could she have known what sort of madness would come upon us all. It makes sense to her anyway. And it helped her make sense of it for me as well. In the end. We can never truly be friends, but at least she doesn't hate me anymore and she says that is the greatest gift that Sister Teresa gave us both. Grace to carry on living and to make a difference, free of hatred. Forgiveness is another matter, because neither of us can forgive ourselves.

Which brings me full circle, sitting outside my room, thirteen years later, watching the Quelea swarm across the dawn, drinking dagga tea. The dreams are back because something new is happening. Life goes on. Christian tells me that there's a new Doctor coming who'll be spending time at the Umbatu clinic here in Umbeke, helping him with the inoculations and the women's clinic. She's an English lady. The one who was going to marry Tom Harrison. Christian says she's going to be working at the Teresa Olatunde Community Hospital too, but she's done a lot of work with tropical disease inoculation with the British Army and so CAMEO wanted her to cover both catchments. He's very excited about working with her and thinks it would be a good idea for me to meet her. I'm not so sure. I didn't kill Tom Harrison, but I don't know if I can face the woman who lost him that day. In a place he would never have gone to if it hadn't been for the sake of a friend. I don't know how she can bear to come here to tell the truth. I know I wouldn't be brave enough to do that.

You see, there's no end to it. No running away, because all I have is the truth and the only honour left is in not letting myself forget what I did. Not for a minute. Except I do of course. I would go mad otherwise. So when I'm working I don't think about what I was. I do the job, because that way I'm wiping away some of the guilt. Repaying the amnesty like Verity says. I don't know what's worse now. To have ripped away the lives of the dead, or destroyed the future of the living. The dead walk with me still and will never leave me. The living - well, they may not know the truth, but they don't have to, because I do. And the truth is that I have no life of my own now. I don't deserve to have a life at all.

Here be Dragons ~ Physician

The pang, the curse, with which they died,
Had never passed away:
I could not draw my eyes from theirs,
Nor turn them up to pray.

The Rime of the Ancient Mariner
by Samuel Taylor Coleridge

Sophie's Diary: Monday 14th May ~ Umbeke, Mgakera River Enclave

It's 5:30am - I couldn't sleep and that, I suppose, was inevitable whether or not I'd gone and done such a silly thing as falling in love in the last 10 days. Tomorrow is a bigger day for me and everyone else here on both banks of the river. The official Day One of the Teresa Olatunde Community Hospital, but today I get to finally meet Christian Kamate and Verity Beleshona in person.

Christian I already feel I know, as we've been in touch by letter and email for some time now - almost three years. Henryk and Helga Zimmerman will also fly in today from South Africa for the dedication. They're both very excited and rightly proud of what's been accomplished here as a result of 'the amnesty'. Teresa's obviously, but also Tom's and the other poor man, Aaron Umbatu, who all died here thirteen years ago tomorrow.

Verity. Mrs Beleshona. I'm almost afraid to meet her in some respects. She's a formidable lady in all kinds of ways, not least because of her work in rehabilitating Matu who were involved in the genocide - the killers. Apparently she's Matu, but her husband was a prominent Lutse who might have risen to high political office.

He and all their children were killed during the genocide. Not the war. That's what it's called in Zyanda now. The war. Genocide isn't mentioned in polite circles there, but people remember naturally. Here, in the Enclave, genocide remains genocide. The Truth. Always. Veritas Semper. This is Verity's town in every sense.

As Chief Executive of the Mgakera River Enclave Co-operative, Verity's the de facto president of this little pseudo-republic. By UN charter, as they're supported by a whole barrage of international legislation and major relief organisations. But this is a community, not a nation - the mission statement makes that very clear. There are no politics. No tribes. Just people who need other people. That's the idea at least and in some ways I can believe in it. I can certainly commit and work within it.

I think I'm excited. I've had butterflies for days now. That too must be expected, because tomorrow's also the day that Luey goes for his interview for the UNESCO job. It's holistic you see, because they're one of the main guarantors of this Enclave as well. Whatever happens now, it's all new. A beginning. Yes, I am excited.

'Dr. Taylor?!' Verity almost ran out of the front door to greet Sophie as the driver dropped her off. Even though she'd seen photographs and been in contact over the telephone and internet, she'd been looking forward to meeting the doctor for so long she was actually shaking with nerves, afraid that they wouldn't match up to each other's expectations. 'Welcome to Mgakera! I hope you have rested well after your long day yesterday - it is not the best of roads here from Mwanza.'

'I'm very glad to be here, Mrs Beleshona. I admit to being too excited to have done more than nap, but my accommodation's beautifully quiet and very comfortable indeed, so I pretty much made myself at home already.' Sophie returned Verity's shy smile with one of her own and reverted to gabbling out a reply. Then they realised they were both chewing their bottom lips and burst out laughing.

'Shall we try again? I am Verity - may I call you Sophie?'

'Oh, yes please... Verity! Shall we do the formal greeting the English, or the French way?' Sophie was chuckling with relief and beginning to relax already.

'We can do it the family way I think - that is what I want more than anything for you and I.' Verity gave Sophie a swift hug, took her by the hand and led her into the boma that served her as both home and office. 'Come and have some breakfast with me - I only just got back an hour ago. Christian and his wife Deborah will join us quite soon, so it'll be more of a brunch I suppose, but I'm so hungry I can't wait!'

They ate on a shady terrace on the other side of the building that backed onto the river. By the time they sat back for a rest and to drink tea both were feeling much more comfortable and finding lots to talk about.

'So what do you think so far, Sophie? Will you like it here?'

'I think that was a foregone conclusion, although primarily I'm here to work.'

'You will have family not so far off in Kenya though?'

'Yes. My sister Claire - they run a safari business out near Lake Naivasha.'

'I have never been there, but I hear it is very beautiful?'

'Yes it is - but then most of the lake lands in the Great Rift are. The wetlands here look just as lovely in fact - the journey in was pretty gruelling, but the scenery more than made up for that.'

'And you have just finished a safari too?'

Sophie laughed. 'I see the CAMEO grapevine's been red hot as usual then? Yes. Claire got me a nice little working tour for a month, with an American party. Hollywood people in fact. They wanted a medic with them as they were doing pre-location work. Well, it was more of a golden 'hello' package thing really, so a bit corporate, but going to some very interesting places that were a little off the beaten track.'

Verity nodded thoughtfully and reached out for the thermal jug. 'We can squeeze one more cup each I think. I will make more when Christian and Deborah get here.'

'Does Deborah work with Christian too?'

'No - she's 'my' side of things. She is an art and language teacher. Well English literature as well. Something I need lessons for when it goes too much beyond Shakespeare and Dickens.'

'If English isn't a first or second language for you, then it's remarkably good. I'm afraid my Swahili's appalling - strictly tourist phrase book standard.'

'That you make the effort is enough. English is a universal language for us, even in central Africa.'

Sophie blushed royally. 'I'm afraid my French is actually worse than my Swahili. My family's got a military background in Kenya and Zambia, so the need for French skills wasn't too pressing as we were growing up. In fact I've never been to anywhere in mainland Europe, except Spain and Greece for beach holidays.' She decided a change of direction was needed. 'Deborah's American, isn't she? '

'Yes, she is - from Dallas, Texas. So at least you have English in common, but she's pretty good in Swahili now.'

'Ah - I know the West Coast better. Claire's husband's from southern California. Claire's ex-CAMEO as well. She was a nurse.'

'So medicine runs in the family a little?'

'Actually no. Just this generation. I was always intending

to teach as well... English and Maths. That was one of the things that had to be let go of, because of what happened here. But then I'm not the only one that had to have a re-think on their career, am I?'

Verity nodded slightly and wondered whether this turn in the conversation ought to be postponed, at least until Christian got here. She decided to give Sophie the option, half hoping that she'd want to leave it until Tuesday when all the excitement of the hospital dedication had died down. 'I've read your file of course. There are some things we need to talk about, relating to the genocide and the work you'll be undertaking with some of the people here. Christian and I have - well, hmm... a kind of confession to make, regarding one of the re-hab cases that we will need to discuss with you at some early stage. Would you prefer to do that today, or leave it until Tuesday?'

'Oh dear - that sounds ominous! I've no objection to today, if it's something urgent?'

'Not urgent - or not exactly. It's more discretionary to be honest. Personal in some ways.'

Sophie held Verity's gaze steadily. The anxiety vibes she was giving off were palpable, almost as though she was embarrassed to be asking the question.

'For me, today's about getting to know each other and I've nowhere else to be, or people to see so... I'm your consultant - no reason for you not to consult me. Especially if it is 'personal in some ways'?'

'Now you have taken the wind out of my sails, Sophie.' Verity smiled at the irony and came to a decision. 'I would honestly rather leave this until another day, but Christian may ask about it too - he is very worried. And in some respects

305

it is more my place to broach this with you than his. So let's do this now.'

'Well you've definitely got my attention - so, yes. Let's do it.'

Verity briefly outlined the situation in respect of David Mukuga, without naming him and then went on to the medical concerns that Christian had for his current wellbeing, pleased with Sophie's engagement, but rather dreading her reaction to the background that she was about to provide.

'I have no doubt in your ability to deal with this kind of thing - the trauma cases you've dealt with back in the UK, with the Army coming back from Iraq and Afghanistan are similar, so it is not that which concerns me. The patient... he is family to me in some ways, although he would say that he was not worthy of that esteem. He was my son's best friend.' She paused to consider how to put this next part, but Sophie replied, thinking Verity was feeling awkward and uncertain and wanting to make her easy on what was after all, the job she had come here to do.

'Then of course I'll help him in any way I can.'

'I know you would - the problem is that Christian and I do not know whether you should treat him at all. You see - he was a member of the militia who killed Doctor Olatunde and your fiancé. He was the boy who guarded the schoolhouse and who let Henryk and Mr Harrison go out to help the doctor. I do not think, in all honour that I can ask you to take his case on but Christian is convinced that he needs help very much and he's run out of options for treating him. Sophie?' Verity felt bad now because Sophie looked tense and pale under her tan. 'I am sorry. Maybe I should have left this for now...?'

'Tom. He's not the one who killed Tom.'

She heard herself speak calmly as though she were asking the time of day. It wasn't even a question. Her mind screamed to back right off, but she made herself consider what Verity was telling her and so she went on, striving to remain professional. 'I'll need to think about this. Thank you for telling me though. What I do want to know now, today is - why he's not stood trial for what happened? I thought they all got away? Or were killed later?'

'All of them, except him.' Verity felt some relief that Sophie didn't appear to be too distressed and so she knew that now she must answer whatever questions the doctor needed to ask. 'He never killed anyone at Umbeke. He helped his grandfather, the man who killed Mbrame - the priest who led them and ordered them to open fire on Tom and Henryk. The boy helped to disarm the others. After they left here, they went north and lived rough until the killings stopped and then gave themselves up to the ZNP. There was still fighting then, but with soldiers. All of the militia who came here were executed, except for this - boy. He was only fifteen years old. The same age as my son. They were born within days of each other. The ZNP took him prisoner and he was jailed for six years. This was all done before I returned to Zyanda at the end of '94, so none of them stood trial for what happened here.'

'Why didn't you give evidence against him?' Her voice was level. Conversational. Even though her head felt as though it would explode, she waited for the answers.

'At first I did not know he was in prison. I thought they were all dead, or disappeared. Things were very confused and a lot of people just vanished. But as I was part of CAMEO by then, and helping with restructuring, I found out about the others and that he was still alive. I thought about going to the Department of Justice, but he hadn't harmed anyone here, and he had been sentenced for what he did in Zyanda. So I decided to leave it at that. He was paying for what he had done.'

'So he was released. Why? Why was he let out, after killing all those people? He did that, didn't he? He should still be there in prison. Shouldn't he?'

Verity was now regretting starting this. Sophie looked wild-eyed and from being pale she now looked flushed and angry. And why shouldn't she be.

'Maybe he should be. But he was released. It wasn't just him - there were too many people in prison and some of them were victims as much as the people who had been hurt, or had lost family. You've read the casework. You know what has been happening here. Is still happening. I was part of the system of local court officials who decided whether 'low risk' prisoners - the ones who were not ringleaders or psychopaths - could be accepted back into their communities. You have read the notes on the amnesty system?'

'Yes. Go on.' Sophie's voice was tight and over-controlled now. She knew this wasn't Verity's fault and she knew that she was here to help anyone who needed it, whether they had been killers or family of their victims, because everyone was damaged. But this... 'You were right to tell me this. Just finish explaining for now and then I'll have to think about it.'

'You will help him?'

'I don't know yet. I need to think. After you finish telling me why you decided to bring him here.'

Sophie's Diary: Tuesday 15th May ~ 'Home'

2am this time. Except I haven't made it to bed at all. I wish I could be angry with Verity and Christian, but I can't. I don't even know who I'm supposed to be angry over. Verity wouldn't tell me his name aside from the obvious, which is David - I remember that from the statements. So every David I meet here I'll be wondering, is it you? That's if he still has the same name. Christian's been told not to talk to me about him yet and let me make my mind up about it all. Verity says he's not based in Umbeke, which means either he's in Mgakera itself, or in one of the satellite communities on the Tanzanian side - anywhere in a 50 mile radius give or take a few miles. So at least I'm not next door to him.

I'll take a sleeping pill I think. I deserve one.

Poor Luey. He called me this evening, all excited to be able to get hold of me on the phone at last and wanting to talk about tomorrow's interview and I really wasn't in the mood for chatting and I can't talk to him in any detail about this side of things. He's being such a darling about all this. I suppose it's not really surprising because he reminds me of Tom so much in his ways, so I do have someone who's always going to be on my 'side'. But as Verity says there are no 'sides' anymore. Just people to help. I do like her. She must have gone through so much and she's so open about it all, admitting she could barely stand to look at this man when he first came to her from prison and could find almost no compassion for him. But she did. Because he mourned her son and because he was really all she had left of herself from the old days. And she's right about the people here in Zyanda too. They're all carrying the guilt, whether they had a hand in the killings or not.

She says she wants to have some therapy as well. Counselling, not EMDR. She badly needs to talk to someone who wasn't involved. That I can do. The other - well we'll see. In theory there's no reason why I shouldn't take the case on. If I was a robot.

Time for the sleeping pill. Need some shuteye - be nice to see Henryk and Helga again anyway. That's not spoiled.

'We must have another toast I think.' Verity was almost dizzy with happiness and had invited Sophie, Christian and Deborah back to her boma for an evening barbeque with the Zimmermans, who were staying there with her for a few more days.

'I agree!' Henryk beamed around at the others gathered around the bonfire. 'To Aaron, Tom and Teresa!'

'To all of them!' Sophie smiled and joined her voice with the others. 'I think we should also toast Christian and Verity for all the hard work in getting Mgakera and Umbeke off the ground. I know Tom would have thought what's been done here is truly wonderful.'

'Teresa would have loved all this today.' Helga's cheeks were glowing with pride and the effects of a good South African Shiraz. Henryk hugged her and planted a bushy kiss on her cheek.

'Would you all like to see the rest of the photographs we brought up with us?' He asked. There had been TV people around earlier and Henryk had shown them pictures of the early days at Umbeke when the refugee camp was still in operation and some old shots of Teresa as a child in South Africa.

'Oh, yes please!' Verity clapped her hands with glee. 'It was so lovely to see Celeste and everyone again.'

They all went back to the terrace to sit at the large table and Henryk brought two large albums out for them to flick through. Sophie, sitting between the elderly couple, was more interested in the later one and to see how Umbeke had grown since the mid 90's, but Helga was keen for her to see the ones of Teresa too. She went along with that more out of politeness, and found herself getting quite absorbed in seeing the woman she had never really liked as a skinny little eleven

310

year old, or the rather serious looking teenaged novice about to go off to medical school.

'It really must have been dreadful out there in Biafra... she was tiny of course, but she's like a walking skeleton in these first ones.' Sophie frowned over the pictures taken while Teresa was still at the mobile hospital set up in her old village. 'And she was getting a little more food compared to some of the others.'

'Without the protein it didn't matter how much they were eating in some ways. That must have been about a month after we found her, I think. It was taken not long before we moved on.' Helga's voice was soft with memory. 'She had started to recover well then.'

'It's a miracle she survived - Youssef said he was convinced she'd die in post-op.' Sophie was almost reluctant to turn the page over.

'She responded well to the penicillin but, as you say, we were only just in time.'

The next pages were full of school pictures, or at the orphanage in South Africa where Teresa had lived for the next five years before returning to Nigeria to join the Carmelites as a postulant.

'This is the picture the TV people took a copy of - but I think the one on the next page is much better. They are both from when we were all together for Easter the following year. It was the first time Teresa tasted chocolate!' Henryk laughed fondly.

Sophie smiled at the black and white photograph that showed Henryk without his trademark beard and Helga at a table with Teresa in between them, looking straight at camera and grinning wide like a naughty cherub, her face more rounded and healthy, but still marred by the burn marks on both cheeks.

'She looks really happy - dreadful scars though. Tom thought they were tribal markings when he first met her.'

'Well you saw that they faded in time, but then the cause was obvious. She was too young anyway to have been scarified - or would have been in peace time if her family had been high caste.'

'Were they?' Verity was looking over Henryk's shoulder

'No, I don't think so. From what we know of the village her family weren't well off and of course we never got too much information out of her as to her life before the war. They were Catholics of course, so a big family with at least four younger children and I think three older - all boys so they had been conscripted with their father. She did tell us about her brother Adie. The one I found with her. She loved him very much.'

'Poor little girl. She was very beautiful.' Deborah dashed a tear away.

Sophie was beginning to feel rather uncomfortable and turned the page to look at the next picture, which was also in black and white, with Teresa in profile looking at Helga mischievously and Henryk, smiling away in the middle behind them hugging them both.

'I see what you mean - that's a much nicer photo of Ter...' Sophie voice tailed off slightly as she looked at a nearly forty years younger Henryk with an almost naked face. '... of Terry.'

'Isn't Henryk handsome in these!' Helga beamed at her husband. 'He had to shave his beard off. It was just growing back in then.'

'You know how I hate shaving - I couldn't wait for it come back.' Henryk laughed gruffly. Sophie nodded numbly, still staring at Henryk's happy smile, but pulled herself together and moved on to the next set.

'I feel a bit like the odd one out today...' Deborah came over to sit beside Sophie who'd decided she needed some time out and was back at the bonfire. 'I never knew them except through Christian. Sorry - do you mind my joining you?'

'I don't mind at all - you're not the only one feeling like they're out of place, so we can share the shame! Joking of course.'

Or was she? Sophie gave herself a mental rap on the knuckles and smiled at the pretty dark-haired Texan. 'I only really knew Tom. I can't even say I knew Terry that well. In fact I couldn't stand her... There! I'm a heretic!'

She laughed, a little self-consciously until Deborah unexpectedly joined in. 'Oops! I can't even pretend to be a little squiffy - this is only my second glass. Seriously though - at the time I thought Terry was a huge pain in the neck. In my silly eighteen year old head she used to monopolise Tom far too much - but I was just a jealous little cow back then of course.'

'But really she's the one who got Tom killed wasn't she? I can totally see why you weren't a fan at the time. Christian idolises her even now, so I can imagine how it would been frustrating for me if she'd still been around when I first met him.'

Sophie laughed. 'Oh, I think we're going to be mates Deborah! The irony is that if I had tried to be more friendly with her, I'd possibly not have been quite so traumatised with it all. She'd certainly have diagnosed me with malaria a lot sooner. But I wouldn't take any notice when she asked me the right questions. I just whined about her to Tom all the time.'

'Goodness! You caught malaria? Is that why you had to go home so quickly?'

'Well partly, yes. We were both due to go back in a couple of months. But - I've learned to get things in perspective more with Teresa and I don't actually blame her for Tom getting killed now. It was an impossible situation they were in and, apart from the psychotic priest, it was no one person's fault. I just wish that they'd never appointed her to the job here in the first place.'

'I don't think I'd be so generous if I'd been in your shoes.'

'Oh, I wasn't at the time, believe me. It hurt like hell losing Tom - our baby too. Took me years to get over it all.'

'Your baby? Oh my. I never knew that either.' Deborah, who was heavily pregnant with her first child, reached out for Sophie's hand. 'I'm so sorry - you were so very young as well.'

Sophie was faintly embarrassed with Deborah's reaction, but put it down to rampant hormones and accepted the sympathy calmly. 'I keep assuming everyone knows my side of the story, but of course really it's all about the three of them and I was just the last gasp of the whole catastrophe. I must say I agree with Verity. That Aaron Umbatu was actually the real hero of Umbeke. But then, if he had been able to turn Tom and Terry back, the militia men may have killed Verity and all those other women straight away and just disappeared into the bush.'

'Or they may have simply run away without killing anyone at all - there's no telling is there?'

'True. What if's are pointless...'

314

She sighed and looked over at the terrace where Christian was recounting some anecdote about one of the orderlies that the Zimmermans had hired several years back. 'So - enough about the past. We can't change it. Tell me about Deborah and Christian falling in love under the rabbit in the moon?'

* * *

Quackers status: Make it quick - I'm pooped

Doc Doolittle

Yo Gorgeous! (((hugs))) How was it?

Oh dear - are you exhausted with all the celebrations?

Quackers

Just come back - yeah v. tired but it was good. The party's still going on at Veritys

Anyway. What have you got to tell me? :-)

Sent at 9:35pm on Tues

Doc Doolittle

To make some room for me in your rondavel - I got it! :-D

Quackers

!!!!!!!!!!!!!!

They told you already? Oh luey! xxxxxx

Doc Doolittle

Brilliant isn't it? ;-)

Yeah I was a little taken aback that they told me there and then but apparently I'm exactly what they want for the Mgakera Conservation project with my stock and wildlife background. Also the part time game guiding will come in useful for one of the long term commercial projects they want to put in place.

315

Quackers

Oh? What's that then?

Doc Doolittle

Probably best you ask Verity about it - in fact I'm surprised she hasn't already told you.

Quackers

?

Doc Doolittle

lol - well you know those game reserves. They're gonna put some exclusive safari accommodation in there eventually. In fact that's possibly why I cracked it so easily because I was telling them about us and how we met and mentioned about Claire as well and suddenly we were talking about exclusive eco-tourism!

Quackers

!!!

So that's why she was so interested in Claire yesterday! lol Any idea when you start?

Doc Doolittle

ASAP
Should be with you week after next :-)

Quackers

Oh wow - so we can start blissful co-habitation! I love you so much! xxxxxxxxxxxxx

Doc Doolittle

Well I must say it's a big relief - it's quick but I've been scared silly some hunky Maasai would whisk you off your feet before I could get there - so I'm glad they didn't keep me dangling with making their minds up

Quackers

lol - idiot! :-p you know I've fallen for you hook line and sinker

Doc Doolittle

Well you women are so unpredictable... :-D

Quackers

You have a real mean streak at times Tarzan :-p

Doc Doolittle

But you love me anyway (((hugs))) Big wet kisses atcha!

Quackers

For some reason my feminist leanings just evaporate around you - will be v. nice to have some real big wet kisses on tap though lol

Doc Doolittle

I could certainly get used to that too babe

Harry says to give you a big kiss from him too - he says he wants to come up and check out the game situation once I've settled - with Claire in the frame through you there could be something REALLY great coming out of this!

Quackers

Reading between the lines of my talks with Verity so far I think she's going to be delighted over this - she says that there's been so much focus on the hospital and self-sufficiency aspects that the long term planning for the various communities hasn't really been touched on yet. They're very keen to get to grips with managing the conservation issues they have and to look at getting mega-tourist dollars in.

Doc Doolittle

Well if they want to get something going with the tribal territories and run it with them in the driving seat more or less then it could be something unique in Africa. I'm even more excited about all this now - it's like some fantastic dream come true!

Quackers

yes it is...

Oh Luey - I wish you were here right now

Doc Doolittle

Me too babe - I can't wait to get there now (((big bear hugs)))

Here be Dragons ~ Truth

Alone, alone, all, all alone,
Alone on a wide wide sea!
And never a saint took pity on
My soul in agony.

The Rime of the Ancient Mariner
by Samuel Taylor Coleridge

10 days later ~ Airport, Mwanza, Tanzania

Luey, reunited with his bags, came into the arrivals area and his face lit up as he spotted his name on the dry-wipe board held by the tall skinny black guy with the greying hair and the cool aviator glasses, wearing a faded denim shirt and dusty black jeans. Verity had assured him that he'd be met promptly and the lady had so far delivered all down the line on the flurry of calls and emails that had been going back and forth between them since he'd clinched the job. He even knew the name of the guy holding the board.

'Hi there. David Mukuga? I'm Luey. Am I pleased to see you!'

David grinned back at him and shook the offered hand firmly. 'Jambo[36] Luey. Pleased to meet you also.' Verity had told him that the Zimbabwean seemed very friendly and these days it made a nice change to get out of Umbeke on a two day round trip like this, especially if there was someone

---

[36] **Jambo** ~ hello in Swahili

interesting to share the journey with him. 'It's going to be a long hot day so shall we get out of here - I just collected a new land cruiser from the depot and I can't wait to try it out. You need a hand with your bags there?'

'I'm good - it kinda balances out, thanks. What're the roads like?'

'For traffic or grade?' David laughed as they went out the door.

'Both - not great, huh?' Luey couldn't stop chuckling now.

'The rush hour's almost over so traffic won't be too bad once we are clear of the city and the ferry. Roads - well maybe not so good as you're used to in the south.'

'They're not so great these days - so long as we're not driving over flint gravel I'll be happy. My back's a bit rough for too much tyre changing. Didn't sleep too well between Harare and Nairobi and the hop over the Great Rift was pretty thrilling, so I'm probably gonna crash on you for a bit for the first leg anyhow.'

'The view is better as we get away from the city, so I won't disturb your rest until we're well on the way. You're lucky we aren't going back in the lorry I came up in - but tyres will not be a problem!'

'Oh? Phew - it's buggery hot already!"

David was leading the way to where he'd parked up. He looked over his shoulder and smiled sympathetically. 'Air con is not far away, Luey. We're going back in convoy and the lorry is carrying a load of supplies - including tyre spares.'

The land cruiser wasn't brand new, but Luey was grateful for the air con as the humidity was high. As usual with a new city and country, despite his fatigue, he was too hyped to get off to sleep straight off, especially as the views were a strange mix of granite kopjes and more verdant wooded headlands that put him in mind of the Matopos in Zimbabwe. And, in a more bizarre way, of the northern lakes in Italy. As they drew away from the city and followed the dragoman they'd picked up with at the CAMEO depot to the east of Mwanza he began to doze off, glad that David appeared to be one of those rare long distance drivers who didn't mind you going to sleep on him.

They'd been on the road for around ninety minutes when he was woken up by the sound of the door closing and saw they'd arrived at the ferry port. David was talking to the dragoman driver so Luey got out as well as he hadn't met the man yet.

'Hey, Luey - I was going to let you sleep, but come and meet Sully.' David smiled over at him as Sully was getting down from the cab. Suddenly Luey, who was a good six foot began to feel a little on the short side as both men were several inches taller.

'Hi there Sully. I'm suddenly feeling my stumpy Mediterranean side. Man - you two are like beanpoles! Are you both Maasai?' The two drivers grinned as Sully and Luey shook hands. David laughed softly.

'Oh no! I'm supposedly Matu and Sully here has Luo blood. But mostly we're mutts - bit of everything.'

'Ah well - nothing new then. I'm pretty mixed up too. Scots, Italian, English, Irish and Heinz 57 no doubt.'

'Well at least you got the brown hair and eyes - best thing living here.' Sully was wearing the light cotton prayer cap that marked him as a follower of Islam. 'Glad to meet you Luey. I know someone who will be even more pleased to see you when we get back to Umbeke! Sophie says you are to do as you are told and not hold us up with nosey questions so we are not on the road in the dark too much.' He winked knowingly at Luey.

'I will just go and see how long we have to wait.' David had been getting fidgety and excused himself.

Luey shook his head and grinned like an idiot. 'I wouldn't mind, but I've barely known Sophie a month and already I'm hen-pecked.'

'Haha - well I guess it would not be too bad to have a bossy doctor for your woman. I did the airport run for her when she first came and she talked about you all the way back to Umbeke.'

'Really?' Luey flushed with a combination of pleasure and the heat and wiped his forehead with the back of his hand.

'You better get back in the car Luey - it's a hot one today and you are not used to lake weather yet. I will keep you company as David's off in one of his moods - get a sneak look at this 'Cruiser as well!'

They'd started walking back to the vehicle and Luey slipped gratefully back into the relative shade and still reasonable coolness of the passenger seat, while Sully moved the driver's seat back a few notches and tried it out for size.

'Oh yes - I could get used to this! David's going to have to keep on pulling rank on the rest of us to keep this baby to himself!'

'David's your boss then? He didn't say.' Luey was suddenly intrigued. Although David was very friendly, there was a reserve about him somehow, although at first he'd put that down to his own fatigue in this awful sticky heat.

'Well, he's not exactly my boss but he's the top man in the vehicle shop in Umbeke - been working for Verity since the beginning more or less and he's a veteran relief driver. Done stints up in Somalia, Sudan, Angola - all the war zones. Most of us back at Umbeke are locals or Zyandans, so he's a bit of a legend with the younger ones.'

'He's Zyandan though?'

'Yeah - from the same town as Verity. She's known him since he was a little boy. I thought he was her son at first.'

'Really? But surely he's as old as her, I'd have thought?'

'Nah. He is younger than I am - in his late twenties. We think he went through some bad shit during that genocide, but he never talks about it.'

'Well... I guess that's not too uncommon is it? Plenty of things I wouldn't want to talk about if I'd gone through all that.'

'Yeah - I told him on the way over he should see your lady. Lot of the Zyandans are already saying she's doing some fine work with them. Might do him some good, but I doubt he'll go.'

Luey frowned slightly. 'Well if anyone can help, it'd be her. She's been through the mill as well and she's trained for years with these various therapies.'

'She is a good doctor - she delivered my youngest son last week. My wife has been praising the Prophet for sending her to us!'

'Difficulties?'

'Our last two children died during the birth. Maryam was terrified for this one as well.'

Luey smiled at him. 'Sophie's a special lady. She loves me for a start.'

'Pity - I was going to ask her if she would like to be my third wife. I like blondes.'

'Hands off, man - I'm not letting her get away!' Luey's smile was a little frosty all of a sudden, but Sully took one look and roared with laughter.

'Just testing - the way she talks about you I know I don't

stand a chance with her.'

'Good - you had me worried there a moment.' He laughed sheepishly. 'So how long have you known David then?'

'From the beginning. About three, four years nearly. He's a good friend, but he needs a lot of space outside of work. Loves his books too much, I think. Spends far too much time with them. That and watching birds. Elephants too.'

'Ah, well - birds and elephants I understand. No girlfriends or wives?'

'Nope - never even looks at a woman, aside from Verity. I think she is worried for him and I know Kamate is. He's the other doctor in Umbeke.'

'That's Christian Kamate isn't it?'

Sully nodded and opened the door. 'Here's David coming back - I better make myself scarce! He's smiling though, so I think the ferry is not so far away. I will see you around lunch time I expect.'

'Look forward to it! Drive safe.'

'Always do!' He waved in farewell and walked back to the truck, pausing to have a short exchange with David.

Lack of sleep, not only for the past twenty-four hours but for several weeks of highs with Sophie and uncertainty over his own future, finally caught up with Luey on the ferry and so David let him go until well past noon. This time Luey slept through them pulling over in a little village just past a major road junction. It wasn't until David and Sully had got back into the vehicle and put the air con on full blast, that he finally surfaced groggily to the fragrant smell of fresh cut pink bananas, mingling rather deliciously with warm curried chicken and steaming hot tea.

'Hey there, Mister Sleepy. We thought you might be ready for some truckers delight!' David smiled at him and passed him a spicy dry-coated chicken quarter wrapped thickly in kitchen towel, put two waxed paper mugs of black tea on the dash holders and gave the other to Sully who had stretched out on the central seating.

'Verity's obviously out to impress you with the travel expenses, Luey. Usually she gets our wives to pack us cold rations.' Sully winked at him then took a huge bite at his chicken, making loudly appreciative noises.'

Luey sniffed at his lunch happily, but yawned widely again. 'Oh, man... I'm bushed. Did I miss the gold mines?'

'Yup.' David nodded through a mouthful of his chapati and pointed to Luey's which was hidden underneath the chicken. 'Two hours ago. You'll see them another time - nothing too much to write home about. Don't let this get too cold Luey. It is good cooking.'

'The owner has her eye on David I think - she gave the biggest one to him... 'This is yours, Mister Mukuga!' Sully did a passable impression of seductive contralto tones while David rolled his eyes. The truck driver guffawed and jingled his keys at David. 'You want to use the bed? Luey and I can just chill in here. Go score us some samosas and we'll say we had to stop to put some water in the radiator.' David shook his head good humouredly, but said nothing.

'I got some US if you wanna get some afters?' Luey said through a mouthful of the chicken, then swallowed and laughed. 'Sorry - this is seriously good grub, guys. Least I can do for being such a duff travel companion.'

'Nah - I was only messing! You're part of the Enclave now, man. We get well looked after - Mama Verity's bit of Africa is one great ride!' Sully was in his element now. 'Hey, David - you found the music system in here yet?'

'CD player - and I didn't bring any.'

'Probably for the best - this is the only African man who's into ABBA, Luey! Mind you that blonde one's tail is something I could never get tired of looking at.'

'Take no notice of him Luey - I like the lyrics, but I prefer orchestral on long trips.'

Luey laughed at them. 'I got some music in the bag. Enigma Variations your thing?'

'Yeah, Elgar's cool. When we're on the road though, otherwise this one will want to go through your entire collection trying to find some Bob Marley.'

'He'll be a long time looking then! I'm afraid I'm a metal head on the quiet - or rather the loud.'

Lunch over, they headed southwest on their new route to join the Zyanda highway, following the contours of the hills, through more rural and increasingly empty landscapes and steadily gaining height. Feeling more refreshed now Luey was determined to stay awake and get a good look at his new home. David also became more animated and they gradually drifted into deeper discussion on the wildlife around Umbeke and the eastern highlands of Tanzania and the Zyandan borders.

'It'll be grand if we have a small sitatunga population, even if it's all the way over to Lake Victoria. They're really rare in Zim now - just in the swamps on the upper Zambezi outside Vic Falls and I've only ever seen one there. Beautiful male.'

'I think they may be found on the smaller lakes nearer to Umbeke still as well. The Luo say they see them sometimes.'

'No Maasai over here then?'

'No - they are more in the Serengeti and up into Kenya, so well east of here. You like the Maasai huh?'

'The lifestyle - what's not to like. Nomadic pastoralists following the grazing and keeping the lions at bay. Living alongside the wildlife, but not depleting it - they're natural conservationists.'

'It is a hard life though. These days they are more into getting tourist dollars into their pockets - getting rich European women to sleep with them is a good career move for some of their boys up on the coast in Kenya.'

'What about here in Tanzania?'

'Well the Serengeti and Ngorongoro clans make their money on the old folkways still. They roam the savannah, but let the tourists take their pictures when they take their rites of passage.'

'The black ostrich feathers and not yelling during the emorata?' [37]

David laughed. 'Something like that I believe.' He paused a moment and decided to get the inevitable question that most newcomers to the Enclave would eventually ask out of the way. If Luey knew Doctor Taylor then he probably already knew a lot about the genocide. 'To be honest where I come from there is not much emphasis given to tribal customs or affiliations these days. I am just a Zyandan now - there never was much of a racial divide between the Matu and Lutse unless you go back five hundred years or more.'

'It was more down to how many cows a man had or something? Or how straight and long your nose was?' Luey opted to be equally direct now the genie was out of the bottle.

'More or less, yes. How much you liked cosying up to the

---

[37] **emorata** ~ the word for circumcision in the Maa language. Both genders are traditionally circumcised around the early teens, although the practice for females (generally a clitorectomy only) is gradually decreasing.

colonialists as well, or whether you preferred cattle rustling - the Maasai wouldn't have been too popular if they'd been interested in moving that far west, but equatorial rainforests didn't appeal much to them of course. The Lutse were more like the Luo. Better dairy farmers and agriculturalists - not so keen on resisting civilisation and Christianity.'

'Sounds like you've studied the history.'

'I was one of Verity's star pupils before the genocide. Regrettably I didn't pay enough attention to the Social Politics modules.' He flicked the CD on again and pushed the Enigma Variations back in. 'This is why I prefer classical music these days. When I was a teenager there was too much propaganda on the radio. We got saturated with it. Soiled. These days I mostly like my lyrics gentle, or not there at all. And I have trouble sleeping, so soft orchestral music is always good.'

They had arrived at the junction for the Zyandan highway and the last leg of their journey. As promised, the road surface improved slightly and David overtook Sully's dragoman with a long and loud horn salute and stepped up the speed as they headed northwest into the slowly sinking sun. He put his sunglasses on again. Luey tore his gaze away from the scenery for a few moments and looked more closely at the obviously complex young man, who appeared to be at least twenty years older than he really was. As they'd been travelling south he'd noticed how tired David looked, with dark circles under his red-stained eyes. If he hadn't obviously been sharp as a tack and coherent, Luey thought, he would have looked like a real dagga-head but it must be just accumulated fatigue. The guy sure looked a bit of a wreck in some respects. Skinny as hell, even allowing for the tall genes. What Luey was sensing more and more, was that David was rather like a wounded animal who was trying very hard to act as if it wasn't, to keep up with the herd, or fool the predators.

'We can make time and put this girl through her paces now.' David looked over at him and smiled. 'This road's graded almost all the way there.'

'If you need a rest I can drive for a bit if you like - if there's not too many potholes to avoid.'

'That's kind of you, but I'm fine. Used to this road and we'll be there before sunset. I'm to drop you off at the staff quarters for the clinic in Umbeke?'

'Yeah. Sophie's supposed to be meeting me there and then I think we go on to Verity's place? Will you be coming with us?'

David shook his head slightly, concentrating on the road. 'No - I have to take the vehicle over to the shop. That's about two miles upriver from Umbeke out near the Umbatu Plantation. Then I'm off duty - back to a good book and sleep the journey off if I can.'

'Maybe Sully's right - you should see Sophie about this not sleeping. You look pretty knackered to me, man.'

'Says the guy who's just passed out for three hours. I am used to it and Christian's my doctor. He looks after me pretty well.' David made light of it. 'Don't worry - I'll not drive us into a ditch. So... what terrible tales has Sully been telling you about me?'

'Nothing really - just that you're a bit of a book worm and need a lot of space. I'd have got the not sleeping bit from the baggy red eyes without your telling me. Us vets know an exhausted animal when we see one.'

'Guilty to being a bookworm. I enjoy my own company though. And the not sleeping... well I guess you get used to it and I've been driving since I was fifteen. My father taught me.'

'Sully said you've worked some rough gigs. Somalia?'

David shook his head more vigorously and laughed. 'He sure has a big mouth that Sully. Yeah - I've done runs to Somalia, Angola... places like that. In relief convoys under UN escort mainly. Somalia was tough, but it's not as though I'm a soldier. But then I never was a soldier. Just a kid with a panga most of the time - I only got to hold a gun for a few weeks.'

'He's just being a friend. I think he was concerned about you getting all 'moody' this morning.'

'Moody?' Again David laughed, but it had a rather hollow ring. The Adagio was playing and he turned the volume up slightly.

'At the ferry this morning. When Sully mentioned Sophie? You took off like a hare.'

David's grip on the wheel tightened and he knew he looked embarrassed. Verity had said that Doctor Taylor was still making up her mind about whether she wanted to see him or not, but Luey wouldn't know about that necessarily. On the other hand if the Doctor and the Vet were together, then perhaps they'd discussed the decision she'd been asked to consider. He directed all his attention on the road, going through the familiar comfortable motions of scanning the mirrors, near and far distance and the road surface, reading it all like a book until his mind calmed again. As always the truth was his friend, so he just asked the question.

'You know Doctor Taylor very well I think?'

'I haven't known her that long, but yes. We're close. I'm hoping we'll get married one day.'

'So you know why she has come here to Umbeke. To work with people like me. People who lived through the genocide.'

'Yes. Sully thinks she's a good doctor and might be able

to help you.'

'She might not want to.' David's voice was soft and sad. 'I can't see her unless she decides that she wants to take my case on.'

'Do you even want her to? Ah... sorry, David. Us Zimbabweans aren't known for our tact. Tell me to and I'll mind my own business?'

What to say. Luey obviously hadn't heard about his unique situation from the new doctor. David's laugh wasn't exactly uneasy and the old days weren't a taboo subject at the Enclave, but even so he didn't really talk about his own experiences to anybody much. With him it had always been about business and his private time was almost exclusively unshared, except with Verity who wasn't exactly a friend and Christian who definitely was, but a very forceful one sometimes. He was always telling him he couldn't keep on huddling himself away from people the whole time. Verity had told him a little about the work Doctor Taylor did and how part of it was about learning to deal with the bad memories, by giving them air with people who weren't a part of them. That was the trouble here - most of the people he was close enough to open up with knew all about him. And even though Doctor Taylor didn't know him, she was too close in some respects as well.

David decided to take a chance on Luey, since he seemed to want to be friendly and was sensible as well as intelligent. He took a deep breath for courage. 'I'm an open book, so you don't have to. I have a very bad past, Luey. I killed a lot of people and I've been in prison. Doctor Taylor doesn't have to see me if she doesn't want to, and I have to stay away from her until she's made her mind up. I told Verity I won't see her unless she agrees to it.'

'Why wouldn't she?'

And there it was. The whole problem in a nutshell.

'Because I was one of the Apostles. The militia who killed the nun and the other two men at Umbeke thirteen years ago.'

There was a taut silence in which Luey must have held his breath, because he suddenly let it out in a low whistling rush. 'Oh, man! That's rough...' Was this why Sophie hadn't been so keen on talking about her work and kept changing the subject when they'd spoken the last couple of weeks? 'So Soph hasn't seen you at all yet.'

'No. Not yet. I didn't want to see her at all. Not even tell her I was at the Enclave, but Verity said that would be too deceitful and that she had a right to know, even if I refused to have treatment. Doctor Kamate says he's run out of medical options for me, so he's the one pushing for a psychological referral. Really, I don't want to cause any trouble, so it is best that I stay away from Doctor Taylor - unless she does agree to take my case.'

Luey was shaking his head, trying to get to grips with the situation.

'Sorry - I know what happened more or less, but Sophie said that none of the men who killed Tom Harrison and the others were ever found? That's what she said anyway.'

'She didn't know about me until Verity told her the day after she arrived. We were never brought to trial for what happened there. My grandfather killed Mbrame straight after he murdered the nun... and Amduna, the man who shot Tom Harrison, killed himself a few weeks later. After we went back to Zyanda. When the ZNP finished off the militias we gave ourselves up and everyone except me was executed for war crimes. I am the only one left.'

'And they just sent you to prison? For killing foreign nationals and non-combatants?'

'I didn't kill anyone at Umbeke. Only Zyandans and only in Zyanda. And I'm still in prison.' He tapped his head manically. 'I locked myself in and threw away the key thirteen years ago.'

'I don't know what to say, man.'

This time David's laugh was harsh and self-mocking. 'You think I do? Verity is the one who tries to make sense of it and I go along with what she thinks is right. In prison all I did was rot. Out here I can at least be of some practical use to the living. And the dead - they make sure I know who to blame for what my own life has become.'

'No shit!' The words were sotto voce. He was appalled at the bald, almost emotionless statements.

'T.I.A. Luey. Black-hearted Africa. I'm still paying because I need to. Have to. Doctor Taylor doesn't. Not for me. So it's her choice and if she wants me gone, then I'll leave the Enclave altogether.'

There was silence between them for a while and the music played on, moving onto lighter, less momentous themes as both men mulled over what had just passed between them. When the Moderato started Luey's thoughts on the seeming collusion of keeping David's part in the Umbeke incident hidden from the powers that be tumbled out, though he tried not to sound like he was judging the man in any way.

'Why did Verity and Doctor Kamate not report you to the authorities, David?'

'Why do you think? Things were in a state of upheaval. We gave ourselves up to the army, but there was still fighting going on in the south. It was a military court and the day after we went in the others went to the firing squad and I was sent to a camp and then the prison a few weeks later.'

There was a large pothole ahead and he stopped talking for a few moments, eyes scanning the road for the best route. 'To be honest I can't even remember whether Umbeke was mentioned - even if it was, they wouldn't have been that interested at that stage. Verity was still here in Tanzania when we turned ourselves in and by the time she had come back and found out what had happened to us, I had been in prison for a year or so.'

'She just left it alone then?'

'Yes. The ones who had done the killings at Umbeke were all gone. Verity and the other women were not harmed. So she said nothing. There was no point with everyone else dead.'

'You didn't kill anyone?'

'Not that day, no. I was holding the gun on the CAMEO people, so I wasn't one of those who chopped Aaron Umbatu. Verity knew all that and so she decided there was nothing left to be done.'

'Christ - you say it like that's nothing! She kept quiet for you - you could still have been hanged...'

'She didn't have to do anything. She thought I would stay in prison until the day I died. So did I.'

Luey had been practically biting his tongue through, so his last remark had burst out like a grand prix winner's champagne cork. No wonder Sophie hadn't said anything to him. He knew that in theory the Zyandan genocide was done and dusted in legal terms and that the Mgakera River Enclave was part of a brokered solution to rehabilitate people who'd survived that brutal period. That it sheltered the killers as well as the victims was taking the moral gymnastics to a point that made his head ache. Taken in isolation, he could deal with it as a concept and even see the justice in it for everyone concerned - hell, he'd been feeling sorry for David practically from the moment he clapped eyes on him but this situation was almost unbelievable. It was too personal that was the problem. He was sitting next to one of the men who had held Sophie's first love at gunpoint and watched him get shot down in cold blood by one of his brothers. And then Verity Beleshona decided, like God Almighty, that Sophie should be told about this man and then left to decide whether she could bring herself to act as David's counsellor, or therapist, or whatever the hell they wanted her to do with him?

He realised with a start that his hands were curling into fists and willed himself to calm down. David was looking as tense, jaw set hard and eyes narrowed and concentrating fiercely on the road. And he had trouble sleeping... bloody hell! But Sophie had known what she was getting into when she took the job. He knew she had taken the time to consider all the ramifications of taking on the work. She knew she'd be working with people like David, even if she hadn't bargained on one of the militia responsible for Tom's death still being around. Had she asked the same things? Of course she must have. She'd been evasive about her work to him so far, but had seemed quite happy about what she was doing in general when he'd spoken to her in the week. He'd put her reticence down to patient confidentiality and realised with a start that this was the only possible explanation. What did he expect her to say? 'Hi Luey, how was your day? Oh - guess what! They asked me if I wanted to shrink one of the gang who killed Tom. Isn't that nice and considerate of them?' A bloody impossible situation for everyone, but especially for the woman he loved.

He chewed his lip in frustration, realising that there wasn't an easy fix for anyone and that probably Verity was dealing with it fairly. And David was even more realistic, in that it seemed he didn't really want to have anything to do with Sophie at all, to the extent that he was prepared to leave if she couldn't take it. All he could do was support Sophie and keep out of the rest of it because he didn't know enough about the background and frankly didn't want to, because someone else poking away at it wouldn't help anyone now. He raked his fingers through his hair, suddenly feeling knackered again and sighed heavily.

'OK - this is beyond me. I admit it. So I'll keep out of it - although I think Sophie's been put in a hell of a position over all of this. It really isn't fair on her.'

'I wish it could have been avoided.' David spoke carefully, anxious not to be misunderstood. 'I don't want for Doctor Taylor to have to do anything that makes things hard for her. Whatever she decides, I do not want to hurt her anymore than she has been.'

'Too late for that, man.'

David swallowed a huge lump in his throat, but held his tongue. Nothing he could do now would make the situation go away or make it easier on anyone. He was actually very angry with both Verity and Christian for wanting to involve Sophie in any way at all. As soon as Verity had told him about the new specialist who was coming to Umbeke he'd asked to be transferred, but Christian had said that the current state of his health was so bad he'd not be accepted as fit for duty anywhere else and he couldn't argue with that because he knew it was true. Sully had had to do all the driving yesterday because he'd been too strung out and had drunk dagga tea from the thermos virtually non-stop until midnight to get to sleep for a few hours before picking Luey up. He was trapped in the Enclave now. He couldn't function anywhere else.

'Where are you quartered at Mgakera David?' Luey asked wearily.

'Not anywhere near Doctor Taylor, if that's what you mean. I live by the vehicle shop out at the Umbatu plantation.'

'That's the coffee farm, yes? Not that far from Umbeke though.'

'No, but it's not near anywhere that the doctors go to regularly. Verity's fixed the schedules so that I don't go into Umbeke too often at the moment - and nowhere near the clinics, or to work on the staff cars.'

'So you really are able to stay away from her? For now.'

'Yes. For now I'm strictly on fleet services. Mechanic jobs and I have people who can do on site work or call outs for the medical vehicles.'

'That's good then, I suppose. At least Sophie can make up her mind in peace.'

David nodded slowly. 'Verity doesn't want to put any pressure on her.'

'Yeah, right. Strikes me Verity makes a lot of concessions for everyone.'

'She has a very difficult job, Luey. She knows what it is like to lose someone like Dr. Taylor did. Verity lost her whole family in the genocide.'

'Sully said you've known her a long time.'

'I was her son's best friend. She was my favourite teacher at school.'

'And now she's like your permanent parole officer.'

'What?' David briefly glanced over at Luey. 'What do you mean?'

'That she seems to pull all your strings, I suppose. Why'd she send you out to bring me in today for one thing. Doesn't seem like too good an idea to me - with wanting to keep you away from Sophie and things. Wasn't there someone else who could've come up with Sully for the supplies and to pick this cruiser up?'

David was momentarily speechless. He hadn't thought anything of it when Verity had asked him if he wanted to do this run, although at the time he hadn't realised that Luey had anything to do with the doctor until Sully had mentioned her at the ferry... But then Verity had said that she wanted him to meet Luey as soon as possible, as he was to be assigned to him as his driver for the out of town work while he was settling in. That had made perfect sense to him until Sully had made that casual remark about the doctor. Confused now, he shook his head.

'I don't know why, Luey. But Verity... she's not like that. Manipulative. Not at all.'

'You know her - I don't. I speak as I find. She's a clever lady whatever, so I'm just wondering whether the likelihood of us having this crop up in general conversation, really hadn't occurred to her?'

'When you put it like that...' David frowned, his mind starting to churn now. 'I thought it was because I am going to be showing you around for the next few weeks.'

Luey looked hard at him, hearing the genuine doubt in his voice. 'OK. She's not like that if you say so. Just as well you're able to deal with things upfront - although it's hardly been a comfortable half hour has it?'

'This is not a conversation I wanted to have with you Luey, believe me.'

'Oh I do, mate. I do believe you.'

'So where does this leave us, then?' He liked this man and had hoped they would be friends. He tried to sound professional, matter of fact, but he could hear his pulse thudding in his ears like thunder. 'Do you want someone else assigned to you? That can be arranged if you like.'

'No - it's alright. You've been straight with me and we both agree that Sophie isn't to be upset by all this. Hopefully I can talk some of this over with her when we get in. I think we can both work together anyway. Whatever she decides about you.'

'Thank you. That is all I want, Luey.'

The CD had finished. Luey hit eject. 'You want this again, or something else? I'm all out of talk for now.'

'So am I. Whatever you want to listen to, Luey.'

* * *

They drove past a signpost saying they were entering the Mgakera River Enclave.

'How much further now David?' It was the first time either of them had said anything in almost two hours. Strangely the silence hadn't been strained, but of course they both had a lot to think about.

'Another twenty miles - about forty minutes, maybe less.'

'Can we stop for a while please. Want to stretch my legs.'

'OK. There's a little river over that next rise with some shade. Sully's probably only about twenty minutes behind us, so we can wait for him if you like.'

'Nope. Five minutes'll be enough.'

David drove a few yards off the tarred road and stopped under some fever trees just short of the rickety wooden bridge over the barely there stream. Luey got out without a word and disappeared behind a trunk, presumably to take a leak, but

David stayed put and wound down his window, switching the engine off for a while. There was a warm breeze and swallows were swooping around the bridge after the late afternoon insects. It must have rained a little earlier as it looked like there were flying ants about, but the red ochre earth was already dried here.

Luey reappeared and walked around to his window. David started to open the door, but the vet motioned that it wasn't necessary, so he let the window right down and twisted to lean out slightly, his forearm resting on top of the door.

'Enjoying the sound of no sound.'

David gave a low chuckle. 'Except the birds and the cicadas.'

Luey nodded and gave him a wry smile. 'I'm glad we talked, David. Just out of my depth with this sort of thing - and where Sophie's concerned I get protective.'

The Zyandan shrugged. 'You are a vet, not a doctor or a soldier - why would you know how to deal with it.'

'Oh, I dunno - vets know enough about animal instinct. Especially sick animals.'

'Animals are not people.'

'No. They're not. They behave better than us, by and large.'

David gave a bitter laugh. 'I won't argue with you on that point. And it is the nature of a male to protect his family.'

'So I don't have to tell you to stay away from her?'

'I told you. I will not go near her until she's decided one way or the other. You have my word.'

'I'm trusting you, OK?'

David was nodding his assent so Luey nudged his arm with the back of his knuckles for solidarity, then moved to get back into the Cruiser again. He settled back down with a heavy sigh as David switched on and slid into first.

'How shall we handle my drop off - if I know my girl she'll come running right over as soon as she hears us arrive.'

'There's a kind of a courtyard - I can put you down nearest her doorway and drive off as soon as you get your gear out.'

Luey chuckled. 'You know where she lives then.'

'Right next door to Doctor Kamate - he's my good friend remember.'

They crossed the bridge and he put his foot to the metal as they crested the slope from the river.

* * *

It was just gone five when they pulled into the square and David swung them around to stop next to a breeze-block boma with some shrubby jacaranda peeping over the top, wrapping around two large oval-shaped rondavels. As predicted a flash of blonde hair was seen through the wide wooden gates at the door of the furthest building as they pulled up, and Luey was barely out of the vehicle before his arms were full of Sophie, laughing and crying happily.

He hugged her close, leaning back slightly so she was on tiptoe and spun her around slightly, shutting the car door behind as he did so with his hip. One hand ran up her back, under her shirt and he buried his head in her hair and neck breathing in her warmth, his lips relishing soft skin.

'Hey, Sophie babe. I made it!' He half whispered, half whimpered with emotion in her ear and then put her down and drew back, holding her shoulders so he could lean down and kiss the tip of her nose and look into those glorious limpid blue eyes.

'Luey...' She couldn't say anything else as she gazed and

gazed into his warm earthy eyes and then ducked aside and burrowed into his chest as he stroked the hair on the back of her head and his other hand snaked its way up her back again, fingers spread and pressing lightly over her ribs and waist.

He heard a click as David unlocked the side door and he gently, apologetically held Sophie away and opened up to reach in for his two bags. David pushed the second one into his grip.

'Thanks, friend. I'll see you tomorrow, yes?'

'Tomorrow after lunch, Luey. Enjoy your evening.'

'Thank you!' Sophie was about to poke her head in as well, but met Luey backing out with the last bag and stepped away, waving frantically. 'Would you like to co...' The door shut with a clunk, the engine purred back into motion and glided away with a dark hand raised in salute.

'Oh! I was going to ask him to come in for a coffee. Who was it? I didn't recognise him?'

'Mukuga. From the vehicle shop on the plantation.'

'Oh, right. I was hoping it'd be Sully again - he's such fun!' She threw her arms around Luey's neck and kissed him long and hard on the mouth.

When she finally let him take a breath, Luey growled in appreciation and bent to pick up his bags again. 'Sully's driving the big truck and he's a half hour behind us. C'mon woman, lemme get inside! I need coffee too - I've only had about three hours sleep in the last twenty-four and I'm about dead on my feet.'

He grinned like a crazy-happy ape as she danced away from him, in through the double gates and past a rather nifty looking long wheel-base green khaki Land Rover with a big red cross in a white circle painted on its bonnet, then in through a cane and mesh frame door. Inside it was light and airy with soft cream coloured walls and honeyed terracotta floors, leading straight into a spacious lounge with a cool-looking tiled terrace beyond double French windows.

'Drop those bags and come right through Doctor Doolittle - we catch the sunset out in the back yard.'

He did as he was told and she seized him by the hand and dragged him out under the thatched terrace. 'Brilliant timing, Quackers!' He breathed as she pushed him down into one corner of the sofa and climbed up beside him to lie across his lap and attach herself very determinedly to his face for one of those very long and very wet kisses they had been promising themselves.

They finally surfaced and Sophie went to fetch the coffee which was fresh, hot and very, very strong, while Luey sat down at the table. He laughed after he'd swallowed the first few delicious mouthfuls.

'I was going to ask if we could skip the welcome wagon thing with Verity so I could grab an early night, but I'm gonna be awake the whole weekend if I have much more of this!'

'Hmm - that's quite a tempting thought - skipping the welcome wagon, but you can dilute it if you like. The coffee...' She pushed the hot water jug towards him as he sloshed a few inches out of the mug onto the grass. 'It's good though, isn't it? The local blend - they've just started to supply one of the Fair Trade groups. Apparently it's going down a storm in Paris!'

'Babe, I'd drink anything if it came with caffeine at the moment.' He grabbed her hand and brought it to his lips. 'But yeah - got a good kick to it. I could certainly get used to it. And this place is gorgeous, but then anywhere you are would be...' He looked at her slyly, his eyes twinkling with desire. 'If we absolutely, positively have to be social, I'll have to grab a shower pretty soon...'

Sophie chortled with pleasure. 'Well of course, that's a given. But there's no hurry you know - I decided that this will be our housewarming so Verity, Christian and Deborah are coming here to us. Around eight - plenty of time for showers and whatnot...'

Luey huffed a little, not sure if he liked the idea of having to share Sophie on his very first night. 'I hope that means you're not going to want to be cooking for hours, or have me helping out - I'm Zimbabwean. I only do braaie! I like the sound of whatnot though...'

'I thought you might...' She leant closer to him across the table and lightly linked fingers with him. '... which is why everything's done and in the fridge! And Christian's going to see to lighting the charcoal on the braai - we share part of the garden with them. Just the bit nearest the rondavels.'

'They're right next door are they?'

'Uh-huh. But we're detached and these are very sturdy earth walls. So long as you don't want to play your Deep Purple albums at top volume it's really peaceful around here... You may have time for a lie down and a little nap if you drink up...'

He stood up, pulling her with him and draining his mug in a few large gulps. 'I'm still feeling pretty woozy from the journey doctor - you'll have to come with me and make sure I don't come over all strange in the shower.' He was backing into the house as he spoke, grinning at her and she started to giggle.

'Well if you put it like that, I'm afraid I shall have to give you a proper examination straight away Mr. Ogil... mmmh!' She returned his kiss with enthusiasm until she realised they'd stopped moving. Luey's mouth trailed down to her ear and his voice was breathless and hot with longing.

'There's a problem I need your help with, Doc...'

'Insurance cover again!? You got the all clear with your medical, you said.' She murmured huskily.

'No... no. It's just... I... don't know where you keep the bathroom?' He sighed deep and mournful into her neck. Laughing like a loon now, she tugged on his hand and half dragged him into the wetroom that led onto the bedroom.

* * *

The scent of burning marula wood wafted in from the garden as Luey was finishing off his second shower. Sophie was about to call him when he came back into the bedroom, rubbing a towel over his head energetically and so didn't at first take in that she'd changed. When he finally looked he stopped dead in his tracks, mouth wide open.

'You have a dress!'

'Really? How did that happen!' Sophie laughed at his surprised face. 'I do own some feminine clothes y'know. I can't always be on safari.'

She smiled fondly at his astonishment fading into admiration as his greedy eyes took in the crisp broderie anglaise sun dress that hugged her bust, then fell loose to mid calf and naked feet. His reflection advanced towards her and he leant down to kiss her bare shoulder gently and lusciously ran his fingers through her loose drying hair.

'I love it - but won't the mozzies be in for a feast?'

'They spray here...' She suppressed a shiver as his breath grazed over her bare tanned shoulder '... and I'm jungle juiced to the hilt!'

'Jungle juiced?' He backed away reluctantly before he got

too enticed again and went back to his towel.

'Repellent gel. Lavender and sandalwood oils and I mix it with DEET[38] myself - want some? It's not too girly and I love the smell on warm skin.'

'Oh that - do I need it, if they spray?'

'Well - they have different bugs up here than in Zim. It won't hurt you.' She caught his eye in the mirror as she went back to brushing her hair. 'Please don't make me do the malaria 'prevention better than treatment' lecture on you of all people.'

He laughed, eyes crinkling at her fussing like a mother hen. 'OK, I know when I'm outnumbered. And you're not the only one who's had a dose, young lady.'

'Sorry...' She got up and kissed him on the cheek as he emerged from inside a billowy dark khaki tee with a be-bereted 'Guevara' chimpanzee print on it. 'One of my little hobby horses. You don't have to slobber it on - just your exposed pulse points will do.' She deposited a squeezy bottle into his hand.

'Yes, Ma'am!' Luey saluted her with a grin. 'Do you want me smart, or slobby, as you're all dressed up? Shorts or chinos?'

'I am not dressed up! Honestly.' She blushed, but was pleased he was asking and not making assumptions on his first night. 'Verity and Deborah don't do trousers too much - well Deborah's six months preggers, so she's being practical more. You can wear shorts if you like, although it's chilly at night here. Christian will be covered up.'

'Huh - these East Africans are pussies about the cold. I

---

[38] **DEET** ~ N,N-Diethyl-meta-toluamide. A yellowish insect repellent oil for sprays or lotions developed by the US Army after WW2 for use in tropical climates where biting insects, particularly mosquitoes spread disease.

have the honour of Great Zimbabwe to uphold, so I'll go for the Kariba houseboat boy look...' He laughed off Sophie's old-fashioned look and plonked down on the bed to get into some ancient beige cargo shorts and slid his feet into his flip flops. 'And before you say it, I know we're up high here. I'll just toast myself by the bonfire if it gets too nippy.'

'Purr-lease don't get all macho over the fire with Christian! He has lighting rights and he's an expert with the kebab skewers.'

She laughed and tangled her fingers in his damp wavy hair. 'Anyway, come on - I'm longing to show you off. They've all been dying to meet you.'

'Ready, bibi!' [39] He stood up and kissed the tip of her nose. 'We going via the fridge for some beer and the braai meat?'

'Oh goodness, yes - I forgot all about that!'

'Just as well I'm here to organise you, Quackers...'

Two hours later and Luey was feeling happily fuzzy and well on the way to being best buddies with Christian, to the extent that they were both burrowing into the depths of Sophie's monster American fridge for the last of the beer. Luey was about to close the door when he spotted some more chocolate brownies hidden behind the salad bowl and made a lunge for them, when Christian slapped his hand away and started laughing.

'No, no, Luey. They're for later after Deborah goes to bed and Verity goes home!' The lanky Tanzanian winked at him, making 'shush' noises. Luey blinked at him owlishly and tried to stifle a yawn.

'Aw, man! That's mean - Debbie couldn't get enough of them. Go on - she loves 'em!'

---

[39] **bibi** ~ feminine equivalent of bwana in Swahili

347

'No - these are special brownies, Luey. I made them for you and Sophie...' Christian had had quite a lot to drink as well and grinned foolishly, lowering his voice to a whisper. '...they're hash brownies, man. Welcome present for you and your lady.'

'Wha...? Haha. Ah, Chris. I'm so knackered man, I think I better pass on them tonight.' He put his hand on Christian's shoulder, shaking his head. 'But thank you - that's a really neighbourly gesture. Good to know you can get some quality dagga 'round here.'

'I have a friend who grows it and lets me have some for medicinal purposes.' Christian winked at him.

Luey suddenly remembered David Mukuga's red stained eyes and instantly blabbed out the obvious question. 'Your friend David over at the Plantation?' He knocked the cap off one of the bottles and took a mouthful. 'I knew he must be into it!'

Christian hastily looked out of the window to make sure the women were all still on the terrace and held a cautionary finger to his lips. 'Hush Luey. Sophie doesn't know David yet.'

Luey's eyes narrowed and he took a deep breath. 'Yeah. Don't worry. Your dirty little secret's safe with me for now. Not sure I approve, mind - but at least he's keeping away from Soph.'

'He told you?' Christian frowned. 'I told Verity she should send someone else to fetch you.'

'Don't blame him - at least he's an honest killer. I meant it. I'm not that pissed. I won't say anything to Soph to make it any more difficult for her.'

'It's as much for David's sake as for hers. He's not a well man.'

'Yeah - I noticed. Poor bastard.'

'It's a difficult situation. Hard to know what to do for the best for everyone.'

'Yeah... Let's not go there. I already had it out with him and the less I know about it the better. So long as nobody pushes Sophie into something she doesn't want to handle...'

There was a slight sound behind then and both men turned to see Verity standing in the kitchen doorway.

'Why would anyone want to do that?' She asked coolly, though she was looking at Luey warily. 'Sophie's a professional. Here to do a job. We won't 'make' her do anything, if she does not want to do it.'

'But you'd send him over to meet me and possibly expose him to a couple of hours of deep humiliation with a total stranger.' Luey had been trying to figure Verity out all evening and was finding it hard work so far, although he could see that Sophie liked her a lot. 'Doesn't seem like a good way to treat a man who's obviously at rock bottom.'

'We should talk about this another time, Luey. Please. Sophie may come in.' Christian shifted awkwardly.

'It's all right Christian. You go take the beers out and Luey and I will talk this over a little.' The older woman moved aside to let Christian escape back into the garden.

Luey leaned against the wall by the fridge and looked long and hard at her. 'Nothing to talk about is there? You called all the shots and now Sophie has to make her mind up one way or the other.' Luey was sobering up fast and had waited for Christian to get out of earshot before continuing, his dark eyes holding Verity's troubled gaze. 'That's all I meant.'

'But you don't know what shots I called.' Verity's voice was soft and sad. 'Please don't pre-judge my motives, Luey. I've known David a long time and I understand him better

349

than his mother.'

'You don't know Sophie though.'

'Maybe not. But then neither do you, for such a short time - even if you are in love. And you're wrong - I do know her a little. I know the young woman who lost the man she loved and the child they made together forever, in the cruellest of ways, thirteen years ago. I know her pain very well indeed, because I have had the same, except I was married to my man for nearly twenty years and lost the three children I bore him in as many weeks. So I know what I have asked of her, and still I had to ask it.'

Unbelievable. The arrogant cow! He was trying to push the anger he'd felt earlier back down, but he couldn't shake the feeling of being manipulated and resented it like hell.

'So why send David, knowing what there is between Sophie and I? Sully would have done as good a job driving the new Cruiser, wouldn't he? You could have avoided this situation altogether then.'

Verity's head sagged downwards and he could see she was shaking slightly. For a moment he thought she was crying, but she looked back up dry-eyed and met his stare squarely.

'To be honest with you - I don't know why. I don't know what to do anymore. David very much wanted to come and meet you and I could not say no to him... He's been so ill recently and only the thought of this new job working on the game management project has been keeping him going.'

'But you 'kindly' neglected to tell him that I was with Sophie - that was obviously a big shock to him. You're so into openness - why couldn't you have 'prepared the way' or even used it as the excuse for him not to come out to the airport?' He tried but failed to keep the sarcasm out of his tone and had the dubious reward of seeing his barbed comment hit the mark hard. Give her due respect though, her eyes didn't leave his for a moment.

'I took a risk. I thought that maybe you could get to know each other in terms of the job. Be friends?'

He let his breath go in an exasperated sigh and his hand combed through his hair in frustration. 'Of all the stupid...' He made himself stop abruptly as Verity seemed to suddenly deflate like a burst balloon and looked over at him hopelessly.

'I am sorry. It just seemed easiest to let him go...' She shook her head sadly, eyes pleading for some empathy. 'You seemed such a nice person from the phone calls and from what Sophie was telling me and I hoped... I hoped you would... like him.'

It was Luey's turn to duck his head, though in part it was through temper as he chewed his lip, trying not to lose it with her. 'You know - I thought you must be a very special woman, Verity. And you are. In fact I think you must be a fucking mind reader.' He surprised himself at how level his voice was, because he'd had to put his beer down on the counter he was that scared he'd bust the glass. Deep breaths. Calm down. 'I do like him. In fact I respect him. A lot. He has real guts - to keep it together like he did with me today. He wouldn't hear a word against you, by the way. He's still your boy through and through. So don't you play games with him like that anymore. And don't involve me if you do.'

'It wasn't a game, Luey.'

'Maybe not. But that's what it felt like to me. I told him I'd work with him regardless of what Sophie decides. I'm telling you that I won't see Sophie yanked around and used as the punishment detail.'

'Punishment? It's not like that. Only if she can't treat him. That's why we gave her the choice. Because we didn't want her to take David on, without knowing who he was. I know it's not fair on either of them. But there's no else left who can help him.'

'Exactly - so she's going to say yes, isn't she. There was never much of a choice, was there?' He looked hard at Verity then and realised that there was very little difference between her and David. They were both profoundly wounded animals trying desperately to survive and fit in with the rest of the herd. She was much better at it, but in a way that was almost worse. She didn't seem to realise there was anything wrong with her.

This time when he spoke his voice was soft and kind, even if the words were still harsh. 'Maybe you don't know Sophie that well after all, Verity. She's a doctor. She'll help him. But maybe she should help you first.'

'She is. I have an appointment with her tomorrow. For counselling.'

'I wish you well with it then. And I'm sorry if I gave you a rough ride - I like David very much and whatever happens I'll work with him.'

'He needs friends, so I am glad. Whatever you think of me, I was not trying to manipulate anyone, least of all Sophie.'

'Yeah. I get it and she can take care of herself so - I'm over being pissed about it. I know David won't mess with her.' He held out his hand to her and tried to smile as warmly as he was able to. 'One thing Sophie may have told you about me - I like everything in plain view. So - we've cleared the air, yeah?'

'Yes. Yes we have, Luey.' She took his hand and shook it, slowly, but firmly.

'I think Sophie and Mgakera are lucky to have you here.'

He laughed, a little shy all of a sudden and handed her one of the beers he'd left on the side while they'd been talking. 'Now, I would say that actually I'm the lucky one - but I'll drink to that anyway.'

Here be Dragons ~ Sorrow

The many men, so beautiful!
And they all dead did lie;
And a thousand thousand slimy things
Lived on; and so did I.

The Rime of the Ancient Mariner by Samuel Taylor Coleridge

Sophie's Diary: Saturday 26th May ~ Home

Luey Ogilvy is a bad influence! Officially...

I'm grinning like a lunatic here. I should be really annoyed with Christian for bringing those hash brownies, but the three of us had such fun last night after Deborah went to bed and Verity's car came around for her. Luey and Christian are like two naughty little boys together already, so heaven knows what they'll get up to when they really get to know each other. As for what Luey will get up to with me - I'm exhausted already! He got his second wind well and truly after clearing the fridge of beer and cracking out the Amarula [40] that he got on the plane from Zim.

I shouldn't be complaining! I'm a very lucky girl - apparently!

I think he's right as well. I love it when he decides to 'do a Harry' and starts off with the tall stories.

He's still crashed out now the brownie effect's worn out, so I'm letting him sleep it off while I go and have this first session with Verity. She seemed a little down for a while last night - I thought at

---

[40] **Amarula** ~ a liqueur made with distilled marula fruit wine and blended with cream.

first that Luey and her weren't going to get on that well, but after he'd 'relaxed' a little and plied her copiously with the Amarula she seemed to let her hair down a little. I hope she holds onto the mellow mood for today - we're getting on really well, but I get the impression she's really nervous about the counselling...

Sophie was coming to the conclusion that the one on one consultation suite at the new hospital was almost her favourite place in Mgakera. It had good natural light all day, with a combination of louvred shutters and reed blinds for privacy as well as ambience. The mood was further assisted by soft oil lamps and essential oil burners, so the room felt muted and intimate. It also felt spacious without feeling too large, something that was really quite vital to her work here, as family life anywhere in Africa tended to be crowded and cluttered with people and purposes. Space, just to talk or to wind down, was a premium commodity even back in England but here, and for the people she saw, it was almost as precious as gold, because all too often the one thing her clients needed above anything else was a haven away from the press of other people and the daily demands of living.

So far she'd seen mostly women as expected. Victims of sexual assault or worse and also of that very specific type of violence that the genocide had engendered. Women like Verity, who had lost their entire families to the killings and many who had all too often seen their menfolk and children, even babies, brutally murdered in front of them. The other good thing about this place, and the larger room next door for group sessions, was that there were no offices and no records were kept in this wing of the building. They therefore belonged to whoever was using them - to the patients as much as to her, or the other counsellors she would train in time. No computer screens or keyboards, just a choice of comfortable seating, floor cushions as well as chairs and sofas and a low table to use if people wanted to write or draw if they didn't want to talk. But having no 'owner' meant that Sophie came to the room fresh each time, as an equal with her client and from there they worked together on what was going to work for them. Her former teachers would probably have had a fit she reflected, but this was Africa and the classic textbook techniques were going to be about as useful as a chocolate teapot to her. What came into this room was different every single time. Even with the same people.

'I feel a fraud coming here.' Verity looked as uncomfortable as she sounded as she slipped past Sophie and, like most people, chose a seat where she could see the door. Sophie smiled gently at her as she nervously looked around the walls for a clock and saw there wasn't one.

'I have an old-fashioned hourglass, Verity...' She reached out to the wall mount just above table level and flipped the double bell-ended container over so the red ochre sand began its fresh falling. '...and we both have watches, so we have two ways of seeing how the time passes. Why do you feel a fraud?'

'Because I shouldn't need this - not after all this time. There are so many people who suffered far worse than I did. Lost more. Got hurt really badly.'

'You're here because you chose to come. Have you asked yourself why you feel you shouldn't be here? Why you feel there are other people more deserving than you 'after all this time'?'

'Because I know there are. They come to me every day, because they need help. So badly some of them.'

'I know. And you've helped so many people, for so long as well, haven't you? Thirteen years is a long time.'

Verity nodded, still sitting on the edge of her chair, coiled and defensive 'You know - we should do this in my office. It feels wrong to be here.' She stopped abruptly as Sophie shook her head slowly and reached out to pour some water from the carafe on the table.

'Help yourself as you like, Verity.' Sophie turned the other glass over, ready to be used, but then sat back again and sipped at her own glass. 'The reason we're here and not in your office is because there's no Verity the executive, the teacher, the politician or the 'fixer' in here. Just Verity the woman who works very hard - too hard sometimes and who makes time for everybody, but never for herself. This isn't an examination, or a consultation, or even therapy in its true sense. It's just you and me and we can talk or do whatever you think is useful for the time we have.'

She looked over at the hourglass. 'That's why we don't have a clock and why I have a half hour gap between appointments ordinarily - in case we need to turn the glass over more than once if we're getting through something that needs to be finished. There's no rules today either, because we start with a clean sheet and decide how you'd like to use the session and we can keep to that for the next one, or try something else. I'm here for you, so I don't dictate what we do, although I can guide you if you need that. But mainly we can just talk about anything you like, what's worrying you, or something you want to share, or to unburden yourself. Whatever's useful for you.'

Verity gave a nervous laugh and went for the water. 'I guess I could do with lessons on how to relax maybe...?' She took a sip from the cool tumbler and sat further back in her seat although she still looked poised for flight. Sophie smiled at her reassuringly.

'Don't worry - it gets easier. I was the same when I went for my first talking therapy sessions. There's a lot of rubbish that builds itself up around psycho-analysis of the Freudian variety. Do you see a leather chaise longue in here?'

Verity giggled. 'And you don't have a beard.'

'Or penis envy. My superego needs some work sometimes though. Counselling is just another word for talking - a special sort of talking in that it's the whole reason for us to be here, but the subject is you and what's troubling you, or what you need to sort out, or unravel, prioritise or just plain dump.' She smiled encouragingly at Verity

'I know. But this is what I meant. If I had been attacked, or raped then that would be something I need help for. How to deal with it. But... nothing. There really is nothing bad anymore.'

'Then why did you ask to have this session? Relax a minute. Put your glass on the arm of your chair and sit right back.'

She waited while Verity did as she asked. 'Just breathe in and out a couple of times - nice and easy and deep. Shut your eyes if you like.' She slowly counted to thirty in her head, watching some of the tension go out of Verity's slim frame. 'OK - now tell me what you can smell.'

'Oh... em... Herbs? And... oranges?'

'Neroli - bitter orange oil. Nothing wrong with your sense of smell then! For the record the herbs are lavender, camomile and rosemary. Essential oils are a hobby of mine - lavender's also great for keeping away mozzies.'

'Useful, then.'

'Very. It's also a mood-lifter, as is rosemary, and camomile's a relaxer. Neroli brings inner peace in case you were wondering.' She laughed softly. 'Now. What's been on your mind recently? You got a little tense last night at one stage I thought, so perhaps we can start there if nothing else is leaping out at you?'

She was a little tense... Heavens was it that obvious? Luey hadn't exactly helped of course, but then he had in a strange way. She had broken one of her own golden rules and made a presumption that he would be a typical white male Southern African, noisy and not too tactful or indeed, deep-thinking. But whilst he may have fulfilled the two former stereotypes he certainly did have a lot going on under the surface and she had been ashamed of herself when he had called her on manipulating David. She truly had not intended that, but as soon as Luey had laid it on the line so forcefully she had realised that her motives might seem rather ambiguous, even if she hadn't meant them to be. As a consequence she'd obviously telegraphed her loss of composure until Luey had given her a couple of generous glasses of Amarula. Even then she couldn't completely relax and had been glad when her driver came to collect her at the end of the evening.

'So many things have been on my mind - opening the hospital mostly and you coming here as well. That has all gone well, so... I thought, once that was all done with and you'd settled in, I could slow down a little and look to the future of Mgakera some more. I was so happy when Henryk and Helga were here for the celebrations, but ever since they left I've been...' She shrugged and fell silent, uncertain how to describe the feeling.

'Un-focused? Demotivated? Management weasel words, but they are a recognised outcome of the end of a long and demanding period of hard work and effort, especially one that means so much to you. How does 'flat and empty' sound?'

'Those last two sound right, Sophie.'

'Would it help if I said I've felt the same in some respects, although that's about a different aspect of Helga and Henryk's visit?'

'Even though you had Luey coming here to look forward to as well?'

'Yes. That's a totally different thing. So I'm very happy about Luey being here - excited and a little apprehensive as well naturally, as it's all been rather whirlwind on every level - but this is the happiest I can remember being, ever. But when I think of this other thing on my mind, I feel sad and ever so slightly ashamed of myself. You're allowed to feel different things, even if you think you ought to be feeling something completely the opposite? Do you see what I mean?'

'I think so - maybe it is something to do with old memories... It was wonderful to see Henryk and Helga again, but it was sad as well. Remembering that day and seeing photographs of Celeste and some of the other ladies who I brought here.'

'Something else we have in common then. I wasn't here, but seeing some of the photos that Henryk and Helga brought with them - of Teresa as a young girl with them in South Africa, upset me quite a lot.'

'But why should it? What happened long ago is something we have both dealt with and overcome. Moved on. I thought I would feel proud and happy with what we've - what I have done since, but really I felt like crying when I saw Celeste smiling in those pictures.'

'Did you cry?'

'No. I did all my crying a long time ago. It is a waste of time.'

'But still you feel sad and empty sometimes?' Sophie topped her water off and sat back, waiting for an answer that wasn't going to come.

Having left a decent gap, she forged on. 'Tell me about you and Celeste - or some of those other women. Share your memories and maybe that will help a little.'

'We were friends - she was a teacher at my school. When we came here Celeste helped me to set up some lesson structures for the children - reading and writing mainly. When more people began to come through, some of the adults came to the lessons as well. The ones where we read from the books here - some Bible or Quran stories, children's books, fairy tales, some Kipling - the Just So stories. Simple things. It was Celeste's idea mostly - the fairy tales and Kipling anyway.'

'You're using the past tense. What happened to her?'

'She died.' Verity stopped for a moment and sipped at her water. 'She found out she was pregnant after we got here. It was her first baby. It killed her... They gang raped her over and over and damaged her insides... Christian could tell you what happened to her.'

Sophie was waiting for tears, but they weren't coming - or rather they weren't falling. She didn't ask how Celeste had died, though she guessed that there'd been some terrible trauma to the uterus or cervix. Probably a late miscarriage, maybe a prolapse. The important thing was for Verity to talk about things that she had probably left unsaid for years and buried deep down, because they were too terrible to think about.

'Could I ask you to share as well, Sophie?' Verity asked tentatively.

'Are you asking me because it will make you feel more comfortable?' The counter question was intentionally gentle and not intended to challenge, but Verity looked worried and bit her lip.

'I'm sorry...'

Sophie smiled and edged forward in her seat, holding out one hand palm up to Verity. 'Don't be - I'm happy to share with you if that's what you want, although that's more usual in a group situation. It's just a question. I want you to be comfortable for this, so sharing is fine. Give me your hand, Verity.'

She put her hand in Sophie's and the doctor softly placed her other hand on top, holding her safe and steady.

'You made the right choice. A group session probably wouldn't be any use to you, because you'd revert to wanting to be responsible for everyone. It's the same reason for not doing this in your office. It makes it about 'work', do you see?'

Verity nodded, her eyes wide and scared now. Sophie paused, giving her time to respond, but when she still said nothing she went on, her tone friendly and inviting comment.

'When we met, do you remember one of the first things you said to me?'

'Yes. I asked you to breakfast.'

Sophie laughed. 'Yes you did, but before that you said you wanted us to be family. Remember?'

'Of course. And I do - I mean I feel like you are my good friend.'

'Well - that was a very pleasant surprise for me. I didn't know what to expect when I came here, least of all from you. I found out a lot about Mgakera from Christian and before that from Henryk and from Youssef, but I really didn't know what to expect from you. In fact I was feeling a little scared of you.'

'Really?' Verity's eyebrows shot up and she smiled uncertainly.

'Oh yes. Because I knew that you had to be a very strong person to have done all the things you've done. Not just survived the genocide, but to come through it with such integrity and purpose. You've changed lives, help to rebuild them. So I didn't know how much you would expect of me and that is quite frightening, especially when it took me so long to get up the courage to come back to Africa again.'

'You didn't want to come here?'

'No. Not at first. But gradually Youssef and then Henryk persuaded me to think about it and then showed me why they wanted me to come out here to work with you.'

'Because of your work with the soldiers? With post traumatic stress disorder and that eye therapy?'

'That was part of it, yes. But most of it was because I needed to stop running away from what happened here.'

'Running away?'

'I never wanted to be a doctor before Tom was killed. I was going to be a teacher. When he died - I crumbled and let his death destroy me as well. And nearly everything, since I got over that first devastating collapse, has been about finding ways to make sense of what happened, but also to stop me thinking about it as well. I went into counselling and they helped me to work out what I would do with the rest of my life, and I chose medicine because I wanted to stop history repeating itself on a very selfish and personal level. How to avoid getting malaria. How not to fall into despair, how not to dream about Tom and Teresa and how they died. How I might have saved my baby. It wasn't so I could help other people, or not at first. That came later, and it did help me a lot because I was good at it, and of course helping other people is addictive - because it's so rewarding. But then you know that as well, don't you?'

Verity nodded, but said nothing. Her grip, which had been quite cold and tight at first, was gradually relaxing and warming up.

'Your solution has been much braver and more direct than mine. You helped those women back then and then the other refugees. You went back to Zyanda and you helped the victims, and then the murderers as well. You found ways to change how people think and act. You found a way to help create this Enclave. But while you were doing all this, maybe you were building walls around yourself? You had lost your family and friends. And even though you were looking after all these other people, maybe nobody was looking after you? Not even yourself. Would that explain some of the emptiness and the sadness?'

'Maybe. But I have friends. And I think I am happy most of the time.'

'You live on your own. Your house is your office. What other things are in your life apart from Mgakera and work? Are all your friends here, or connected with Mgakera?'

Sophie watched Verity shake her head and did not resist when she pulled her hand away, almost regretfully.

'I love my work. It means everything to me.'

'I know. You give it everything, but sometimes you need something back in return and that's why you said you wanted a family. You need to share your work. Your life. It's too much for one person to do on their own, isn't it?'

'I do share! Christian and Deborah are like my children and I have many friends here in Tanzania and Zyanda - all over Mgakera on the farms and up country as well.'

'Do you have people you're close to, who have nothing to do with Mgakera and what you've been doing all these years?'

Verity opened her mouth, but nothing came out. It was not an objective question, but then this wasn't going to be that way. It was personal, in which case it also wasn't a fair question, because how would she have people she loved who had nothing to do with Mgakera and her work. She took another breath and was about to say that she had lost everyone she truly loved before the genocide when she stopped herself, realising that this was what Sophie meant. She had good friends, people she trusted and loved, who shared her life, but if her life was her work...

'I know what you mean I suppose, but it's not that simple is it? Not really. My family were lost and when I came here first, I couldn't go back to Zyanda, so I chose to stay and help with the other refugees who followed us. There was so much to do. There still is...'

Sophie was nodding and let her talk it through at her own pace, making a small comment here, sometimes asking for clarification on some point she wasn't familiar with. Medical training was a similar treadmill if you let it be and, in the past, Sophie had used that to fill up the howling gaps left in her own life for more years than she cared to acknowledge, so she knew all the attractions and pitfalls that a vocational profession offered. She also knew how easy it was to lose sight of activities, emotions and goals, away from the job and how hard it was to take time away from a self-imposed cycle once you'd poured all your effort and devotion into it. Recognising that you had done that was half the battle, and so the more Verity talked around what made her life 'tick' the better. Competent people were very good at identifying patterns.

The hourglass was roughly on the forty-five minute mark when Verity stopped to pour more water for herself and gave a little sigh.

'I think you were right about not doing this at the office - even if all I have done is talk about work.'

'It's important. Important to you and everyone who lives here. But you don't just work and talk about work all the time, do you? You and Deborah were talking about Coleridge last night when Luey said about how he and I were like albatrosses? I know that's partly work related, but then Deborah started going on about the Romantic Period. You were getting quite animated about Jane Austen - I thought you made some very insightful comments. But, before that, you'd been very quiet after you'd come back out with Luey?'

'I know - it's a little embarrassing...' She squirmed a little as she sat back with her water, then she laughed. 'Not about Jane Austen of course. I only wish she had written more than she did - I meant about being quiet...'

'I wondered whether Luey had been a little insensitive? He was so tired last night and what with all that beer...'

'We had a slight misunderstanding, but he wasn't insensitive - just honest.'

'Honesty's not always too gentle though.'

'No. But we sorted ourselves out. I can see why you love him - he cares a lot about you.'

'Maybe you shouldn't tell me anymore - if you were arguing about me?'

'Not about you exactly, no. But he made me see something differently. That was why I was quiet for a while - seeing it with someone else's eyes.'

'"O wad some Power the giftie gie us to see oursels as ithers see us!"[41] That or take up mind reading?'

---

[41] From the poem 'To A Louse, On Seeing One On A Lady's Bonnet At Church' by Robert Burns

Verity looked at her sharply and then laughed ruefully. 'Strange you should say that as well - he said I was a mind reader. Or trying to be. Trying too hard anyway.'

'Just a figure of speech.'

'Maybe. I'll tell you what it was about, I think. I have a guilty conscience and although we weren't talking about you specifically, it does concern you quite deeply. We were talking about David. David Mukuga.'

'Mukuga?' Where had she heard that name recently... 'Oh - the man who drove Luey here? David...'

'The David who was in the militia. One of the Apostles.'

Sophie frowned at the oddness of the situation. Verity ran through what had passed between her and Luey last night, sounding ill at ease over what she now felt was a serious lapse of judgment in sending David out to do the airport run. Trying to explain this to Sophie made her feel the whole affair was completely ludicrous, what with Luey feeling it had been underhand and then David telling her this morning that he thought it was better that he not see Sophie at all, whether or not she agreed to it. On this last point she had managed to persuade him that he'd be foolish to pass up the opportunity of help if it was on offer. Finally she held Sophie's gaze, knowing she must be looking as guilty as sin.

'I'm sorry. Luey felt that it wasn't fair on David or you, so that's probably why he's not said anything - because he didn't want to interfere as well.'

Sophie shook her head. What a silly hash they were all making of this, trying not to tread on people's toes. 'Typical man - doesn't want to make a fuss. Well - never mind. I was going to tell you today anyway. I will take David's case on. Does that make you feel a bit better?'

'Oh, yes! It does... You aren't annoyed about it?'

'No. Well - maybe a little at first. I just said I was going to think about it. I didn't know you were going to keep the poor man away from me - like he was some kind of leper. I assume that's what Luey's got cross about.'

'I think so. It was actually David's idea to stay right away from you. He didn't want to upset you in any way. And stupidly I agreed to him going to meet Luey because they'll be working together.'

'And I didn't exactly help matters when I got all snappy with you, when you told me he was here...' Sophie sighed heavily and shook her head. 'Well this is a good lesson for us all, isn't it? We're all rushing around trying not to upset people and that's exactly what happens.'

She looked at the hourglass again and considered turning it over. But another idea occurred to her and she acted on it impulsively.

'I actually haven't got anyone else to see today, so we've got plenty of time to get back to you and what we're here to talk about. When you were saying about Celeste and Henryk's pictures, it struck a chord with me as well. There's something I'd like to show you, but it's at home. Would you like to come over again? We'll give you some dinner and just have a good chat - get over all this awkwardness?' A smile passed over Verity's face, only to be replaced by a frown. 'What's the matter? We can do it another day if you like - if you've got something else on.'

'David might have called in on Luey this afternoon. They were going for a quick tour of the farm, but David had to cancel - he could still be there at the moment. He was going to see Christian as well...'

'Christian's doing a polio clinic this afternoon. Oh look - this is happening again.' Sophie reached for her bag and pulled her phone out. 'I'll call Luey and if David's with him, then I'll get Luey to keep him there, so I can meet him while you're there too, can't I? That way we can get our first meeting out of the way on a social basis, where David's not the focus of everything - that won't spook him too much will it?'

'Alright... Yes. That will be a good idea. He likes Luey.'

'And he trusts you. Don't worry - this'll work out fine. Whether David's still there or not.'

Here be Dragons ~ the Deeps

And the fifth angel sounded, and I saw a star fall from heaven unto the earth: and to him was given the key of the bottomless pit.

Book of Revelation ~ 9:1 (King James version)

Luey woke up to a mercifully empty bed, mouth wide open and drooling into the pillow he had a tight hold of. Groggily he moved his cheek onto something less moist, but smiled contentedly as he inhaled the sweet ingrained Sophie-scent of jungle juice and sex, then snuffled deeper into the bed linen, like a truffle pig in ecstasy. Remembering dimly that Sophie had said to have a sleep in while she went to work, and still feeling rather fuzzy after a long eventful Thursday, he drifted for another half hour or so before hitting the shower. Refreshed after a long leisurely wet shave - something he rarely did, but generally vowed to make more time for when he did, he dressed quickly and went out in search of coffee and a very late breakfast.

Another hour and he was stretched out on the terrace sofa in the shade reading an economic paper on hunting tourism models, when he heard muted voices from next door. In due course a door opened and Christian came out into the garden with another man, who turned out to be David.

'We come bearing gifts!' Christian was beaming as they manhandled an humongous crate of beer across the lawn. 'But they need cooling down, unfortunately. Deborah said I was a real pig drinking so much last night, so we ought to

370

help you re-stock!'

'Gah!' Luey leapt up to open both doors into the rondavel so they could stagger through to the kitchen with their burden. 'Man! I'm still sobering up...' He shuffled ahead of them and grabbed the leading edge of the crate so they could all hoist it up onto the counter beside fridge-zilla, as he'd dubbed it. 'Blinding! Are those pint bottles?'

'Half litres! Good, yes?' David smiled at him. 'They were on the dragoman from Mwanza.'

'Cosmic! Namibian beer![42] And here I was expecting Red Cross rations.' Luey grinned at them as he began reloading from the bottom compartment upwards.

'Isn't that supposed to be the salad drawer...?' Christian looked over Luey's shoulder, smirking superiorly. 'Looks like you are a good luck talisman - last truckload we had was some Tusker from Nairobi. Pot luck with CAMEO provisioning sometimes.'

Luey had slowed down and looked speculatively at the labels. 'Oh no!' He gave a mock groan 'Only a month on the sell by! Well two dozen'll keep me and Soph going OK for a week or two. I hope you kept some for yourselves lads?'

'Of course!' Christian laughed and David nodded.

'You guys want some juice or lemonade - or a coffee?' He was looking at David as he spoke. The man looked even more exhausted than when he'd dropped him off yesterday evening.

'Nothing for me, thanks Luey.' Christian grinned at him.

---

[42] Namibian brewers famously follow the Reinheitsgebot having been a German colony between 1884 and 1919 (officially - the South Africans having expelled the Germans in 1915). The 'beer purity law' remained in place after WW1 and today breweries in Namibia still hold licences to produce many high quality European beer brands, such as Becks, Amstel and Guinness.

'I'm starting a clinic in ten minutes and I think David has plans, so I'll leave you both to it. Maybe catch you for some sundowners later, yes?'

'My liver!' Luey wailed theatrically as he waved Christian off. 'So what would you like David?'

'Juice with some lemonade sounds good - I've had far too much coffee today already...'

Luey grabbed a tray, glasses and a pitcher which he filled with mango juice and lemonade in equal measures, then led the way back onto the terrace. 'I won't ask if you slept well - you look knackered. We can give the tour a miss if you like?' Luey poured the drinks and pushed a glass towards David with a worried glance.

David wrapped his fingers around the cool condensation on the glass and then rubbed his eyes slowly with his fingertips. 'Would you mind very much if we left it until tomorrow? I can't drive too far today. Sorry.'

'Do you work weekends here?'

'Every day. There's nothing else much going on and something always needs doing in the garage, if not on the road.'

Luey frowned, but didn't comment on that. 'Well, there's some reading I need to do that I didn't get through on the flight over from Nairobi - too much turbulence for my taste over the Rift. So, yeah, tomorrow will do. What do you work on in the shop?'

'General mechanic stuff - there's machinery from the farms to maintain as well as the dragomans and the personnel fleet. We have a couple of ambulances and some old army fire engines we're re-furbishing as well.'

'For the new air strip?'

'Yes - that is somewhere I will take you as soon as possible.

You have a pilot's licence, Verity says?'

Luey nodded. 'Just light aircraft. Cessnas, that kind of thing. Learnt to fly when I studying at Davis in the US.'

'I would like to fly a plane. Maybe one day...'

'Is that the sort of skill they're looking for here then?' He laughed at the silly question. 'Of course it is, else why are they building an airstrip.'

David smiled at him. 'Yes. Lot of the farms and tribal lands will need services like crop spraying or air ambulance - even exec jets in time perhaps. So Mgakera will have a little airport and they'll have strips up country on the reserves for the guest lodges.'

'Some exciting times coming...' The phone started ringing and Luey chuckled. 'Sophie checking up on me, I bet! 'Scuse me a mo'.'

He came back a few minutes later looking thoughtful and took his refilled glass over to the sofa, motioning for David to take one of the comfortable camping chairs.

'Well - we're both stood down for the tour of Umbeke and environs today. That was Sophie, but she had a message for you from Verity as well. Soph's decided that she'll take your case on and Verity wants you to meet her as soon as possible, so they're both on their way over and Verity wants you to wait here for them.'

'That is very sudden...' David eyes were wide and his voice shook and tailed off as he sat down heavily.

'Verity just had her first counselling session with Soph - I assume that's what's pushed this forward.' He frowned slightly, taken aback at how stunned David looked. 'I kind of locked swords with Verity last night about our journey in yesterday - if this is down to my thumping on her buttons then I'm sorry.'

David nodded absently, barely seeming to listen to Luey's confession.

'No. It's alright, Luey. Best to get this thing going I think.'

* * *

Luey heard the gate scraping and the low murmur of the Land Rover and went to the front door to greet the two women. He walked onto the gravel giving Verity a rather tense smile as she got out of the vehicle, kissed Sophie briefly on the cheek and then spoke low and urgent into her ear. 'Minor emergency babe. He's recovering now, but David crashed on me just after you phoned - his BP was rocketing and he says he's been hammering the coffee.'

Sophie looked over at Verity as she walked across to the open door. 'David's not feeling too well apparently.' She looked at Luey for more information as they went inside.

'I've been getting some fluids into him and he's just been sick, but he's in pretty poor shape. I put him in the spare bedroom for now.' Luey steered Verity to a chair in the living room and went to follow Sophie into the bedroom.

'Is he disoriented?'

'Not too much - trembling and nervous, but... well, he would be, wouldn't he?'

David had heard the women arrive and had tried to get up but felt dizzy, so he was sat down on the bed and looked up anxiously at Sophie and Luey as they came into the room together.

'Here's the proper doctor to look at you, mate. Hey... don't try to get up - what are you like?' Luey put a firm hand on David's thin shoulder and sat down beside him.

Sophie saw a stethoscope and what she supposed was a vet's blood pressure meter on the nightstand and smiled reassuringly at David. 'Hello David. I'm Sophie - of course. I hear you've been hitting the coffee a bit too hard?' He nodded at her slightly, but said nothing. Luey's pronouncements were right on the nail, but it looked like David was stabilising. She wondered how much he'd drunk. Probably not that much judging by how skinny he was.

'I see Doctor Doolittle's already had a listen to your heartbeat, but I'd better have a go as well. May I, Luey?' She grinned at him as she reached out for the 'scope.

'Be my guest, babe - the BP was about 140 over 85 earlier, but it's come down since.'

'Uh-huh...' She knelt in front of David then slipped the diaphragm through the top of his shirt and onto his chest. 'OK - that's not too fast, but a little skittery still. Now... Luey does this work the same as a human BP cuff?'

'Yeah, you get it on and pump it up like normal - it's all set up. I did the last one about ten minutes ago.'

'Brilliant.' She smiled at David as she pumped the cuff up and nodded towards Luey, her eyes twinkling cheekily. 'Did you ask him what sort of animal he used this on last?' Again all she got was a shake of the head. This was so not the best way of starting a good rapport with a client she thought sourly. Luey came to her rescue yet again.

'It was a bull I think. It goes around the top of the tail. Don't worry - I cleaned it afterwards.'

That got a laugh from all of them and the reading dutifully came up on the monitor. 'Yup. That's good...' Sophie let the cuff down again and took it off. '... almost back to a respectable 115 on 70. Looks like the animal doctor's done the trick for you, David.' He did look pretty flushed though and his eyes were very red and tired looking. 'Luey said you were sick earlier - how are you feeling now?'

'OK. Just very tired and a bit edgy...' David made an effort to look at Sophie and smile, not wanting her to feel he was being unfriendly. 'My head feels - like it is fuzzy. It aches. I did not sleep too much last night.'

Sophie nodded, holding David's gaze and returned his smile. 'I can see that you're pretty exhausted. Having me and Verity spring this surprise visit on you didn't help either I expect?' He hung his head at that and shook it slowly. She looked over at Luey for inspiration.

'I've got some bread baking, so why don't I go and make some tea and take Verity out on the terrace. Then you two can have a quick chat and join us when you're ready?' He winked at Sophie and stood up to go. David looked a little panicked, but didn't object.

'Good idea, Luey. We'll see you soon I expect.'

She waited until he'd gone out of the room and then pulled a chair over from the wall so she could sit facing David. 'This wasn't the best way for us to get introduced, was it?'

'Not really. The whole thing took me by surprise.' David tried to make his voice sound relatively calm with some success, but Sophie could tell he was making a huge effort for her. His hands were shaking a little and he looked like he wished he was anywhere but here.

'Yes - I'm sorry. That's mostly my fault for having taken my time deciding on whether to have you as a patient. Luey's told you that I want to work with you - but I think you must have been feeling quite ill before he told you that?'

'Yes. It was a long drive yesterday and then I could not sleep.'

She nodded. 'Christian's been trying to help with your insomnia, Verity tells me. But it's pretty chronic? Long standing?'

376

'Yes. Christian has tried his best for me, but it never really goes away.'

'Are you taking any medication or herbal remedies?'

'Not really. I drink coffee if I need to be alert - for driving. If I'm not, then I drink herb tea.'

'So how much coffee did you have today?'

He shook his head. 'Five, maybe six cups. I made it strong though.'

'The local coffee? How strong?'

'An extra spoonful.'

'That's pretty strong then... What sort of herbs do you take in your tea?'

He dropped his eyes, but answered clearly. 'Dagga - cannabis. It is not so strong in tea though.'

'That's *sativa* isn't it?' An immediate nod. Whatever else he was, this chap was no dummy. 'You're right, it's not as strong as some varieties and pretty weak if it's infused. When was the last time you had the tea?'

'Last night. Just one cup about ten o'clock...' He hesitated then plunged on. Best he give her the full picture. 'I wanted to relax and get some rest, but I was drinking it from a thermos most of the time on the way up to Mwanza on Wednesday - Sully did all the driving then. I don't take it on days when I drive - that's when I have coffee.'

'How much dagga tea in the thermos?' Sophie was looking at him closely now. She'd have to talk to Christian about this later as David must have been abusing his system for some time and she wanted to know what other, if any, medication he'd been on.

'About two pints - so four small spoons. Not that strong.' He rubbed at his eyes briefly.

'OK. So that was to relax you overnight and then set you

up for the long drive with Luey yesterday?'

'Yes, that's right. I had two big mugs of coffee for breakfast yesterday and then I had ordinary black tea - or water, the rest of the time.'

'Until last night - then dagga tea to wind down, and the coffee this morning to kick start you.' He looked at her, eyes haunted but cogent and nodded.

'What's Luey been giving you to drink while you've been here?'

'I had some mango juice and lemonade - but I threw that up. I've had a couple of glasses of water since.'

'And what have you been eating today?'

'Some mielie-meal[43] with fish relish for lunch.'

Probably not enough she reflected - he really was underweight, though obviously not starving. 'OK - worst's over, but I think Luey or I had better take you home later, just in case. You'll need to cut your caffeine consumption right back for a few days and try to keep to two or three mugs a day in future - and no double spoonfuls, OK? You need to watch the dagga tea as well for a bit, even though you know the hazards with that. Really you shouldn't have to be relying on it this much, so that's something we can work at another day.'

'I don't want to be any bother to you or Luey. Christian will let me stay with him tonight I expect. I know I should not be driving when it's this bad.'

She smiled as she stood up and put the chair back. 'That's sounds a better plan then. Are you feeling well enough to

---

[43] **mielie-meal** ~ a staple food in Southern and East Africa similar to polenta or grits. It is a kind of thick porridge made from white maize (corn cobs) or millet and used as a carbohydrate accompaniment to various 'relishes' such as meat, fish or vegetable sauces and stews.

come out and join us and Verity for something light to eat and counteract the nausea? We'll be having some cold meat left over from the braai last night and salad later on and I can do some rice as well if you like - no trouble honestly.'

'Thank you. You will not do this therapy today then?'

'Oh no! No - I just wanted to meet you and have a chat. Nothing heavy at all - we can start therapy when you're ready for it. Doesn't have to be straight away. I'll see how Luey's getting on with the tea-making - think you'd better have a fruit one though.'

There was a light tap on the door so Sophie went over. 'Oh hello there, Verity. He's feeling a bit better now.' She turned to look at David again. 'You up to having another visitor, David?'

'Of course, if it's Verity.'

'In you go then! I was just going to see what's happening with this tea.'

Luey was in the kitchen taking a round of bread out of the oven and getting a tray of tea things ready. She leant against the door looking at him fondly.

'I thought you didn't do cooking, Doc?'

He poked his tongue out at her. 'I'd have starved long ago if I couldn't turn my hand to it when I have to - Harry's bloody hopeless at it unless it involves a braai or a frying pan.' He laughed and put the pan down. 'Do we have some fruit teas, or decaf?'

'I have some bags - hibiscus and some mint and camomile in here I think...' She opened a cupboard and fished out a couple of bags of each. 'Yes. The rest of us can have normal tea if you don't like those.'

'You have ordinary too don't you? Bags. We can have a

jug of hot water and take what we like then, babe.'

'Genius!' She reached up and kissed him briefly on the lips. 'You're full of surprises my love. The bread smells yummy - there's some jam and stuff in here as well. All the breakfasty type preserves. Just the thing to soak up what's left of the caffeine. Good job you were with him, Luey.'

'Yeah - luckily I roomed with a couple of serious caffeine addicts out in California, so I knew what it was straight off. Although he's fond of the dagga too.'

'Yes, he told me. Only in tea apparently.'

'Even so, he was wired as hell half an hour back. Trembles and everything. Verity was worried.'

'She's gone in there now. It's a strange relationship they have though - she was telling me more on the way over. She's almost like his mother in some respects.'

'Yeah. I thought that as well, out there just then. He's in absolute awe of her - won't hear a word against her.'

Sophie slipped into his arms, rubbing her forehead gently against his chin. 'Yes - she was telling me all about you playing Grand Inquisitor in the kitchen last night earlier on... I think you've guilt-tripped her actually.'

'Me?' He frowned down at her, but then kissed her sweetly on the forehead. 'Well... she really stitched him up sending him out to meet me - he had no idea we were an item and it really freaked him, though he covered it quite well.'

'Crossed wires all over. I didn't mean for them to forbid him to come into contact with me at all - but I was sending out some rather confusing signals too.'

'I just saw he was really stewed about it, but when he told me why I was mad that they'd put you in such a compromising position. And him too.'

'Well - we can put it right I expect. He's in a shocking

state though. Imagine living with all that awful baggage for so long.'

'He seems to be able to talk about it a bit though. I thought that not being able to was part of the problem with PTSD?'

'Usually, but - if it's the wrong sort of talking... Verity's got a milder case of it I think. Anyway - patient confidentiality etc!' She eased herself away from him. 'I'm starving again and the smell of that bread is driving me wild... so I'll go see how our guests are doing.'

David was lying down and Verity was sitting on the bed beside him, holding his hand. Sophie smiled at them both.

'How are you feeling now, David?'

'A little better, thank you.'

'Hungry he says - but then he can stand to have a few good meals inside of him. Something smells good from the kitchen?' Verity turned to Sophie with a strange mixture of guilt and concern on her face. Sophie came over to stand beside her and put a reassuring hand on her shoulder.

'Luey's made some bread and we're going to have an Umbeke version of afternoon tea I think. Are you up to coming out on the terrace, or shall we bring it to you in here, David?'

'Actually, I need the bathroom again please... and I can go out on the terrace I think.'

'Not feeling sick again?'

'No - just a full bladder...' He gave a nervous chuckle which had Sophie giggling as Verity moved off the bed.

* * *

Conversation out on the terrace centred around bread-making and the general merits of orange marmalade against ginger preserves for a little while. However, when a family of warthogs suddenly made an appearance in the garden, Luey went into 'Harry mode' with the highly dubious tall tale of how, when a warthog is chased by a predator they automatically scrunch up their eyes in panic and, because their skin is allegedly so tight, their tails get pulled into a vertical position like a car aerial.[44] More silly anecdotes along those lines eased any lingering tensions away and eventually got them onto the topic of wildlife in general.

'Can't wait to get you out on a game drive, David - you've got really sharp eyes!' Luey grinned at the younger man who'd got his sunglasses back on again. 'Where'd you get into birds though - most Africans I know aren't that into them?'

'It's the flying I think. They always seem so free - able to get themselves out of trouble.'

'What are you like with waterfowl - we have a biiiig kingfisher fan here. Soph lurves them!'

'I like them too, yes. I prefer herons and egrets though - something about the way they fly.'

Luey laughed. 'Once they're up, yeah. They have a nice unhurried flight pattern.'

'I like tracking as well - needed it sometimes upcountry in the past, because it gets quite hilly and the cover's thick. There is a lot of good game up there now there's not so much encroachment from Zyanda - it got pretty bad after the genocide. People were having to hunt up there because all the farms had been destroyed, or weren't productive...'

At some stage during this turn in the conversation Verity had disappeared inside. When Sophie realised she'd left, she

---

[44] The real reason for this is simply to act as a visual marker for the young hogs to follow their parent's dark tufted tail through long grass to safety.

gathered up the plates as an excuse to go in too and made her way into the kitchen. No Verity there so she went back into the living room and bumped into her coming out of the bathroom. She looked quite upset and Sophie wondered if, despite what she'd said earlier that afternoon, she'd been crying. Whatever else she looked ill at ease, so Sophie opted for the diplomatic approach.

'I thought we'd leave them to their animal stories, so would you like to stay in here for a while Verity?'

'Um... yes, if you like. You were going to show me something I think?'

'Of course! All the excitement distracted me... Have a seat and I'll get the pictures I was saying about.'

She went to a chest of drawers, took out two photos and came to sit beside Verity on the pale tan chesterfield, placing both on the coffee table. One was the black and white picture Helga had liked of the almost beardless Henryk in between her and the ten or eleven year old Teresa. The other was a later one, which vaguely echoed the same grouping, but in colour and taken outdoors with Tom in the middle with his arms around Teresa as an adult and a rather dishevelled and scruffy teenage Sophie. In both photos Teresa was smiling up at Henryk or Tom, although she was on different sides.

'This is what had me a little rattled at the party the other day. I asked Helga for a copy if you remember?' Sophie's voice was soft and sad.

'Oh my! Yes. I remember you went quiet for a good while after we looked at those photographs. Strange how it's alike, yet not.'

'Teresa's pose is similar yes, but you're looking at it without knowing Tom at all. I nearly burst into tears when I saw it...' She reached out a finger and traced it lightly around

Tom's lower face. 'We'd been playing hide and seek with the school-kids just before this was taken, which accounts for all of us smiling - normally I didn't do that much around Teresa. I didn't like her at all.'

'Did you not? But you always speak well of her.'

'Now, yes. But not when she was alive. I didn't know her very well at all - that's all come since. I was jealous of her friendship with Tom. They were like brother and sister, but I felt threatened and couldn't understand that it didn't hurt what was between me and Tom.'

'You were young and in love - sometimes it is hard to see things justly.'

'Maybe - but you see, at first I blamed her absolutely for getting Tom killed. Totally illogical I know - he died because Mbrame ordered the shooting, but if it hadn't been for her behaving so stupidly... She wasn't of course - although it was rash, she was incredibly brave. I didn't know how brave at first...'

'So this brought those bad memories of her back to you?'

'No, not exactly...'

How to explain something as slight as a smile on two different faces. Tom's and Henryk's. Two separate people, but the exact same smile more or less and it had blighted her perception of this tiny, tragic but driven woman and created so much resentment and distress for her down the years. She traced the smile on Tom's face and then on Henryk's.

'I never saw Henryk without a big bushy beard, so I'd never have noticed this until the other night. Do you see that they're smiling the same smile?'

'Goodness! Yes - it is! How extraordinary.'

384

'It's the explanation for all my envy and ill-will towards her. I couldn't understand why she was that close to Tom you see. He said it was because he reminded her of her little brother.'

'The poor little one she was found with?'

'Ah, of course - you knew her background too.' Sophie smiled and put the older black and white picture on top of the later one. 'Did Henryk ever tell you about how Teresa was when he first found her? Not her injuries - her state of mind?'

'Yes. She was semi-comatose. Couldn't remember her name.'

Sophie nodded. 'It was more than that though. Did he tell you that she was convinced she was dead and that she'd gone to heaven? That she thought he was God with that big beard?'

'Oh! The poor child!' Verity looked at the little girl's beaming face in the old photograph. 'I think he told us something like that, but I'd forgotten the details.'

'Well - I think that it wasn't her little brother so much as this smile that they shared... Tom and Henryk. Because this was the first kind thing that she'd seen for so long in that awful time, back in her village in Nigeria. People who cared for her and loved her... Made her well... Gave her the courage to live again.'

'A happy memory. Would it be that simple?' Verity's voice in turn was soft and rueful as she looked at the happy child who had survived against appalling odds.

'Yes - they get forgotten when terrible things happen. And sometimes you lose sight of them altogether. But this one must have stayed with her. I'm glad it did. She and Tom always had a great rapport and of course he knew her for a few years before I met him. I got it all wrong and blamed her for it.'

'But you didn't know then. You can't like everyone you meet after all.'

'True. But I was such a bitch to her. If I'd tried to be friends more then things might have been different. I'd have got the malaria confirmed a lot sooner for one thing - if I'd just listened to her when she said she wanted to check it out.'

'She was a very good doctor, Henryk said.'

Sophie nodded. 'Yes. She was an excellent doctor... but they still shouldn't have sent her here. But if they hadn't - then maybe you and the other women would have been massacred. Buts and what ifs are such dangerous things...'

Sophie's Diary: Sunday 27th May ~ Home

Well what an intense end to yesterday! Verity and I had a long chat about Teresa and other things - we both had a good cry together. Big, big breakthrough for her, although she'd already been crying because of some silly thing that David had said about watching the animals up in the Mgakera Highlands in Zyanda - that was where the militia went after they left Umbeke apparently.

David... how he's survived this long without a major crack-up is positively amazing, only just short of miraculous. I think to some extent he's been able to rationalise himself into staying functional through the work, in the same way that Verity has - but of course in his case the burden of guilt is colossal. Hopefully he won't be quite so wound up now I'm not some kind of avenging angel figure in his head! Poor thing! He must have been so scared of meeting up with me. He did calm down quite well with us, thanks mainly to Luey, but also Christian coming over later on was good for him. I was feeling quite cross with Christian for not supporting David better over the insomnia at the very least, but I think in the circs he's actually done a pretty good job considering that, apparently, David had a really bad dependence on cannabis when he came out of prison - at least he doesn't smoke it any more. The tea habit's more beneficial for the 'wind down' aspect anyhow.

Verity and Christian having a good heart to heart with him during the evening has done some good as well - Christian's a real rock of a friend to both of them. He told them both they were being really silly living on their own and that they'd both feel better if David moved in with Verity. That way she can have someone to look after and he'll have someone to keep him occupied without getting too obsessive. They've agreed to try it for a couple of weeks anyway. David's also a walking encyclopædia - reads literally everything he can get his hands on, vehicle manuals, IT techie stuff as well as classic literature - Christian says Deborah's running out of things for him to read! I'm sure he must have a photographic memory, I think to the point where he might have something like Aspergers perhaps, although his motor skills are excellent, so perhaps not - will have to do some investigation on that online. Verity says that he was the brightest student she ever had - that's another thing to do with her guilt burden - overdoing the punitive part of his rehab. She thinks it's her fault he's so damaged, but we can work on that as well.

I guess Youssef, as usual, had it right all along - this is the one place where I can do more good than I ever thought possible. And I get Luey as a bonus prize - how lucky am I?!

Hard Rains

David ~ five months later

Steadily the silver-capped pen moved across his line of sight, rhythmically back and forth and David's eyes followed it faithfully from side to side, over and over as he spoke or listened to Sophie's calm voice. It wasn't hypnotic exactly and he certainly wasn't ever unconscious, even for a moment, but what it did do, despite his own early misgivings, was send him into a kind of removed reality. The sensation during the EMDR sessions was actually pleasurable at times, but he hadn't been convinced of its effectiveness, even after he'd researched it on the internet, until they were about four sessions in. It wasn't just the pen and the eye movements of course. It was the talking over, and re-examining, and writing that were all feeding into the re-processing of his memories of the genocide, of Misha, of his father, grandfather and of the nun, Teresa Olatunde.

Starting with that evening back in May, when the insomnia had finally pole-axed him, Sophie had been a touchstone for him. Luey too, but the potential for friendship had been obvious there almost as soon as they'd met at the airport. With Sophie, there had been too much dread and needless concerns about how she would 'see' him, so she had come to be a forbidden grace to him; someone whom he was not worthy of knowing, or even approaching. From the moment Sophie had come into that bedroom, she had gone out of her way to put him at ease and encouraged him to talk about things he'd rarely voiced, even with Christian or Verity. It was strange because he'd never been around Europeans too much before, but he almost felt closer to her and to Luey now than to people he'd known for years. They were colleagues of course and Sophie was now his doctor, but they were both most definitely his friends. It felt good, especially now Christian was a father and spending more time with his family. Even that was a joy David thought he'd never know, as he was without doubt little Dawn's favourite uncle.

The pen stopped moving and his focus returned to Sophie's face.

'You still feel this is helping, David?'

'Yes it is. I'm sleeping better, although maybe the meditation is helping more with that... but the flashbacks are becoming less frequent and painful. Is there a problem with continuing?'

'No problem - we can carry on indefinitely, provided it's doing you good. But it's slightly unusual to keep up the actual EMDR this long.' Sophie's smile was reassuring as she gave a small shrug. 'But then the trauma's very deep-seated and been stagnant for such a long time, so it's not too surprising that you want to go on. So long as you feel you're getting enough out of it still?'

'It's everything really Sophie... It's hard to think how I was before sometimes. I wasn't really alive anymore and then you come along and it's just talking things over at first. It's got me thinking about it all without the despair somehow.'

'Well that's the trick of course, but you'd be surprised how hard it is to move away from the memories for some people. I think really, even though you'd lived with it so long and in some ways had done some of the re-processing yourself already - so you could function just well enough, you must have known you were at a dead end. In a way it was sink or swim and you chose swimming...'

He laughed at her mischievous grin and rolled his eyes. Swimming was not something he liked too much, although Luey was trying to teach him. 'Well you know how good I am at that! But I was almost dead - or might as well have been.'

'Going to live with Verity's done you a lot of good as well - for her too.'

'I think we both missed having a family - and now we have Dawn to fuss over as well... It's good to have people you love around you.'

Sophie smiled gently at him and relaxed right back in her chair. 'Amen to that! Being with Luey's been so wonderful for me. If you'd asked me around this time last year what I thought it was going to be like working in Africa again I'd have told you that I must need my head examining coming back to it all.'

'But you came here anyway - I knew you had to be a brave lady.'

'Brave?!' She shook her head. 'I was scared rigid I think! Right up to when I got on the plane in April to come out to Kenya - I'd never even seen Claire's place there before, I was that afraid to come back. Don't forget I've been on the receiving end of this therapy as well. It's taken me this long to come to terms with what happened back in 1994.'

'You moved on though - got through it in a very purposeful way. You've given a lot of people back their lives, Sophie. I'm very glad you decided you were strong enough to come here.'

David looked at her seriously, though his mouth was curved into an affectionate smile, wanting to express his gratitude and admiration for what she had done for him. She was going pink now, so he went on more earnestly.

No, really I mean it. My life had become nothing, even though I was doing a worthwhile job here. I had no joy for anything or anybody, except my books and even they were starting to torment me. I was breathing, but I wasn't really living like other people.'

'Well you've certainly taken to this like a champion - you're a very intelligent guy and I think part of your trouble previously has been that your brain has been too confined...? You needed to stretch it out more. The way you've researched the subject and how you've approached the writing aspects has been astounding at times - Luey says you're like this great big brain sponge soaking up everything you can cram into yourself!'

'*Isodictya elastica*?' David laughed geekily. He'd looked it up last week when Luey had made the joke.

'Show off!' Sophie smiled at him. 'Really - Verity ought to send you away to University and give you something to apply yourself to.'

'No fear. I'm happy here and I have everything I need to keep my mind busy now you've helped me out of the black pit.'

'Well at least you didn't need chemical assistance - be thankful for small mercies!' She was silent for a moment as a lateral thought struck her. 'You can do degree courses online now you know - that might be something for you to look at? Do you good to have something terribly cerebral to tackle.'

'I've spent enough time in my head these past years, Sophie. Besides - I'm enjoying the challenge with the game management project support with Luey and the tribal lands liaison work with Verity. I don't have the time to get a formal education!'

Sophie laughed, though she was looking at him closely. 'I meant for enjoyment more than practical or career purposes really - but I guess your OCD's[45] working for you positively now, so I'll let it ride I s'pose.' She chuckled some more as David got the giggles and gave him a gimlet look. 'And don't think your roleplay habit's escaped my notice either, young man! I've been reading some of your fanfic lately - you're getting quite the compelling wizarding style...'

David blushed a little and grinned sheepishly. 'I don't see how you can nag me about that - you started me off on the fantasy genres, so it's your fault I got hooked! Anyway - just because your soppy elf lady's got a complex about mortals dying on her, doesn't mean you can have all the fun with the angst writing...'

'Touché!' Sophie was getting breathless with hilarity now and took a few deep breaths to calm herself. 'I think that's this session done with anyway. You're doing really well - it's good to see you so upbeat and energetic. Now... let's see about the next appointment...' She clicked her work palmtop open and scanned her diary. 'Looks like next month I'm afraid. I'm out on this inoculation mobile clinic up north for a week on Monday and then there'll be more here and in Umbeke. I'm really hoping the rains'll hold off a bit longer now, much as we need them.'

'Forecasts are saying they'll be heavy this season when they finally get here - Sully's driving you isn't he?'

'Yup - should have some fun, but lots to cram in.'

'Luey and I were intending to go up there soon too. Been

---

[45] **OCD** ~ Obsessive-compulsive disorder. This can manifest in those suffering from PTSD as a coping method in dealing with other symptoms such as flashbacks or avoidance measures.

some reports of malcontents hanging around the Duma[46] Flats. There's Luo camps in those areas, so I'll mention it to Sully so he can keep a look out.'

'Poachers?'

'Could be, although they've not found any signs of traps. Doesn't hurt to be cautious anyway - I was talking to the police over in Mwanza last week and they said there's reports of activity on the borders down south as well...'

'... and if Burundi sneezes, Zyanda comes down with a cold! Don't worry we'll be extra careful up there.'

* * *

Long day today. The therapy is working, but what Sophie said about my OCD working for me now is not really a joking matter. Not for me. But she is right of course. My obsessions now are mostly cleansing and borderline 'normal'.

Keeping this journal for the EMDR visualisations is something practical and disciplined, allowing me to organise the memories. But there's pain in here of course and also a creeping and unexpected bewilderment. It isn't having to go over the killings, or the other violence. I already know those intimately - have 'processed' them to some extent already. My own conscience and need to atone had started that before Umbeke. Maybe even before the night Misha and Fleur were murdered. I always knew what I had done was wrong and so it follows that I know who was responsible for the guilt. Even so, it wasn't just myself who carried the blame and it's been this knowledge that's caused me most distress when I finally had to face something I had buried away so deep I no longer knew it was decaying inside of me. My father. My

---

46 **Duma** ~ Swahili name for cheetah

grandfather. Their part in what I had become. They were dead, but I still carried their guilt and their crimes, which meant - I had finally realised - that I was their victim as well as my own.

It's easy to accept guilt on your own behalf, I suppose. You can't escape from your own actions, no matter how many excuses or explanations you find, or invent, as to why something you chose to do was inevitable. That doesn't matter really. You made it inevitable and there's no getting away from that. No matter how much evidence you can pile up to mitigate the something that you should not have started, or thought of, or wanted. The genocide was something that was generated and carried along by hatred and fear and mass hysteria. These things happen. It has happened many times in history and who's to say where it starts. Who it starts with. You can't. Not really. Except with each individual who succumbs, when they decide they must collude with the obliteration of a whole people. Even maniacs like Hitler, or Pol Pot. Mbrame too. And me, because I was too afraid not to.

And then there is forgiveness for me. For a mass killer there should not be any, surely? I don't know anymore. I know the truth for sure, but I got so lost in examining my most dreadful actions that the 'softer' ones, that were even more horrific in some respects, in turn got lost inside of me, to lie forgotten. I loved my father and my grandfather, but they had done the same things I had done. Led me to them in fact, because I would never have gone to St. Antoine's that night unless they had come for me. In that at least I was blameless. They could have left me alone but did not. Perhaps it was their misguided way of protecting me - making sure I was on the 'right' side? I had never questioned it before, but now, in preparing for my visualisations, writing them down and reading the words back again, my examination of the memories got me thinking about how it had started and why I had fallen so deeply into the webs of a psychopath like Mbrame and others like him. So my therapy journal is not just for me, it's for my father and grandfather too. Because I want them to be freed as well. And for me to be free of them, I suppose.

Sophie's been to some trouble in getting me interested in different ideas, philosophies even, that might help bring me out of the self-crucifying tunnel I have dug myself into. Different ways of looking at the meaning of life and, because she's also gone through EMDR herself, she's offered some of the solutions she found helpful, as suggestions for me on how to 'goof off', as she calls it. How to zone out of destructive cycles and let your mind fly and have some fun. Or just get some kind of exercise that doesn't feed into the crippling, hermit-like habits I've clung to for so long.

It was a very simple idea of course. She asked me what I liked to read. And the answer was - anything. Everything. So then she asked me to make a list of books I'd read and, more importantly enjoyed, then look for the gaps. I sort of got what she was doing and so I wasn't altogether surprised when she asked to see the list and looked for patterns...

'It's very college library, isn't it?'

'Well, yes - it's mostly things I've got from school. Deborah's lent me a lot as well, since I came here. I like Dickens and Austen a lot. Hugo too. Shakespeare is... odd, but admirable in terms of language.'

'Why do you say Shakespeare's odd?'

I couldn't answer that to my own satisfaction, so we talked about it later on, after the session, as I had to go out with Luey and he invited me back for supper with them. Just friends

talking. Something I had missed out on for almost half my life.
Luey nailed it - he said that I was all rote and no wild cards.
Everything I read had something to do with my narrow rut of
self-improvement and need for discipline. Required reading
for a classic education. Classic. Shakespeare. Dostoyevsky.
Voltaire. Tolstoy. Even manuals to do with my work - I used
to read them over and over until I knew them by heart almost.
Luey was breathless with laughter when I told them this, but
then he sobered up and shook his head.

'Ho, man! That is really anal, David! Don't you ever read
something light or pulpy - like... I dunno - Mickey Spillane,
or Agatha Christie? Silly, fun books?'

All rote and no wild cards...

I knew of Spillane and Christie, but it had never occurred
to me to read them, or others of the mainstream paperback
genres. Of course my access to books had been very limited,
but I'd been using the internet since I'd come to the Enclave
so, like the true geek I was beginning to realise I was, I
went online and researched the world of pulp. I read some
Poirot stories and liked his meticulous analytical style (of
course!), but it was too dated and removed from my world,
so I gravitated to Desmond Bagley and Wilbur Smith, who at
least wrote about Africa, historical and modern. I discovered
Tom Sharpe as well on Luey's recommendation. His scathing
satirical books on apartheid were hard for me to read at first.
I couldn't get my head around how you could write a 'comedy'
over such a terrible regime and disgusting atrocities. But
gradually I began to see how holding something up for
outrageous ridicule and deconstruction showed the thinking
and justification behind that oppression up for exactly what
it was. Luey lent me the Wilt series and that helped me

understand the world of parody some more in the pillorying of more comfortable, but still idiotic English social mores. Looking at the 'familiar' from a different angle. And it is was, of course, fun to read, if a guilty pleasure at times as some of the observations verged on the grotesque.

It also brought me back to Shakespeare and his tales within tales. I thought about it some more, then talked it over with Sophie and we got into The Midsummer Night's Dream and The Tempest territory. These were works I had not dismissed exactly, but had found hard to accept the spell-binding and mystic side of things. Those themes made me uncomfortable and so, of course, that was something else to look at away from the EMDR. We discovered we had a mutual fascination with classical and also Norse mythology, and so I suppose it was inevitable that Sophie suggested trying more modern fantasy classics, Tolkien and Lovecraft and others were mentioned. Our conversations spilled over into the virtual realms - it was Sophie who found a fan site that was heavily into genre writing and roleplay and started playing at being an elf woman. She had so much fun she made me join up as well and... well, it was like being reborn almost. Regaining a purity I had forgotten, I suppose. And a way to wield power if I wanted as well - the world of wizards drew me mightily. I was tearing through the books, devouring new concepts and delighting in how another world could be drawn so far apart from ours, but still keep to a truth that I could recognise, even when the story sank into evil or depravity. And dramatherapy is a valid treatment for those who have PTSD, if you want to look at it more practically.

Some of it was very juvenile, but also liberating as well, especially with the evil creatures in a way, because they were incapable of being anything other than what they were created to be - mean, or depraved, or crazy. The older veins of fantasy writing came from another era of course, with antiquated attitudes and prejudices. But the social divisions and racial borders were familiar in their simplicity, and suddenly I could make a jump into fantasy that felt 'right', even though it wasn't my own truth, because I could re-write myself, or the characters I wanted to write, and nobody could get hurt because it was fiction and a dream that couldn't be real, but nevertheless was habitable in my head. I could start over and make me a new story, even if it was just for a fantasy self.

In some ways I think this was how we all got through the genocide. Not just the killers, but everyone? People like Verity, and like Misha as well. Every day was a new story. You chose your 'side' and off you went, doing what you needed to do to keep going along the path you'd forged for yourself. We were all afraid I think - even Mbrame at times. So I walked the terrible killers' path a day, or an hour at a time, losing myself, my humanity along the way. Some of the time maybe. Partly it was automatic, especially at the end leading up to Umbeke. We didn't think anymore, just like my grandfather had said - we let Mbrame do all the talking, make the decisions. Even when it got us killed.

The night my father was gunned down was a watershed for all of us. We had been on our way back to our truck from our latest extermination of Lutse adherents, when some rebel snipers opened fire on us and we were pinned down behind the mosque. I hadn't stayed with the vehicle as usual because they'd needed more ammo and we'd been late and couldn't park up close enough. So there we were, behind cover with plenty of bullets, but gunmen on the rooftops better hidden and too much open ground for us all to make a run for it. Mbrame was never too great at tactics, so as usual it fell to my grandfather to work out how to get us out of it. It was nearly dark when he and my father crawled off on a circuitous route while the rest of us kept the snipers busy. My father was shot in the head as he drove the truck between us and the snipers.

Before he'd gone he'd smiled at me and said they'd be back in no time. That we'd get out OK. But his eyes were sad and tired. It was almost as if he'd known what was going to happen? I think for most of us that was the point at which we all began to really get the jitters about what we were doing. My grandfather and I took it bad of course. We had to throw father's body out of the truck and leave him there because the gunfire was so heavy and Mbrame was screaming that we didn't have time to see to the dead. We just left, with me sitting on the floor of the cab trying to drive and grandfather sprawled across the seats shooting and shooting; and Paul Amduna cringing down at the other door trying to peer over the dash, yelling out directions to me so I didn't crash into the wall. I remember nearly everything, except the rest of that night on that nightmare journey back to our camp. I know I was crying and my grandfather was talking to me non-stop. Only I don't know what he said and then when we got back I suppose we all drank and smoked until we were unconscious.

I won't remember it. I don't want to. All I know is that from that point I was numb with it all. Even at Umbeke at first. Like it wasn't happening almost. Just something I had to do.

Sophie says to try and get it all down in here if nowhere else. Maybe I will take it to the sessions eventually. We could use the headphones instead of the pen - what has stayed with me is the noise for that day, so that might help me do a visualisation, but really I'd rather leave this one be. I already forgave my father and grandfather for what they did to me, so it's not as though there's an issue left to resolve. And I do have good memories of them as well as the bad. Especially grandfather while we were in the Highlands. I just wish we hadn't had to abandon my father. But then it's not as though anyone got a decent burial back then and he wasn't the only one we left that day. If war is hell then what comes after for the survivors? But I did survive and I've been given a reason to live and, finally, a way to live properly. The therapy is helping for sure.

Time to call it a day - so far as the keyboard is concerned anyway. Tonight I have a new world to explore, courtesy of Luey this time. The Saga of the Exiles, an epic time travel sci-fi and fantasy of inter-galactic, prehistoric and future Earth with a bit of the Celtic Bean Sidhe and mind-bending super-powers thrown in! Sounds right up my street. Time too for camomile and wind down into sleep finally. I like my new life.

Verity

Sophie's Diary: Wednesday 31st October

Luey's birthday! He knows what his main present is of course, but not that Claire got the rings Dad sent over for us last week and forwarded them here to Verity. All he's expecting is a Halloween party for him tonight and also to celebrate our engagement. Can't wait to see what our rings look like finally, even though we won't be able to wear the wedding ones until next year.

Only have to work this morning and that's mostly taken up with a session with Verity, so I'll have plenty of time to get things ready before he gets back. Chris and Debs are seeing to the BBQ stuff (she does a wicked Tex-Mex marinade that Luey adores) so all I have to do is rustle up something for dessert that tastes wildly alcoholic even if it isn't and stick it in the fridge. Amarula bread and butter pudding might be a good idea - use the last of it up.

Still only a few days late. Will wait until I'm back from the clinic trip until I do the test though - don't want to jinx things by getting carried away too soon.

'So what are we going to talk about today Verity?' Sophie settled back into the cushions and sipped at the cool water. Verity beamed a quizzical smile at her and held up the small brown parcel she'd brought in with her.

'Don't you want to look at these first?' she laughed, holding it out to Sophie. 'I'm dying to get a sneak preview!'

'Nooooo!' Sophie blushed as she took it from her friend. 'You can see them tonight when Luey opens them - well the ones with the jewels anyway. The other two are going into storage until next year.'

Verity shrugged and shook her head with a resigned sigh. 'In that case I admire your self-control - I'd want to rip it open straight away and have a look.'

'Oh I will - just as soon as I get it home! But then I know what they look like already. Now,' she looked sternly at the woman, 'back to business madame.'

Verity's sessions were often a struggle to wrestle her away from the daily concerns of the Enclave, but gradually she had been letting Sophie have glimpses of her past relationships, primarily with her husband and two youngest children. These obviously still carried a lot of pain for Verity, but as the memories were mostly good ones, she found it easy enough to talk about her old life in Zyanda as a mother and teacher.

Sophie knew a little of the fate of Angelique, Verity's eldest child, but so far she'd volunteered very little information, except to say that she felt responsible for sending the young woman to her death. So it was something of a surprise when Verity suddenly started talking about her daughter.

'It would have been Angelique's birthday today as well. She would have been thirty years old. All Hallows Eve.' Verity gave a hollow laugh. 'Sometimes I find Deborah's fixation with Halloween a little tiresome, but that's just a cultural thing - I shouldn't let it bother me now.'

'Does it?' Sophie looked concerned as Deborah had been busily making jack-o'-lanterns out of gourds and melons for the party, but she kept her voice even, knowing that Verity had very little tolerance for any kind of religious or cultural observances, even African ones.

'No - not really. It's like Christmas or Ramadan. Family festivals centred around gift-giving, or getting the harvest in, or whatever. I don't mind all that so much - Robert always used to like Christmas when the children were very young. Halloween's not really known here, but we have similar celebrations in the syncretic beliefs, so it's not alien exactly. Did you ever hear of Imana the Creator, or the witch peoples?'

'A little bit - nothing too specific. Wasn't Imana supposed to have hunted Death so men would be immortal?' [47]

'Some such nonsense. The Matu are supposed to be one of

---

[47] In the legends of the Congo rainforest, Death is a savage animal and hides from Imana the Creator under an old woman's skirts. All unwitting, the woman takes Death into her home and dies. After she is buried, her son's wife notices there are cracks around her grave and, fearing the old lady will come back to life, for three days the younger woman fills in the cracks so the spirit cannot return. Because of this, Imana decides that he will no longer hunt Death and from that day on men can no longer come back to life when they die.

the tribes that were descended from the witch people Imana chose to prevent the dead coming back to life, so I suppose we do have a kind of Halloween tradition, except here it amounted to ritual necromancy and cannibalism. And sowed some the seeds for the genocide because that was another reason for the Lutse and the missionaries to hate us.'

Verity tailed off into silence for several moments. Sophie was going to wait for her to carry on, but decided not to let Verity's last comment lie and spoke mildly, not wanting to make a big deal of querying it. 'You don't usually make much of being Matu, Verity.'

'It shouldn't be something to be made much of - there's been no real distinction since the first World War, but it made enough difference to fuel the genocide. And actually I have a Lutse bloodline as well, on my mother's side. And Matabele come to that. I'm as much a Bantu as Nilotic in origin.'

'Matabele?'

'Ndebele - same difference. 'Mat' was the old way of saying it in colonial Rhodesia, which is where my mother's paternal family came from originally. They moved north during the nineteen forties - after her father left the RAF. I was born in Zyanda though and that's enough ethnicity for me. I'm Zyandan and that's an end of it now.'

'Genetically there's very little difference these days - not over here in central Africa anyway, with the bloodlines merging over time. The Nilotic population's still more marked physically in southern Sudan and East Africa over to Somalia, but I guess the main differences in most nations now are linguistic.'

'And as we all speak English, or French - or German even, that's getting less and less important as time goes on. Some good had to come out of European colonisation eventually.'

Verity sighed and patted Sophie on the knee apologetically. 'Thank heavens we don't let politics into the equation here in the Enclave - there are enough difficulties to try and survive here in Mgakera without constantly worrying over what our grandparents kept pecking away at and holding grudges for it all. Even now it makes my head ache and my stomach heave when they have elections back in Zyanda - at least I don't have to vote anymore! Robert would be mad as hell at me, but I don't ever want to get involved in another national political rally. Community council elections are bad enough, but at least we've got around that here with the clan accords.'

'Well I must admit to thinking it all sounded pretty feudal when I read up on the Mgakera constitution, but it does work remarkably well in practice.'

'Most people will behave themselves on a family and township level provided they don't have too much interference from outside of the community. When it was agreed to take down the borders around the river country, it took away a lot of the problems between the Matu and Luo villages over territory for the herds, and they're both happy to work on the farmlands and profit share. And of course this was such a sparsely populated area already, it wasn't too difficult for the governments to cede the land and power to UNESCO and lo! Mgakera is remade as a Utopia that only has invested citizens and no rulers. Well - administrators perhaps, but I'm a community employee all the same.'

'You'd win a vote for president if there was a vacancy I think - but yes, I'm all for cutting down on electoral paperwork and keeping profits where they're made, instead of hiving all the money off to investment houses or petty despots.'

Verity grimaced at the latter sentiment and laughed

resignedly. 'Well Black Africa got along for long enough with a thousand kings and no border delineation most of the time, give or take tribal migration and conquest. There's enough to contend with just with the weather without hitting each other continually on the head because you'd rather milk a cow than drink it's blood and make shields out of the hide.' She dipped her fingers into her cup of cooler water then dabbed them onto her already damp forehead. 'Wretched air-con! I really wish the rains would hurry up and break - it's getting too hot to think almost.'

'Amen to that! I'm glad we're not closer to the Lake - the humidity must be killing over in Mwanza.' Sophie paused a few moments and then went on tentatively, not wanting to push too hard at Verity and lose the opportunity to steer back to Angelique somehow. 'I'd like to know more about the witch people - as you mentioned them and if you don't mind talking about the old customs too much?'

Verity gave a hard laugh, then shook her head ruefully. 'OK - as it's sort of seasonal to talk about them and I like to pour scorn on the subject... Unless you'd rather I saved it for this evening?' this time her laughter was more conciliatory. 'Where to start with it?'

The hourglass had already been turned once when Sophie saw it was well on its way to emptying again. Their conversation had skirted around what happened to Verity's eldest child and touched on other, more recent conflicts in Central and Western Africa, where the war rape and abuse of women and children was seemingly forever finding new depths. 'It's really weird how cannibalism gets justified, even today.' her voice was soft and sad. 'What was it someone said - we're all just a good hot meal away from turning into savages? Except in Africa where people are too used to living at the edge of starvation.'

'All too true, yes, but at least in some places we're working on that.' Verity smiled at the doctor, 'It was barbarians I think, but savages is a better word for what some of the Matu witches were in the 1500s. You can hardly blame the Lutse for hating them so much when they first reached the central uplands and were systematically slaughtering them into submission. Or for being afraid that it could happen again. God and Allah were supposed to have stopped that possibility by bringing the old ways to an end, but I think in a way it made it worse? With the Catholics in particular...'

'Men like Mbrame?'

'He was a disaster waiting to happen I think. Quite mad, even before the killing started. Robert said that Mbrame's family were mixed up in some witch smelling[48] scandal a few generations back, so who knows - maybe it was a tradition for him to indulge in ritualistic sadism and sacrifice and a simple thing to screw it all up into a half-baked biblical jihad?' She sighed and paused to pour more water for them both. 'But really I think with Mbrame it was more to do with rites and sanctity than actual power-tripping so much. Did David tell you about him? How he baptised them all the night before it began, to make them his 'apostles' - holy warriors?'

'He hasn't told me, no, but he's written about it in his visualisation journal. I thought it was rather mixed up, but I suppose it was a way to justify what they were doing. Making it God's work?'

---

[48] **witch smeller** ~ in Africa they were (and are) generally female and themselves used 'magical' techniques to detect evil doers. As the innocent were sometimes maliciously accused, witch smellers were often more feared than the witches they hunted. In Rider Haggard's King Solomon Mines, Gagool is primarily a witch smeller, rather than a shaman or medicine woman.

'The god of love and tolerance?' Verity's voice was harsh with contempt. 'My Misha was there too - he came home reeking of dagga and communion wine, singing hymns and saying he would be an angel. At least the animals who killed my poor Angelique didn't try to hide their hatred behind idiotic bible thumping, or twisted crusading ...

She stopped abruptly, breathing hard. This time Sophie waited for her to calm in silence, just reaching out to stroke her hand gently while soft tears fell.

'I thought I was sending her to safety. Away from what happened to my little ones. I let her out of my sight because I didn't want her to go the same way as Misha and Fleur, herded into a church hall where they were supposed to be protected. Better to flee with friends than stay and wait to be killed. I thought I was doing it for the best...'

'There was no way you could have known what would happen. Everything was so frantic and confused. It wasn't your fault, Verity.'

'I could have gone with her. I should have...'

'But you didn't. Because you were needed so desperately where you were. A few days before - or afterwards - and maybe they wouldn't have run into that militia patrol and Angelique and the others would have got across the border. It was war - you acted for the best to give her a chance, just like you took a huge risk to get your other friends to Umbeke a week later.'

'While she was being raped and mutil... Ah, hell!'

'We can stop if you like, but it might be better to go on for a little if you can?' Verity had finally stopped sobbing but was still trembling and Sophie wasn't about to turn the now empty hourglass a second time, even if they were going to carry on. 'I won't tell you that crying is cathartic, but this

407

may help to release some of the pain you've had dammed up inside you for such a long time, Verity. It's not weakness to let it go now - this is really the first time you've been able to talk about her at any length to me, and you've done so well. Up to you anyway.'

Silence again, but Verity's grip on her hand tightened and Sophie waited some more.

'You wanted to go back and start getting ready for the party, didn't you?'

'Plenty of time for that - Debs and Aisha are helping me. I can stay with you as long as you want.'

Another pause, but then Verity seemed to come to a resolution. 'You're right of course. I know it wasn't my fault, but she was my daughter. She didn't want to leave me but I made her go anyway. Told her I couldn't bear for her to stay where there was danger, even though she wanted to. The way should have been safe enough, but it wasn't. We didn't know that.'

Verity's head had been bowed while she said all this, but now she looked up to meet Sophie's gaze. The tears had stopped and she tried to smile. 'And you're right about holding all this in for too long, but I don't want to carry on for now, please.'

'That's OK...' Sophie started to say, but Verity wasn't quite done and interrupted her.

'What I would like is to be busy with something that has nothing to do with the past, or with Mgakera for a few hours.' The smile grew a little stronger, though her eyes were still sad. 'I'd like to come back with you and help you with the food, or whatever needs doing and think about being happy and celebrating something good. Angelique was only a couple of years younger than you - did you know that? I'd hoped to help her prepare for her marriage some day and it would mean a lot to me - to help you, my friend.'

Sophie hugged her firmly and simply said, 'That's what we'll do then.'

Sophie

Sophie's Diary: Friday 2nd November ~ evening

Yesterday was almost a blank for me, although I did manage to get some work done in the pm. So glad we decided not to leave the party until this weekend - have been throwing up the last 2 mornings, but Luey was out for the count until about 10 yesterday. Have attributed my continuing jippy 'tummy' to the chilli butternut squash which also had Luey hurling for a bit and he has the constitution of a rhino! I know I should tell him but I don't want to until I'm really certain - and I have been later than this before since I met him...

Verity and I managed to have another chat today, just in her office for once, so she could break off and potter about if it got rough. I've offered her some EMDR sessions, but I think she's right in continuing with just the counselling as it's mainly to do with getting things out finally with her. We talked some more about Celine and Teresa as well - when she was a little girl and what could have happened to her in Nigeria. I'm so glad I saw that photo of her when she was young with Henryk - no use in wishing that I could have understood sooner how it was with her and Tom, but at least now I can remember her fairly and for what a great doctor she was - she'd have made a brilliant medical consultant on the team here. This vaccination tour is going to be so useful - I'm doing TB and DPT[49] plus yellow fever, as well as doling out the contraceptive

---

[49] **DPT** ~ Diphtheria, Pertussis (whooping cough) and Tetanus

goodies, but it's the so-called childhood illnesses like polio and measles that we take for granted at home that will be so vital...

The rain had dwindled away to a soft mizzle for now as Sophie and Sully finished packing up the vehicle and Luey had come out to help and see them off.

'Look after her, Sully - and don't let her take a turn driving if it starts chucking it down again. She's far too fond of that gas pedal!' Luey winked at the lanky driver as he gave Sophie another 'last' hug goodbye.

'And of course you never put your foot down, Mr. Speed Demon!' Sophie planted an irritated kiss on Luey's scratchy weekend chin and disentangled herself with some reluctance. 'Time to let me go, Doolittle - I'll call you tonight from main camp if the signal's OK.'

'You'd better, babe.' Luey shut the door of the Defender smoothly after her and leaned in through the open window for a proper kiss, then stood back and waved jauntily as Sully pushed into first gear. 'Take care both of you - see you in a week!'

Had that only been an hour ago? Sophie sighed and pulled her khaki jacket close around her as she watched the wipers struggle to keep up with the incessant battering of the rain, even on double speed.

'You want the heater on, Doc? Can't have you coming down with the chills.'

'No, it's OK Sully - I'd rather have the window open, but then we'd both get soaked. I don't like this sort of weather out here. Gets so muggy and it feels like the whole world's crying.'

'Just think of all those happy coffee beans! This is just 'breaking day'. Tomorrow or the day after it'll blow itself out for a few days until the next lot arrives. The first storm's always the worst and this one's very late!'

'I think Mgakera gets the worst of the equatorial forest and savannah weather with bells on!' Sophie muttered sulkily, but then laughed because she could never stay moody with Sully for long. 'Sorry - just feeling sorry for myself.'

'You'll be back with Luey in no time - these vaccination trips always fly by. And I brought some Bob Marley with me, so we don't have to talk to each other!' He flicked the CD on as Sophie thumped him on the arm, laughing all the while.

'You get the dagga out and I'll tell on you, Suleiman Mustafa!' she said sternly and then spoilt it by laughing again.

'Ah no, Doc. You're one of my little birds! No worries!' he started to sing along and Sophie smiled at the rain streaming down the windows.

She let her thoughts wander over the past few days as they drove north east, barely noticing the rain now as Sully's growly voice lulled her irritation away. Verity was over the worst now, but it had been tough at times as she let the dams walls fall, talking in the main about her three grown children, but sometimes about the other four babies that she'd lost. Two of the miscarriages had been due to placental malaria, and this of course had opened old wounds for Sophie. She'd come to terms with her own loss as inevitable long ago, whether or not Tom had been killed. Malaria really was a killer so far as babies were concerned, and Sophie now knew how lucky she had been not to die as well, since she had had no natural immunity after her medication had failed.

If she was pregnant, this time it would be different. She had prepared thoroughly for this week away, packing a small camping bed net and a good supply of her meds and sprays, and the anti-mozzie spraying regime at Mgakera was exemplary. But, but, but... mozzies hatch and develop in water, so the rains were always a dodgy time; although incessant downpours did help a little, especially during twilight and dark, as at least the little buggers couldn't swarm too well in a deluge.

She'd been talking a lot about the equatorial rains and mosquito life-cycles with Luey and David too. A smile crept over her face as she thought about the unlikely friendship the three of them shared and the strange way their conversations span out and ranged over such a wide area of life experience. With being pre-occupied with the vaccination clinics and infant mortality, Zambia and Tom had been on her mind as well, and somehow the talk had turned to him several times since the party - both Luey and David were curious about her first love, though for different reasons. She was beginning to think that, if things had been otherwise, Luey and David might have been friends with Tom. They all had things in common for sure but then so did she, though naturally things were platonic between her and David, especially with the doctor-patient relationship. In some respects David reminded her more of Tom but that could be down to his passion for trucks and birds.

Weird how things turned out. Since that night in Kariba her recurring dream of Tom and their baby had ceased, but sometimes she had the feeling Tom was still close to her at odd times. When Luey looked at her in a certain way, or David pointed something of interest out as they were driving. If David felt he had been given a second chance at life, she too was regaining feelings she'd thought would never come back to her, that had died with Tom. But they'd only been waiting for her she realised. Lying just below the surface, waiting for her to recover. People were resilient and needed each other.

She'd been good for Luey and David too of course. For Luey, in his capacity to love and be loved and in all kind of ways for poor, stunted David. His progress really was astonishing - she'd never encountered such a success story, not only with the EMDR but with the dramatherapy that the roleplay forum was supplying. For herself as well - it was really silly how much pleasure she was getting from messing about being an elf! Luey had been teasing them both about their online 'am-drams', steadfastly refusing to join in, although of course he was just as bad really with his WoW [50] habit. But then some people needed body counts and a Rambo hierarchy and didn't 'get' the attraction of self-written roleplay and being totally in control of character development and goals instead of working with the game infrastructure the whole time. It wasn't even exercising the imagination so much as finding out what really mattered to you. What you could believe in. Maybe she'd see about taking an online module in transpersonal psychology [51] - that might be something to stretch her mind a little in between wedding planning for next year and the new baby...

She pulled herself out of the reverie sharply, cheeks hot with embarrassment, even though Sully had no inkling of the cause and started rootling around in her bag to cover her discomposure.

'Need some coffee? I'm falling asleep here.'

---

[50] **WoW** ~ World of Warcraft. Possibly the most successful and certainly ubiquitous online fantasy battle gaming environment on the planet.

[51] **transpersonal psychology** ~ a branch of the science that investigates the spiritual aspects of human experience including the visionary.

'You read my mind - I can pull off after this hill.'

Sophie sank back into her seat again and tried to concentrate on the scenery as she hadn't travelled up here too much yet. Far too soon to start thinking about baby showers when they were driving through an actual force of nature of monsoon rains.

* * *

Sophie's Diary: Monday 5th November ~ main Luo encampment west of Lake Tembo

Well I suppose it was worth the awful day travelling up - today we got everyone who showed up inoculated by teatime and they've been lovely to us hospitality-wise. Delicious goat curry and rice last night and yummy warthog with roast yams this evening. But I blame David and his ruddy long range forecasts! Early rains like wretched Calcutta monsoons - yesterday it bucketed down from start to finish and we apparently only just made it over the pontoon bridge as we crossed the Tanga on the way up. It's kaput for now, but at least the weather cleared this morning and they said they'll re-jig the anchors tomorrow if it holds, as the river's gone down a little. It looks like they really caught the downpour over the border though - couldn't see the Mgakera Highlands on the Zyandan side for murk on the Uganda highway as we came north!

Sully says there's another way over to the Flats, although it adds about an hour to the journey time for the trip out to the Lake camp tomorrow. He's not too happy about going there I think. Not because of these reports of illegals but I'm guessing that it's not a great place to be in if it starts flooding - very low country there lakeside, although I don't think the Luo have a permanent camp down there as there's plenty of high ground. It's spectacular up here in the dry season as the water supply's permanent - great for growing coffee, but that's mostly off Enclave land to the east of the Lake. Luey was a bit disappointed not to be able to come out with us - Lake camp's not far from this biggish island he's got his eye on for some breeding scheme. He's being really cagey about telling me what it is they're up to and David's suddenly clammed up on me as well...

Ephraim struggled up again, fighting the panic down. He was shaking with the effort and steadied himself against the boulder as he checked the makeshift tourniquet above his knee for what must have been the hundredth time and offered thanks to Allah that the blood loss from the wound on his calf seemed to have been stemmed. The last thing he needed now was a predator to catch the scent. He wasn't too far from where the herd was and maybe the others would be on the lookout by now, as it was past noon and they'd been gone for hours. He passed his fingers across his eyes, dashing away sweaty tears. At least he had escaped with his life. Painfully he pushed himself off the rock, leaning heavily on his staff now, hardly putting any weight at all on his right leg for fear of setting the bleeding off again.

* * *

'What on earth's the matter, Sully? Sit down - get your breath back...' Sophie was alarmed at how strained her driver looked as she finished swabbing the needle mark on the little girl's arm, gave her a hard-boiled sweet and steered her back to her mum.

Sully shook his head, but leaned over slightly, holding his arm across his ribcage and took slow breaths before speaking. 'No time, Sophie. Got to go out and collect a casualty right away - one of the herders been shot and they're saying another's been killed...'

'I'll come with you then...!'

'No! Sorry. No - best you stay here and I'll bring him in.

415

It's only a few miles and you'd have to set up again. I'll be gone fifteen minutes at most.'

'OK. I'm nearly done here anyway. Do we know how bad he's hurt?'

'Leg injury and they said something about a bullet lodged in the shoulder? He's weak but conscious.'

'Get going then - and be careful!'

The Enclave

Verity happened to be in the comms office when Sophie came on the radio. Quickly she took over from Henri.

'Verity here. Say again Sophie? You're breaking up badly... Over.'

'Bloody storm! ... can you hear me now? Over.'
Henri fine-tuned and the crackling died away slightly.

'OK - yes we have you now. It's raining hard here too. Over.'

'Really bad here. Not just the rains - we have a big problem! I just took a hunting rifle bullet out of one of the herders up here - from his shoulder and he's got what looks to be a terrible ragged wound from an automatic weapon on his leg... very worried it might get infected...'

There was a crackle and what sounded like someone else talking. Verity looked at Henri anxiously and nodded when he asked if he should get the police on the phone. Sophie came back on.

'... Sorry that was Sully. We're going to take a few of the men out to where Ephraim was shot - he says his friend Okot went down and he thinks was killed. Over.'

'Roger, Sophie. Be careful please. We'll call the police over in Rufighebwe... Do they know who was doing the shooting yet? Over.'

'Em... Sully's saying they think they were Zyandan mostly - not local tribesmen? Militia... Oh god... They had chainsaws! Were taking ivory - elephants... They saw smoke and vultures and went to investigate... were on their way back when they got Okot and Ephraim just ran for it. Yes! Get the police definitely. Over.'

'Thanks, Sophie. Just to confirm - you're at the Lake Camp on the Duma Flats, yes? Over.'

'Yes - but they're moving off the plain as I'm talking to you. River's almost burst its banks here but the road's passable Sully says, and we're going back to main camp after we retrieve Okot. Ephraim found vehicle tracks, so Sully says the poachers won't have stuck around. Hopefully I can call you from main camp later tonight? Got to go now. Over an...'

'Sophie! Are you there? Sophie!!' The line crackled thinly to itself.

'Sounds like she was signing off anyway, Verity.' Henri said and held out the phone to her. 'I have the desk sergeant on the line for you.'

* * *

'Luey - calm down and listen to what Verity's saying!' David pushed Luey back onto the sofa in Verity's living room and held him down by the shoulders until he was certain that the Zimbabwean wasn't going to kick off again. Verity sat down beside Luey and took both his hands in hers, squeezing his fingers gently.

'Try not to worry, Luey. Sully's there and he'll look after

417

her. They were taking some villagers with them - they'd were armed as well and, like I said, these poachers will be long gone by now. She said they'll call in again in a few hours when they make main camp - and the police are on their way up there already. There's nothing we can do now without more information. No point in our driving up there until we hear from Sophie and Sully tonight. OK, Luey?'

David was crouched down in front of him now, looking anxiously into Luey's face as he struggled to regain his composure.

'Sorry...' Luey mumbled raggedly. 'This godawful storm's not helping either.'

'T.I.A - anything that can happen, will...' Verity broke off as her phone rang and she motioned for David to get it. He was back within a minute, looking even more concerned.

'That was Henri. He's just heard reports on the news of a 'quake over at Lake Kivu an hour ago and some aftershocks already in the Zyandan Highlands...'

Luey groaned 'Cosmic! That's all we bloody well need with the rains as well!' He patted Verity reassuringly. 'OK - I promise I'm not going into orbit again honey, but I think I'll go home to pack a bag and come back here for the night, if that's OK with you? See what they say when they get in tonight and then maybe David and I can go out first thing tomorrow morning?'

Verity was nodding as he stood up and jingled in his pocket for the car keys. 'Yes, come here for tonight, but the police will be calling as well. Best we see what they say before you go charging around. Drive carefully - the roads will be getting very muddy now.'

'No fear. I'll be good!'

Just over an hour later David went to the door to let Luey

back in. Verity was talking to the police at Rufighebwe on the phone, her voice low and anxious. The rondavel seemed shrouded in darkness as the last of the daylight was swept away by the rain.

'A little good news - Sophie and Sully arrived at main camp OK, but there's more trouble up there and the comms are all out. The police are co-ordinating on a portable mast from there, but we won't be able to go up until tomorrow at earliest.' David looked tense but animated, as he took Luey out to the kitchen where he was making some relish to go with their mielie-meal supper.

Luey's anxiety levels were almost through the roof with frustration. 'What the hell else can go wrong, now! Are they sure they're OK - and what about those bloody poachers?'

Both men looked around hopefully as Verity came into the kitchen, still holding the phone and about to speed dial one of the CAMEO distribution hubs. She spoke quietly and urgently, not looking at either of them. Finally she finished the call and shook her head sadly.

'There's been a massive landslip at main camp and the telecoms mast has come down. The officers that were sent up there met Sophie and Sully on their way in. It looks like the Matu who killed the herdsman headed north-west for the Zyandan Highlands.' She met Luey's worried gaze. 'There's flooding now on the Flats, so their trail's mostly likely been wiped - that's all come from the Luo who went with the Cruiser... The damage is bad up there - several people were crushed in the landslip and almost all the permanent dwellings went down. Sophie and Sully are doing the best they can with the wounded, but they need supplies and shelter as soon as we can get them up there. There's around a thousand people without a roof and about a third of them have injuries of some kind.' She stopped and stabbed out the number viciously.

'How bad's the flooding up there, Verity? Did they repair the pontoon?' Verity shook her head at David, then turned slightly as her call was picked up and immediately launched into a torrent of French.

Luey looked at David in dismay. The Matu smiled grimly back at him.

'There's other ways around, Luey, but it sounds like we'll need to take some of the big trucks up there for the casualties.'

'Can we fly in...? Get some med supplies in there if nothing else...' The Mgakera airstrip currently had two crop sprayers that Luey had been borrowing a little for game-spotting.

'Depends on the flooding - not a lot of landing strips there away from Lake Tembo. Verity's on to Bujumbura[52] - they're co-ordinating for the earthquake - best chance for getting hold of NFI aid in a hurry. Mwanza's further and the road around Geita's always hell in the rains. The damage is really bad all around the south-west area of Lake Kivu apparently.'

'Yeah - I heard on the radio as I was coming back. What's NFI?'

'Non-food items - so meds and equipment. Tents, rescue stuff.'

'Of course...' Luey flushed in mortification and looked anxiously over at Verity who was now listening more than talking.

'At least we know where Sophie and Sully are and they're not in any great danger now. Could be worse...' David was taking pains to keep Luey reassured.

---

52 Bujumbura ~ capital of Burundi

Verity had finished and motioned for them to join her at the kitchen table. Her face was sad but calm and she squeezed Luey's hand briefly as he pulled a chair back. 'Try not to worry - nothing much we can do until the morning now. The weather forecast for tomorrow is an improvement on today, although we could still have rain up here. That's why they moved the aid co-ordination over to Burundi - the earthquake epicentre was to the west of Lake Kivu, but they've missed out on the rains so far so the roads are fine.' She looked over at David and went on. 'You'll need to get on the road as soon as it's light and take three dragomans to the airport at Bujum - they've got fuel and the usual humanitarian supplies at the depot already and there's some specialist boxes with tents and survival gear being shipped out from the UK tonight. That'll be arriving not long after noon tomorrow - they're flying it in from one of the military bases to save transit time. They said they can let us have some of that emergency gear and maybe some people to help with the set up, so you'll be able to go straight from there cross country to the Highlands and get to main camp that way. Even if they get the pontoon up again you won't be able to get the dragomans over it, so that'll save some time. How soon do you think you could get to main camp from Bujum - the roads up country in Zyanda aren't too bad apparently.'

David was nodding as this last part. 'They've just finished laying asphalt end of September, so it's as good as it gets. Depending on these survival boxes clearing the airport...'

'That shouldn't take that long - CAMEO have worked with this disaster relief company lots of times before in other places - floods and earthquakes. Everything.'

'OK - hopefully we'd make it back up there midday or later the day after tomorrow. Maybe quicker if the weather holds and we can drive safely after it gets dark.' He glanced over at Luey. 'What about getting a plane to main camp - maybe take Christian and some more med supplies up in the morning?'

Verity hesitated a moment, but then grinned. 'Yes - the police said that Gobengwe's still above the surge and they can get a vehicle there to pick up Christian. Luey - will you be alright to fly him?'

Finally Luey stopped frowning. 'Yeah! Course - I know Gobengwe pretty well now. The strip's not too close to the river there, so it ought to be fine, so long as it's not too stormy.'

'Good!' Verity got up again, taking the phone with her and heading for the living room. 'I'll call the police back to set this up and then Christian and the guys over at the vehicle shop so they can get the lorries ready to go first thing. You two can finish cooking dinner and then we'll all get an early night. Busy day tomorrow and I need my rest!'

Angels of the Abyss

And I saw an angel come down from heaven, having the key of the bottomless pit and a great chain in his hand. And he laid hold on the dragon, that old serpent, which is the Devil, and Satan, and bound him a thousand years

Book of Revelation 20:1-2 (King James version)

As none of them slept too well they were all up before dawn. Verity went off with David to the vehicle shop to help supervise the loading of provisions for the journey to Bujumbura and beyond, leaving Luey to go and pick up Christian and the medical supplies to supplement what Sophie had with her. As the two men headed back to Mgakera's airstrip, the rain eased off somewhat and Luey began to anxiously watch the cloudbase.

'Is the visibility going to be a problem?' Christian was not a confident air traveller.

Luey grinned over at him. 'Gobengwe's lower than here so it should be OK mate. I wasn't planning on taking her up too high anyhow and it looks like the rain's gonna fizzle for a bit.'

'Will we have that thing...? The bumps...?'

'Turbulence?' Luey laughed. 'A little, but that's normal for a small plane. Don't worry, I need to keep below the clouds so it won't be real bad. Besides which it's only a short hop - we'll be landing about twenty minutes after take-off.'

'Those are the worse bits.'

'Promise I'll be as gentle as I can.' He decided it was probably best he didn't tell the doctor that he'd need to follow the highway and rivers to avoid getting lost since he'd only flown there a few times and always in clear weather...

As luck would have it the larger of their two refurbished Polish crop-dusters had just come through its regular checks the day before the rains had started and so had still been snugly tucked away in the hangar at the 'rocky' end of the Mgakera airstrip, so they at least had a nice dry start and no worries about having to get pushed out of mud before they even fired up the engine. Their destination, Gobengwe, was an ex-WW2 base from the old colonial days and had a rather ancient, but still viable concreted runway, so Luey was reasonably confident that they'd not have too much trouble getting there and back.

'There you go Chris - told you it wouldn't take too long.' Luey had done a quick low level pass to make sure there were no hazards on the Gobengwe strip and waggled their wings at the Mgakera Land Cruiser that was parked outside the large rambling shack that passed as Gobengwe's Air Traffic Control Tower and hangar.

'Good... Just tell me when it's safe to open my eyes again.' Christian was squeezing the hell out of his worry beads, head bowed.

Luey tutted softly and tried not to smile too much, even though his friend couldn't see him. 'Anyone would think you didn't rate my flying, mate. It's been smoother than your daughter's gorgeous little bottie all the way so far, so I'm not about to let you lose your breakfast now!' He started the descent, keeping her level and glanced over at the doctor to see his reaction.

'I didn't have any breakfast. If you see anything come up it'll be my supper!'

'Ingrate! OK. We're nearly there now... just one little bounce...'

The front wheels hit the deck and then a lighter bump as the back came down. 'Reckon you can risk a wave out of the window at Sully now! We're not on fire or anything... ouch!' Luey was having a good laugh until Christian thumped him on the arm.

'Looks like we've got a police escort.' Luey frowned slightly as he peered out of the windscreen. The rain was starting to tip down again, but Sully and another man in dark blue fatigues had got out of the Land Cruiser. Christian nodded but still hadn't got much to say for himself as they rolled up outside the ramshackle building.

Sully had waved to them and was opening the back door of the vehicle as Luey jumped down. He turned and to his delight saw Sophie running over to him. 'Hey, babe - am I pleased to see you!' He whispered in her ear after she'd finished kissing him and hugged her tight again, running his warm hands soothingly down the damp back and arm of her waterproofs, because she was sobbing with relief.

'It's been horrible not being able to get thuh - through to you!' Her voice was stumbling with fatigue... 'It was so awful Luey... the herdsman and all those elephants...'

'It's OK, babe. I'm here now, sweetheart.'

Sully had come up with the policeman who looked to be in his mid-thirties. 'Hey Sully - thanks for looking after her.' He clasped the driver's arm gratefully and gently turned Sophie around so she could see Christian was with him. 'I brought you some help see? And we've got some more med supplies in the hopper and there's more coming through tomorrow on the trucks. David and a couple of other guys left to get them at first light.'

'We've heard from Mgakera about the relief shipments this morning. Mr Ogilvy, isn't it? I'm Sergeant Mohammad Abdullah.' The policeman saluted him and then put out his hand. Luey took hold of it, a little taken aback at the formality, but the cop gave him a lopsided grin and turned to greet Christian who'd finally made it out of the cockpit and onto terra firma with evident relief.

'Dr Kamate? My father would want me to pass on his regards. He'll be getting up here in the next day or so, but he says that you can rest assured we'll do everything we can to get the aid convoy through without any hitches - there'll be an extra squad coming in from Mwanza by then to meet them on the Uganda highway.'

The policeman kept talking as he saluted and shook hands with Christian, then turned back to Luey who was still hugging a shivering Sophie, trying to warm her up against the chill damp of the early morning. 'I'm afraid I have to break up your reunion for a little while longer, Mr Ogilvy. I've had permission from Mrs Beleshona to requisition you to pilot myself and Sully on some aerial recon - to see if we can pick up the trail of these killers from yesterday...'

Luey's head snapped around to look at Abdullah irritably. 'Not in this plane you can't - it's a two-seater. I can take you or Sully - not both.'

'That won't be necessary - we have a light aircraft in the hangar. A four seater.'

Luey was still frowning, but responded to that more positively. 'OK. But Sophie comes with us... What, babe?'

Sophie had backed away slightly, eyes wide and shaking her head. 'I can't. Got to get back to main camp with Christian

- still so many people to see to, Luey. Sully's the one who knows the area best. I'll see you later though.' She patted his hand then let go as Christian came up to her. 'Work to do first, Tarzan!' Her smile was tired, but strong enough and so he nodded and reluctantly turned back to Abdullah.

'Let's have a look at this plane then, Sergeant.'

Sully had unloaded the supplies as they were talking and so Christian and Sophie went to help him get it all into the Cruiser while the Sergeant walked Luey over to the dilapidated hangar. There was an engineer inside who'd been running the checks for the Skyhawk and Luey's concentration was tied up with that for a little while, even though he was familiar with the model, as he hadn't flown one since the late '90s. Once they were through he found Sully and the policeman waiting patiently by the cabin steps.

'They couldn't wait - we'll see them later though.' Sully looked at him apologetically. Luey nodded quietly, looking past the driver at Sgt Abdullah standing impassively to the side.

'Well we've got about two hours fuel so it'll have to be short, whatever happens.' He gestured for them to get aboard and followed them up the steps. Quickly he went through the final checks and turned to make sure Sully was settled beside him and finally to the cop in the rear seat.

'What's the flight plan, Sergeant?'

'If we could fly eastwards towards Duma Flats and Lake Tembo - Sully will direct you to the place where they first found the poachers and then we need to fly over the road they took back to the north west.'

'Will we be landing at all?' Luey asked as he started the engine up.

Sully shook his head. 'We won't be able to by the lake and

then the road runs beside ravines a lot - we're looking for a crash site...'

* * *

The rains had stayed away from Burundi so far, something David was thankful for as they rolled up at the CAMEO depot near the airport at Bujumbura after a gruelling seven hours out from Mgakera. The naval transport plane had landed a little ahead of time and the CAMEO relief consignment had already been offloaded at the depot, so they had a reasonably quick turnaround and were back on the road north in the early afternoon with the ShelterBox[53] gear, supplemental food and fuel supplies to those they'd brought with them and half a dozen CAMEO disaster relief workers, two of whom were sitting up in the cab with him.

Once they'd cleared the traffic away from the outskirts of the capital and were heading upcountry they began to relax and get to know each other. Abel and Magdalena were both Malawian and were full of warm praise for the cargo of sturdy plastic boxes that were split between the three dragomans. They had helped to distribute them the year before, during severe flooding down in Kigoma on Lake Tanganyika. They were quick to reassure David when he expressed concern over there being enough boxes to go around when they got to Lake Tembo.

'The tents are big enough to shelter a family of ten people...' Magdalena explained '... and just wait and see what's in them! Even the box is useful once it is emptied.'

---

[53] **ShelterBox** ~ an international disaster relief organisation founded in Helston, Cornwall in the UK, specialising in emergencies where shelter is an issue. They supply boxes containing tents, basic toolkits, multi-fuel stove, cooking and water purification equipment, blankets and warm clothing - and a children's drawing pack.

'Well I'm very impressed with how quickly they got them over to the depot from the airport.'

'Oh no, David.' Abel smiled over at him. 'These were all in prepositioned storage already - the ones that came over on the Hercules all went off directly from the airport with the Response Team from the UK. Don't worry - we learned from them when they sent boxes over for the Kigoma floods and your local people can see to the NFI relief. These tents are really easy to get up and the other equipment's excellent - all you have to do is get us there in one piece.'

David shook his head and laughed softly. 'Well pray that the rains hold off when we get to Zyanda - it was looking like it was in a competition with Noah's Flood last night.'

'Forecast's not so bad.' Magdalena said evenly. 'What was it like this morning up there?'

'A little lighter, but the sun didn't get through until well after ten. Means that we'll have dry roads over the worst part of the mountains, although I'm not too certain how it is on the road north of Rukare - we came in on the highway south-east of there. Not too many clouds then.'

'How long before we get to Tanzania?' Abel asked.

'Depending on the light and whether or when we get rain, between noon tomorrow or early the day after. Too risky to drive for long in the dark anyway.'

* * *

Luey eased back on the yoke and turned back westwards away from Lake Tembo, still flying quite low and following the barely discernible road trail that Sully and Sophie had driven along yesterday. The place that Sully had just shown them was frighteningly close to the islands that he was hoping to use for a rhino breeding project with a possible site for a small safari lodge and sitatunga reserve. For now all they could think of were the seventeen elephant carcasses that Sully was telling them the poachers had left behind. Four of those were very young calves who would have had negligible ivory. With mounting fury he listened to Sully talking about the now washed out trail that they had followed after retrieving the corpse of the unfortunate herdsman Okot Oduya.

'That's the end of the road we met you on yesterday sergeant, but they must have turned off and we missed it because of the rain.'

'Is there another road off this one?'

'Not exactly - but there's a narrow trail that leads up north to one of the old ensete[54] plantations and from there another, better road onto the Uganda highway.'

'They had a lorry though? As well as their Land Rover?' The policeman sounded tired now as well. Neither Sully nor he had got any sleep last night. 'Would they have been able to drive them both through a bush trail?'

'Put it this way sergeant - I wouldn't drive anything bigger than a land cruiser on that road unless I really had to, especially not when it's this wet. It's very steep and narrow in places and I'm sure that the smoke we saw was in that region.'

---

[54] *Ensete ventricosum* or *Ensete livingstonianum* ~ also known as the false banana tree is cultivated primarily in north eastern Africa, particularly in Ethiopia, but found as far south as the Transvaal and westwards into the highland jungles and lakes of central Africa. Its green fruits are inferior in taste to true bananas but the rest of the tree, especially the roots, have a variety of uses including feed for livestock and fibre for rope and baskets, so it has been farmed as a staple crop for centuries, most recently in combination with coffee or tea. The tree itself was a feature in murals in Ancient Egyptian temples depicting the goddess Isis.

As they had been talking Sully had been looking down trying to spot where this smaller trail snaked off. After a few more minutes he found what he'd been looking for.

'There! Go north east of that ravine on the right - the trail goes down and then up the other side away from this road.'

Luey peeled off as Sully had said. He could see the trail quite easily now as there was not so much tree cover on the steep sides of the river defile, before the little road zig-zagged up again and disappeared over the northerly ridge. Abdullah was craning his neck around following the line of the road they had just left and then turned to look out of the window on Sully's side of the Skyhawk.

'I think you're right about this road Sully. The spot we met overlooks that valley where we saw the smoke from the crash. How far ahead of you do you think they were?'

'In time? About an hour - not much more than that I'd say.'

'Would that tally with where we think they've gone down?'

'Could be - it would take them best part of that time to get to there on those gradients, especially in these conditions and if they weren't sure of the road...' They were rounding the ridge now and Luey's eyes followed the little road as it swung north-west back into the hills; then he cried out and flew away from the ridge into a wide circling pattern.

'There's your crash site, guys!'

Both vehicles had evidently failed to make a tight corner where the road had crumbled away and then nosedived into the ravine. The lorry had slipped right into the river, not far from a small stone bridge and the cab had all but disappeared into the swollen waters and lodged itself into a rocky cascade. The Land Rover was further back on higher ground and looked to be burned out.

Sgt Abdullah was craning around Sully trying to get a better look. 'Can you fly in lower to get a better look please, Mr Ogilvy?'

'Sure - and Luey's fine.' He manoeuvred smoothly and whistled as they all saw the extent of the wreckage. 'Doubt there's any survivors from that though!'

* * *

Sophie's Diary: Early Wednesday 7th November ~ main Luo Encampment west of Lake Tembo

2:30a.m.- This has to rate as one of the worst nights of my entire life. Am so tired and it's likely we'll be up again in a few hours time. Glad we radioed Verity before we left the Lake after I'd patched up Ephraim. If the police hadn't been on their way up when the landslip hit then I think we'd have lost even more people. As it is there's still around 70 people pretty badly injured and about twice as many with minor stuff that have been seeing to themselves. We don't know what the death toll is yet, but only a half dozen for sure so far (not including poor Okot) and another eight people missing still, three of whom were likely not on the hillside.

Most of the encampment went down like matchsticks, but luckily the chapel's not too badly damaged and the school house beside it is as safe as it can be, though it's a little crumbly out in the yard. We've made a makeshift shelter for the badly hurt and the babies whose parents are missing in there anyway, with the chapel as our morgue for now.

Sully is an utter angel - I don't know what I'd have done without him. I was in a real panic when we first got here about an hour before sundown and saw the mess. The Methodist minister, Elias Llewellyn and his wife luckily have some med training and they'd started triage for the people they'd already got out of the debris, although they had bugger all to use in the way of bandages etc, as all his first aid stuff went down with his cabin. Mo and his guys were

432

an absolute godsend - now I know why they carry these portable radio masts with them. They managed to get a generator going as well. They've been passing messages to Mgakera too and Verity is going to send Luey up in one of the crop dusters with more supplies early tomorrow. Can't wait for him to get here.

Will have to try and get some sleep now.

4 a.m. - No good. Am doing this instead to pass the time and stop me going crazy, although I think this camping lamp battery's not got too much juice left in it.

5:30 a.m. - In the school hall again. Eli came to get me as an old woman was having a crisis. Nearly lost her but have managed to stabilise again. Dehydration's going to be a big problem but Mo says we can get some more clean water supplies when he goes to the Gobengwe airstrip this morning. I begged him to let me go with them too and he finally agreed - I really need to see Luey as I'm feeling a little shaken up with everything. Probably just knackered. Who wouldn't be?

'I'm worried about you, babe. Is it just because of all the drama and not much rest?' Luey drew Sophie gently to him on the back seat of the land cruiser that they'd flattened so it was a little more comfortable to stretch out on. They had been talking in hushed tones as Sully was crashed out in the front passenger seat, exhausted after being almost constantly on the move for over thirty-six hours. Sophie didn't answer straight away, relishing his warmth and really wanting to be able to relax and drift a little. Eventually she gave a little sigh and hugged him close so her head was cushioned into his neck and he wouldn't be able to look at her without shifting drastically.

'Yes. It's tiredness mostly I think. I was almost there as well before you started with the mother hen thing.' She gave his hand a gentle squeeze to show she was teasing. 'I hardly got a wink last night, but Chris made me have a quick snooze after lunch. Sully's the one you should worry about really - he was dead beat after you got back. He was out all night with the cops down at the generator shed trying to get some power back on.'

'Yeah - Mo said there's a load of damage there, but some of it's not completely wrecked.' He kissed the top of her head gently and turned slightly, pulling her around as well so they were loosely spooned together for their mutual comfort, emotional as well as physical. 'I can't help it, babe. I was so worried about you last night.'

'I know. More than half my problem was that I wanted you here with me...'

She trailed off, shutting her eyes in surprise when a couple of fat tears suddenly welled up and escaped, the salt stinging as they rolled down her nose. Silently struggling to compose herself, she took a couple of deep breaths until she was sure her voice wasn't going to wobble.

'I nearly lost it when we found Okot and the ellies yesterday.'

'Sully said you were upset. I wish I could have been there for you - it's never nice to see what those bastards do. And for them to have murdered someone as well.' He tried hard, but knew he'd failed to keep the venom out of his voice. Sophie tensed in his arms, so he lowered his lips to where her neck met her shoulder and murmured an apology into her skin. Gradually she relaxed back into him again. He wished he could slowly make love to her without having to talk and make things worse - even if they'd been alone it wasn't the right time.

'What do you think of Mo?' Her question, seemingly out of nowhere, made Luey chuckle.

'I'm serious, Luey.' Sophie persisted, though she was smiling now. 'I thought you were going to punch him this morning when he said you had to pilot him.'

He grimaced with embarrassment, blushing furiously in the dark. 'Well... as a rule I try not to deck officers of the law within ten minutes of being introduced to them.' He got an elbow in the ribs for that and clasped her closer to him with an exaggerated whimper. 'I'll behave now, I promise!' He smiled, whispering in her ear. '... He kinda grew on me when we got airborne, after I heard about what happened when you met them yesterday afternoon.'

'That was really weird. He'd just run over to us and got in the cruiser - we could hardly see to drive by then with the rain, and then there was this massive bang echoing up the valley and then all that smoke.'

'Must have been the tank exploding - looked like both vehicles were total burnouts. He was really impressed with Sully - they didn't even know there was a road up there.'

'I think it's more a cart track that the Luo have been widening recently from what Eli was saying when we got back.' She paused a moment and then it all came out in a rush. 'But what I meant was - about Mo... It's really silly, but it's creeping me out that he's here now?'

'Why? He seems fine. Very efficient and he was singing your praises the whole time I was with him almost?'

Sophie cringed, then went on though she felt so daft. 'Yes I know - and I do like him, but... It was just strange the way he greeted Chris? Like they'd met? He said something about his father, so... on the way back here I asked Chris and that's when I got the creeps?' She let out a sigh and rubbed at her eyes which were feeling rather gritty from her earlier tears. 'I'm being stupid - forget it.'

'Oh no you don't, lady! Out with it, if it's bothering you.'

'Shush - you'll wake Sully...' The exhausted driver chose that moment to start snoring loudly and determinedly.

'Yeah, right! C'mon Quackers - you can't just leave it hanging now.' He brushed his hand gently through her hair and kept quiet then, letting her take her time.

Finally she told him about how the sergeant's father had been the chief investigating officer into Tom's and the other murders back in '94 and that Christian and Verity had met him several times since. Apparently Abdullah Snr had been promoted to the regional command for the Western Lake District a few years back. Luey remained silent for about a minute, just stroking her arm and shoulder gently until the tension left her and then spoke soothingly.

'You've had a hard few days, love - no wonder you're feeling jittery.'

He felt her nod slightly and, reaching up a finger to stroke her face, found it was wet. Saying nothing he shifted and sat up, propping himself against the door, gently pulling her up and back into him as he went, then cradled her head into his shoulder again.

'Will you tell me the rest of it now, babe? I know you've had something on your mind for over a week now, so don't try and brush me off.'

'Since when were you psychic?' Her voice was calm enough anyway, but he kissed her hair, knowing she was still crying.

'Hey! Bluff macho Zim guy here. Nothing psychic about me. Just noticed you were going easy on the beer and wine on my birthday? Trust me - I'm an animal doctor and I can usually tell when females are in season.' She laughed a little

436

and he smiled into the night. 'Have you done a test yet, Sophie?'

'No. Not yet.'

'Why the hell not, silly woman?' His voice was soft and full of affection now and he waited patiently for her to tell him why, half-knowing the answer.

'Too early. Well it was. I was going to do it this morning actually, but... Well you know.'

'Things happened and it didn't seem too important? But it's been nagging away in there anyway?' He sighed then and turned so he could look at her. She rolled into him and tried to evade his gaze but he put his fingers under her chin and turned her back gently, dipping his head to kiss her briefly on the lips.

'Do it first thing in the morning, Soph. Before I have to go back to Mgakera. We can radio Verity and have them ready to refuel me so I can come back with more supplies, just in case David doesn't make it over tomorrow afternoon. Mo wants me here again anyway if we can get down to the killing ground at the weekend.'

'I didn't want to tell you until I was sure. The last time ended so...' He silenced her with another, slightly longer, deeper kiss.

'Last time you were sick. Really sick. This time it'll be different, babe. I love you and I know what this means to you - means to both of us come to that.'

As he finished talking the clouds were covering the rabbit in the moon and the rains started in earnest once more, so they snuggled back down onto the seats and pulled the blankets over them.

* * *

Eli and Christian were taking the night shift over at the school house, talking softly over Sophie's hastily scrawled notes and Christian's updates. Apart from the rain hammering down on the corrugated roof it had been a quiet evening. They'd been able to stabilise everyone that afternoon, putting the worst cases onto drips, which meant that everybody could now relax a little and get some rest, knowing their severe cases were sufficiently hydrated. As it was Christian had had to call on Luey to drag Sophie away that evening, having already practically yelled at Sully to go and get some rest when he all but collapsed on them a few hours after they got back from Gobengwe.

'I hope the sergeant got back before the rain started again.' Eli's usually strong voice was subdued. Christian looked up from the desk and tried to sound reassuring.

'Mo's very sensible - don't worry about him. He wasn't going to be driving.'

'I know, but those men could still be at large. We don't know for sure how many there were - Ephraim cannot be sure that he saw them all...'

'Did he not? I thought they were at their camp.'

'They did, but they only saw the big truck - there were four men there for sure, but there could have been more out in the rover.' Eli Llewellyn was an old time Methodist preacher and had known Christian for nearly thirty years, ever since he had started school. The doctor had rarely seen the minister this low before, but then he had close family hurt in the slip - Sophie had only just been able to save Eli's sister-in-law last night.

'You think they may have been with the same gang that were seen last month?' Christian asked, raising an eyebrow. There had been some trouble at Gobengwe market where blows had been exchanged and one man had his jaw badly fractured.

'Maybe - those men were driving a Land Rover as well.'

'But there are lots of Land Rovers - Mo will find out more when he comes back tomorrow.' If the flooding started to recede the police were hoping to get to where the poachers had set up camp as soon as they could, though how much of the grisly scene would be left to inspect was debatable. For now Christian tried to reassure the clergyman. 'Some of our people who are coming in with the dragomans have experience with tracking - Luey too, so I'm sure they'll be able to help the police account for all the murderers.'

Eli nodded, trying to look positive. 'Maybe they have already paid for their sins, but it is wild country out there.' Plenty of places to hide with the deluge wiping out their trail...

* * *

And he opened the bottomless pit; and there arose a smoke out of the pit... and the sun and the air were darkened... And there came out of the smoke locusts upon the earth: and unto them was given power, as the scorpions of the earth have power...

Book of Revelation 9:3 and 11 (King James version)

The explosion had echoed in his dreams when he had finally sunk into a rest even more troubled than usual. Jules lay huddled and shivering feverishly in the dilapidated storage hut that stood near the old plantation drying sheds and tried to order his thoughts for what came next. Of his injuries, the cuts and burns on his legs were now causing the most concern as they had stiffened up during the night and he still had several miles to travel to reach their other vehicle. He knew he couldn't chance going off-trail in his condition, so he'd have to risk it and keep to the easier gradients of the road. Maybe they'd have called off the air search after they'd seen the vehicles yesterday. The rain had eased off again after first light and if he took it slowly, trying to keep to the brush cover beside the track where he could, then he ought to make it by nightfall OK.

He stroked the long muddy canvas package beside him. Ditching the ivory wasn't really an option he was prepared to take just yet. Even though the rest of it was lost now, these two matched tusks would be enough to clear his debts when he made it back to Zyanda and maybe stake the hire of another crew. That was the least of his worries though. First he had to get to their camp in these damned hills and then find someone to patch him up.

* * *

Sophie's Diary: Thursday 8th November ~ Luo Main Camp

Death count's gone up to 77 but the good news is that Mo picked up the 3 guys who'd hitched to Rufighebwe market at the weekend, so they're safe and back with their families. The other 5 people who went missing had been out trying to shore up some mature Arabica shrubs down near the bridge and got caught in the main slide, so they'd been buried under a load of rubble. The river level's up again too and the pontoons are either gone or beyond repair, so the only way in for the foreseeable is from the north.

David and the other drivers got in about 3 o'clock this afternoon with some more CAMEO personnel - just as well as it started to pour again just after sundown. We sent the emergencies off to the hospital in Rufi as soon as we'd got a dragoman offloaded. The boxes of tents they've brought over are marvellous - so easy to put up and the equipment packed in with them is brilliant. Nearly all the able-bodied and some of the less injured have been able to get under canvas, so it's just the bed rest cases in the school and chapel now.

Luey flew back to Mgakera around noon, but he's coming back tomorrow because Mo wants to do another aerial check over the crash site and then see if they can land over at the Lake where Okot was killed. David's going to take the Land Cruiser down there too - Sully's busy helping Eli with the burials now.

And it's official - I'm pregnant. Luey's really pleased, although it's such bad timing with how things are here...

'Sergeant Abdullah?' He shook the tall policeman's hand firmly. 'I'm David Mukuga. Sorry to miss you yesterday.'

'Pleased to meet you Mr. Mukuga. And no problem - I was caught up with paperwork over identifications and taking more statements for the poaching incident.' He smiled ruefully at the gangling Matu. 'Change of plan for today though - I'd like to come down with you in the cruiser to the airstrip while the Mwanza squad go on down to Lake Camp, please. I understand you know the area up around the old ensete plantation quite well?'

David coloured slightly. 'Yes - I used to go hunting up there back in the '90's...'

'Well - it's been all but deserted in the borders for nearly a decade now. Don't worry - this has nothing to do with what happened in Zyanda, although we think some of these hyenas may be ex-militia. Or rather may have been - looks like they got wiped out already.'

'Sully told me about the crash last night.'

'Yes - if any of them did survive it they're likely to be in bad shape, so I want to make sure we can account for them all and check that they didn't have another camp up there.'

'There were some old buildings in and around the periphery of the plantation they might have been using - would it help if I came up with you and Luey?'

Mo's smile came back broader than ever. 'I was just about to invite you along! Luey said you've had some experience as a tracker too?'

'Some - mostly for game though.' David said quietly. That was true enough, despite his earliest experiences with two-legged prey.

'Let's get going then - Luey said he'd leave at sunrise and I want to make sure the Skyhawk's ready to go a.s.a.p.'

* * *

Mo had talked some more with David Mukuga on the way down and, despite the man's reserve, he was pleased that Mrs Beleshona had agreed to let him be co-opted onto the police search team as he seemed very capable. That the man probably had a less than squeaky clean record sheet was not something that worried Mo - Sophie, Christian and Sully had all impressed him these last few days and they obviously regarded David as a seasoned professional, even if his so-called military experience was dubious. Mo was also glad they'd come down early as the mechanic had still been asleep about ten minutes before they heard the throaty throb of the crop-dusters engine.

Despite not getting too much rest the past three nights, Luey was keen to get on with things and so the fifteen minute wait for the flight checks to be done saw him pacing around outside the hangar like a caged lion, leaving David a little puzzled as to what was bothering him so much.

'Hey, relax my friend - a few more minutes won't make much difference will it?'

Luey shook his head abruptly, then cracked a smile finally. 'Sorry mate. I'm just keen to get this over with so I can go and see Sophie.'

David laughed sympathetically. 'Well I guess she's looking forward to seeing you as well Luey - she was grumpy as hell yesterday evening when we were told the police wanted to be up early to go over to the Lake.'

As he was talking Mo appeared at the doorway to the hangar and beckoned them over. 'We're good to go now.'

Ten minutes later and they were back over the crash site, which wasn't that far from the airstrip. Luey circled a few times, gradually getting lower as David got his bearings and had a good look at the two vehicles.

'They didn't have too much rain over this side yesterday so the river level's gone down. Better than it was on Wednesday anyhow.' Mo's deep voice was calm and measured. 'We can see where the road slipped better today - it must have come down at the same time that Main Camp went.'

'Same aftershock probably - there was one about that time on the Zyandan side of the plateau as well.' David had been listening to the local radio almost non-stop since leaving Bujumbura. 'Luckily not many people live up there, so there wasn't much damage and there's less topsoil to slip on that side.' He turned to look back at Mo who was once again relegated to the back seat. 'Looks like the truck may have ignited as well, but the rain and splash-back from the river may have doused it - I'd need to get a closer look.'

'You'll get it. First though I want to get a look at those other buildings and see if there's any signs of activity there.'

'OK - Luey if you follow the trail up the other side of the ravine heading west north west roughly, there's some outbuildings in the next valley.'

They were nearing the Uganda highway, having flown over some of the old drying sheds when they spotted the main farm building nestling amongst some false banana trees, but the north slopes had coffee bushes planted so they got a good view of the end of the trail and the better road that led out of the plantation.

'You want me to get us in real low, Mo?'

'Circle it high and wide first, Luey, then go in for a closer look.'

All three of them craned to see the ground as they banked over the farm buildings. Suddenly David gave a low whistle and jabbed his finger at a clump of ensete not far from the tumbledown house and the telltale glinting of a headlight mirror in the sunlight breaking through the morning mists.

'Looks like another Land Rover!'

* * *

In the end the decision was simple. As soon as they landed back at Gobengwe, Mo radioed back to police HQ in Rufighebwe for his team to set up a road block on the main road out of the old plantation and then to send a vehicle down the northern trail to the crash site if they discovered the farm was deserted. He'd brought two AKs in the vehicle and Luey, as promised had brought his hunting rifle with him, so they wasted no more time and roared off in the land cruiser, heading for the ravine to check out the wrecks and look for signs of any survivors. It all depended on how many bodies they could find, as only four men had been seen by Ephraim who had all been at the lake with the truck, and of course there could have been more he hadn't seen. There had been the definite sighting of seven pugnacious strangers in Gobengwe market, but again that wasn't conclusive. It mostly depended on whether they'd all gone off hunting elephant, but Mo couldn't be a hundred per cent sure until the team confirmed whether the farm was clear.

'Well - this was an engine fire for definite, Mo.' David shook his head as the three of them stepped away from the shell of the rover, which had rolled over mostly onto the driver's side. The tank was intact and two of the four bodies in the vehicle had only superficial burns. 'Once the canvas went up the rain would have put the fire out, so these two must have suffocated if they didn't die in the impact.'

The driver and the man behind him were charred, but had been partially thrown forward, so had almost certainly been killed outright, which left the front seat passenger. He had gone through the windscreen and his mangled corpse could be seen about ten yards down the slope. Predators and vultures had already moved in and the flies were busily at work at the remnants as the sun rose higher in the sky, burning off the last of the mists left by the rainfall. The ground was already drying out, but the smell of smoke and burnt rubber filled the air still.

'So it must have been the truck's tank that blew up then?' Luey asked the question, but they were all gazing down at the river bed at the other vehicle.

'Looks that way - the noise alone would have meant an explosion...' Mo's voice was thoughtful and he looked back up the trail. 'Would the rover have been in front if they were in convoy do you think David?'

'Could be - there's more slippage higher up, so the rover might have gone down ahead, but the trail probably crumbled in both places at once.' David looked uphill again, trying to picture the descent of the lorry from the scarred brush and debris on the slope to the river about a hundred and fifty metres farther down from where they stood. 'Yeah - must have been. The rover had just started to turn on the corner and it looks like the lorry went down about twenty metres back from that.'

Mo nodded, noting some impact damage where it looked like some glass had shattered away from where the rover would have rolled. 'OK - I think that there were no survivors from this one with all the doors being intact or crushed. Let's go get our feet wet I suppose...'

They walked onto the part of the trail below the Land Rover that hadn't collapsed and carefully made their way down to the river. It was still running fast, but the level had subsided somewhat and the water now barely made it up past the concertinaed hood to the footbrakes of the truck, with what was left of the flatbed clear of the river altogether. What load there had been on the lorry was gone, although some of the tarpaulin had snagged on the brush or tangled on rocks nearby. Mo and David were having a good look at the area around the tank, which had definitely blown but wasn't quite ringing true for them.

Luey decided to leave them to it and made his way down the bank a little to see if he could find anything that might have been blown clear, or washed away downstream. The river broadened into shallows, though still bloated around the bend and he spotted some twisted remains of part of the tank, half stranded on a gravelly spit. He quickly checked for signs of crocs or hippos and then waded slowly out to the strand and kicked at the charred metal a little. As he looked around him he spotted a thin streak of dirty white caught under a boulder and some rope flapping in the water churning past it. Further investigation revealed a broken piece of elephant tusk about six inches long. Swiftly he scrabbled at it and found the rope had also wrapped itself around the same rock.

Having liberated his trophies, he splashed back onto the bank and made his way back to the others.

'Look what I found guys!' Luey hailed them, holding up the rope in one hand and the ivory in the other.

'Was the rope cut?' Mo was propped up on the door of the cab and holding himself steady with another length still tied to its housing.

'Yeah! Yours too?'

'Yup!'

'So what have we got here d'you think, David? You're sure there was no fire in the engine or cab?' Mo was frowning now as they sat on a rock in the sun, drying off a little after poking around in the submerged parts of the truck.

'If there was, between the river and the rain it would likely have gone out very quickly. Only signs of scorching are on the tarps and in the flatbed, so I'd say the tank must have been set off deliberately. And someone cut those ropes so the load would break loose for sure - the river was definitely over the cab end of the flatbed at one stage.'

'Well you've got your seven corpses - they're all accounted for aren't they?' Luey sighed, sweeping his fingers through his half-dried hair. He was beginning to fret about getting back to Main Camp and Sophie.

'Maybe - but both doors were open and the cab could easily hold more than two people.' Mo scratched his chin absently. 'The passenger door wasn't too damaged in the crash and the window was down, so it could have been opened fairly easily afterwards. The seat belts hadn't been used...'

'Or were undone.' David had a sick feeling in the pit of his stomach. The two bodies they'd found, one of them the driver probably, had most likely died on impact but hadn't been carried away in the flood, though their corpses had been

447

swept into the lower corner of the cab. 'Someone had to have been alive after it hit the river. Those two wouldn't have been able to cut ropes or stuff a burning rag in the fuel tank.'

'So there had to have been one survivor at least from this wreck, if not from the Land Rover you think?' Mo got a sour nod from David and got to his feet with a grunt of frustration. 'Why blow the tank up? It's crazy!'

'Not necessarily...' David's head was bowed and he was examining the length of rope Luey had found. 'During the genocide... sometimes when we had a vehicle crash, we used to torch it - so no one else could take it. Or think nobody had escaped, if we lost any people...'

* * *

Luey was all for going back to the land cruiser and Main Camp, but Mo decided they should inspect the far bank and up as far as the ridge to see if they could find any other signs of a survivor; reasoning that even if there had been, they may not have been able to get away too quickly if they had been injured in the crash.

'No point in looking for signs here after all the rain that's fallen - the trail on the other side's more sheltered though and we might pick up on something.' Mo was obviously determined to eliminate all possibilities, so David and Luey followed him up to the nearby bridge without further argument.

Their progress was silent and sweaty as the gradient was quite steep, until David found some muddy slippage and beaten down brush near the trail, where the terrain got even tougher and overgrown.

'Could have been an animal, but some of this looks as

though it's been pulled on rather than broken...' He looked around him carefully and then examined the ground even more thoroughly. Luey was about to press for them to move on, when David spotted some more disturbed earth right below an overhanging rock and gave a cry of satisfaction. 'Partial boot print! That must have been made recently... The boulder would have maybe stopped this getting too wet.'

They'd just set off up the trail again when they heard an engine in the distance.

'That could be my men, but we'd better get off the road just in case.' said Mo. They hunkered down about ten metres off trail, well screened from above by mopane scrub.

'Well it's certainly a Land Rover.' David murmured as the vehicle drew nearer.

'Would your guys have got here this quickly, Mo?' Luey asked, wondering if he should start loading his rifle.

'Depends on what they found, but yeah - could be them. Load up anyway - we might not have much more time.'
Barely a minute later the vehicle crested the ridge and, mercifully, was police force navy. Even so Mo waited until he could see who was inside before he let them break cover and hail the Land Rover.

'Well you guys have saved us a long walk! What did you find at the farm?'

The answer was nothing and nobody, so with the road block in place and the poachers' other Land Rover having nowhere to go, they'd decided to scout down as far as the old outhouses by the drying sheds. What they found on the way confirmed that they'd found a fresh trail and evidence of a survivor from the crash.

Mo looked speculatively at the bloodied canvas covering

the ivory. 'They wouldn't have ditched these unless they'd really had to - they have to weigh more than fifteen kilos each.'

Luey gave a low whistle. 'That's a lotta tusk - must have come off a big cow too.'

'And they were armed still - they found some AK casings at the scene as well. We haven't got an experienced tracker so I'd like to take David with us. You can come if you want Luey, but I can't guarantee we'll come back this way too soon unless we find them quickly.'

'You reckon there'd be no one else who stuck around here?'

'I doubt it, Luey.' David answered. 'This is too heavy to carry that far if they had an AK as well - even if there were two of them. I think they'd make for their other camp and the vehicle with this. There can't have been more than four people in that truck.'

'OK - I'll go back to the cruiser then. Where do you want me to meet up with you, Mo? Gobengwe or Main Camp?'

Mo thought quickly. 'Main Camp - I'll want to talk to the herdsmen again. I'll bring David back with me.'

'Take care guys.'

* * *

He'd started off well, but the rain had done nothing to cool his fever and now he just felt hot and giddy. Jules rested again, his breath sawing and his legs screaming agony. He knew there was at least another three more miles to go and it was well after noon now. Spending yet another night out here was not an option - he had to get to the abandoned farm before sundown. If only the rain would stop. The noise of it dripping through the trees made his head ache and stung his eyes as it mingled with his sweat, so everything was blurring in front of him. There were other, quieter noises as well, but he paid no attention as he limped onwards again, hardly caring whether he left a trail to follow or not now.

Yellow-green eyes watched Jules through dark branches, paying no heed to the rain and slippery bark as it crouched high up. Perfectly camouflaged, the panther simply waited for the interloper to come to him.

* * *

'It must have been a leopard I think. Lions get confused with how to kill animals on two legs - they tend to eviscerate first, rather than go for the throat.' David had noted the gouges on the shoulders and upper body and, with the number of trees on this part of the trail, a leopard could have easily attacked the poacher from above.

'Well - whatever it was didn't make a good meal of him.' Mo was holding the AK which they picked up about a hundred metres from where his men had found the ivory and shell cases. 'He let off a few rounds before it brought him down anyway.'

'Wildfire - I doubt he was aiming, let alone hit it. Pretty sure it must have got him very quickly - some of those blood spots on the canvas were arterial. From the size of the bites to the throat it was probably a male. I guess it must have dragged him off while he was still holding the AK.'

'Big, strong brutes, leopards. Not an easy way to go - but appropriate, some would say.'

David frowned and shrugged unhappily. 'Who knows what his story was. In different times that could have been me lying there.'

'That was then. You made different choices than this one did, I think.'

* * *

Sophie's Diary: Friday 9th November ~ main Luo Encampment

The extra CAMEO people have helped a lot. Chris and I were really knackered yesterday and poor Eli was on the verge of collapse with the additional anxiety for his family - his son was one of those who'd gone off to Rufi and he was worried sick about him.

Luey finally got in about 2pm, having been off with Mo and David all morning and then he had trouble trying to turn the cruiser around. Poor thing - he had to reverse uphill on that tiny track nearly back to the top road before he could go into forward gear again! But at least he got here well before dark. Chris practically ordered me to take a few hours off and rest, which cheered Luey up no end. He had great fun showing off his camping skills putting up one of the tents for us and made me a lovely mug of tea on the little wood stove in the box. Did us both good to have a rest and a little privacy as well - I forget how much it takes out of you when there's so much to do and so many people to look after, even if they're really quiet and still stunned like most of the people here are, whether or not they were injured.

We'd just started to have our supper when Mo got back with David and a new corpse for the morgue. They were both ravenous so we finished eating with them before I went off with Chris to do a quick and dirty autopsy after Ephraim had identified the dead man as one of the poachers who'd shot at him and Okot...

'You're certain that the burns and lower wounds were there first?' Mo sounded exhausted now the adrenalin rush had faded.

'Uh-huh.' Sophie nodded. 'If you look at these cuts on

his thigh here... See how they've seared and puckered and the cuts vary in depth and spacing? That's similar to wounds I've seen on soldiers who've been in IED [55] incidents; so I'd guess these were done by burning metal shrapnel from the tank explosion, where he didn't get out of the way quickly enough maybe?'

'And they are older than the bite wounds on the upper body and throat.' Christian spoke softly. 'By one or two days probably, looking at the swelling and infection.'

Sophie was looking anxiously at Mo as he was talking and stepped back to grab two chairs. Bringing them back to the make-do slab, she reached up a gentle hand to the sergeants' shoulder. 'Time out for you, Sarge! Can you get us some water please, Chris - we skimped on that at supper and I need another drink too.' She sat down with Mo and smiled at him. 'You've had a long day - you can afford to relax now. You got your man and all the others are gone as well.'

'But how did it take him so long to get to where he was found? It couldn't have been more than five miles away from where they crashed?'

'There's not just the burns and metal wounds - he has bruising all over that was probably done when they crashed - and I'm pretty sure he must have broken some ribs as well, so there might be internal injuries. I'm actually surprised he got as far as he did with what he was carrying.'

'So how recent do you think the bite wounds are?'

'Probably two days at most, but the examiner in Rufi will be able to give a more definite conclusion on that for you. Did you say that he may have sheltered somewhere for a time?'

---

[55] **IED** ~ Improvised Explosive Devices or roadside bombs

'Yes - there was an old shed near the road over the hill from where they crashed.'

'Well here's my best guess then. I think he was running high on adrenalin after the crash, and his injuries didn't start to bother him until he got away from the truck. From what Luey told me about the road out of the ravine, he'd probably have taken several hours, even the next day, to get as far as the shed, and probably he'd have had to rest there for some time too.' She paused as Christian re-joined them and took a welcome sip of chilled water from the temporary meds infirmary they'd set up yesterday. With a smacking of freshly moistened lips she went on. 'So - assuming he'd been trying to make the old farm since the Tuesday afternoon, and judging by how clean the exposed bite wounds are, he probably got attacked yesterday at some stage. Before it stopped raining anyway.'

'Yeah - that would fit I suppose.' Mo smiled at her slowly. 'At least Ephraim has given us a positive identification.'

'So this chap is the one who killed Okot you think?'

'Almost certainly - if the bullets you took out of him match the one for the AK we found today. We'll be sending this one to Mwanza for a full autopsy and the forensics will be done there too. If the follow-ups we're having done on some of their ID we found back at the farm pan out, this gang could have been part of a much bigger network that's been operating in Rwanda and Uganda as well. Orders from the District Commissioner's office - we don't want them thinking Tanzania's an easy target.'

'No - it would be horrible if they tried to move in on somewhere like Gombe Stream.'

* * *

When Sophie left Christian talking to Eli and got back to the tent an hour or so later, Luey, David and Sully were waiting for her.

'You didn't all have to wait up!'

'We wanted to, babe.' Luey gave up the camp chair for her and stopped to kiss the top of her head before reaching into an ice bag and handing her a can of cola with a sly wink. 'Verity packed a goody bag for us!'

She smiled wistfully at the cans of lager they were drinking, but relished the first frothy mouthful. 'Well I doubt the caffeine will keep me from sleeping tonight. Are we all in here?'

David and Luey exchanged sneaky glances and David answered her. 'Sully and I are off to the cruiser in a minute - we need a bit of luxury seating after running around after poachers and grumpy pastors all day.'

'Eli's been stressing about getting the Muslim dead seen to properly.' Sully said. 'He was worried about getting them all buried before the weekend - took me a while to get it across to him that Allah will understand if this cannot be done quickly.'

'Poor man - he's had such a lot on his plate with his son and his wife's family as well.' Sophie replied thoughtfully.

'Well things are getting sorted - I'm amazed at the difference here since yesterday even. Those CAMEO guys that came over with David and the other drivers are amazing - getting all those tents up. At least everyone can get under cover now and the kit that comes with these boxes is pretty impressive.' Luey was sitting on the floor holding Sophie's free hand as she sipped her drink, trying not to make too much of a show of trying to get rid of the two drivers.

Soon enough David wanted to get some sleep, so he and Sully left them to it. Sophie gave Luey a relieved smile but was blushing quite brightly.

'I thought they'd never go... Can you have a look at the back of my waist please - I think a botfly's got me!'

Luey burst out laughing. 'I thought you were squirming around a lot at supper! Sure it wasn't a mozzie?'

'Definitely not - there's quite a big bump by the feel of it...' She was rapidly peeling off her outer garments as she spoke, much to Luey's amusement as he went round behind her to examine the afflicted skin. 'I put some anti-histamine on it just before you got back here and that stopped the itching, but it started again at supper. It's been driving me insane!'

'Have these knickers of yours been wet? I've told you about getting your laundry ironed - flies love clean wet clothes.' He gently prodded the angry red bump then patted her bottom comfortingly. 'No worries - definitely not a mozzie. Looks like a putzi fly[56] probably.'

'They're clean and dry on this morning, thank you!' Sophie protested furiously. 'But it did rain hard after dawn and I got soaked running from the cruiser to the school. I put the cream on as soon as it started itching - in fact I swear I felt the little devil chomping on me!'

Luey was still crouched behind her, having moved the lamp closer for a better look. He was having some trouble holding back the hilarity, but managed not to laugh out loud.

---

[56] **Putzi Fly** ~ the female will often lay eggs in damp clothing. When the maggot hatches it bites the wearer and feeds just under the skin raising a boil which can become enlarged, painful and itchy. The maggot does not burrow too far into the host as it leaves an air hole to breathe and expel its waste. Ironing destroys the egg, but if a boil develops the maggot can be killed by blocking the air hole, either by bathing or sealing it with medicated cream.

'OK babe, I believe you. Good news is I think you killed it already - I can see its little butt sticking out - want me to take it out now?'

Sophie exhaled explosively. 'Yes! YES! Get it the hell out of me!'

'Don't panic - I'm a dab hand with putzis! You got some antiseptic wipes in your wash bag?'

'Yes! Hurry up! There's tweezers in there too.' She was squirming impatiently now and Luey grinned to himself as he went through her things.

'There you go - all done!' He wiped the boil clean and then liberally applied some more of the anti-histamine that Sophie had fished out of her jacket pocket. 'Want to have a look at the monster?' He'd put the tweezers and the maggot on another camp chair while he finished ministering to her. He held it out for inspection.

'Is that all it bloody is!' Sophie's eyes narrowed to steely blue slits as she glared at tiny larva, not even as big as a grain of rice. This time Luey couldn't keep it in and roared with laughter.

'TIA Soph! It's only a baby remember - and even little things can cause a load of grief down in the deepest darkest parts of the Great Incontinent...'

'I hate you, Luey Ogilvy.' Sophie sulked adorably and he pulled her into his arms with a happy smile plastered all over his face.

'Well our little one's going to cause you at least as much pain and irritation as this guy did - but I'll be here to help you with that too.'

'Damn right you will!' She smiled up at him and kissed his stubbly chin. 'Thanks for getting it out for me, love.'

'You're welcome, sweetheart.' He kissed the tip of

her nose and sighed with contentment. 'Now - how about grabbing some kip. I'm feeling tired as hell after all that running around in the gorge and nearly twisting my neck off getting out of it.'

'OK - I'll even massage your poor shoulders for you before we go to sleep.'

'Pure genius - just what I was hoping you'd say...'

Omega and Alpha

Solstice Day, 21st December, Lake Naivasha, Kenya

Luey slipped his hands around Sophie's thickening waist and kissed her gently where her shoulder met her neck.

'Alone at last, Mrs Ogilvy Taylor. Much as I love your family...' He gave up talking and nibbled softly on her ear.

'Well - you covered your impatience very well, Mr Taylor Ogilvy...' Sophie's fingers grazed his warm cheek then tangled lazily in his thick dark hair, holding him to her.

The sun was fast descending to the hazy tree-lined horizon and still they stood in silence on the veranda, holding each other and watching the failing light stain the lake in constantly moving jewelled tints of aquamarine, apricot and glinting palest gold. Finally Luey spoke low and loving.

'I never thought I'd say there's a place lovelier than Kariba at sunset, but...'

Sophie silenced him again with a brief kiss and then laughed softly. 'Ah - but you get your money's worth in the tropics! See - blink and you'll miss the sunset.'

'Well - that's the equator for you, I guess. All maximum spin and no messing about with silly seasons. Still beautiful, if brief.' He smiled at her and stepped back a pace. 'Let's sit out here a while, shall we? See if Hugo comes up to pay his respects to my beautiful bride?'

Hugo was a very old, very grumpy hippo that Claire had warned them about conscientiously the day they arrived but, so far, he had failed to appear on their lawn and justify his reputation. Sophie nodded and took his hand to lead the way over to the swing bench and the table, where they'd left the last of the champagne that her parents and Harry had brought over from the hotel to the small party after the ceremony in Claire's garden.

'I also like your family's presents. Tasty as well as practical.' Luey poured them both orange juice cooling in the ice bucket and then added some fizz to his glass.

'Spontaneity has its advantages - bringing the wedding forward was a lucky decision with Old Mother Lucas cutting up rough and demanding to see her grandkids for Christmas! And it was good that they could give Verity a lift back to Nairobi.'

'I also love rich relatives. Claire and Grant are included in that by the way - this house is exquisite!'

'I still prefer our little nook in Umbeke - just the right size for a small family...'

'Talking of which, how's our little darling doing?' He put his hand on Sophie's tummy and rubbed gently. She laughed at him.

'Nothing happening in there just yet. No stirrings for another month or so.'

'But some sensation is starting - can't begin with the stimuli too soon, Doctor!'
She put both hands on his and smiled happily.

They fell into companionable silence again, sipping their drinks and watching the distant silhouettes of pelicans and darters on their way to roost, flying low over the darkening water that was just beginning to shimmer as the waxing moon rose high in the early night sky. After a while Luey took her left hand and brought it to his lips, then held it out for them both to admire their rings, which were finally in unity.

'You are a very clever lady, Mrs Ogilvy Taylor!' He murmured, his voice replete with contentment. 'I thought that Harry would be teasing me forever over getting designer rings, but nobody in the whole world has anything like these. I love them almost as much as I love you...'

She snuggled into him as he spoke and his voice trailed off as he stroked her hair with his other hand.

'Baobab's are magic and precious - like you are to me.' She whispered. 'My tanzanite ring is very special, but it has too many sad memories. I needed to move on and make a statement. These ones are full of potential and built to last. Gold and diamonds from Tanzania. Our first home.'

Her engagement ring was a plain gold band with a larger, roughly oval shape in the centre resembling the cross-section of a baobab fruit. It held a dozen 'seeds' each containing a tiny diamond that glittered in the moonlight. The ring Luey wore had the same central design, standing slightly proud of alignment on one side of a wider band than Sophie's, which was etched to look like the gnarled bark of the magic tree. Their wedding rings were again simple bands, but reversed, so Sophie's had the bark effect and Luey's was plain. They both slotted onto the engagement rings exactly, so they sat as one on the finger and would turn together.

David had given her the idea after he'd driven them out one afternoon, to a small lake a few miles out of Mgakera to look at malachite kingfishers, egrets and shoebills amongst other birdlife. On the way back they'd stopped at a little village where some enterprising local had set up a bottle shop in the hollows of an enormous baobab and David had regaled them with various stories about the magic tree that held water even when rivers dried, and nurtured life sustaining fruit and seeds. It also got her thinking about Syamenga's tales in Kariba and how the souls of the ancestors inhabited the baobab's branches, so they could continue to look after the living.

A light wind off the lake stirred the leaves on the trees. Luey turned and looked at her again.

'Have you been thinking about names again, babe?' She smiled but didn't answer yet, so he went on. 'I've been having a bit of a ponder. If we have a boy, would you like to call him Tom? It's my father's middle name as well.' Sophie's eyes widened, but her lips curved with pleasure and he gave a small sigh of relief.

'That's a lovely idea - if you're sure?' She answered and he grinned back at her in delight.

'You get to choose a girl's name then!'

'How does Teresa sound?'

'Perfect... Surname can be Taylor-Ogilvy - bibis first and all that!'

They laughed happily and after a while went inside to continue their wedding night.

Glossary (of acronyms and unusual terms)

CAMEO   **Co-ordinated Aid, Medicine and Education Organisation**

An entirely fictional logistical umbrella group for several humanitarian organisations working all over the world.

Dragoman   Very large robust trucks of the types used by Aid Agencies and haulage companies in places like Africa, to carry supplies of food, fuel, medicines and other supplies, including people, where they cannot be flown in due to the roads being rough or non-existent, or because of other environmental and/or political prerogatives. Travel companies also now use similar vehicles for back-packing style holidays all over the globe.

EMDR   **Eye movement desensitisation and re-processing**

a large heavy-bladed knife like a machete. Generally used in Africa for cutting through thick vegetation, or butchering carcasses of bush-meat.

Panga   a large heavy-bladed knife like a machete. Generally used in Africa for cutting through thick vegetation, or butchering carcasses of bush-meat.

PTSD   **Post-traumatic Stress Disorder**

A severe anxiety disorder that is sourced from any   situation where a psychological trauma is caused. Often the causative event involves physical or emotional violence and occurs most commonly in personnel returning from active service in conflicts, or in cases of domestic violence especially if rape is a factor.

T.I.A   This is Africa. The plaintive cry of many a frustrated ex-pat of whatever hue, or hailing from any other corner of the world, who comes up against the multitude of problems that beset the continent to make the absent heart pine for their own native soil.

Lightning Source UK Ltd.
Milton Keynes UK
UKOW05f1909260114

225268UK00003B/9/P